Fatal Rain

RT French

authorHOUSE®

AuthorHouse™
1663 Liberty Drive
Bloomington, IN 47403
www.authorhouse.com
Phone: 1-800-839-8640

First published by AuthorHouse 9/1/2009

ISBN: 978-1-4389-9930-2 (e)
ISBN: 978-1-4389-9928-9 (sc)
ISBN: 978-1-4389-9929-6 (hc)

Printed in the United States of America
Bloomington, Indiana

This book is printed on acid-free paper.

Dedication

Accomplishments are never single-handed conclusions, regardless of how they appear. Driving forces behind the scene dictate the tempo and mood and help articulate the outcome. So it is, especially with me. I owe much to many, but two in particular.

First and foremost, I want to thank God for breathing essence into me. It was his love that brought me here and his love that marks each and every day on the course I run. Please help me to finish the race.

And I am especially indebted to my wife. She has raised me, taught me, loved me, and selflessly supported each and every project I have undertaken. Her encouragement has more than made up for any doubts I have ever entertained. Thank you Ronni, you will always have my love!

Destination

It had always been a delightful spot in the black, measureless abyss. A blue orb shimmering in between irreconcilable distances and black holes that required unimaginable dexterity to navigate. With its ever present quilted patches of white, drifting clouds, Earth was a coveted mission, especially now that critical mass had been achieved.

The mission was simple yet delicate: document the calamity about to happen and protect and nourish a particular human girl child that exhibited extraordinary capabilities. In fact, she was, in all probability, the next evolutionary link in the frail human chain. Some of the members on the High Council had asked, "Why invest resources in following the events of a primitive people on this distant planet?" Eventually, after much debate, the majority of the High Council felt that the beautiful blue oasis was worthy of consideration because of it's diverse life forms, proximity to their planet and that from time to time humans were capable of exquisite thoughts and great compassion when not constantly plotting one insane war after another.

The crew was experienced and handpicked. The ship employed the latest in technology and was the pride of the homeland. So advanced was the ship that it could literally be called the fifth crew member. With its ability to plug into each of the crew's cumulative experiences, coupled with its powerful reasoning capabilities, it was performing far beyond the engineers' expectations. Interplanetary travel was now as comfortable and easy as a leisurely, if lengthy, planetary picnic.

Strict protocols had long ago been developed concerning contact with the blue water planet (#42907AZ632), better known as Earth. Field work had been ongoing for over two hundred years, and with the rather consistent weather patterns and the clearly irrational yet predictable behavior of the inhabitants, the final outcome was already well established through binary-computational statistics and the most advanced quantum logarithms, combined with highly developed intuitive processes. The High Council had voted and authorized the project. All that remained was an objective, sterile documentation and a little proactive evolution thrown in for good measure.

In less than one cycle around Earth's rather smallish sun, the crew would be homeward bound with a virtual archive of data for further consideration. Golic, the acknowledged primal of the ship, set the automatic controls for the landing coordinates, ensured that normal stealth procedures were in place, and settled back into his body absorption control seat with his favorite drink. Taking nourishment orally had been obsolete for several centuries, but everyone conceded that the act was nonetheless calming and enjoyable. The pale green glow of the flight deck was comforting and offered a dramatic backdrop in the control room, featuring a viewing monitor that comprised the entire forward wall. Great care had gone into the design of the ship. No sharp edges or corners could be seen. The interior was smooth wherever possible. No need to risk bruising the fragile, yet exquisite exoskeleton that evolution had fitted them with. Evolution took strange paths as it curved and wove its magic. At just over four feet tall, Golic's race was weak by human standards. Debate still raged as to whether or not physical labor should be outlawed on their home planet. With their mental capabilities and life assisted robotics, his people could perform any task. The exoskeleton needed to handle their planet's atmospheric pressure had gradually become weaker as they spent less and less time outside. With a cranium approximately 25% of their mass, they required large feet for balance and only three lengthy and elegant digits on each hand were needed to manipulate the most demanding of their machines.

Much had changed in the last phase of their civilization and it was now anticipated that one could reasonably

3

live to be three to four hundred years old. This dramatic change roughly doubled previous life expectancies from studies completed only twenty years previously and brought with it a whole new set of problems. More time meant more resources were needed for each life unit. Financial, educational, career, family and a whole array of issues avalanched onto their society. One constant remained however: knowledge. Knowledge had long ago become the most sought after commodity. This expedition would add much to each of the crew's intrinsic value. When not working, all had priority access to the communications cloud on their planet. Unlimited access to the synthetic learning center guaranteed each crew member would be able to remain abreast of current events while giving them the ability to further their own particular areas of expertise. This gave them a tremendous advantage in future assignments. Knowledge fulfillment was not only an essential fact of life, but it also became the prime recreational outlet and on this trip they had ample opportunity to purse that endeavor.

Golic was glad there was a diverse and engaging crew. The actual work could, at times, be tedious and drawn out, but all onboard knew the prestige of this undertaking and wanted to impart their own special touch to the expedition. Nimore, Kosh and Dra were near clones of each other. Physical differences were hard to detect without examining the hand. A light blue color could be detected on the bottom half of the first digit; an evolutionary after-thought that indicated gender. Gender had actually been obsolete for several hundred years and procreation was now handled by the Commission. Physical contact was no longer needed for any reason. Their lives were mainly mental and social oneness.

Golic watched as the three crew members, alerted by the ever watchful ship, drifted to their seats and took in the breathtaking panorama, as their ship dashed unher-alded into Earth's atmosphere. The craft soared over the Pacific Northwest coastal location picked specifically for its anticipated effect rates. The Pacific Northwest was the perfect Petri dish for the clinical scientist. These lush, green tree-covered, undulating mountains would bear the first impact. This was to be the vanguard of the poten-tially life ending event.

The craft took a circuitous route Golic had plotted as a bonus for all the bleak, dark days in transit. They skimmed over the majestic, rocky coast line and watched the ocean waves relentless beating of the shore. Hovering unseen above Portland, they observed the migration pat-terns of the inhabitants and mused at the obsolete build-ing structures. Turning inland and exploring the deep emerald Columbia canyon, they approved of the soaring canyon walls that controlled the strong rivers surge to the ocean.

Finally, the ship settled in a quiet, damp valley, secluded from most curious eyes. No humans noticed their coming and only a few of the indigenous animals sensed any change. Silent, unseen, and mostly passive was their role. Golic informed base of their arrival, as the crew readied the time honored and proven observation techniques and began the wait for the chosen one.

Changes

Shelly was only nine. A tomboy, precocious, wide eyed lonely nine. Brown pigtails, jeans and a T-shirt with tennis shoes tied in double knots. Gangly, still no hint of puberty, with her mother's engaging smile accented with a cute upturned nose full of freckles that bled off at the side like snowflakes caught in a breeze. Possessing a love of all animals, even slithering snakes, signs of attention deficit disorder and a classic cluttered room that only she could navigate, she was all her father could ask for.

Everyone had noted the changes since the accident. Not everyone thought she could overcome them. Dan did. He knew she was cut from the same bolt of cloth as her mother and that she would again run through the house with no regard to the mud on her feet or concern that she might wake her napping Dad. Time would heal her. But for now she had her special sharing moments in the comforting back yard. When her father would ask her where she was going, it would invariably be to the back yard—to share. He knew it would take time. It would take

7

time for him, too. He wanted it to be soon. He needed her back in his life. He was as lonely as his daughter.

The Enveloping Woods

Oregon was a cacophony of adventure. An outdoors with as rich a pallet of colors as one could imagine. Trees of every description, streams, roaring rivers and wild blackberry bushes taunting the domesticated strawberry patches. Tulip fields lay in glorious passion alongside wide sterile highways with the ever present, beckoning woods roaming free over the hills. Huge trees danced in the wind within sight of the boisterous ocean waves. Beaches cluttered with the remnants of logged trees tossed from the sea like pickup sticks.

Shelly felt alive outside. She could breathe the deep mossy smells and rich wet bark and know she was only a whisper away from her mother, her lovely waiting mother. She longed to again wrap her arms around her mother's waist and feel those soft, warm, gentle hands stroking her head and bask in that special motherly aroma. Shelly had retrieved several scarves from the clothes her father had boxed up for Goodwill. She needed the comfort of those rich, deep, meaningful smells as she lay huddled in the dark. Lost in a flash of black ice on a lonely road, her mother had skipped off the winding path and plummeted to an icy death. She was gone now, never to return, but Shelly knew, that somewhere, she was watching and praying for them.

But only in the woods, away from others, could Shelly whisper for her mother and, with certainty, know that loving eyes gazed upon her and smiled from the height of the swaying pine trees. If she concentrated and held her breath, she could almost hear her mother whisper back to her. She needed to be in the woods. Her father called it the back yard, but the trees knew no fences and boundaries. The thrusting trees roamed the land at will and they alone etched the borders of their territory. Shelly was transformed in the solid grasp on the mighty trees. She relaxed that grip that held her heart so strong. She opened up like she could never do at home and she exhaled the pent up tensions of a motherless world and soaked in the nurturing woods. The release gave her strength for the next minute, hour and day. The woods were almost as consoling as her mother's hands.

First Encounter

'First impressions are lasting impressions' or so the saying goes. Always brush your teeth, comb your hair and never leave the house without a fresh pair of clean underwear. You never know what might happen and what affect it could have on your life. Greet everyone and each situation with special regard. Certainly in this instance, it could not have been truer.

On February 6th, about 5:30 PM, just after dinner and right before Dad started the dishes, Shelly said, "Dad, is it okay if I go to the woods for awhile? I won't be long."

"Will you come when I ring the bell?"

"Yes."

"Right away? Or will I have to come out there and get ya?"

"I'll come right away. I promise."

"Fine, get going and stay in the range of the bell," said Dan Brown, Shelly's father.

Shelly hit the door on the run, making sure to take a flashlight with her, along with a bright yellow jacket with a whistle in the zippered pocket; items her father insisted upon when venturing into the woods. More than once, Dan had to go out looking for his daughter. Frantic each time, fear eating at his gut that he might lose the rest of his soul. He made sure to remind himself that she was just out in the backyard, but the fear was always there. What if she got lost? What if a bear roamed into this neck of the woods? What if some sick bastard kidnapped her? Such were the thoughts that Dan struggled with. He knew Shelly needed time and freedom to sort out her mother's death, but it took a small toll on him each time she dove into the deceptive labyrinth just fifty feet from their back door.

Shelly was actually an accomplished woods person at this early age. She had spent more time in this part of the woods than anyone else in the near vicinity. She knew every rock, every tree and what secret each valley held. She knew the animals she would encounter and which ones would gladly eat out of her hand. She feared nothing in the woods and could whisper her mother's name and feel complete.

Today was different, though. It was more than a need to go—she was expected. She felt it deep inside her, at her very core. Shelly headed for the deep valley, where few of her friends had ever gone. This was clearly out of the bell's range, but she vowed to be quick about it and broke into a sprint to conserve time. She was being drawn there for a specific reason. Clearing the crest of the hill and looking down into the deep valley, she carefully scrutinized the area, Shelly saw nothing unusual. She remembered how once her mother laughed when she had seen deer droppings and had called it deer raisins. And when Shelly had picked one up and threw it at her, the chase was on. Of course her mother caught her and gave her nuggies. Good times, Shelly thought, as her heart warmed a few degrees. Shelly continued down the side of the valley until it opened into a small meadow.

Walking and having an imaginary conversation with her mother, Shelly ran right smack into something. She had hit her head and right hand on some unseen object. She had bounced off of it hard and landed awkwardly on the slightly browning pine needles. Surprised, she looked around and saw nothing. She got up, straightened her shoulders and turned a full 360 degrees to make sure she had not overlooked something. She was in the middle of the meadow and there was absolutely nothing she could have smacked. Did she imagine it? She touched her throbbing head where a small welt was forming and felt the slight abrasion and knew something real had happened. She cautiously reached out her right arm and felt nothing. Am I going nuts? Is this what the school counselor calls a breakdown? She shook her head and laughed softly to herself and started off again. Thump. Again, her head bounced off of something right in front of her. Fortunately, she had not generated any momentum and the bump was less severe. She reached out her hand and came into contact with a warm, smooth surface. But she still saw nothing. It felt like a glass window, only curved. She could feel the smooth warm curve that was gently tilting inward in all directions. She took several steps to the left and right, feeling the tilting warm thing in all directions. Putting her left hand on the object, she set off to find the end of it. She walked and walked and ended up making a complete circle. It seemed to be a giant ball, about the size of a house, but she couldn't be sure because she couldn't see it. Weird, she thought. Is this a dream? Just then, she thought she heard the last drifting notes of her father's bell. Did she hear it, or did she think it? Nonetheless, she dug in her coat and answered with the chrome plated police whistle, not knowing if she was in range or not. When she finished she distinctly heard the invisible glass ball whistle back to her. It was soft and more mellow but nonetheless a whistle. Not wanting to whistle again because three whistles is a row was a danger signal and that meant that Dad was to come quickly, instead she snapped her fingers using both hands, a newly learned talent that had gained much respect from her third grade class. Again,

14

softly, yet distinctly, she heard two snaps back. With de-light, she laughed out loud. Soon, her laugh returned to her. This was very, very cool. Wait till she told her Dad and her friends.

With that thought in mind, she carefully noted the lo-cation and backed away slowly making a mental map for future use. She gathered three rocks and stacked them on top of each other and, when completely satisfied that she could find the place with no problem, she spun on her heals and ran. She sprinted the quarter mile to her home, as fast as her size five feet would move. She had to get to Dad before the sun was completely down. Wow, she thought, this is way cool. Her instincts had been correct.

The Skeptic

Great truths are seldom received warmly by the mob. Instead, doubt tied to tradition passes as knowledge. Open minds and age are inversely related. Usually, only the innocent see the world as it could, should be, and truly is.

Shelly arrived breathless and in halting speech addressed the mob, "Dad! Dad you gotta come see!" yelled Shelly as she opened the back gate and came running full steam into the house. "It's a glass ball. It's as big as a house and you can't see it," said a breathless huffing Shelly.

"Slow down. First of all young lady, I had to hike way back in there, ringing the bell before you answered me. Didn't I say to stay in range of the bell?" asked Shelly's father, clearly agitated.

"Yes, but ya gotta see what I found. You won't believe it."

"And just what is that? Another tree that looks like your teacher?"

"No, you can't see it, but you can feel it and it makes noises."

"What makes noises?"

"I'll show you. Let's go," urged Shelly.

"Girl friend, it's already late and you have school to-morrow and I still haven't checked your homework. After that, you need to start getting ready for bed."

"But Dad! You don't understand. This thing is cool. It's big and it even makes sounds," pleaded Shelly.

"Sounds? What sounds?"

"Well, when I whistled back to you, it whistled just like I did. And then, I laughed and it laughed."

Dan squinted his eyes trying to remember what the psychologist had told him about what to expect from his fragile daughter after Lisa's death. He knew overreacting was not the thing to do. He should let things pass at their own rate of speed.

"Well Shelly, if it's that big it will be there tomorrow. You can show me then," said Dan rather proud of his reply.

"Dad, what if it's gone? This is important. It won't take long. Please, let's go now!"

"Shelly, what did I say?"

When ever Dad used that phrase, "What did I say?" Shelly knew exactly what it meant. The discussion is over. It is now law. Live with it.

"You don't believe me do you?" pushed Shelly.

"Get the dictionary and look up the word skeptical." He spelled it for her, S K E P T I C A L. "Right now I am very skeptical." This was a game Lisa Brown had always played with her family. She would use big words and then make one of them look it up. It undoubtedly accounted for Shelly's unusually large vocabulary. "Right now, young lady, we have things to do. So start doing. Tomorrow, you'll get a chance to prove me wrong. We will go on a dinner/picnic and find your whistling invisible whatever. Okay?"

"Sure. Have it your way. It's always your way," said a terse Shelly as she stomped from the room and paused to pickup RutButt, an abnormally large, neutered Tabby. "At least RutButt loves me."

After her bath and a review of her homework, which showed that she wasn't exerting nearly enough effort at school, Shelly queried her father, "Are you really a cynic?"

"What?" laughed Dan.

"A cynic. The dictionary said a skeptic is a cynic. A doubter, one that doesn't believe."

"Let's just say I'm from Missouri and seeing is believing."

"Okay, Dad, get ready to eat your words. Do you want to bet something that I'm right?"

Betting was a tradition in the Brown family. Nobody passed up the opportunity to bet. Rarely did the wager involve money. Mostly it revolved around chores, back tickles or food. "Yes, how about you raise that C in math to an A."

"Okay, and if I win, I want a week hiking trip with you and a friend, in the redwoods," said a confident Shelly.

"Deal. Pinky promise," said Dan as he and Shelly intertwined little fingers and kissed.

"Oh, and one more thing Shelly, don't tell anyone about this until you and I have explored it together. Until then, it's a secret. Okay? And that means Miss Martinez too."

Juanita Martinez was the deal of the century. She was the housecleaner, cook and companion for Shelly in her father's absence. Dan had economically coerced her to stop cleaning houses for several families and come to work for them full time. She was nothing short of wonderful and badly needed with the absence of Shelly's mother.

"Okay Dad. Tomorrow, please don't work late. I want time to investigate."

Protocol Review

Rules and normal conduct are part of the fabric of intelligence. Regardless of where you come from in the Universe, there will always be operational standards. Order is highly valued by all living things. Ants, deer, monkeys, crocodiles and hawks all operate in a regulated fashion. It is only logical to recognize that accepted practices touch the most distant of us.

Contact this early in a mission was rare unless intentionally initiated, as this was, by the probe. Earlier missions had identified thirty nine evolutionary anomalies within the entire human race. Of those, more than half had been eliminated from the selection process solely due to geographic location. Twelve had been deselected due to mental imbalances that would tilt the process negatively. The four remaining males were removed from selection because the females of this life form seemed to be better at nurturing and therefore more highly prized at this time. Two female children were left in queue owing to the chance that one of them might have developed unexpected problems since last contact. A beacon devise had been discretely implanted in both girls for rapid identification. Both girls were truly exceptional. Their instincts were first rate and the slowly blossoming sixth sense each possessed was just now beginning to exert itself in their personal evolutionary process.

Shelly had been selected over the other female child because of her father's considerable survival tendencies. She would stand the best chance of surviving the pending disaster, the fatal rain. Humans would be greatly tested in the upcoming months and years, and the ideal candidate would need reliable protection. The girl's paternal unit was most capable and made the decision an easy one. The other girl child would still be monitored but only sporadically.

While she couldn't predict the future, she nevertheless seemed to sense it. Shelly was vaguely aware that she was changing much like a larva into a butterfly. The urge to go to the woods was yet another example of her metamorphosis. Following her almost uncontrollable need to go deep into the woods, Shelly had simply walked right into their ship, merely hours after site acquisition. Sensors had alerted the crew well before the initial head banging that she was in the area. They had all been in the control room watching the small female human with the remarkable aura. As they scanned her, it was obvious this child had some emotional issues that needed reconciling, but, nonetheless, her aura showed amazing clarity and depth. They wondered if she was a transplant, but reconsidered that as improbable.

Dra reflected that, "She seems to be a perfect subject. Too bad she isn't older, with more life experiences."

"She is everything we were anticipating," replied Nimar, the scientific coordinator. "I'll send a probe to her habitat tomorrow evening and gather additional data."

"Kosh, intersect with the town's communications systems and select your remaining test subjects. Have them discretely assemble after we scan the immediate animal life sources," directed Golic. "Now, I suggest we venture out into the environment and gather our vegetation DNA samples and insert some data probes. As you are all aware, the ship will monitor your time in this gravitation, it could be deadly." The entire communication effort between crew members was thought driven by directive. That meant, only those thoughts specifically designated, would be transmitted. That left the mindless thought clutter that all beings seem to possess, out of the transmitted range. This development was much needed, as earlier mind communication methods were at times far too personal and occasionally dangerous.

Golic noted the sense of pride swelling with the crew. The mission was on target and ahead of schedule. Each member excelled in their area of expertise and none experienced any negativity from the other. Missions of this length and importance often created internal issues with the crew. But, to date, all was running optimally.

Setting the Stage

Events transform us all. Our personal environment plays a key developmental role in our lives. Shelly and her father had recently been challenged by life. Unwanted changes had bullied their way into their lives and made themselves at home. Now, like unwanted relatives, they wouldn't leave.

Dan hurried Shelly off to school and started his twenty minute commute to his plumbing company. Shelly was more than a little responsible for his new career. Several months ago she had suggested that he call Bill Oppenheimer, the previous owner of the shop, and ask him if he wanted to sell. Dan asked Shelly, "What are you talking about?"

"I think he is sick and needs the money for an operation."

"How do you know that?" inquired Dan, wondering what the kids in school were talking about.

"I felt it when we drove past his store last week."

"You felt it?"

"Yeah. Sort of a sad, brown feeling. I think it's called leu-something."

"Leukemia?"

"Yeah, that's it."

"Girl, you're beginning to scare me", said Dan. But he made a mental note to check up on Bill and see what the story was. Sure enough, Shelly was right. He ended up buying the store and, finally doing what he had always wanted to do, manage his own business.

ЖОЖ

As he drove to the shop, he called Bruce Sonwix, his daughter's psychologist, "Hello Bruce, this is Dan Brown, you have a moment to talk?"

"Of course Dan, how are you and Shelly?"

"That's why I'm calling, Bruce. Shelly is claiming to have seen something invisible in the woods. She still spends a lot time there whispering to her mother and I'm worried. I don't want to over or under react. Any suggestions?"

"Dan, like we discussed, Shelly will take time to internalize losing her mother. It's a momentous change in her life. Imaginary friends are an easy way for children to help them cope with their problems. They aren't capable of relating everything they are feeling to adults. From that standpoint, imaginary friends are a good thing. However,

Dan, it's almost always a person that's imaginary and not a thing. What else has she told you?"

"Well, she found it, whatever it is, in the woods yesterday. She can touch it but can't see it. Oh, and it echoes sounds that are made. She wants to show me tonight."

"This is interesting. Usually children don't want to bring an adult into their imaginary world. Go along with her, but don't pretend. If you don't hear it or see it, say so. She needs you to be the constant in her life. She needs reality. Dan, don't get too hung-up on this phase of her mourning. Every child is different and they all solve the issue in their own time and way. Let me know how it goes."

"Thanks Bruce. I'll get back to you soon. Have a good one."

"You too Dan. Talk to ya soon."

Dan arrived at his office just as he concluded the call to Bruce.

Premonition

The past three months had seemed a blur to him. Shortly after their tenth anniversary, Lisa had decided to visit one of her clients up the coast from them. Shelly grew pale as Lisa moved to the garage door. She ran to her mother, fell on the floor and wrapped her arms around her legs. She began yelling about the ice and the wreck. Both Dan and Lisa were caught totally off-guard. Lisa did her best to calm Shelly as Dan picked her up off the floor and carried her to the couch and held her in his arms. Shelly continued to plead with her mother and, despite Shelly's outburst, Lisa informed her that she had scheduled an appointment and she would be going. She reassured her that she would be careful, kissed Shelly on the head and headed for the door.

Shelly, now in tears, shouted, "Whisper to me, Mom. Whisper to me."

Both Dan and Lisa looked at each other not knowing what she meant. Lisa left the house. Shelly, ran to the bathroom, locked herself in and threw-up. Dan tried to coax her out and finally resorted to the emergency key to open the door. Dan called in to his office and said he would be staying home today with his daughter.

One hour later, Lisa was deep into a shadow cloaked valley rounding a gentle curve when she hit black ice along the river. Black ice is so named because all you see is the black asphalt beneath the ice. It appears as if the road is dry and very navigatable. Her car didn't even swerve as it exploded through the roadside steel fence and dashed itself on the rock strewn stream one hundred feet below. The car immediately began to sink and slow- ly rolled onto the driver's side as Lisa sat unconscious from the crash. As the cold water lapped at her face, Lisa gradually awoke and realized her situation. Trying to free her arms to unlock the safety-belt, she discovered that neither arm responded. One arm was pinned by the crushed door and the other appeared to be broken. She struggled for several minutes to keep her head above the water and finally relaxed and accepted her fate. As she blacked out from lack of oxygen, she whispered, "Shelly, I love you."

According to the police, the car never changed direc- tions and simply bashed through the road barrier and right into the river a hundred feet below. She never made it out of the car. An eighteen wheeler, with the height to see over the edge of the raven, had spotted the car around 5:00 PM and notified the state police. They found her pinned in the car with her seat belt still on. The air bags had deployed and she had drowned in the cold dark waters of the Wilson River. The car had half filled with water and was lying on the driver's side. Dan wasn't notified until 9:00 PM that evening.

He was already worried and had placed several calls looking for Lisa. Shelly informed him the police were on the way before they even pulled onto the farm lane. When the police car pulled up to his house, he was looking out the window, hoping against hope that she would come around the corner. Instead, a young, big highway patrolman knocked on the door and requested, "May I talk to Dan Brown?"

"I'm Dan Brown."

"Sir, is your wife Lisa Brown?"

"Yes," said Dan, turning white with fear.

"Sir, is this her driver's license?"

"Oh my God. Yes," whispered Dan.

"Sir, may I step into your house?" Dan opened the door and motioned the officer in. "Mr. Brown, I am sorry to inform you that your wife had a fatal car accident. She has died." The officer searched Mr. Brown's eyes for the hint of acknowledgement. Dan just stared off into the distance with no expression on his face. Understanding that this is not an uncommon reaction, the officer continued,

"Mr. Brown, your wife died when her car left the Highway 6 about fifteen miles east of here, sometime this morning. I am sorry, but we will need you to come to the hospital and identify the body. Are you here alone or is there someone that could drive you?

No answer came from Dan.

"If not, I can take you to the hospital," said the officer, knowing that the man had not heard most of what was said as soon as the word 'fatal' was uttered. He also knew his message had just destroyed this man.

Dan's knees momentarily buckled and he uttered, "Oh my God! Where is my wife?" said Dan as he grabbed the door knob, looking for support.

"We have taken her to Tillamook County General Hospital. Just ask at the front desk where you can view the body. I am so sorry Mr. Brown. Are you going to be alright? Do you need me to drive you?"

"I'll never be alright again," moaned Dan as his thoughts raced to Shelly.

The officer caught some motion over Mr. Brown's shoulder and his eyes met a small girl huddled along a wall. She was in her pajamas and was looking straight at him. Apparently, she had heard every word and now sat frozen in space with the most painful expression the officer had ever seen. He motioned to Dan and, seeing Shelly, Dan went to her and caught her up in his arms and they both wept and shared their pain. The officer, now fighting back tears, gave them several minutes before he again asked if he could assist by driving them to the hospital. Dan indicated no and that he was going to get someone to stay with Shelly. He did not want her going to the hospital.

The rest of the story was still being played out, day by day, often hour by hour. Each of them had a lot of healing to do, but Shelly seemed to be coming around, and if he could just keep her happy without imaginary friends, it would be even better. Her premonition about Lisa's accident and the police arriving on her cue, he had simply pushed to the back of his mind and he wanted to leave it there.

Pre Picnic

Expectations are tricky things. You focus too much on them and the results never seem to live up to the hype. You ignore them and pretend that something special isn't waiting around the corner and you end up dulling reality. Expectations are very tricky indeed.

Dan had his usual post Lisa day at work. He went about his work as a robot in a rusty tin can factory. Things looked familiar, but nothing made a lasting impression. Nothing seemed worthwhile. His employees had been more than kind and had taken up the slack where and when they could. But it was clear to all, even his customers, that his heart wasn't in it anymore. Nonetheless, with bills to pay and people counting on him, Dan did his best to stay afloat. He worried about the picnic this afternoon. He couldn't lose his little girl to this tragedy. As bad as it was, he knew it could have been worse. Lisa had talked about pulling Shelly from school and taking her along for a day adventure. Somehow Shelly sensed that the trip would end badly and had tried to talk her mother out of going. She had ended up in her father's arms, never giving a second thought to going with her mother. Thank God, for small miracles.

For the first time since her mother's accident, Shelly actually felt good. Today was going to be alright. Her father would see that she was right and then they could both figure out what the thing in the woods was.

Her best friend, Monica, could see the difference.

"Hey Shelly, you look different."

"Oh Monica, if only you knew."

"Knew what?"

"I can't tell you yet. But soon I can and then I'll show you," grinned Shelly.

"Girl, you're acting nuts. Think you can sleep over this weekend? My Dad said we are getting G-movies," implored Monica, sensing a chance to reconnect with her best buddy.

"I don't know. I can ask," said Shelly shocking herself and Monica with the reply. Since the accident, Shelly had barely acknowledged that anyone else existed. This was a good sign to Monica. Monica's mother said it would take time and once again, she was right.

Monica and Shelly had known each other since the first grade. Shelly was the second tallest kid in the fourth grade. Monica was easily the tallest. She was a head taller, with credit going no doubt to her two Amazonian

parents. Shelly's father had called them Amazons because they were both over six feet tall, with the father
being at least 6'8". When Shelly learned what Amazon
meant, she was furious with her father.

"That's mean Dad. Bet you wouldn't say that to
them."

Recognizing his blunder, he apologized and said, "I
should have just said they were uncommonly tall. Sorry
Shelly." Dan placed a lot of importance on being responsible and acknowledging when you were wrong.

Monica was bright, cheerful, and loved animals as
much as Shelly. They had bonded immediately and began seeing as much of each other as possible. Both sets
of parents became good friends because of the girls.
Monica's only shortcoming, no pun intended, was the im-
mense dislike for the color red, undoubtedly because she
had the reddest hair anyone had ever seen. It was absolutely brilliant. No Irish girl had ever had hair a shade
redder than that that sprouted from Monica's lofty head.
Shelly would tease her and ask her if she had been eating radioactive cereal again. Then she would say, "I
bet it glows in the dark. Bet you never needed a night
light." Teasing that only true friends could get away with.
Consequently, no red could be found at their home. She
didn't like anyone who wore red and, therefore, Shelly had
to redo her wardrobe. It was a reasonable concession

for such a strong friendship. Even Dan recognized the worth of it all.

The day dragged slowly by for Shelly. It was as if the second hand on the oversized Weston clock was teasing her. The minutes squeezed painfully by like an oversized dog trying to get through a doggie door two sizes to small. Why did they even put clocks in school rooms, she wondered? Was it a grown up form of torture to make you aware of how much of the day is wasted in school? Probably, she thought, because teachers needed to know when they could take a break and sneak down to the teacher's lounge and sit around and talk about how dumb you are.

Actually, Shelly didn't have to try very hard at school. She had been reading at a ninth grade level while still in the third grade. Her vocabulary was off the charts and boredom was the biggest enemy she had. Still, just beneath the oversized vocabulary was a little girl struggling to fit into life. Dan and Lisa had discussed skipping her a grade or two to give her a bigger challenge, but with the accident, Dan felt that now was not the time.

Finally, the last second slipped off the face of the clock like a drop of water sliding from a leaky faucet and the bell rang liberation. School was out! Order and decorum was required in the school building, but as soon as the kids cleared the main entrance, it was a harrowing, noisy sprint for the bus. Windows were coveted and the best seat, the back of the bus, was reserved for the big kids. Shelly was one of the last kids on the bus route. Her Dad had teased her that her name should have been FOLO, first on and last off. As soon as the bus came to a stop at the end of her road, she lunged out the door and began running to her house. Halfway down the road she slowed and stopped. Where was RutButt? The crazy cat always met her halfway down the road and shot up his eighteen inch antenna tail as a sign of undying love and eager anticipation. He would lace himself between her legs and rub his head deep into her calf. She would laugh, reach down and stroke him under the chin and then together they would race to the house. Shelly would throw herself onto the long green couch and RutButt would jump onto her chest and settle down with his nose so close to hers that she could feel his breath. A certain amount of cuddling and petting was due the lovable cat for deserting him all day. After about five minutes of purring love, Shelly would pat the big Tom on his hind quarters and say "Food?" RutButt would leap from her chest and dart for the kitchen. He would sit patiently at the oak kitchen table and nervously twitch his tail in anticipation. Once fed, her desertion for the day would be forgiven and all was right with the world.

But today, no RutButt. She searched the house and asked Miss Martinez, "Juanita, have you seen RutButt?"

"No, Shelly. Now that you mention it, not all day. Is the pet door open?"

Shelly checked, and the door was open. She promised herself to not get all worked up about him. He had vanished several times already, only to come home hours later. He was probably in the woods. She would find him later.

"Shelly, the Coles and Websters called and asked if we had seen their dogs. I told them no. Maybe you can look around some and see if you can find them while you're looking for your big tom cat," said Miss Martinez.

"Okay, but first I have to pack a picnic." She intended to save Dad time and surprise him all in one. Peanut butter and grape jelly sandwiches with Fritos, a big dill pickle and a can of pop each. For dessert, a Snickers. That should do it.

Dan called home and found Miss Martinez laughing at Shelly's picnic menu. "Mr. Brown, Shelly is very excited about the picnic," said Juanita Martinez. Dan had hired Juanita after having her clean his house on recommendation from Monica's parents. She had worked out wonderfully and Dan had quickly hired her full time to watch Shelly when he was gone and to clean house and prepare meals for them. Dan wondered if she was documented but somehow didn't feel right asking her, so he didn't. She sure seemed happy with the money and it kept her off the house cleaning circuit with steady income and a Christmas bonus. Shelly adored her in a distant sort of way. Juanita appeared to be a little younger than Dan, somewhere around thirty. She was slender and had midnight black hair usually arranged in an elegant, supple French braid. Dan had never really noticed how pretty she was. Her English was excellent, but clearly not her mother tongue. She drove an old triumph motorcycle, even in the rain. And most important of all, she cared. She cared for this broken family. She wanted to help them heal.

"Oh I knew she would be excited," said Dan. "Tell her I'm on my way and should be there around 5:00."

With the picnic out of the way, Shelly took a look around the house and the outbuildings for her kitty and any dogs that might be in the area. Living in the country had its advantages and disadvantages. Just a few close neighbors to worry about, but most conveniences were five miles away in town, with the exception of four family farms that eased up to the Brown property lines. Shelly's family didn't farm and had let the strawberry fields go fallow. They had wanted the land for land's sake. Both of her parents loved being outside of town. They loved the quiet and style of living that country life gave liberally. As she had often been told, you had to be self sufficient to live in the country, and didn't have to worry about kids gunning their cars up your street, gangs painting their signs on your fences, sirens wailing through the night, checking the newspaper to see what crimes had been committed in your zip code and, thankfully, no door to door evangelists. Lisa had been an insurance agent and could easily work from home. Dan's business was starting to slowly sprout and both needed the down time the country afforded.

Shelly's search turned up no dogs and more importantly, no cat. *Oh well,* she reflected, *he'll show up later.*

Dan arrived home right on time and barely had time to talk to Miss Martinez and go to the bathroom before Shelly was grabbing their coats and putting her back pack on with the picnic in it. She literally shoved her Dad out the kitchen door as Miss Martinez laughed and said, "I'll lock up and see you two in the morning."

Adventures in Picnicking

Picnics are underrated. Good things almost always happen at, during, or after a picnic. Sure there can be petty annoyances; rain storms, forgotten hotdogs, ants, or even minor arguments. Still, if you look with just a little bit of joy, you can find very delightful things. The sun as it etches its rays across the trees, the low flying birds that sing as they soar on feathered wings, the occasional sighting of a favorite animal and their caution turned to ease as they recognize your motives, the way food always tastes better after a hike, or the way people look deeply at each other with no distractions to gain their attention.

"Slow down Shelly. If you think I'm going to run all the way, you're sadly mistaken little miss who should know better."

"I'm just excited Dad. I can feel something neat is going to happen. I've been waiting all day and it just seemed like forever to get here. By the way, keep an eye out for RutButt, he didn't show up at the bus."

"Really? You excited? I never would have guessed. The Rutster is gone? That's not like him. He probably found a little girl cat to play with," teased Dan.

"Right," said Shelly, "and wouldn't he need testicles to do that?" inquired Shelly, who actually liked and paid attention in biology class.

"What? Who told you that?" said Dan, regretting ever starting this line of thought.

"Oh Dad, I've heard all about the birds and bees. It's no big deal," informed Shelly.

"Well, if you ever have any questions, please ask me first. I promise to tell you the truth," said Dan realizing that more conversations of this type would be even more necessary now that Lisa was gone. "Now, how much farther is this mysterious thing?"

"Over that hill by the giant pine tree down in a valley by a little stream," pointed Shelly.

"How many minutes?" asked Dan.

"I don't know. A lot less if we run," urged Shelly.

"Not a chance, girl. I had a rough day and I need a relaxed evening."

Fifteen minutes later they crested the gentle ridge of the valley and began their descent. As they drew closer to the meadow, they saw one of the strangest sights. Gathered in a large circle were cats, dogs, raccoons, two deer, a coyote, numerous rabbits, uncountable squirrels and birds of every description perched in the trees. All were silent, sitting and transfixed on nothing. At least nothing Shelly nor Dan could see. Friends and foes sat right beside each other and as the couple drew closer to the circle, Dan noticed snakes, frogs and insects also gathered around the circle. Undoubtedly there were others that Dan had not noticed. None showed even the least acknowledgment of the two interlopers. Most had their heads slightly cocked to one side or the other as if listening intently. Dan felt the hairs on his legs and arms standing up. He was scared, but he didn't even begin to fathom why. There was an eerie silence in the woods that Dan had not noticed until now. It was as if you could actually hear the plants growing. Shelly had a grin across her face bigger than when she got her ten speed bike last Christmas. She kept walking towards the animals but Dan held her back. "Stay right here. Do you hear me," said Dan in his most serious I'm not messing around voice.

"Okay, Dad," said Shelly, recognizing the need to obey. Dan eased himself closer, step by step, and not a single animal moved even when he was directly behind a coyote and three squirrels. He twisted his head from side to side, trying to pick up any sounds whatsoever. He heard nothing. He had a clear, unobstructed view of the entire circle of animals. He saw RutButt and softly called to him. No response at all. Dan reached out his hand and ran his knuckles into something about six feet high. He placed his palm on the smooth warm surface and pushed his hand as high as he could and still felt it curving ever so slightly away from him. He reached down and felt the glassy smooth surface again curving inward toward the center. Carefully, so as not to step on any creatures, he side stepped around the entire unseen orb as Shelly stood frozen, as if turned to salt. Whatever Dan was feeling, it managed to not distort his vision. It was completely invisible. While on the other side of the object, Dan picked up a small rock and told Shelly he was going to throw it to her. He drew back his arm and let fly. The rock traveled about five feet and clanked to the ground. Something was definitely in-between both of them. "Shelly, when I threw the rock, could you see it?"

"Yes. And I saw it bounce at your feet." The object was indeed there, but thoroughly invisible. Dan returned to his starting point and backed away slowly till he stood beside Shelly.

"I'm not a skeptic any longer, kiddo," said Dan with his mouth slightly open, his head tilted and both hands on his hips.

"I told ya Dad. It's pretty neat huh?"

"That's putting it mildly."

"I wonder how high it goes," posed Shelly more inclined to investigating than Dan.

"Well, let's see," said Dan reaching for another rock by his feet. With a soft arching toss, Dan heaved the stone twenty feet up and in toward the circle. Clink. The rock hit something and began rolling off the orb as they watched with their view undeterred.

"Way cool," shouted Shelly. Soon, 'way cool' echoed back at them. Dan took a step back and prepared to run if necessary. Nothing happened.

"Shelly, if I say run, head for home and don't look back. Go as fast as you can and call 911 and tell them an airplane crashed in our woods."

"Why would I say that?"

"Because they won't believe you if you say you saw a UFO. Now get ready." He placed his thumb and index finger in his mouth and issued a loud, long whistle. Nothing. Shelly tried the same process her Dad had taught her years ago and immediately bouncing back at them was a purer whistle of the same duration, but clearly a mimic of the first.

"Okay, so it echoes, too," said Dan. "You were right about everything honey. But why isn't it echoing our conversation?"

"I don't know Dad."

Just then it echoed back what Shelly had just said and not Dan's words.

"Wow," uttered Dan, "This just keeps getting stranger and stranger. Let me try and see if it will echo what I say. Hey, is anybody in there?"

Nothing again.

"It doesn't seem to like me."

"Oh Dad, maybe it doesn't know what you want."

As soon as Shelly uttered the last word of her sentence, the invisible globe echoed her entire statement.

"It only echoes what you say Shelly. Maybe it's because you found it," said Dan not believing he was actually saying something like that.

Suddenly, all of the creatures relaxed their heads and looked around the circle and turned and went their own ways without so much as a bark or chirp. RutButt walked right past Shelly and didn't even seem to recognize her even as she called to him.

"I think the animals may be hearing something we're not," said Dan.

"I know they are Dad. It's talking to them in their language."

Dan looked at Shelly for a long time and then said, "And I think whatever this thing is, it wanted us to find it."

"Of course it did Dad. I just wish I could see it." And as if on command, the invisible became visible. It was drenched in a rainbow of colors that constantly changed.

Dan had a grasp of its size now and just said, "Wow. Somebody pinch me." Shelly laughed with delight. Something Dan hadn't heard since that dreadful day. The orb again echoed her laughter, but Dan noticed that even though close, Shelly's original voice was better.

The orb was roughly seventy feet across. Large to be sure. It seemed to be a ball flattened at the top and the bottom, with the colors playing on it; it appeared to be a very big soap bubble languishing on a faint breeze. The colors disappeared after only a few minutes and it again became invisible. Dan knelt and looked under the ball and could see no compaction of the meadow grass. He reasoned it must be floating. He stepped up to the surface again and tried to push it. Nothing happened, except the harder he pushed the warmer his hands became. Crazy he thought to himself. Now what do I do?

They backed up by a large pine tree and sat down and stared at nothing. Shelly suggested they eat their picnic, and when Dan made no reply she began handing her Dad things from her backpack. Dan never took his eyes off of the spot where the object had sprung into the visible spectrum.

"What do you think it is Dad?" asked Shelly, still at that age where parents are the smartest things in the world.

"I don't have a clue honey. But I know this: it's intelligent. Somebody or something is controlling this thing. Let's finish our sandwiches and get back to the house. Hopefully it will be here when we return."

"Don't worry Dad. It's not going anywhere for quite a long while."

"How do you know that Shelly?"

"I just do. I feel it. It's here for us. It is going to help us somehow," replied Shelly gazing at the invisible orb with joy written all over her face. Dan hadn't seen her contented or happy in months, but here she was making predictions again. He felt a shiver run up his spine.

"Now finish your sandwich daughter and let's march."

Both finished their messy sandwiches with the colorful ooze dripping down to their hands, packed up their backpack and began walking out the valley and over the hill. At the top of the hill, both stopped and took one last look at nothing. Comfortable sounds had returned to the woods. But the mood of the valley seemed to hold sway on everything. It was as if the forest was holding its breath. There was a new tenant in the woods, or maybe a new landlord.

Taking Stock

We all do it; we take a baseline of our everyday situations and hardly even know we are doing it. You walk into a room and note the noise level, the temperature and if the faces appeared friendly or not. You take a quick survey of your immediate environment. Everyone and everything does it.

The expedition's excellent progress continued. Not only had the small human returned, but she had brought her male adult unit with her. They observed them for a long period of time as they inspected the ship and consumed nourishment. Rather strange behavior, Golic thought, to bring a meal to what surely was an enormous event by earth standards. But that is exactly the kind of observation they were here to make.

The crew had successfully gathered the DNA of the plant life in the local vicinity. The plants had been imaged, cataloged and scanned for the contamination. What so often happened in this region of the planet was rain; that's why it was selected as the target site. Oregon, as the humans called it, receives annual rainfall ranging from 120 to 6 inches per year. The Cascade Mountain Range was the determining factor. Hugging the coast line, it captured most of the moisture and deposited it on the western side of the range. The habitation of Tillamook was just such a location. The average rainfall for this area was 120 inches per year, with the record being 204 inches in 1996. Remarkably, they received 27 inches in one thirty day period with the strange sounding name of November of that same year. That's roughly 1 inch per day! Rain was a part of life for the inhabitants of this region. Humans had been observed playing games, walking in the woods, gathering consumables in buildings they called shopping centers, and going to the beach in the rain. Most traveled with a garment to ward off the moisture and some had portable roofs called umbrellas within easy access. The humans had adapted well, and, to them, it didn't matter if it rained or not. Things needed to be done and they were. That is what made the humans such an interesting species to study. They adapted so well and so completely.

As far as contamination was concerned, only slight trace elements were being seen. But change was in the wind— literally.

Walking and Talking

What makes humans so amazing is the way they process life. Something identical can happen to three people and they will all react differently. They internalize the event and try to make sense of it. They put it in various boxes in their minds until they find one that fits perfectly. There it will lay for however long it takes before they feel safe to take it out and play with it.

All the way back to the house, Shelly peppered her father with questions: How much do you think it weights? Is it light as a bubble or heavy as a house? Do you think people are inside it? How many? How do they get in without doors and how do they drive without windows? Why is it warm? Are they cold blooded (a term she had just learned in biology)? I bet they're herbivores.

Dan just kept on walking and occasionally shook his head. Finally he said, "Look sweetie, I don't know what this is or what it does. Honestly, you know as much as I do. You are asking a lot of good questions but I have no idea how to answer them. Let me work on this a while.

Now listen very carefully to me Shell, do not tell anyone what happened. And I mean anyone. If you do, people will laugh at you and think you're crazy."

"But Dad, we gotta tell somebody."

"I'm working on that also. I'll make some calls tomorrow and see if we can get some help."

"Won't they think you're crazy?"

"They may, but I'm an adult and might have an easier time convincing them. Okay?"

"You bet Dad. And by the way, I love you."

Dan stopped in his tracks. His jaw tightened, a tear began to form. Shelly hadn't said she loved him since the accident. He picked her up and held her tight and kissed her all over her face until she filled the woods with her laughter and she was desperate for air and pleading for him to stop. For a moment, they both felt on top of the world.

Dan gently placed his daughter back on firm ground and said, "Race ya to the back door." Shelly darted off through the undergrowth. Dan jogged along careful to let her win but just as careful to make her try real hard.

At the backdoor with his head sticking out of the pet door was ole RutButt. He gracefully stepped outside and intertwined himself in Shelly's legs. She picked his twenty two pounds of sinew and muscle up and he buried his large head in her long brown hair. Dan watched and knew that RutButt, as much as it hurt him to say it, had really been the one thing that kept Shelly going these past few months. Dan had emphasized her responsibilities to the cat and told her that her mother would expect nothing less than pure love and attention to that kitten. The bond couldn't be stronger if they had been real brother and sister. They needed each other in so many ways. They slept together, nearly bathed together with RutButt sitting on the edge of the bathtub and dipping his paw in playfully, they ate together with a chair at the dinner table reserved for his highness, and they cuddled and preened each other whenever they could. RutButt had an unusually large tongue and would start licking Shelly's face, and if she moved he would put a very strong large paw on her as if holding down a kitten. It was a joy for Dan to see. He loved that old cat almost as much as Shelly.

Together they all went into the house. Dan and Shelly both took one last look towards the woods before closing the door. Neither felt anything ominous, but instead a curious relief settled upon them.

"Oh Dad, tell the Major I'm looking forward to seeing him."

Dan just looked at his daughter in disbelief.

Just the Facts, Sir

It is amazing the difference a real friend makes. Regardless of how much time has passed since you last saw or talked to this person, immediate rapport is established by just saying hello. Real friends don't need, want, or expect excuses; they just want your friendship and the hope that you will call them whether you're in need.

Dan and Shelly lived off of Highway 6 about five miles east outside of Tillamook, Oregon. A great place to raise a child, Lisa always said, except for the colossal amount of rainfall. "Oh well," she would say, "that's what makes it green, and you know when you're green you grow and when you're ripe you rot." Then she would laugh the same hypnotizing laugh and brandish a gleaming white smile punctuated with a dimple smack dead center in her chin. Thankfully, Shelly had inherited all.

Dan had met Lisa when he was stationed at McChord Air Force Base and Lisa was living in Tacoma. McChord AFB is located about 35 miles south of Seattle and a mere 10 miles south of Tacoma in North West Washington.

Dan had not been some hot shot pilot; instead he was an excellent logistics officer. Lisa was a college student in her last year at University of Puget Sound, majoring in Business Administration and Management. They had both happened to attend a "Woodsy". A Woodsy is basically a party, set deep in the woods, or someone's backyard, where you drink all you can until you throw up. Neither was into the drinking scene but they did enjoy the boisterous crowd and funny antics a woodsy with lots of booze can manifest. Gradually they began seeing more of each other until Lisa, not Dan, got down on her knee in a pizza parlor and proposed marriage on the condition that Dan leave the military. Dan had given more than just a few hints that while he liked his job and the people he worked with, he was not a spit and shine kind of guy. The regulations the military dealt out with their especially large and nasty tasting spoon seemed to always go down wrong. Lisa sensed this and felt a good push might help. It did. He accepted on the spot and they were married within a year and settled just outside of Tillamook, a town known for its crabbing and local cheeses.

Now, tucked away in nowhere land, Dan needed help. His first option was to call his old unit Commander, Major Johns, a good man with a consistent approach to life. Honesty is the best policy in all situations.

"Major Johns, can I help you?"

"Major this is Dan Brown, do you have a moment?"

"You old shit. How they hangin bad boy," said the Major dropping his usual protocol. "Oh course I got some time. By my calculations, five years and thirty seven days and a wake up. What's up, drain buster?" said the Major taking a swipe at his plumbing business.

"Glad to hear you're the same sorry ass I always knew. You sure sound good Johns," replied Dan referring to the Majors last name as most military men did. "I got a situation that I need your expertise on."

"Must be nasty shit if you gotta call me."

"It is buddy. Are we secure on this line?" inquired Dan.

"Damn straight."

"Okay. Here goes. Now don't laugh and let me finish before you lay into me. Last night I saw a for real bona fide, certified, absolute, without-a-doubt UFO."

"Oh shit and I thought this was serious," gruffed the Major. "I seen two of them myself. So what?"

"Well I know that and I believed you. That's why I'm calling. What the hell am I suppose to do?"

"How foolish do you want to look, compadre? Cause they're gonna make you look mighty stupid if you go public."

"Johns, I touched it and it answered Shelly's whistle with its own whistle."

"What? No shit? You touched it? Don't mess with me Dan!" said the suddenly serious Major.

"Scouts honor. Swear on whatever I need to swear on Johns. It happened. Scared the bejezus right out of me."

"Dan, listen carefully and take notes if you can't keep up. Remember the show Dragnet?"

"Yes, I'm not completely brain dead."

"Detective Friday always had that one great line in every show: 'Just the facts sir, nothing but the facts.' If you intend, and I think you do, to go public, better have your facts lined up in a pretty tight little neat row. Verify, verify and verify again. No sloppy work. Know exactly what you're talking about and know how much you want to say. It's one thing to see a UFO, it's a whole nuther can a worms to claim personal contact. Remember that poor bastard that claimed he and his wife, somewhere in the Deep South, got beamed up to the mother ship? Damn near drove him crazy going public. Think about it, son."

"I have, and there's more. This UFO is invisible but feels like a large ball about seventy feet across. And last night, every kind of animal in the woods was gathered around the damn thing just staring at it. And, at Shelly's suggestion, it became visible. I can't be any more seri-ous Major, this is for real."

"Anyone else comes to me with this cockamainy story and I'd personally certify them 4F. But you, my friend, I trust. What do you think it's doing in your backyard and why in God's name are you taking Shelly out there?"

"She took me, Major. She found it and I wish I knew what it was doing. Think you can spring a three day and come see it?"

"Ohhhh, so that's what you want. Why didn't I see it before? Dumb shit plumber won't be believed by the lo-cals, but big shot, everything to lose Air Force man lends credibility to this screw ball séance."

"Sure, that plus maybe convince me that Shell and I aren't cracking up or seeing mighty slick swamp gas. I'll have lots of beer, and not that cheap stuff you drink."

An agonizing quiet descends on the line as Dan waits until the Major says, "Ah shit, why not? Who needs a retirement? Call me tomorrow and if it's still there, give me the green light and I'll fly the base Cessna over for a few days. In the meantime, my wacky friend, I hope you plan on documenting what you got. Pictures, mea-surements, maybe ask it a few questions, etc. Can you handle that?"

"I'm covering all those bases, sir. Hey, what about notifying the Department of Defense?"

"Where have you been? Don't you know the military is out of that business? All you got left is loonies and their less than trustworthy web sites. No, for now keep a lid on it. Call me if the meatball is still there tomorrow. Now get to work and let me get back to my nap."

"Thanks, Major. Talk to you soon."

A Friendly Get Together

Dan didn't want to take Shelly on his next excursion to the valley. He wanted to do it on his own. No telling what he might turn up, and he didn't need her underfoot. He excused himself from work and left Bob in charge. Bob was a no-nonsense kind of guy. He had lived in Tillamook all of his life and literally knew just about everyone and the names of their dogs. He was a natural hire for Dan. He not only was a certified plumber, but with his contacts it made it a heck of a lot easier for Dan to get his foot in the door with the community. His plumbing business, called PLUMB CERTAIN, was doing alright for a business on the rebound, and Bob was a big part of that success. Bob was big in a lot of ways. He was 6'5", and although he wouldn't tell anyone, he had to weigh at least three hundred pounds. Nevertheless, he was nimble when he needed to be. He carried his size gracefully, and, except for the unkempt mustache, he was neat as a pin, efficient and polite. Dan trusted him explicitly.

"Bob, I've got some things to take care of today. I have sent all the bills and invoices out, and we have enough supplies to last through the month. If you run out of any-thing, just buy it on the company credit card. Keep the crew running and call me on the cell if you have an emer-gency. I'll try to call you this evening for an update."

"No problem boss. Is there anything wrong?" Usually Bob would never ask such a question, but everyone at the office knew Dan was under a lot of stress after Lisa died and with Shelly being so remote and worrisome lately, he felt he needed to pry a little bit.

"No, Bob. Actually, things are looking up. Shelly seems to be coming around and I just have to get some things in order for a visit from an old Air Force buddy this week. I'll catch ya later." With that, Dan rose from be-hind his desk and exited the side door and headed for his van. Bob and Shirley, the receptionist/office manager, exchanged glances and went on about their business.

Dan headed for the camera store to pick up a video camera for the afternoon's work. He needed to docu-ment everything that was going on. He was able to find an excellent Canon Mini DVD Camcorder that could do more things than he possibly could understand. It was pricy, but a quality rig, and it was just plain necessary. Arriving at home, he explained to Miss Martinez what he was doing home, "Juanita, Shelly and I found something in the woods yesterday and I want to film it. If Shelly comes home, make her stay until I return. Okay?"

"Okay Mr. Brown. What did you find?" asked a naturally curious Miss Martinez.

"I'm not sure. That's why I intend to take some pictures of it. I should be back in a couple of hours. If I'm later, can you stay till I return?"

"Claro que si, Mr. Brown," said Juanita, slipping into her Spanish, "of course I can. But can I see the pictures?"

"Sure. Why not? I'm going to grab a few things out of the garage and then I'll head out. Keep Shelly here, please."

Some Things Better Left Alone

Most people like to think they are special. The rules, however well meaning, somehow don't apply to them. They think they will be able to tame the surly dog, or simply show the bully how to get along with everyone, and the all time favorite, smoking, regardless of what it says on the pack, won't give them cancer. Looking through one's own lens on life doesn't ensure a rosy outcome. It does, however, often guarantee an up close and personal, get your fingers dirty, and wish you hadn't touched that experience.

Dan took a backpack and put the camcorder, a tape measure, a notepad and pen, a pocket tape recorder, a flashlight, and a rope into the backpack. He was sure there was something he was forgetting, but for now this would have to suffice.

The walk to the valley seemed to fly by. Dan had taken the pocket recorder out and was giving a play by play commentary of the events leading up to yesterday's events. He noted the date and time when he finally crested the hill overlooking the valley. He froze. He stared in disbelief and then dropped to the ground. Surrounding the orb were now thirty or so people. Again like the animals their attention was fixed on where the invisible ball hovered. They also had their heads slightly tilted. Dan recognized several of the people. Some were neighbors, the police chief, the owner of the grocery store, that good-looking red headed cheerleader from the high school and others he couldn't see well or recognize. He began fumbling with his backpack trying to get it off his shoulders so he could retrieve the camcorder. Careful not to make any noises, he brought the camera to his eye and pushed the record button. Nothing happened. He had neglected to read the instructions on the new electronic gizmo. After a few agonizing moments he was able to turn it on and start recording. As he did, he whispered into the mic and gave a running commentary on what was unfolding before him. Actually, nothing was unfolding before him. No one moved, no light show, no noises, nothing. What was going on down there? Suddenly, an extremely bright oval opening appeared in one of the sides of the orb. The light beamed outward from the ball and seemed to have a different quality to it, almost as if it were alive. It didn't look like any lighting he had ever seen. A woman, who Dan did not recognize, straightened her head and stepped into the light and disappeared into the opening. About five minutes later, a dark puff of smoke could be seen coming from the bottom of the cloaked ball. Five more minutes passed, and then all the people straightened their heads, turned, and began walking out of the woods. They went basically two different directions: toward Dan and off to his right cutting into the Webster's field. About seven of them were coming right at him. Dan rose up from the ground and dusted himself off as they approached. He kept the camera rolling. None of them talked to each other and they didn't seem to even notice each other. As they walked by Dan, he tried to talk with them but they had a strange faraway look in their eyes and just kept moving. Dan kept the camcorder on the progression as he tried to communicate. At least he would have some evidence of the strange goings on. He worried about the people but he also needed to get some data for Major Johns.

When the zombie-like people had cleared his field of view, he turned his attention back to the ball. He wanted to get some close up photos and measure it. He started down the hill to the valley. It was actually a beautiful day and the rain had been kept at bay by a wind shift and a curiously aggressive sun. He kept the camera running as he descended the hill. Once in front of the orb he said, hoping the ball would glimmer in existence, "I wish to see you." Nothing happened as Dan kept filming. He let out a loud whistle, and again, nothing happened. He tried one additional thing; he tossed a rock up on top of the object and thankfully, he heard it careen and clunk down the object and fall at his feet. *Well,* he thought, *I guess it doesn't like me.*

Without further delay, Dan squatted down and systematically began looking under the orb for the dark cloud that it emitted after the woman had entered the contraption. To his left and about three feet in front of him, he saw some discolored grass and was able to lie on his stomach and stretch his arm as far as possible to retrieve a small handful of grass. His fingers were now coated with the gray material. He put the grass in his pants pocket and stood up. Stepping back from the ball he said, "Is there somebody in there?"

No reply.

"Can I ask you some questions?"

No reply.

"Why are you here?"

No reply.

"Okay, then I guess you won't mind if I take some measurements," said Dan. Since the craft was invisible, he found two large fallen branches and leaned them up on opposite sides of the UFO. Then, he began to dole out his tape measure to get a more accurate account of its size. He came up with sixty six feet as his best estimate of the diameter of the sphere. He grabbed more branches and stripped away as much as he could so that he ended up with relatively straight poles. He started leaning the poles, equidistance from each other, against the ball until he had eight poles surrounding the ball. He stepped back and turned the camera on. The branches gave the invisible object some dimensions and allowed him to better grasp its size. He put his camcorder down on a stump as he adjusted the focus to include all the branches and he stepped into view to add additional perspective. Then he remembered the newspaper he had purchased for this occasion to verify the date. He had left it in his truck. *Oh well, maybe next time,* he thought. He stated his name, date and time. Dan gathered a few leafy branches and tossed them up onto the top of the ball and filmed once again. It looked like a magician's trick. Everything was caught on camera.

Returning to his camera, Dan once again asked, "Does anyone or anything want to say something to planet earth? This is your last chance. I've got to go home and eat." No response.

Dan backed away from the ball and couldn't help but think that this was almost fun. Then he remembered the zombies leaving the valley and "'fun" no longer seemed the best choice of words. Dan gathered his camera and loaded his backpack. He couldn't help the sensation to keep looking at the thing. He half expected that a monster would rush him as soon as he looked away. Dan hiked out of the valley and turned to have one last look at his handy work from the top of the hill. Dan's blood ran cold as he stared dumbfounded at the scene below. The branches had been quietly and artistically rearranged. Now, hovering in front of the object, they had been bent to spell out, in cursive, *Shelly*. Dan raised his camera to film the magic unfolding before him and the sticks immediately fell to the ground in a jumble. Dan turned and ran all the way home, praying that Shelly would be waiting for him.

A Gathering

Get-togethers can be fun; holiday meals, birthday parties, anniversaries, and the ever popular bunch of friends out on a Saturday night. In most cases there is implied consent to be at the occasion. Gatherings at other times can be purely involuntary; military roll call, quarterly business reviews and traffic court appearances. It's important to remember that, regardless of the occasion, someone is always in charge and you need to know who.

Kosh had followed Golic's recommendations with excellent results. He had been able to patch in to the local tele-communications system employed in this region and, by cross referencing, had developed a list of two hundred potential survey candidates. Calling each person and asking for them directly, the ships computer system then determined if they had reached the right party. If not, it simply terminated the connection and moved on to the next one on the list. If it reached the correct individual, a two second sub audible tone was emitted that directed the human to proceed to the ship at a certain date and time. It was a most effective means of inert compulsion. An advanced type of hypnosis.

The electronic burst also instructed them to develop a logical alibi for their absence and that all was to be forgotten except their need to be at the coordinates on time. Eventually, forty subjects were contacted and the ship's computer, named Neep for its prime inventor, notified Kosh. Now all that remained was for one outsider to be selected for the survey. They needed an outsider because this human was expendable and they did not want to raise suspicions locally.

The scanning of the forty subjects had gone well. They had learned new information about the area and a great deal of trivia concerning local politics, entertainment, and sporting events. Not much real usable data, however. Golic had been able to supply the expendable human and a complete body analysis had been performed.

The only surprise was that Shelly's parental unit had reappeared and filmed some of the activities. In addition, the human noted basic measurements of the craft and witnessed the expulsion of the analyzed waste. It was assumed he took samples of the end product with him. Lastly, the parental unit tried to communicate with the ship. Unfortunately his aura is typical and much less impressive than the girl's. To date, none have come close to her luminous intensity.

Finders Keepers

Shelly saw her father running towards the house and eagerly ran toward him. She closed the gap in no time at all. Grinning widely, with pigtails flapping, Shelly really was a very strong runner and overall athlete. She had inherited that from her mother's side of the family. Dan picked her up in his arms and pulled her close to his chest.

"Oh Shelly, I am so glad to see you."

"I'm glad to see you too, Dad," said Shelly slightly surprised by her father's embrace. "Did you go to ball? Did you take pictures? Miss Martinez said you would show her. Can I see 'em too?" blurted Shelly in her typical run-on sentence style.

Dan gave Shell one last kiss on the cheek and put her back on terra firma. "I got some pictures and it's still there. I have to call Major John's right away. He will be coming to visit," said Dan, purposefully ignoring the pictures question.

"Let's get the pictures developed, I want to see them," implored Shelly.

"Actually," said Dan, sliding the camcorder out of the backpack, "no need to develop. I've got it all on a disc."

"Wow Dad! When did you get that? Can I try it?"

"I just bought it today, and no, you cannot try it. It's off limits. Do you understand?"   "Yes father," said Shelly in her patronizing voice. "But we need pictures of you too."

"Maybe later. But I have a video on the disc and it's important. You could accidentally erase it. It's off limits for now. Let's go in. I need to call the Major and let Juanita go home."

Dan dismissed Juanita and told her she would have to see the video some other time. As he told her, he noticed her rather large chocolate brown eyes. Funny he had never noticed before. He hurried to his study and closed the door and called Major Johns.

"Hello Major. This is Dan."

"Well Dan is it go or no go?"

"Definitely a GO Major. Got pictures, dimensions and I saw a crowd of people standing around it acting like zombies. They acted like they were in a trace, only vaguely aware of themselves and no one else. Very strange stuff Major. I'd like to get you out here ASAP."

"Dan, did you view the film yet?"

"Actually, it's a video, and no, not yet."

"While I've got you on the phone, take a look. I'm curious," said the Major.

"Hang on, Major. I'm going to put you on the speaker phone while I figure this thing out."

"You never were much good with anything with more than one button," joked the Major. "I'm surprised you didn't have to get Shelly to show you how to use the speaker phone." Dan laughed but secretly knew it was indeed Shelly who had figured it out and not him.

"Okay Major, it's coming up. I can see everything on the little screen that pops out. Yep. I got it and you know what, it's scarier the second time around."

"If you know how, make a copy now. If you're not absolutely sure, just leave it alone and I'll do it when I get there. I assume you have a PC with read and write disc capabilities," replied the Major.

"I'm gonna leave all of that for you Major. Now get here and call me when you are thirty minutes out and I'll come get ya."

"Roger that, I will leave early tomorrow morning. Should be there around 11:00 AM. See ya then."

"Thanks Major. Blue sky and fly safe."

Dan emerged from the study with the distinct impression that Shelly had been listening at the door. *Only natural*, he thought. "How about some dinner, girl?"

"Sure, then can we see the video?"

"Not tonight Shell. I want to review it with the Major first and have some sort of plan ready before we start showing this to anybody and that includes you."

"Ah Dad, that's not fair. I found it and told you about it. It's more mine than yours. Finders keepers and all that stuff."

"Actually, Shelly, I don't think it considers itself anybodies property. This thing could be very dangerous; dangerous not only to us, but to everyone. We need to be careful around it."

"But Dad, I already saw a bunch of people coming out of the woods. Now lots of people know. What's the secret?"

Crap, Dan thought to himself. *I had hoped she wouldn't have seen them. She is way too logical for her age.*

"Shelly, I don't know if those people know what they saw, and we don't want to try and remind them. Leave them all alone for now. Got it?"

"Yes sir," replied Shell with dejection etched in her eyes.

"Now let's eat, feed your kitty, do your homework and take a bath. Then it's lights out."

Bath and Bed

At *least,* thought Dan, *Shelly is acting more alive than she has since the funeral. Now I just have to keep her away from the woods and under control.* Dinner was delicious, the usual for Juanita. Chicken enchiladas, fresh refried beans, a great spinach salad and a crumb cake made from a box, all a wonderful treat. Without Juanita, Dan couldn't have made it the past several months. She was a godsend.

RutButt sat as his chair and stretched his neck as far as possible to take in every molecule of aroma that wafted off the casserole. Shelly enjoyed the discipline game she played with the oversized cat at every meal. RutButt would try to massage the etiquette rules for eating and Shelly would gently reel him in and keep him from pouncing on the table and lapping up all in his path. Their companionship was essential to each of them. They formed an extension of each other and regularly made sure to tease one another. After supper, when the dishes were cleared, Shelly prepared her bath water and slipped beneath the seven inches of lavish soap bubbles that accompanied every bath she took. RutButt sat on the edge of the bath tub and squinted his Egyptian eyes in contentment. His Cleopatra eyes were enormous tonight and his expression was one of wonder and love. Shelly was chest high in suds and Dan knew it would only be another year and the bathroom would be off limits to him. But for now he enjoyed watching his little girl bathe under the watchful eyes of the majestic and protective King RutButt.

They say that dogs believe they are people, while cats think people are part of their pride. Dan wasn't sure where he fit in the equation, but he knew Shelly belonged to RutButt.

With the bath over, Shelly headed to bed and Dan to the study. First he called Bob and told him he was taking a week's vacation because his old friend was coming to town. With that white lie out of the way, he reviewed the video and got all goose bumpily again. It was creepy. Two hours later, Dan made his way to the emptiest room in the house, his bedroom. Without Lisa by his side, Dan no longer immediately fell into a deep, satisfying sleep. Instead, he tossed and turned. Occasionally he cried and often awoke with a start as he relived the trooper coming to the front door. Now, anyone coming to the front door automatically elicited that one terrible moment of his life. He hated the front door and tried never to use it. Hopefully tonight he could escape the past and not repeat the all too familiar routine. Tonight he wanted blissful sleep. Total unawareness would be welcome.

Late Night Caller

Visitors bring much into our lives. Good memories, late night talks, a chance to hear tales about your family or share photographs. Tonight, a different kind of visitor arrived unannounced and intent on perpetrating its own agenda. Not exactly what anyone had in mind.

At somewhere around 2:00 in the morning, Shelly was awakened with a warm sensation on her body. It wasn't RutButt because he usually slept under her covers, curled up by her feet. No, this was a warm like a blanket that had just come out of the clothes dryer, deep and snugly satisfying. Sensing a light in the room, she opened her eyes and beheld a fuzzy, round, soft green ball slowly moving down her body. Scared at first, Shelly clutched her fists and started to scream, but then, the light changed colors and glowed a deep red. Shelly relaxed and just watched as the ball slipped and hovered around the room. RutButt, deep into a kitten dream about mice or catnip, sensed nothing. The light glided over her furniture, clothes, pictures, knickknacks and stopped over her school books and backpack and hesitated a few moments before moving on. It drifted into the hall and toward her father's room. Shelly slid out of bed and quietly followed a few feet behind. The light paused by the closed door and then effortlessly ducked under the crack at the bottom of the door and eased into her father's room. Shelly, as quiet as a leaf fluttering down to the ground, gingerly opened the door and pushed it aside. Her father was sound asleep and didn't stir as the light again replayed its stealthy tendencies. It seemed to be taking an inventory or maybe taking pictures of everything in the room. Like before, it moved over her father's body, as it had hers. Then, she noticed it spent more time over any book or magazine it encountered. In only a few minutes, it exited the room and Shelly feared it might run right into her, but at the last moment it lifted silently above her head, paused and moved into the living room. The process was repeated in all of the rooms, even the garage. Seeming to have all the information it needed, it moved to the fireplace and, before leaving, approached Shelly again and hovered face high for several seconds before shooting up the fireplace and into the night.

Shelly stood in front of the red brick fire place with her mouth wide open for several seconds, and then the glowing orb reappeared at the back door window and seemed to be waiting. It moved to the back of the yard and again waited. It raced at the back door, stopped, and bolted for the backyard fence where it paused. After several more passes, Shelly got the hint and ran to her bedroom and slipped her sneakers on and grabbed a jacket and a flash light. She hoped her father wouldn't be mad.

By Invitation Only

Shelly raced to catch up with the glowing fuzz ball. It now was a much lighter shade of green, almost yellow, and seemed to be helping in lighting the path. Patiently it waited. Satisfied the child was in tow, it proceeded up the trail towards the woods, the valley, and the summoning ship.

The woods were eerily quiet. The squishing and crunching of Shelly's sneakers and her slightly irregular breathing were all that could be heard. The pace to the orb was steady and very manageable. Shelly had the feeling that the now yellow fuzz ball could accelerate to unbelievable speeds if it wanted, but it was courteous and waited for the excruciatingly slow bi-pedal Shelly. As they neared the crest of the hill that led into the valley of the orb, the yellow fuzz ball zipped ahead and Shelly saw it center itself above what must be the invisible orb. It changed color to a deep ruby red and then blinked out. It vanished. Gone in a flash. Lickity split, as her grandpa would say.

Shelly instinctively knew the ship wanted her here and alone. The specific reason was unknown but, frankly, she liked the adventure and attention. As she approached the usual resting spot of the globe, it flashed into life. The most beautiful color Shelly had ever seen, and she knew her colors. She had been the proud owner of the largest Crayola box in third grade; boasting a whopping 96 colors. In addition, she portioned out some of her allowance and eventually acquired the Crayola Colored Pencil set of 50. She was a **connoisseur** of color. Her room had four distinctly different colored walls and a ceiling full of glow in the dark stars. Color was her friend, except red in deference to her best friend Monica. Now she was stumped. What was this color the orb gave so gently to her? It wasn't quite blue, not an aqua, definitely not an azure, closer to cobalt, but sort of navy with a tinge of sapphire or perhaps indigo. It was glorious to behold. As she bathed in its vibrancy the color abruptly changed to a silver metallic surface and a figure could be seen assembling itself to the side of the sphere. It was hazy at first but soon grew distinct and very real. "Mom," yelled Shelly as she ran to the image! She ran right through the image and spun on her heels. "Mom, is that you?" Again she tried to reach out and touch the vision but felt nothing but air as her hand effortlessly passed through the apparition. In that sweet voice that Shelly dreamt about, and had almost forgotten, the ghost said, "Shelly, this is the image and voice of your mother, Lisa Brown. It is not your mother, but instead what you on earth call a hologram."

Screaming as she cried, Shelly uttered one word, "Why?"

"Because we thought this would be the most effective way of communicating with you. We have scanned you and your father's memories and have constructed this hologram for you."

"But you look like Mom and sound like Mom."

"Yes. That is what was intended."

"Can you talk to my Mom?"

"No. She is dead. She died in a vehicle accident. If this image is too unsettling, we can shift to something else. Perhaps someone you never knew personally." The hologram immediately changed to Bugs Bunny and said, "Eh, what's up doc? Are you more comfortable with me?"

"No!" screamed Shelly. "Bring her back." Lisa Brown again resumed her role as hologram.

"Shelly, please remember this is just an image. Do not get emotionally attached. May we continue now?" Shelly was sitting on her knees in front of the image taking in every nuance. Without waiting for an answer the ship resumed, "We did not select this site randomly. We have been monitoring this town for some time and became aware of your talents while doing so. You have an ability and clarity of thought that is far ahead of most humans. This and your unusual aura make you a natural selection for our survey. We need current input into our data that takes into account the emotions and decisions of those affected by the pending environmental and cultural changes. We would like to study you, and, indirectly, your family."

"You mean like in biology class? Are you going to dissect me?"

"No, we have a thorough understanding of human physiology, and therefore dissection is not necessary. We are more interested in how you cope with the coming events."

"What events?"

"The changes that involve your environment and social issues. We would like you to be our guide."

"We? Are there more than one of you?" requested Shelly.

"Very perceptive of you, Shelly. Yes, there are four of us."

"Will I get to meet you?"

"We'll see," said the hologram, looking and sounding like Lisa Brown, but not acting like her. The hologram was stiff and emotionless. Shelly's Mom could cry during a TV commercial. She became very upset with actors that played the bad guy in movies and refused to like them again no matter what role they played. She was an emotional volcano, spewing love, laughter and hugs with remarkable frequency. Shelly could not remember a single day that her mother had not told her that she loved her, usually followed by a kiss and a big, warm, smothering hug. The hologram was lifeless. Effective, but lifeless. Shelly sat motionless, staring at the hologram which had crouched down and appeared to be looking at her. Again, Shelly reached out her hand seeking a solid body, and found none.

"Why are you doing this to me?" asked Shelly now growing visibly angry.

"We have told you. We need to know more about the human condition."

"What do you mean, 'human condition'?"

"What drives your decision making process? How concerned are you about the life of the planet and its various species? What is your understanding of a higher power? These and many other questions."

"Why don't you talk to my Dad about this stuff? He knows a lot more than I do."

"We have observed that with age comes a loss of the natural essence each human is born with."

"What does that mean?"

"It means older humans lose some of the innate abilities they are born with. They become sterile in their ability to understand certain things. Most mature humans rarely see life as it really is. We need to study those more open to new possibilities. Yesterday we scanned many humans from your area and found them to be quite normal and of no further interest. We have limited time and need to exchange data with you. But, we need someone who freely wants to help us understand the human condition. Are you willing to help us?" Shelly sat quietly and thought about what they were asking, whoever they were, and she decided to help if her father would let her. Before she could answer the hologram said, "Don't worry about your father, we will persuade him. Thank you Shelly."

"I prefer to talk instead of think to you," said Shelly abruptly.

"We understand. You do not want to communicate with your mind. You would rather use vocalization. Is that right?"

"If you mean talk instead of read my mind, yes. You creep me out when you read my thoughts. Please stay out of my head. Do I get to ask questions?"

"Of course. We will do our best to answer you. Are you comfortable with our arrangement?"

"I guess. Shall I start?" solicited Shelly, intent on learning all she could.

"Not now Shelly. It is late by your earth days and you should be resting. Before you leave we want to enhance your mental capacities. You currently have skills most people don't. You can see things that will happen before they do. You can meet other humans and understand intimate things about them. You see people's auras. We are going to help you evolve to an even higher place. You would have gotten there eventually, but it probably would have taken you thirty or forty years to achieve. With our help, it will take you just a few minutes. When the yellow ball passes over you, you will notice a slight warming and dizziness. Do not be alarmed. Tomorrow you may have some headaches and want to stay in a dark place. This is quite normal. Do not be afraid. You will also begin to sense things about your surroundings and the people you come into contact with. It will be much stronger than before. Be careful who you tell about this ability. It will frighten some and may even cause them to distrust you. Are you ready?"

"I guess. Do I just sit here?"

"Yes. Relax. It will only take a moment."

The yellow orb floated out of the top of the ship and hovered just over Shelly's head. She could feel the warmth calm her body and the glow somehow made her smile. There was no noise or smell, just a calm feeling.

"Thank you Shelly. Please go home now and we will start tomorrow. Thank you."

"Okay, but I doubt I can sleep. See you tomorrow. Sleep tight, don't let the bugs bite, but if they do, get your shoe and beat them black and blue."

"What does that mean, Shelly?"

"It's just something nice to say before you turn out the lights and go to sleep."

"Is beating bugs a devotion to your God?"

"If you mean a prayer, no. It's not like that at all."

"Very well," said the hologram as it blinked out. Shelly turned and headed for home.

"She is a most interesting human," said Dra. "Did you notice the passion in her aura when she first recognized the hologram as her mother?"

"She is a very strong life force. A very good choice for our main contact," replied Kosh. "It will be interesting to see how she assimilates the next few days and months."

After Glow

Reflection is a thing of beauty. It affords you the opportunity to remove emotion from an event and more closely unravel happenings objectively. White can become black if emotions cloud the sky.

Clothed in velvet black, with sequin stars lighting the way, Shelly walked back through the shrouded woods. Shelly kept the flash light five feet in front of her and occasionally she would peek behind her and look up the trail to see if she was being followed by the ball of light. She remained very alone in the woods. Considering all that happened to her, she thought she was doing remarkably well with the new responsibilities she had. She had to keep secrets, make important decisions, and even keep some things from her father. She felt some guilt about that, but didn't see any real good that would come from telling her father that she had been out of the house this evening, at least not now. Now if she could only sneak back in. The walk home gave her some time to think about the questions she wanted to ask. She wanted to ask it all sorts of things, but wanted to make sure she asked the kind of questions that her Dad would approve of. She wanted to show him how grown up she could be. She wanted to show him how responsible she was. That was a key word for Dad; responsibility. He was always talking about people being responsible for their actions, and that included him. Shelly knew it also meant her, and she intended to show him. She would make a list of every question she could think of and then sit down with her father and show him how she was planning ahead. She hoped he would be impressed. She whispered to her mother, "Mom, please help me to do the right thing. I know my decisions will help or hurt us. I need to be right."

She arrived back at the house around 4:30 AM, quietly opened the back door and slid into the kitchen. RutButt was waiting for her and let out a loud meow. "Shhs," said Shelly quickly picking the cat up to quiet him. "No need to wake everyone up," whispered the now tired girl.

ЖОЖ

Shelly rose the next day with a killer headache. Apparently the aliens weren't kidding about the aftereffects of the enhancements. She quickly took three aspirins before her father came into the bathroom and then headed for the kitchen. All during the Saturday morning breakfast she was busy writing on a yellow pad she had found in her fathers' office. She did, however, pull the blinds in the kitchen to shield her from the morning sun. She must have presented a peculiar picture to her father that day.

"What are you doing, daughter?"

"I thought we better be ready to talk to them if we get the chance," said Shelly. "So, I am putting together questions for them. That way, I won't forget anything."

"Good idea. But I am not sure if you will be going back out there again," said Dan, preparing for the fight that was sure to come.

"What?" said Shelly in total disbelief. "I was the one that found it and told you about it. It likes me. It wants to talk to me, not you."

"Shelly, I don't want to put you in a dangerous situation, and anyway, what makes you think it will talk to anyone?" asked Dan.

Recognizing that she was about to open a can of worms she would rather not, Shelly saw no choice. "Last night it sent a little ball of light into our house. It wanted me to come with it back to the valley."

"Oh God, tell me you didn't go," pleaded Dan with fear etched in his unshaven face.

"Dad," said Shelly holding her hands up as if fending off sword thrusts, "it seemed the responsible thing to do." There she had worked the word responsible into her defense. Maybe that would help.

"How in the hell does that make you responsible?" said Dan raising his voice while pushing back from the kitchen table and beginning to pace back and forth.

"Mr. Brown," interrupted Juanita, "what is in the valley?"

"Juanita, not now please," said Dan. "Young lady, you will not leave this house without me. Do you understand?" directed Dan with absolutely no patience.

"Yes father," kowtowed Shelly. "But you really do need to know what happened last night."

Just then the phone rang.

Before Dan could answer the phone, Shelly said, "It's the Major Dad. He's here."

Dan stopped before answering the phone and gawked at Shelly, he picked up the phone as he shook his head, "Hello."

"Dan, the eagle has landed. My ETA was a little off but the scenery was magnificent. Come and get me and let's take a look at your little friends."

"I'll be there in twenty minutes Major. Meet me in the terminal," said Dan hanging up the phone. Turning to his daughter, he said, "Finish your breakfast and stay in the house till I get back with the Major. We will finish this conversation when I get back."

"Dad, can I go with you to get Major Johns? I really want to."

"No. You need to learn to listen to me. When I tell you to do something, DO IT!" Shelly knew enough to keep quiet and not look her father in the eye. The last thing she wanted to do was challenge him.

"Juanita, please see that she stays in the house. I should be back in about an hour and a half. I'll have my cell phone if you need me." With that, Dan grabbed his car keys and left.

"Chica, you better learn to handle your father better than you just did. You might as well pour salt in his eyes. Let him cool down and let him start the conversation. Let him be in control. Trust me on this. It's the same with all men," said Juanita with knowing eyes.

"You're going to like the Major, Juanita. You really will," said Shelly as she kept writing down questions.

The Major

Never judge a book by its cover, for there could be treasures within. Likewise, never evaluate a person by their frame. Looks, in the long run, mean literally nothing. Beauty fades, strength diminishes, teeth fall out and hair ends up on your pillow. Humor, persistence, and ingenuity eventually rule the day.

Major Patrick Johns was the son of a rancher in Austin, Texas. He spoke with a slightly detectable twang that revealed his cowboy heritage. Short and stocky best described this Air Force man. No more than 5'7" tall and weighing in at 180 pounds, he certainly appeared squat. But when he took his shirt off, you could see the hours at the gym had paid off handsomely. He was head to toe solid muscle. Muscles on top of muscles. The girls sure liked it. Even Shelly, as young as she was, had responded with a "Wow, look at that Dad," when he pulled his shirt off to go swimming in the ocean on one of his visits. Ruggedly handsome, and beneath his good ole boy routine, was as bright a man that ever wore Air Force wings. Major Johns had no problem attracting the opposite sex.

His dance card was full and punched. He was a content and happy man.

The Major almost hoped Dan was dead on when it came to the UFO. He would rather wrestle with that problem than face a man coming apart at the seams after his wife's death. He also had a soft spot in his heart for Shelly. She called him Uncle Major and he smiled every time she did it. What a wonderful child Lisa and Dan had raised. He worried for her also, especially if her old man was cracking up.

"Dan, over here," said the Major spying Dan as he entered the terminal. After manly handshakes and eventual heartfelt hugs, Dan grabbed the Major's travel bag and said, "Let's grab a burger and get out to your place. I want to see what has you so stirred up."

During the ride to the burger joint and continuing till they arrived at Dan's home, Dan reviewed all of the relevant facts to the Major, except his daughter's most recent revelation. Major Johns wanted to see the video as soon as he hugged Shelly.

"Uncle Major," shouted Shelly as she ran and jumped into the Majors arms.

"Wow! What a great reception. Shelly you are getting bigger every day. Look at you," said the Major putting her down. "You're getting prettier by the minute. You look like your mother. Why, I'd be surprised if Dad don't put a shotgun by the door real soon."

"Why would he do that?" grinned Shelly. Dan and the Major exchanged glances as the Major couldn't help but notice the lovely woman by the kitchen table.

"Juanita, I'd like to introduce my best friend, Major Johns."

"Please, you can call me Patrick."

"Nice to meet you Mr. Patrick," said Juanita before she could correct herself. Her formality brought smiles to everyone, including a blushing Juanita.

"Well Dan, let's have a beer and look at this video," said the Major in his typical take charge fashion.

"Me too," said Juanita. "You promised me, and a promise made should not be broken."

"And me too Dad. It's mine after all."

"Why not? Look, everyone in this room is sworn to secrecy. You cannot, I repeat, cannot tell anyone. Not your best friend, your neighbor or mother. Understood?" said Dan looking for a verbal yes from Shelly and Juanita.

"Yes sir," they both answered in unison.

"Alright. Let's go into my office and see a scary movie," said Dan, leading the way.

Dan, with Shelly's constant interruptions, explained to the Major and Juanita what had led up to the video and then he hit the play button. As the screen jumped to life, Dan again was upset with the quality of the video. He had been herky-jerky with the camera and the constant motion of the subjects and the lens made it hard to not get dizzy as you watched. The camera work improved as the video continued and it was clear that Dan was getting the knack of his new toy.

"Right here I have just crested the hill and I'm looking down into the valley. You can see the people in a circle around it."

"Excuse me," interrupted the Major. "There is no 'it'. I only see a bunch of folks standing in a circle. If you show this to anyone else, only describe what any normal person could see. At this point of the video, there is no UFO. In fact, I would not use that word, ever. Let some-one else use it."

"Point taken," said Dan. "Okay, here you can see a bright light and a woman going into the bright light. She is someone I have never seen. And about five minutes later, here I'll speed up the video; right here you can see a black puff of something hitting the grass."

"What do you think that was, Dan?" asked the Major.

"Not sure. Hate to speculate, but I do have a sample. I can run it over to a friend of mine at the court house;

they have all sorts of resources available to them. Pretty sure they can analyze this."

"Good answer," instructed the Major.

"Now here you can see the group of people leaving the valley in several directions. Some of them came right by me and you can hear me trying to talk to them. They didn't respond. Kinda like they were in a trance or something."

"Don't use the word trance," said the Major. "Just say they didn't respond when you tried to talk to them. Believe me; someone else will use the word trance, sooner or later."

"Why can't he use those words, Uncle Major?"

"Because Shelly, this is hard enough to believe without telling people what they should or should not believe. Let me put it this way; if I tell you the candy tastes good, and you try it and don't like it, then it becomes my fault. If, on the other hand, I ask you if you'd like to try some candy, and you don't like it, it's not my fault. You didn't have to try it. Ya see, let people draw their own conclusions, especially with this!"

"What are you doing here Dan," asked Juanita.

"I am leaning sticks up against it to get a better idea of its size, and I am measuring it. Here I am telling you the date and time to give some reference to what I am filming."

"A newspaper would have helped, but it really doesn't add any credibility to the sighting," said the Major. "Hump," grunted the Major. "Anything else you want to show me before we get up close and personal with your artifact?"

During all of this, Juanita stared at the monitor without talking or blinking. Eventually, she looked from person to person trying to get a grip on the situation.

"Is this for real?" she said.

"Absolutely," replied Dan. "Do you understand now why we are so secretive?"

"Yes. Oh my God, is this really happening?"

"Calm down Juanita," comforted the Major, "we don't know much about what is really happening. We need to be very clear headed when we get up close and personal. Understand?"

"Yes," answered Juanita in a very small voice.

Shelly asked, "Dad, can we talk about last night now?"

"I guess we better. Unbeknownst to me Major, my misbehaving daughter slipped out of the house last night and visited the craft," began Dan.

"Actually Dad, the light ball visited us first," corrected Shelly.

"What light ball?" asked the Major.

"Last night a ball woke me up with its light. It was right above my head. It was about the size of a tennis ball and it glowed. It went all over me and then all around the room, it seemed to be snooping. Then it went out of my room and squeezed under Dad's door and snooped around his room. It did the same thing all over the house and finally shot up the fire place and waited for me in the back yard."

"Madre mia!" exclaimed Juanita.

"And what did you do?" asked the Major as he eyed Juanita and wondered how wise it was to involve her.

"Well, I didn't know what to do at first. But it seemed to want me to follow it, so I did."

"Without waking me up, I might add," said Shelly's father.

"I already said I was sorry, Dad. Really."

"Okay, Shell, go on," urged the Major.

"Well, the little ball of light stayed just in front of me all the way to the valley. Then it went up on top of the space ship and disappeared. The UFO turned on its rainbow lights and lit up the area. It was beautiful."

"Rainbow lights?" asked the Major.

"Yeah. Sorta like a soap bubble. Very pretty. Anyway, then the scary part happened. Standing right beside the ball was Mom." You could hear Dan suck in his breath.

"I ran to her and tried to touch her, but my hand just went through her. She even spoke to me in Mom's voice -- she said she was a holygram."

"Holygram? What's a holygram?" asked Juanita.

"Do you mean hologram, Shelly?" asked her father.

"I guess. She was just a fancy picture that could talk. They even changed it into Bugs Bunny when I started to cry, but changed it back when I asked for mom again. It was nice to see her, even if it wasn't her."

"What did you talk about, Shelly?" pressed the Major.

"They wanted to let me know that they liked me and wanted to talk to me. They said something about a survey and that I should come back tomorrow and I could ask them questions."

"Is that what you were writing this morning?" asked her father.

"Yes. I did some while you were picking up Uncle Major.

"You said 'them' Shelly. Did they say there was more than one?" asked the Major.

"Yes," grinned Shelly, obviously proud of herself for finding this gem out.

"Did you see them?"

"No. But mom said there were four of them."

"Well then, let's take a look at your questions," said Dan.

Twenty Questions

One single good question can tell you more about a person than a resume full of hyperbole. Pay attention to the questions; they are usually more important than the answers.

"I started with things that I was most interested in, but some of them may be silly," said Shelly looking for support in their eyes.

"Let's just call it brainstorming for the time being. No such thing as a silly question now. We will refine the list as we go along. Now, what have you come up with?" said the Major in as supportive a tone as possible.

Shelly read the questions from her list and occasionally glanced up to see if the three of them approved.

* Where did you come from?
* Why are you here?
* Are you like us?
* Can we see you?

* How old are you?

* What do you like to eat?

* Are you ever scared?

* Is my Mom in heaven?

* Do you know God?

* What is your space ship made of?

* Is there anything we can do for you?

* Do you have pets?

* How do you have fun?

* Are you real smart?

* Is big foot real?

* Did you help build the pyramids?

* Do you play games?

* Do you miss your families?

* When will you leave?

* Are we going to die soon?

Juanita, Dan and the Major listen thoughtfully. The innocence in Shelly's questions rang through. Dan fought back tears as Shelly read her questions headlong without pause. Juanita noticed Dan's sensitivity and was warmed by his compassion. When Shelly finished, she looked around the room, deep into each person's eyes trying to decipher what they thought. "Well, are they good questions?" asked Shelly.

"Absolutely," replied the Major as he patted her shoulder. "I think it's a great start. In fact, let's go see this ball and run some of these questions at it. That should tell us if we need more," directed the Major as he gave Dan a look that meant *I am ready to see this thing.*

Column Left, March

Military organizations are the optimum of social order. You know who is in charge, what your duties are, and what will happen if you fail to perform as expected. Punishments and rewards are visible for all to see. It is the perfect Pavlovian example of Stimulus/Response.

Dan organized the group. Before they left, he made sure they all had a quick snack in case they were gone several hours. He outfitted everyone, including Juanita, after her loud protests at not initially being part of the expedition. Each had rain gear and flash lights. He put new batteries in his video camera and made sure he had his cell phone.

They assembled in the back yard and Dan insisted that he lead the group to the valley. Shelly took up the second position and the Major was more than happy to bring up the rear, following the lovely gyrating Juanita. They made good time and were soon at the valley's entrance. During the walk, Dan had laid out the rules of engagement such as;

* Keep a safe distance from the ship, I don't want anyone sucked up by the light

* He would be in charge of the questions, everyone else should just be quiet and observe

* Major Johns would be in charge of the camera duty

* Everyone was to mentally observe all they could and individually write down the experience as soon as they returned to the house

* If he said run, everyone better hightail it back to the house

* And lastly, when he said they were finished, they were finished and nobody better complain.

Most of the directives were aimed squarely at Shelly. Dan was being very careful, and for good reason; he had pulled three of the people closest to him into this game and he wasn't sure what the rules were or how you could tell if you won. It was dicey at best, but strange events called for strange action.

"So Dan, it's supposed to be down in that valley?" asked the Major.

"Yes, right in the middle. We are going to stop by that stump to the left and try to make contact," answered Dan.

"Mr. Brown, is it alright if I just stay up here on the hill?" asked Juanita with her voice slightly quaking. It was interesting how people responded when it was time for action.

"Actually, Juanita, I would prefer somebody stayed on the hill with the cell phone in case we needed help. Would you do that?" asked Dan, giving Juanita an opportunity to save face.

"Oh, would I ever! I'm getting chicken flesh all over thinking about that thing," replied Juanita.

"Okay. But remember, don't call anyone unless I or the Major give you this signal," where upon Dan raised his fist high over his head and made a big circle with it. "Got it?"

"Yes sir. Got it," answered Juanita.

Q and A

Shelly, Dan and the Major advanced down the hill in single file and stopped by a rotted out stump, with moss the final tenant, about thirty feet from the center of the meadow. Dan looked at his two comrades, gave a glance back up the hill to see if Juanita was still at post —she was— and then said in a loud voice, "Hello. Is anyone home?" No reply. "I'm going to throw a rock where I think you are. It's just to find out if you're home." Major Johns was smiling, wondering if any of this was real. The rock clinked off of something and rolled back toward them.

"Holy mother of God!" said the Major.

"See Uncle Major, I told you it was real," said Shelly.

"Do you want to talk to me?" asked Dan.

No reply.

"Look, we believe you want to communicate with us. Please let us know you are there."

No reply.

"Can I try, Daddy?"

"Why not? Looks like no one's home."

"Hello space ship. I'm here to ask you some questions," said Shelly, fully expecting an answer.

"Hello, Shelly," answered the ship. All waited as Shelly turned and asked, "Did you hear it too?"

"Hear what?" asked the Major.

"It's speaking in my head. It said hello."

"Major, I think its communicating with her telepathically," said Dan.

"Go ahead and ask it something Shelly," encouraged the Major.

Major Johns took a step backwards and was staring with his mouth open—just staring, barely breathing.

"Can you show us the ship?" asked Shelly. The ship instantly displayed its soap colored bubble which gradually faded to a sort of white porcelain.

"Major, turn on the camera," prompted Dan as the hologram of Lisa Brown took shape to the side of the ship. Dan's knees momentarily buckled and he audibly moaned at the likeness.

"My God it is her," stammered Dan.

"Hello Mom. Did you miss me?" asked Shelly in a playful manner.

"I suffered no distress at your absence," responded the ship telepathically. "I see you brought more humans with you. Do you think that is wise?"

"It's just my Dad, our friend the Major and Juanita our housekeeper."

"Shelly, do not bring anyone else back here or we will have to take steps to keep our location safe. And, know that we will only transmit to you alone. Are we agreed?"

"Yes. Sure," said Shelly bending down to pick up a leaf.

"Sure what?" asked Shelly's father.

"They don't want to talk to you; only me. They think older people don't have the right color."

"What color?" asked the Major.

"I don't know. It's not in my Crayola box. It's called aura," replied Shelly as she held the leaf up to the sky to see the veins networking their way through the now fallen hero.

"The more humans that know of our existence, the more it will compromise our mission. We must insist on this requirement. Now, did you wish to ask some questions Shelly?" motioned the hologram of Lisa Brown. Too bad nobody read lips, because the lips did move synchronously with the telepathic messages and were quite lifelike.

"Yes. I have a list. I hope it's not too long."

"We have ample time. Please proceed," encouraged the hologram.

"Okay. Where did you come from?"

"We came from the galaxy you call the Virgo Cluster. Specifically, what you call 'M87'. Our home planet is called Creum."

"I better tell you the answers because I don't think I can remember all of this," said Shelly indicating that she would pass along the information as she got it. Shelly proceeded to replay the conversation as best she could.

"Why are you here?" asked Shelly, not fully understanding that this was the key question. It would determine the future, if any, of Earth.

"We are here to record a very unique event that is already happening to your planet. We wish to observe the event and learn from it."

"What is happening?" asked Shelly with anticipation only matched when opening Christmas presents.

"Most of the life on this planet will die and become extinct."

When Shelly passed along this answer, Dan exploded. "What?" he yelled. "Are you saying we are going to blow ourselves up?"

No reply from the ship.

"This is crazy! Why in hell won't you talk to me?" screamed Dan.

"Dan, get control. Shut up and listen. Let Shelly ask the questions," ordered the Major. "Shelly, ask why they only want to talk to you and then ask what is going to happen to the earth," instructed the Major.

Dan, beginning to pace, kept quiet as Shelly asked her questions.

"We will not respond to questions from anyone but you Shelly. Prompting from the others will elicit no response. Shelly, you may tell them that your aura is uniquely vibrant and luminous. We feel sincerity, directness, and innocence with your communications. It is really quite an honor to meet someone of your caliber. Communicating with those with improper auras leads to much mental anguish for our kind. Please tell the two adults that if they persist in directing your questions, we will erase their memories and send them home. We will allow them as your guardians, for your protection, as long as they remain passive in relationship to us. We hope that is clear."

"Yes thank you. It is very clear." Shelly relayed the message as closely as she could and carefully watched her father for his reaction. Dan Brown could become quite excited, as Shelly had witnessed on more than one occasion. Major Johns moved over to Dan and had whispered to him to calm down and listen.

"Now, we would like to hear the rest of your questions," beamed the hologram.

"Good. Can you tell me what's going to happen to the earth?" asked Shelly not realizing she had slipped into the personal *I* versus the *we*.

"Your planet is undergoing a significant environmental change that is water-related. Nuclear pollution has directly affected the evolutionary process of one of your lowest links of the food chain. The consequences will be felt by all life on this planet."

"I don't know what that means," uttered Shelly. Dan and the Major stared on in disbelief as they continued to witness only one side of the conversation.

"Humans have been dumping nuclear waste in the Sea of Japan and the North Pacific Ocean since 1950. Eventually, a specific red algae growing in the area mutated into a virus. The sea life ate it and it slowly spread. The algae and virus can now be found throughout most of the Pacific Ocean, parts of the Atlantic and is beginning to appear in the Indian Ocean. Through evaporation, the virus breaks down and soon finds itself in clouds, falling as rainwater on your land masses. It has now reached critical mass and will start by killing the grasses growing on your planet. Not only will sea life be affected, but, through the rain, the entire food chain will be vulnerable."

Shelly gave the men the bad news as quickly as she could and then continued as they stood in shock.

"Can we do anything to stop it?" Shelly asked.

"No. And within days, major changes will be seen by all. Water will become the main commodity for the remainder of your planet's life. Riots will break out, and mass migrations will follow."

Shelly's mouth had dropped open and finally she issued a barely audible whistle. She continued to relay the information as she received it. Shock, turning to fear, was deeply etched into the furrowed brows of both men.

"Do you believe in God?" whispered Shelly.

"God is an abstract that cannot be proved or disproved. While it is acknowledged that the intelligent design theory carries weight, the randomness of destruction can be seen to counterbalance the argument. Most intelligent life forms have come to the conclusion that the pursuit of God is wasted time." Shelly did not pass along that answer. She needed God. God was where her mother was. How would she ever see her mother again if there was no God? After a long pause, Shelly asked, "What should we do?"

"For short term survival, we recommend storing pure water and substitute liquids in large quantities. In the next few days, rainwater in this area will be contaminated. No standing water will be safe. It is also recommended that you store up food supplies. With fear, hoarding will begin within days."

"Can you help save our planet?"

"No. We cannot get involved and in any event; the time to save the planet was decades ago."

Shelly sat down on the ground, hunched her shoulders forward and started slowly rocking as she plucked grass from the meadow floor. She wished she had never found this thing. She wished she could take it all back. She wished this was all a dream. Dan stepped over to Shelly and sat down beside her and took her in his arms.

"Shelly, I don't know how, but we will get through this. You'll see. I'm not going to let anything happen to you."

"I told you what they said; it's not going to be the same. We are all going to die. Me, you, RutButt, the trees, everything," sobbed his little girl.

"We just need some time to think about this. Let's go home now and collect our thoughts." Dan stood and helped Shelly to her feet and motioned for the Major to join them in their retreat. "Let's get out of here, Johns. I need a beer."

"Make that six," said the Major giving one last look over his shoulder at the sphere as they hiked back out of the valley.

The Eyes Have It

Nothing tells a story better than the eyes. If you risk direct eye contact, you can see fear, joy, hate, love, seduction, sadness and more, vividly expressed in the windows of the soul.

The solemn group collected Juanita at the top of the hill. Their faces and hollow eyes told the whole story and warned Juanita away from unnecessary explanations. At the house she prepared sandwiches while Dan got everyone something to drink. Juanita functioned, but just barely. The concern for her was visible in everyone's eyes as Dan began running through the questions again with Shelly. He wanted to make sure that Shelly passed along everything they had communicated. Each question was played back on the video cam and Shelly would recount the answer as best she could. When they got to the question about God, they realized that Shelly had not answered the question.

"Shelly, what did they say about God?" asked Juanita.

Shelly held her breath as she tried to find the right answer. Was it better to tell them what was said, or was it better to lie? "They said they don't think about God. They think he is an abstack."

"An abstack?" questioned Juanita.

"What the hell is an abstack?" asked Dan.

"Shelly, did they say abstract?" injected the Major.
"Yes! That's it, an abstract. Where is the dictionary?" said Shelly rising from her chair and stomping off to the office. She wasn't sure of its exact meaning, but she instinctively knew she didn't like it. Five minutes later, shoulders tense, she shuffled back to the kitchen table. "The dictionary says abstract is considered apart from concrete existence: an abstract concept. Does that mean God is hard to figure out?"

Both Juanita and the Major knew this was Dad's question and their body language told the story as they deferred the question to the parent.

"That's exactly what it means. God is too big and wonderful to fully understand. We can only understand him by enjoying the beauty in the world or his many incredible creations. Like RutButt. Those UFERs should have spent more time thinking about God and less time on their space ship."

"UFERs?" queried the Major. "Pass me a beer Dan," said the Major. "This whole situation sucks!"

"Is that what you'd call it? A situation! I'd say it was more of a catastrophe," replied Dan. "Just what in hell do we do with this information? And by the way, what do you want to call them if not UFERs?"

"UFERs is fine, but I'll tell you what we can't do," said the Major as he headed for the study. "One: we can't panic. Two: we still can't tell anyone. No use looking like the village idiots. Three: we can't speculate. We need to know exactly what we are talking about; we can use the internet to do some research. Let's start there."

"You need to get supplies now," said Shelly.

"Wow, you're right Shelly. That's a great idea. Why don't you and Juanita go to town and buy some soda, juices, bottled water and some canned food. Go to several stores so it doesn't look like we are stockpiling. Here is my credit card, Juanita.

Are you going to be okay?" asked Dan, seeing the concern in her face.

"Yes, Mr. Brown, I'm just a little scared," replied Juanita.

"Trust me, we are all scared. Try to focus on getting us some supplies. Load up the van with whatever you think we will need. Fill up the whole van if you can. Come straight back and we will put the supplies in the garage."

Dan and the Major settled into the study and went on-line to do some research as Juanita and Shelly headed for town.

Girl's Day Out

"Shelly, was that a picture of your mother I saw by the space ship?" inquired Juanita as they made their way toward town.

"Yes. They call it a hologram. It looks like Mom and even sounds like her, but it's not. She hasn't told me she loves me even once. It's just a video."

"Doesn't any of this scare you, chica?"

"It did at first, but I know they don't want to hurt us. They are just like reporters for a newspaper and we are the story. But I didn't like what they said about God. How can they not think about him? I know that's wrong. He thinks about them," said Shelly, shaking her head in disbelief. "That bothers me most of all. God made everything, even them."

Juanita crossed herself and said a quick Hail Mary under her breath.

"Juanita, how come you never talk about your family?"

"Shelly, I have been on my own for a long, long time."

"What's that mean? Don't you have any family?"

"Well, I think I have a brother somewhere in Chicago, but I don't know for sure. Our parents died when we were little kids and we ended up in an orphanage in El Paso, Texas. My brother was adopted a couple of years later and I ran away from my foster parents when I was thirteen. I lost touch with him. I wouldn't know how to find him."

"Don't you have a boyfriend or cat or something?"

"No, chica, just me and some flowers."

Shelly could sense the loneliness in Juanita's voice and said, "Well, then you are part of our family. Just like Uncle Major. And someday you and the Major will be a family."

"What do you mean?"

"You know what I mean. I saw you looking at him and I saw him looking at you."

Juanita didn't think a nine year old could make her blush until this moment. Laughing, she said, "Shelly you are too much girl. And I do thank you for including me in your family. That's sweet," replied Juanita not knowing how important family would be in the coming crisis.

"It's not sweet, Juanita, it's the truth."

The shopping duo hit the three main grocery stores in town, and concluded their spree by patronizing two quick stop gas stations to round out their collection of beer and soda. With a considerably heavier van, they headed back to the farm.

Circumstantial Evidence

The internet had already had a potent impact on civilization. Positive or negative is still to be determined. Will it be an incredible resource for the thoughtful or a wasteland for the indulgent?

Dan and Major Johns needed data, and lots of it. Would it be possible to tie together the bits and pieces of the impending doom into a coherent story? Or would they find no way to make sense of the events unraveling around them? Where they doomed? Would the cockroaches inevitably rule? Their visiting neighbors had told them it was too late, unstoppable, a foregone conclusion. But they had also said it would make *most* of life extinct. Not all of it. Maybe pockets of people could survive if they knew how and where their chances were best. That seemed to be the ultimate mission at hand.

Major Johns sat down at the PC and said, "Right. What do we know about nuclear dumping? Let's just see what old man Google will tell us." Within seconds, the Major had more information at his fingertips than he could have imagined. "Man! Look at the links. Obviously someone has been very busy. Not surprising Greenpeace is all over this."

"Hit that link," said Dan. A web site crawled to life on the PC. Clearly, this site was not intended for thrill seekers or voyeurs. It was full of statistics and scientific data. As he read through the paragraphs, Dan was able to glean the shell of truth. "We're screwed," said Dan. "Look here Major, Russia has been dumping nuclear waste in the Sea of Japan since the 1950's. And even Japan got into the act later. Oh my gosh, there are at least six nuclear subs sunk on the ocean floor, four Russian and two American, not to mention other bits and parts unintentionally lost while at sea. We have turned our own oceans into a cesspool of radiation."

"And here's the scary part, Dan: Plutonium 239 has a half life of 24,000 years. For all practical purposes, it ain't going away any time soon. And look here, you know what's ironic about all of this? Plutonium is nonexistent in the natural world. Man created it, and now it's going to kill us."

"So let me get this straight," said Dan, sitting down on the desk and massaging his temples, "our UFO buddies said that the nuclear waste polluted the red algae and somehow it's getting into our water supplies and the food chain."

"That's right," responded the Major, "let's look up red algae." The PC flickered as the sequence of keys was struck and then it glowed to life. "Here we go. Oh great! Let me read you what it says. 'Also known as the Red Tide, Red Algae is the most advanced group of plants. They are so advanced they can be found both in tide pools and at depths of over 600 feet, due to their ability to absorb longer wavelengths of light.' And get this, we use it in everything from toothpaste, ice-cream, lipstick, jells, etc. It's apparently all over the place. Oh, and here's more not so good news, according to the Scripps Institution of Oceanography in la Jolla, California, the red tides are so unpredictable there is absolutely no way of forecasting when or where one might appear. They aren't associated with any particular weather or ocean patterns at all. Over the past 100 years that they have been keeping records, they have been seen in every month of the year and in all kinds of years. It does say that a microorganism called Salps eats them."

"That's probably what they meant about the food chain. I bet ya Salps get eaten by something and so forth," injected Dan.

"Yep," twanged the Major. "Okay, if it's going to hit us via water, what do we know about water? Let's see what the trusty internet will tell us. Here's some stuff: 70% of our planet is water, which gives it a blue color seen from space. I am sure our space critters enjoyed that. That equates to 326 million trillion gallons. I knew it was a lot, but not that much! How many zero's is that? Try to imagine that many gallons of milk."

"Who cares?" quipped Dan.

"Don't get your feathers in a ruffle at me buddy. I'm in the same boat you are," replied the Major.

"Sorry. This is freaking me out. Go on."

"I am sure you know this one; the human body is two-thirds water and it is essential for keeping our body operating. We need eight glasses or two liters each day to remain healthy. And we use about a quarter of a liter each day by just breathing. And obviously, the more active you are, the more water you need. You can live several weeks without food, but less than a week without water."

"Okay. That's stuff we pretty much knew. What else ya got?" urged Dan.

The Major stroked the keys and called up another site on water usage. "Oh this is scary, as if we need more reasons to be scared. Each day in the US, we use 1500 gallons of water per capita, culminating in a yearly per person use of 500,000 gallons. That's huge! I think a normal swimming pool has around 10,000 gallons, the same as in a big gas tanker. Let's see, that would be 50 pools worth of water per person. Man, are we water hogs or what?"

"We never have been very smart with our water. We use it to flush our toilets for crying out loud. Talk about creating problems," added Dan.

Reading ahead he listened to Dan, the Major said, "Oh, and I sure didn't know this. Here is how water is used in the US: 40% for irrigation, 39% for hydro-electric power, 13% for public use, and the remaining 8% for industry. And, of course, California uses the most— 22% of all irrigation water in the US. Huh, Canada has 20% of the world's freshwater but represents only 0.5% of the world's population. China, on the other hand, contains 21% of the world's people and only 7% of its water supply."

"Ya know what they say about surpluses?" posed Dan.

"Yep, the prime cause of all wars," answered the Major. "If this thing happens, we are going to see some real caca hit the fan."

Color Me Red

It is interesting how we have assigned value to colors. Black cats and the black plague pretty much said it all. Purple was for royalty in Rome, yellow denotes a coward, while white embodies purity. Blue is just blue and green is calm and relaxing. Red signifies stop, communists, zits, and danger. No wonder we have race relation issues.

As Juanita prepared one of the Browns' favorite meals, meatloaf with baked potatoes and corn, Dan turned on the TV, hoping to escape from the drama of the day. The CNN anchor was reporting on the spoiled surfing in LA and San Diego. Never before had a Red Tide covered this much of the North American coastline. Broiling rust colored waves pounded the sands of Laguna Beach where chiseled young men draped in black wet suits waited with little patience for the blue swells to return. Mothers collected their wandering children in soggy disposable diapers and ushered them away from the nasty looking water. Seagulls seemed indifferent about the tinted ocean and maintained their ever present patrol, looking for anything small enough to ingest or, better yet, something recently dead. Pictures from satellites gave a much more somber view of the situation. A pale red hue drifted on the Pacific Ocean like drops of blood in a bathtub. Patches of the red algae could be seen nearly circling Japan, lapping at the shores of Hawaii and etched like scarlet lip liner on the south west coast of America. Large fish kills were being reported in Japan and Hawaii, but so far the carnage had not reached America. Dan had summoned everyone into the room when the story began and soon regretted drawing them into this web of darkness. Juanita was gently pulling on her left ear, Shelly was biting her lip, and Major Johns had set his jaw tight as if about to receive a punch to the face. Dan maintained a steady pace across the room. The Major thought to himself, *what a sorry crew they made. How were they possibly going to deal with this in a positive manner?*

Just when everyone was feeling about as low as they could get, it began to rain. Woe upon woes. Lightly but steadily, the rain coated the road, fields, trees, and the future with silent death. A more perfect assassin could not have been designed than to have death measured out in the very resource you depend on most. The rain caressed each lowly target without remorse or joy. It was mute to its own power. Just another journey in its never ending cycle between Tierra Firma, streams, rivers, oceans and the clouds.

Dan walked to the wide picture window in the living room, with the drapes Lisa had so carefully picked out, and touching the window with his palm, he leaned heavily against the transparent protection and said loud enough for everyone to hear, "Stay out of rain. Drink only from the supplies in the garage. Don't brush your teeth with tap water. I don't even know if we should be bathing in the stuff. Maybe that's something you could ask the UFO Shelly. I think this rain could be fatal. Imagine that, Fatal Rain."

"Shouldn't we tell everyone else what we know Dad?"

"Not yet Shelly. I know they wouldn't believe us and you heard what they said. If we bring others back there, they will be gone, we look like idiots and, more importantly, we lose contact with the only ones that know what's going on. Eventually we will have to tell someone, but not now."

"A lot of people are going to die very soon. It won't be safe to go into town. We need to get the neighbors and form a group for protection," said Shelly as she looked at the carpet, directing her comments to no one in particular.

They all looked at her as if she were an alien herself. Dan and the Major seemed to be staring through each other in some kind of secret communication.

Breaking the silence, Dan asked Juanita, "Can I talk with you in the kitchen?" She followed dutifully, not sure of his intentions.

"Juanita, please have a seat," said Dan as he pulled out a table chair for her. "I have been thinking about what is going to happen in the next few days, weeks or months and was wondering if you might consider moving in with us. You would have your own room, rent free, I would continue to pay you, and I think it might be more secure for you with what might happen down in town."

"Oh, Mr. Brown, I don't want to cause you any unnecessary trouble and I already have my own apartment."

"Juanita, if what I think is going to happen does happen, food, gas, water and everything else will become very hard to get. I doubt our legal system will remain intact and it will be survival of fittest. The Major and I can protect this place. We are at least a little bit isolated from the town and we have specific information from the space ship that should help us survive. Do you have family in town that you would like to bring?"

"I am by myself," uttered Juanita, ashamed of how it sounded when said aloud.

"Look, Shelly and I think you are wonderful. We already consider you part of our family and it really would be best if you moved in here."

"Shelly certainly is your daughter. She also said she thought of me as part of her family. Let me think about it Mr. Brown."

"Fair enough," replied Dan. "Now, how can I help you with supper?"

"Actually, it's almost ready. Just call Shelly and Patrick and we can start. I hope you don't mind, but I intended to eat here. I love meatloaf. It's from a recipe I stole while working at a restaurant," smiled Juanita with just a touch of devil in her eyes.

"Juanita, you can eat with us anytime you like, and you don't ever have to ask. We are lucky to have you."

When they were all seated, Shelly requested to lead them in a prayer, something she had not done since the accident, "Dear God, bless this food. Keep our water clean and stop what is happening to our world. Oh, and bless Uncle Major, Juanita, my Dad and RutButt and the UFO people. Amen." An earnest amen was echoed by all.

Consequences

Scientists are a curious lot. When research yields data that is expected, unexpected, spectacular or ho-hum, they remain steadfast in their underlying belief in repeatable experimentation. It's universal. Hypotheses are at stake and grants may follow.

Nimar, the scientific coordinator and Dra, the impact analyst, had been eagerly awaiting the first heavy precipitation to contain the deadly mutated agent. It arrived that evening in a light, persistent drizzle. Monitors picked up the virus, although currently in trace amounts only. Initial studies indicated the virus could live for as long as three months without losing its effectiveness. Additionally, their studies had shown that the virus had a cumulative effect and, in essence, its virility grew exponentially over time, right up until its death. Nimar transmitted to Dra, "It will only be a matter of days before notable effects become evident to even the humans."

"I have statistically determined that they have no more than one month before social breakdown occurs," said

Dra. "They have no frame of reference for this type of catastrophe. Their history records only two major viral situations that even approach this event: the Black Plague and Spanish Flu. But they pale compared to this contaminated rain. With no hope of banding together, they will blame each other. Ultimately it will be chaos followed by death."

"I concur," nodded Nimar. "But what is most significant about this species is its diverse languages. That is what has doomed them. The humans must know the importance of their grasslands, yet they have allowed its size to dwindle. In the recent past, 40 percent of the earth was covered by grasslands. Today, the figure is down to less than 20 percent. They call it everything from African savannas, Australia rangelands, Eurasia steppes, North America prairies, and in South America they call them pampas. They cannot even name it uniformly. Their antiquated communications are the blame for much of their problems," concluded Nimar.

Dra continued more as a refresher for himself than to enlighten Nimar, "Interestingly, of the fifteen major crops that stand between the humans and starvation, ten are grasses; grains like wheat, rye, sorghum, corn, rice, oats, and millet. When the grasses die, so will the life forces that depend on them and it will continue to cascade to extinction. Too bad their scientific community was focused on war and individual gain and not on their own people and the quality of life," eulogized Dra.

Social Climate

Monica, Shelly's best friend in the world, called that evening and Dan answered the phone. "Hello, this is Dan," expecting it to be one of his employees.

"Mr. Brown, this is Monica. Can I talk to Shelly?"

"You sure can. Hang on a second," said Dan putting the phone down and seeking out Shelly and whispering in her ear. "Don't mention a word about this," reminded her father.

Shelly gave him a look that could have boiled eggs, "Jeeze, Dad, duh." Shelly ran to the phone and did their secret whistle to authenticate her identity. It was responded by the same ultra secret whistle.

"Hey Monica, what's up?"

"What's up? Oh boy, I bet you forgot didn't you?"

Shelly quickly ran through all of their conversations this last week and then meekly said, "Yes. I'm sorry Monica."

"I have been sitting here waiting for you to call. I wanted to know if you could stay over tomorrow night."

"I know. You remember me talking about my Uncle Major? Well, he flew into town today for a visit and I really want to see him. Maybe we can do it next week."

The phone went silent as Shelly held her breath. She really didn't want to upset her best friend, but now was not the time to go on a sleep-over.

"Don't be mad Monica. If Uncle had not come into town, I'd be there right now. Promise."

"Okay," said a resigned Monica, her voice betraying her frustration. "Next week for sure then. No backing out."

"Deal. Love ya, gotta go," with that Shelly gave the secret whistle and hung up the phone.

Dan had been listening to the whole conversation leaning against the door jamb of the kitchen.

"Thank you for keeping the secret. No one else can know. What did she say about next week?"

"I promised her that I would spend Saturday night with her. I hope that's alright," replied Shelly, half wondering if she would want to with all that was going on.

"It should be fine. By the way, since I have you here, I wanted to let you know that I asked Juanita to move into the house. She could have the extra bedroom. I just would rather have her here if things get nasty in town."

"What kind of nasty are you thinking of?" asked Shelly, now wide eyed.

With Shelly it was hard to remember that she was only nine. Sometimes it felt just like talking to an adult and other times the child sparkled through. Realizing he had unintentionally alarmed his little girl, Dan sought just the right words to calm the situation, "Shelly, sometimes good people get very excited when things don't go just the way they expect. They can get angry and even violent. People can start doing things they never would have considered before. I'm not saying anything is going to happen, I just feel it would be safer if Juanita didn't have to go into town every day, that's all."

"Dad, it is going to be war out there. People are going to start killing each other and even themselves. And yes, Juanita needs to be here with us. Anyway, I think it would be wonderful to have another woman in the house. And I think Juanita is the right one."

Dan was surprised at his daughter's matter of fact approach to the disintegration of society. She wasn't the same little girl any more. The space ship had somehow changed her. Shelly's visions were tending toward prophecy. In addition, he had no idea that his daughter would react so positively about Juanita and refer to her as 'another woman'. My, how things had changed in such a short period of time. Nothing would ever be normal again. He needed to refocus on his priorities. Survival of his family was his main concern now.

Dan had other issues that needed to be resolved. Who and when would he tell what he knows? How much evidenced would there have to be before he could take others into his confidence? So far, outside of the red tide and some fish kills, nothing much out of the ordinary was happening. He would have to begin monitoring the news much more closely, including the local rag, the Tillamook Headlight Herald. Headlight. Dan scoffed. We are going to look like deer in the headlights if the UFERs are right.

The Major came into the room and asked Dan if he was ready to talk about their next steps and a contingency plan.

"Yes," replied Dan, "now would be the time."

Preparations

Ant or grasshopper? Which are you? Prepare or procrastinate, or worse yet, ignore the facts lying at your very feet? Woe be to you who puts off till tomorrow today's work.

The Major led Dan into the office and shut the door. "Dan, I have been giving a lot of thought to the next few weeks. I hope you don't mind, but I contacted the base and requested to extend my leave."

"Thanks, Major. I certainly can use the help. What have you come up with so far?" said Dan, sliding into a small couch that Lisa had picked out last year. It was plush, very comfortable and the site of RutButt's afternoon naps. A poof of cat fur rose on unseen air currents as Dan descended in the cushions.

"First, we need another trip to the UFO. We need to ask more specific questions, but if the questions are not initiated by Shelly, they will know. We need to covertly coach her," continued the Major. "For example, we need to know what effect the rain will have on us. Is it hazardous to our skin or just if we ingest it? We should also find out how best we can protect ourselves. Seems to me that this doesn't have to be a species ending event, at least not for Homo Sapiens."

"Agreed, Major. I think we can help Shelly down the path. What about our immediate survival?"

"Well, I overheard some of your conversation with Juanita. If I heard you right, you want her to come and live here at least for the short term. Correct?"

"Yes. Both Shelly and I think she is a wonderful house-keeper and person but, more importantly, she doesn't seem to have immediate family anywhere. I am nervous about any of us going into town if things start going bad," replied Dan.

"Actually, she's pretty easy on the eyes too ole buddy," nudged the Major.

"There is nothing going on. It's just the best solution, that's all."

Smiling, the Major continued, "Sure Dan, I under-stand," with a twinkle in his eye. Dan just smiled back and slowly shook his head. The Major had always been a tease and, at times, a bit of a jerk, but you always knew where you stood with him.

"Anyway, I caught you checking out the territory a time or two, so don't start pointing fingers at me," laughed Dan.

"Alright, enough of that. It is a good idea. Get her here if at all possible. Now, we need to continue to stockpile food and drinking supplies without drawing notice. I suggest I make the next trip and then a day or two later, you should go. Buy as much as we can without drawing attention to ourselves. In addition, both of us should visit a local gun shop and pick up some protection, good sleeping bags, tents, hiking boots, you know, and survival stuff. I can visit some survival web sites and get additional ideas about what to procure. And, by the way, if you need any drugs, better get them now. I suspect pharmacies will be hit hard when the looting starts. That reminds me, we will need lots of TP, toothpaste, hand and clothes soap," said the Major as he checked off things he had jotted down on a note pad.

"Looting? My God, we're talking about looting. You believe it's going to happen don't you?"

"Buddy boy, you betcha, yeah. After seeing what we have seen and corroborating some of their assertions, I give it at least a 75% chance of happening. Oh, and we will need basic hand tools, nails, spare gasoline, and I heard of a water filter that was used by missionaries in Africa that could purify anything, even urine. We need to find those and get some," rambled the Major, clearly with more on his mind.

"Major, I have a problem. I am still trying to run a business and my credit cards aren't inexhaustible."

"Dan, I never meant for you to bear the brunt of this alone. We will use my credit cards until I max them. I have a substantial retirement fund set aside. I'm in good shape."

Dan lowered his head into his hands and sat there wishing this was just one of those extra vivid bad dreams that you wake up from in a cold sweat. He looked up and the Major had a very sympathetic look on his face.

"Friend, you've been through a lot the past few months. It must seem as though you are Job from the Bible, only on steroids."

"Kinda, although I know Job had it a lot worse. The only good thing is that Shelly seems to see this as a big adventure and is thriving. It's good to see her engaged again. And yes, it certainly is overwhelming. I am glad you're here."

"Okay. That's enough pity talk. Let's get to work. I'll go to town in the morning and you hit the internet and make sure we have all we will need. Both of us should start dropping hints to Shelly so she will ask good questions. Now, I suggest we get some rest. It's going to get hurriered and hurriered from here on out," twanged the Major in his best hillbillyese.

Dan ushered Shelly into bed, made sure RutButt had been fed and his litter box emptied, and the dishes put into the dishwasher. By the time he finished the mundane, end of day chores, he was exhausted, not so much physically, but emotionally. This type of preparation was vaguely similar to all the prep work in finalizing Lisa's funeral. Everything was so negative and black. Hope had not only faded but was difficult to recall at all. An oppressive weight bore down on him and reduced his mortality to mere fruitlessness. His daughter, that one shinning lovely fresh soul, kept him going. He lived not so much for himself as for his seed. She was too good to die, too young, too special. He would find a way to go on. He would give her a chance at life.

"Good night, Dad."

"Good night, Shelly. I love you."

"Good night Uncle Major."

"Good night, Shells Bells."

"Sleep tight, don't let the bugs bite, but if they do, get your shoe and beat them black and blue," giggled Shelly.

Juanita's Adjustment

Few times in a person's life do they have the chance to establish the terms for their employment. If given the opportunity, one should take ample time and think through what is really most important. Then be sure to include those important things as part of the bargain. Life is short and work can be all consuming and may very well define your existence.

Dan had a relatively good night's sleep. He woke early at 5:30 with the first hint of sunlight and initially sat up, but then stretched and yawned wide before settling down into one of the matched pair of big down stuffed, double ticked pillows his aunt Ethel had given Lisa and him for a wedding gift. The pillow was especially comforting and conformed as no foam pillow could. With the clean, sweet smell of fabric softener lingering on the pillow case, Dan managed a half smile. As he burrowed his head deep into its receding feathers, he almost cooed with contentment. For the first time in a long time, he was at peace. Funny, now that everything seemed to be turned on its head, that he should be calm.

With eyes closed he reviewed the list of things that needed to be accomplished today. And there he found the answer. Action, any action, is better than sitting on your behind and worrying. The plan that the Major and he outlined last night had given him the clarity he needed. How many times had he heard that if you are having trouble sleeping, that you should keep a journal by your bed and jot down your worries and to-dos for the next day and forget them? He wasn't 100% convinced, but he would certainly give it a try next time insomnia slid its dull worries into his head. He dressed and proceeded to the kitchen where he found Juanita already sipping a cup of coffee.

"My, you are here early," said Dan, stopping by the Mr. Coffee machine and pouring himself a dark brew of wake-up.

"I had trouble sleeping last night and so I got up early and came on out to the farm. Mr. Brown, I have given quite a bit of thought to your offer to live here. I want to make sure I understand how it would work. I have a place and my own things; if I give the apartment up I may not be able to find another that I can afford when I need to move back. That makes me a little nervous."

"Juanita, I hope we have that problem to face. I seriously doubt that is going to be an issue. If everything settles down and it is safe for you to move back to town, I will personally see to it that you find a place that you like for the same money you are spending now. In addition, because you will be living here, your room and board will be part of the deal, so you can pocket the money you would have been spending on the apartment and utilities. Financially you should be way ahead of the game."

"I do appreciate that Mr. Brown, and I don't want this to sound selfish, but I enjoy having my own time. I don't want to be on call 24/7. I like to do things on my own. I've been on my own since I was thirteen and I like calling my own shots."

"Juanita, first of all, we know each other well enough that you can call me Dan. Secondly, I do not want to run your life and it's not my intention for you to be on call. Think of it as a job with regular hours; say 7 to 4 with weekends and holidays off. Throw in a two week paid vacation too. And most importantly, Shelly and I think you are just great and we don't want to do anything that will cause you to leave, but until we know what's going to happen in the next few months, I would just feel so much better knowing you are safe and here at the farm. That's all. I don't want you to feel confined," said Dan fixing Juanita with sincere eye contact.

"Alright Dan," said Juanita, still not comfortable calling her boss by his first name, "if I can use your van, I will move my stuff out tomorrow."

"No problem, the Major and I will help you. Now, how about I get the other two up and let's have breakfast."

A Glint of Hope

Everyone seemed in good spirits at breakfast. Only RutButt seemed annoyed by not having his regal place at the table. He kept busy weaving between the legs under the table with a special emphasis on Shelly's. He was especially fond of runny egg yolks and Shelly regularly offered him her plate when she was finished, careful to leave ample yellow slurppies to enjoy. Shelly loved watching the feline clean up after indulging in his egg drizzles. His rather large and rough tongue would meticulously caress all parts of his mouth, nose and eventually front paws for extensive work on his handsome, wide face.

"I have an announcement. Juanita has agreed to move in," informed Dan with obvious satisfaction.

Shelly bound from her chair and embraced Juanita with a smothering hug. "This is awesome Juanita. Can I help decorate your room?"

"Shelly, we have to remember that her room is her private area. You are not to go in unless invited," said

Dan, eager to lay down the ground work for a successful transition.

"Yes, Shelly, you can help me," replied a now smiling Juanita.

The Major nodded his approval and taking a last draw on his coffee, said, "Time we got busy Dan."

Patrick, as Juanita liked to think of him, was certainly a leader. She had given him the best plate of breakfast without even knowing she was pandering to him. She had always liked take-charge kind of guys. She suspected it was her knight-in-shining-armor complex that she had read about in one of her psychology classes. Nonetheless, there was something about him that was attractive. That, plus her general uneasiness, spurred her to ask, "Patrick, would it be alright if I rode along with you?"

Dan jumped in and said, "I think that's a great idea Juanita. You know the town and can direct the old military guy around. But please don't go in the stores. They saw you yesterday and we don't want to alert anyone to our plan." This, thought Dan, was also a way of showing Juanita that she wasn't tied to this house and her job.

"Great, I'll get my purse."

"What about me, Dad? What am I going to do?" implored Shelly.

"Well, you could help me or maybe get hold of Monica and hangout with her," guided Dan, hoping she would opt for Monica.

"I think I will call her. Maybe we could take a bike ride."

"No. Go over to her house. Stay out of the rain and the woods and be back for lunch. Don't bring Monica for lunch. I want to keep everyone away from the house. I don't want prying eyes."

"Aye aye sir," replied Shelly snapping to attention and garnering a smile from her Dad.

With Juanita and the Major on their shopping trip, Shelly playing at the neighbors, Dan finally had some time to devote to the internet. What he found was indeed hopeful. He started by Googleing water filters and ended up hitting a site that talked about a water filter that was commissioned by Queen Victoria in 1835. Apparently, the London population was becoming ill by drinking water from the Thames River. Diseases including Cholera, Typhoid, Salmonella, E. Coli and Fecal Coliform were threatening anyone who drank from the river. John Doulton invented a gravity fed ceramic filter that is still being manufactured today and in use all over the world. It boasted that you could pee in it and later, with confidence, drink it. Dan didn't intend to test that hypothesis, but did order two of the large units to be delivered, ASAP.

Dan wondered, *where in the world could you be safe from water and yet, still have enough to drink?* Then it hit him: glaciers. Melt the ice and you have water, in fact really old water with few impurities in it. Maybe arid locations like Nevada, Arizona and Northern Mexico weren't the best suited for survival. Maybe the wide open expanses of Alaska were safer. True, it snowed, but perhaps it was less dangerous than rain. He would have to discuss this with the Major.

Provisions

You get what you pay for and there is no such thing as a sale. Everyone needs to keep these two principles in mind when hunting for provisions. Since man no longer has to hunt for food, shopping has taken its place. Rituals are preformed, special garb in donned and proper attitudes assumed before the hunt. In tribes of Africa, alcoholic beverages or mild hallucinogens are consumed as a sacrifice to the hunt. The custom continues to this day as we prepare for the mall. And as long as you keep in mind the two above principles, you should do fine.

The dynamic duo headed for town in the plumbing company van. The Major drove because that's what men do. He never even considered asking Juanita to drive. She was fine with that. She gave directions when necessary and dutifully waited in the van while Patrick loaded up on supplies. Actually, the Major considered them provisions and not supplies. Major Johns always thought in military terms. Having been in the service for nearly 25 years, it was habit, and, as far as he was concerned, a good habit. The Air Force had taken a scrawny kid out of high school and given him the opportunity of a lifetime. He was the poster child for a lifer. College paid for by the government, assignments all over the world, involvement in important situations, the chance to prove his metal, financial security, thirty days of vacation a year, and healthcare. What more could he ask for? But even he thought 30 years was enough. He could retire comfortably at three quarters his regular pay and still be under fifty years old. Not bad.

He made an unscheduled stop, but before going into the sporting goods, store he called Dan.

"Hey Dan. I'm going to pick up some survival stuff. I should have asked before we left, but I need to find out what you already have. Do you own any guns beside that 12 gauge shotgun your father gave you?"

"No, that's it. I was thinking along the same lines when I ran across a survival site on the internet. I think we should have a couple of Glock 9mm's, maybe some sort of assault rifles too."

"Roger that. How you equipped for camping provisions?"

"We have three great sleeping bags, a propane stove and lamp. Probably need the little cotton filaments and more propane. We have a large two man tent and a couple of hatchets and an axe. Oh, and we have two binoculars and of course the obligatory cooler on wheels."

"Do you have outdoor clothing?"

"Three down ski coats, Juanita could use Lisa's. Oh crap, I gave Lisa's to Goodwill. Anyway, we have good boots and long underwear for Shelly and me."

"Got it. I'm gonna stock up, just in case. See ya soon, we filled up the van and are nearly out of room."

No question, The Major enjoyed this game. Preparing for the worst and expecting the best was his motto. No need to keep Juanita in the van, so they locked the vehicle and headed in to put a major dent in his wallet. First he headed for the guns. He picked out two Glock G17 9mm pistols for just under $500 each. Next, he wanted a rapid fire assault rifle. He chose the Bushmaster A2 M4 for around $850, and lastly he needed a scoped rifle for long accurate shots in case they had to hunt meat. He found a beauty in the Winchester Savage 308. With the scope, he stole it for $825. Of course he laid in plenty of ammo including shotgun shells. He signed his life away and knew he would have to wait for the handguns. The Brady Handgun Protection Act said that he had to wait five days, allowing the feds to check his background. The waiting period did not, however, cover the rifles, something he never quite understood. From the gun counter he and Juanita moved to the clothing section and then on to the camping gear, first aid supplies, portable generators, emergency hand crank radios, and plenty of batteries for flashlights. Two hours later he had dropped a cool $4,700 in just the sporting goods store. He hadn't totaled up the food and drinks yet, but he had a $15,000 limit on his credit card and was confident they would contact him if he ran over. One last stop at a liquor store and they would be set. Like the other outlets, Patrick loaded up on the provisions, beer and whisky mainly. Alcohol was always valuable. It could be traded or drank. Either way, it was valuable and the Major was sure he would need a drink somewhere down the line.

Juanita had been quietly evaluating Patrick all through the outing. He was witty and a good conversationalist. Very conservative and courteous, something she usually didn't find in men. He was roughly fifteen years her senior, but he confided that he had only been married once, to the Air Force. She could almost picture herself with him. Yes, she knew this was being silly and romantic, but that's what she did in her spare moments. She tried to visualize herself in a relationship with whatever face in a crowd she saw. Being alone for most of her life had left her longing for a real bond. And not one where she earned more money than the guy. One that didn't come with the standard question, 'Can I borrow the car?". All things considered, the move into the Brown house may not be so bad after all.

As they headed back to the farm, Juanita asked, "How scared should I be, Patrick?"

Turning to look at her as they edged into the traffic, he said one word, "Very." Silence was the third passenger for the rest of the ride home.

A Visit to the Boys

For Shelly, Sunday afternoons were often reserved
for exploring with Monica. They would grab a cold can
of soda, their Hollywood shades, and mount their waiting steeds. Both had mountain bikes that were perfect
for their deep sorties into the many bike paths etched
into the forest carpet. On these expeditions they sensed
when a rest was needed and, in unison, would hop off
their bikes and plop themselves onto the ground. They
would play make believe games as they rode. Often they
were pursued by one bad guy or another and only their
heroic acts could save their families, the town or even the
world. At this age they hadn't yet developed the mind set
to spend much time thinking about boys. Boys were an
inferior interruption into their otherwise idyllic lives.

On this Sunday, Shelly spent only a few hours with
Monica. Her normal time spent with her best friend was
being usurped by the white lie to spend time with her be-
loved uncle. True, she did love him, but all things being
equal, she would rather spend time with Monica. Now,
however, all things weren't equal. Soon she would be

going off to the spaceship to see if they could learn anything new. The excitement and fun of playing the UFO game with the elusive unseen extraterrestrial beings had turned into a scary prophecy for Shelly. The UFERs didn't seem to be concerned for what was about to happen to the life on good old planet earth. In fact, they seemed to relish the opportunity to be here for the big show. That just didn't seem right to her. She would be sure to mention that to them when she got the chance. It was also obvious that Dad and the Major had some questions that they had been giving not so subtle clues to. Shelly remained fixated on the God question. It had been bothering her ever since she heard their answer. *Abstract*, she thought, *what a bunch of bull hockey*. She had heard her father say that and didn't quite know what it meant, but it sounded very appropriate.

After a quick sandwich lunch that only Juanita could turn into an excursion to heaven, they equipped themselves for another trip to the valley. All fell into a rhythm and executed their responsibilities without being told. Dan again took the lead with Patrick bringing up the rear, with a steady eye on Juanita as she moved fluidly through the forest. Shelly walked along, quietly anticipating the questions and answer session. At the top of the ridge, Dan handed Juanita the cell phone and demonstrated the call help sign once again. She nodded obediently as the three continued down the hill.

As Uncle Major worked the video cam, Shelly began, "If you are here, will you please show us?" The orb pulsed into view. Sleek and seamless it floated effortlessly and as silent as a snake in the grass. "We would like to ask some more questions if that is alright," requested the girl.

The hologram took shape and Lisa Brown once again danced in mid air. "Of course, we were expecting you," transmitted the ball directly and only to Shelly.

"Is the rain going to hurt us if it touches us?"

"Prolonged exposure to contaminated water in any form will cause skin rashes and burns that will easily become infected. Water on your surface is not necessarily fatal; however, prolonged exposure to your orifices or open cuts or sores could lead to death. To ingest contaminated H2O would certainly lead to death."

"What about water filters? They are always advertising them on Daddy's radio. Wouldn't they work?"

"Most available filters can improve the appearance and taste of water, but none that we know of are capable of removing the virus."

Shelly, no longer wanting to pursue the questions her father and Uncle Major had been prepping her for, took dead aim at her real gripe. "Do you love?"

"If you mean do we feel closeness and affection for others, yes we do."

"Doesn't it hurt your heart to see us die?"

"The cycle of life is endless. It is neither good nor bad that things cease to exist. The death of one thing brings life to another. One goes, one comes. It is the way it has always been, both on the micro and macro level. The theory of chaos is very real."

"It hasn't always been that way."

"What do you mean?" replied the hologram.

"There was nothing until God made it. He can do what he wants, when he wants. I am surprised you don't know that," lectured Shelly with hands on her hips. Dan and the Major were left to wonder where the conversation had gone as Shelly was not giving them the ships responses.

"It is good that you believe in a higher life form. We too believe in the possibility of evolving into higher forms. We choose to not spend valuable time meditating on that possibility."

"Are their others out there like you, watching us?"

"Some. Not as many as you would think, but then we have only explored a small portion of the universe."

"Do any of the others know we are going to die?"

"Doubtful. We have reached an agreement to explore certain sectors and periodically release data to each other. Our next gathering is not for another thirty two of your planets years."

"So, you're the only ones that can help us and you won't?"

"It is not our place to change your world. It is your responsibility."

There was that word again, responsibility. It seemed to have tremendous implications no matter where you went. It was our responsibility, no one else's. How many did Uncle say? Six billion people and we can't seem to fix our own planet?

"What will happen to the earth when we are gone?"

"After thousands of years, another life form will ascend to the top of the ladder and begin their reign. Again, the cycle continues."

"Is there anything we can do to stop this?"

"To stop it; no. To preserve yourselves as long as possible, you have already taken some initial correct action. Store as much food and water as possible, wait for the riots to die down and migrate to safer coordinates."

"Dad, I don't want to ask any more questions. Can we go home now?"

"You bet Shelly. Let's get out of here. Ready Major?"

Irritated at not getting all of the information he wanted, but still supporting Shelly, the Major had no choice but to say "Yes. I'm finished filming. Let's go."

With little fanfare the ship blinked out of existence as they turned to exit the meadow. Shelly seemed to be metamorphosing into a grey listless cloud as she clumsily plodded along the path, head down, not saying a word. All three seemed especially somber to Juanita when they climbed out of the valley. Dan shook his head slowly, as if to say, no questions now. Juanita fell into line after the Major and this time got to appreciate his graceful gluts rhythmic gate. RutButt waited at the door. He had not wanted to venture past the yard for days now. No wonder!

Illness and More

The four horsemen of the apocalypse are a terrifying concept. The Pale horse in the bible is portrayed as weak, instead of strong and healthy, because it is carrying sickness, decay, drought and famine. The Pale horse had ridden in with the rain!

Shelly went through the ritual debriefing as Patrick replayed the video. Shelly would rub her temples, as if massaging a genie out of a bottle, eventually she was able to access the far reaches of her brain and dig out the answers to her questions. Not verbatim, but certainly her understanding of the conversation was right on. The rehash with the UFERs once again killed any party atmosphere for the day. A gut ringing resolve darted from each person to the next. They were in this together and together they intended to stay.

"I've got to check the news. We need to know what is happening," said the Major as he grabbed the remote off of the coffee table and hit the green on button. Several cities along the Washington, Oregon and Northern

California coastline were reporting high numbers of people flocking to emergency rooms with severe rashes and internal bleeding. Livestock in these same areas were being found dead in the fields. Fish kills were spreading rapidly as the size and scope of the red tide expanded. The Gulf of Mexico and the waters around the Philippines now had their own version of red death at their doorstep. Hawaii and Japan had both been declared disaster zones and were reporting significant loss of life that appeared to be directly related to the red tide and possibly the water. Scientists were declining to say that the water was directly involved, possibly for fear of riots. Japan had already declared martial law and Hawaii had requested the National Guard and any additional governmental support possible. Congress was in special session to deal with the problem and the President was on his way to California for a first hand assessment.

"Looks like somebody put two and two together," said the Major, "Besides the red tide reference a couple of days ago, this is the first time I heard that water might be a factor."

"Dad, it is time to tell people?" said Shelly matter-of-factly.

"Major, what do you think? Should we go public?" asked Dan.

"Not quite yet. Let me call some of my friends in the DOD (Department of Defense) and give them a heads up. This is going to be tricky," replied the Major, understanding the questions they would probably ask him. "Dan, let's you and I use your phone in the office." Dan and the Major motioned for Juanita and Shelly to stay with the news as they headed into the office and closed the door.

"I'm worried about Monica and her family. They are going to get sick and we can stop it," stated Shelly.

"Let your father and Patrick handle this. They have more experience with big problems. Let them work it out. Don't go and do something you will regret," cautioned Juanita.

From the secluded office Patrick placed the call, "Hello, General Jacobs, this is Major Johns, how are you?"

"Not at all good right now, Major. Not much time to talk. Lots of static on the radar, if you know what I mean."

"Actually, I might, General. I have come into some mighty alarming information that I frankly don't know what to do with."

"What kind of information Major? And be advised this is not a secure line."

"Can't wait for a better connection. My sources tell me that the red tide is the product of nuclear contamination emanating from the Sea of Japan. This tide is creating a virus that is transportable in water. It is literally falling on us in the form of rain. Rashes and burns on the skin are painful, but if you drink any water with the virus in it, it's fatal. It is spreading fast and will affect the food chain, starting with anything that eats grass. It has the potential to wipe out life on earth."

"Whoa. Slow down there Major. You're not the type to run amuck. Who is your source?"

"You wouldn't believe me if I told you. Just watch the news, and see what happens when riots start to break out. We are headed for chaos and portable water will be the main ingredient for survival."

"You sound a little paranoid, old buddy. Do you really want me to run this up the flag pole? It could mean the end of your career."

"I've got a little more than five years till retirement. I didn't plan on receiving any promotions. Shoot the moon sir."

"If someone wanted to talk to you, are you still at your command site?"

"No, sir. I am now on leave with an old buddy of mine in Tillamook, Oregon. But my cell number is still active and listed on the base directory. General, please get back to me and tell me I'm crazy. Right now, I feel like a prophet of doom."

"Hang in there, Johns. I'll make some calls. Your reputation is still highly regarded and I'll make damn sure they know it. We'll talk."

Hanging up the phone, Patrick filled Dan in on the missing parts of the conversation. Nothing they could do now except get Juanita moved in as soon as possible.

Changes in Attitude

It is amazing how quickly attitudes can change. Pearl Harbor changed everything for much of the world. To defend his family a father would do what was unthinkable yesterday if it became necessary today. Attitudes drift on the wind of survival.

All four loaded into the van and headed for Juanita's apartment. On the way to town, traffic seemed to be heavier than normal. Not a large town, Tillamook, nonetheless, experienced traffic problems in the peak tourist season. But at this time of the year, this was unusual. As they passed a Fry's grocery store, it became evident that the volume had been turned up a notch or two. The parking lot was unusually full. Everyone coming out seemed to have the shopping cart piled high or even a second one in tow. Vehicles were being loaded quickly and tempers seemed short as horns could be heard all over the lot. Yelling, pushing and at least one fist fight was visible from the road. Noticeably absent from the scene were the police. Not a cop car in sight. In fact, as Juanita stared, she saw store employees pushing carts to their cars and getting in. The run of the bulls had started.

Driving by the hospital, the panic was highlighted by most, if not all, of the police keeping order at the emergency entrance. Lines of people, perhaps as many 200, stood waiting with little or no patience. Without the gun-toting heavy weights, the gates would have been breached. Approaching Juanita's apartment, the upper floor of a two story house, the street seemed almost normal, except no one could be seen outside. No movement whatsoever, not even dogs nor cats. As Dan slid the car beside the curb, Patrick with his pistol in hand, said, "Does your key open the door at the top of the stairs?"

Juanita nodded and handed the Major the appropriate brass key. "Let me check it out. If it is clear I will signal you. Dan, have your pistol ready and stay in the van. Someone might want to take it. Do not let people walk up to you. Pull your gun and tell them to leave. Don't hesitate to shoot. We all need you," sternly advised the Major. Easing out of the van and not closing the door, the Major made his way to the stairs on the right side of the house. He kept his gun alongside his leg as he walked. Lightly making his way up the creaky wooden stairs in need of a good coat of paint, along with everything else in Tillamook, he noticed a light on in the kitchen. He peeked in the window of the door and noticed a small boy, about ten years old, going through the cupboards. The Major slid the door open and poked his head and gun inside the door.

"What are you doing in here, boy?" snarled the Major.

The boy dropped a can of baby snow peas as he turned in shock. "Dang mister, you scared the hell out of me."

"Answer my question. What are you doing here?"

"My father said to take a look and see if the lady needed any help. If she wasn't there, then get whatever food I could and go back home."

"Where's home?"

"Other side of the street about five houses up by the stop sign."

"Anybody in here with you?"

"No. Look I'll leave, it's no big deal."

"You will sit down on that couch and shut up. Understood?"

"Yes sir," answered a clearly shaken and scared boy.

"Come," mouthed the Major as he motioned Juanita to join him upstairs.

Juanita exited the van and ran across the lawn and took the stairs two at a time. She entered her apartment breathing heavily and saw the boy, "Jimmy, what are you doing here?"

"My Dad wanted to check on you and told me to grab any leftover food I could."

"Look, Juanita, I don't know how much time we have, but I suggest you only get the most critical items and do it fast." Juanita immediately went into her bedroom and took out two suitcases from the closet, opened them on the bed and began throwing her life's most prized possessions into the blue worn Samsonites. Pictures, some jewelry, clothes, bathroom implements, beauty supplies, and a special box hidden on the top shelf of her closet. Lastly she grabbed a CD walkman with about twenty discs and shoved them into the corner of the last open suitcase. Turning and carrying the bags to the living room, she had finished in less than ten minutes. A horn honk from the van alerted the duo to trouble. Shelly had her head out of the window and was yelling for them to hurry. Juanita told Jimmy to help himself to whatever was left as she and the major cautiously went down the stairs. Peeking around the corner, the Major saw about seven young men advancing up the street. Not armed, but clearly announcing their intentions to own this area. They were coming straight for the van. Still about 100 yards away, they broke into a run and spread their formation out. Patrick grabbed one of the suitcases and told Juanita to run! The side door was opened by Shelly as Juanita and two suitcases seemed to sail in like a line drive at a baseball game. The Major took the front seat and told Dan to reverse as fast as he could. By now, one of the young men was within throwing distance and he sent a fist sized rock ricocheting off the hood of the van and careening over the roof. The Major stuck his Glock out the window and fired one shot into the air. The young men's aggression seemed to dissipate as fast as air out of a needled balloon. They hit the ground and hugged it for dear life.

"Jesus Major, what's happening?" said Dan, dumbfounded as he kept accelerating back down the street.

"Anarchy, Dan, anarchy. We're just lucky they haven't gotten around to guns yet. My guess is after our confrontation they won't make that same mistake again. But I am surprised it's happening so fast."

Prophetically, Shelly said, "Uncle, next time you will have to shoot to kill."

"I hope you're not right Shelly. But I'm afraid you are. Let's get back to the farm and stay there."

On the way out of town they passed two gas stations with lines wrapped around the block. Gas was already recognized as a vital necessity. They also encountered several accidents with all the cars abandoned. No signs of police or ambulances. Twice they heard gunfire but couldn't tell where it was coming from and Juanita pointed out the large number of dead dogs and cats littering the lawns and sides of the pitiless roads. It was happening. It was happening now and it was happening too fast.

When they arrived at the farm, Monica's father was waiting for them. He was pacing back and forth as they parked the van.

"Dan, do you know what's happening?" asked George Achers.

"We were just in town and it's not safe in there anymore. Don't go in unless you have to and then, only if you're armed," answered Dan.

"But why?" asked George clearly unable to assimilate the recent events.

"I don't know, George, but I heard something on the TV about not drinking water. They think it's poisoned somehow," said Dan, giving him vital information if he would just heed it. "Stay inside and keep out of the rain. If you have a gun, keep it handy. Now you better get back to your family. Check in with us when you can. Oh, and George, obviously I am keeping Shelly out of school until all of this blows over. I suggest you do the same," encouraged Dan.

George had paused in mid step when he heard the last suggestion and almost stumbled. He hadn't even thought about keeping Monica out of school. He reminded himself that he needed to get a grip and deal with the situation. He nodded to Dan and turned and jogged home.

Stacked on the front porch were two large boxes. Patrick saw the labeling and confirmed Dan's guess, "It's the Berkefeld water filters you ordered. I'll bet that is the last delivery truck in this area for a very long time."

"If we ever have to choose what to save first, save the water filters," informed Shelly as if she were the authority on valuation in a society gone amok.

Dan let his thoughts slip uncontrollably out of his mouth, "Thank God we got 'em. Now how do we test em?"

The Source

Bad information can get you killed, but, then again, so can good information. Sometimes it's better to know someone who actually knows what information is best to know. Ya know what I mean?

"General Jacobs, this Major Johns actually used the word virus in connection with radioactive leaks around the Sea of Japan?" asked Vern Smith, the liaison to the Secretary of Defense.

"Indeed he did Vern. He is a solid guy and wouldn't go screwing around with bogus intel."

"He wouldn't tell you his source?"

"Said I wouldn't believe him if he told me. Sounded unusually guarded about the whole deal. Didn't ring true for him. Out of character."

"Well if he knows, who else does? We have to get a lid on this before panic hits the street."

"Vern, we're too late. It has not only hit the street, it hit the fan, the ceiling, and your shoes. Have you seen the national news lately? Riots are starting to occur at our west coast hospitals. Japan and Hawaii are shutting down. Nothing is going in or coming out of them. This damn red tide is beginning to show up everywhere."

"General, get him on the phone now! I need some answers for the Secretary. He has a conference with the President later today."

When the Major's phone rang, it actually startled everyone. They were all sitting around the kitchen table collecting their thoughts and figuring out what they would eat for lunch. No calls had come into the house in the last day, and when the Major's phone rang with the traditional, albeit unnecessarily loud phone sound and not some cheesy show biz song, all four literally jumped. Uneasy smiles dotted their faces, except Shelly, who blurted out a laugh to cover her jitters.

"Major Johns here."

"Major, it's General Jacobs and I have Vern Smith, the liaison, to the SOD with me. You are conferenced in. Are you in a secure place?"

"Give me a minute and I will be," replied the Major as he motioned Dan to follow him, but also raising his index finger to his mouth signaling him to keep quiet. "Okay sir, I am now in a secured room," confirmed Johns as he closed the office door behind Dan and himself.

"Major, this is Vern Smith. You seem to know more than you should about recent events. I want your source. This is a national security issue," ordered the liaison.

"Sir, you won't believe me. You will only believe the information I give you. I know what is happening. I know where this is all going to end. My source will cloud the issue," warned the Major.

"What in the hell are you talking about? You're no damned journalist protecting your precious source. I just gave you a direct order, soldier, during a very dangerous time for the U.S. I want the source," demanded Vern.

"Alright, you asked for it. I came out to Tillamook as a favor to a friend of mine. He swore his daughter had found a UFO in the woods behind her house. My friend had also seen it and videoed it. He wanted me to verify he wasn't going nuts. I came out here and low and behold, we got a UFO."

"Oh come on Major. What a bunch of bull," shouted the General.

"Not quite sir, more like a herd. It gets better. We talked to them. They are here to watch our planet die. They even told us how it would happen. And by God, it's happening. Now you don't have to believe it, but we felt we needed to tell someone and I picked you," lectured Patrick in his best professorial, non-condescending tone.

"So, let me get this straight: a UFO landed in your back yard, with, I am assuming, little green men, and they told you the planet is going to die. You have had a close encounter of the fourth kind, never before recorded, and now they are sharing secrets with you. How nice," laughed Vern.

"I can prove it, gentlemen. The virus is in the rain. Everything it touches will eventually die. Already we have livestock falling over dead and people are coming out of the woodwork with rashes and burns from the rain. You cannot drink the water. It will kill you. If you don't believe me, try a glass or water where the red tides have been. It is going to spread and eventually wipe most life out. Do your homework and you will come up with the same answer."

"Give us a minute, Major," said the General, hitting the mute button on his three legged star trek looking conference telephone. "Vern, we gotta check this out. It sounds like horse shit, but Major Johns is a solid career man—as good a man as you will find. Send some guys out there to check it out. Maybe homeland security or the NSA. What have we got to lose?"

"Alright, you set it up. Keep my name and the SOD out of this for the time being. Report back to me when your boys show up and die of laughter," responded Vern as he stormed out of the room.

The General adjusted his chair in front of the conference telephone and hit the mute button again to bring everyone back on line, "Major, we are going to send some folks out your way to check up on your story. You should see them sometime tomorrow. I'll be in touch."

"General, your boys won't be able to see the UFO. They have warned us that only the four of us can see it. But, we do have some video for you to look at, and by the way, we don't know what color they are, but there are four of them."

"Great. Nonetheless, keep your cell phone handy. You may have to pick 'em up at the airport."

"Will do, sir. And thanks for listening. This is real."

The General hung up without so much as bye. Patrick returned his cell phone to his hip holster and said, "Well that was pleasant," as he repeated the conversation to Dan. "Something tells me this is all for naught."

Loose Ends

Calling from the courthouse, Dan's quasi scientific friend phoned, "Hey, Dan, how you doing?"

"I've been better, Jerry. Any news on that sample I left with you?"

"That's why I'm calling. I gave it to the crime lab and they did a preliminary analysis and came back with ash. Most likely human remains. You been cremating people out at your place, Dan?" said Jerry with a slight laugh.

"No, Jerry, I have not been cremating people. It is just something I ran across in the woods while fishing and it looked suspicious," lied Dan. "I guess I better let the police know where I found it."

"Go ahead, but don't expect any action in the near future. They are swamped with the run on the hospital and the stores. They haven't even had time to investigate the missing person that came in a couple of days ago."

"Who is missing?"

"Well, some woman sales rep was coming up here to meet with the bank and never showed up. Her husband logged a missing persons report with the Portland police and they tracked her activity up here. But, not much anyone can do with the way things are."

"Thanks, Jerry, for getting back to me. How is the general scene in town?"

"Bad and getting worse. This is the worst thing I have ever seen. All these illnesses and dead animals. And now the looting is starting. It's got everybody, and I mean everybody spooked. I doubt there will be anybody in the office tomorrow. I was just cleaning up my miscellaneous tasks before I head out indefinitely. Stay safe Dan."

"Thanks Jerry. You too."

Dan didn't want to spook Juanita or Shelly so he confided only in Patrick the nature of the phone call.

"So, our nice little UFERs are experimenting on us," stated the Major.

"Looks like it. Another reason to be very careful around them. Can't let Shelly go back there alone. Not that we could stop anything, but I certainly feel better knowing we are there with her."

"Not to change subjects Patrick, but I have to call my business and see how they are doing."

"No problem. I'm going to check on the girls."

The phone at the *Plumb Certain* rang seven times before Bob answered. He was out of breath, "Hello."

"Bob, this is Dan. What's going on down there?"

"Holy cow, Dan, looks like the Chicago riots. People running around in the streets, stealing cars, breaking windows, looting. They even came in here and took some stuff. Don't know what in the world they will do with it, it's just plumbing supplies."

"Bob, tell everyone to go home. Clean out the safe, and lock up the store as best you can. Do not put yours or anyone else's life in danger. Get out of there."

"That will be easy; I'm the only one here. Are you okay?"

"Bob, we're fine. Don't worry about us. Oh, and Bob, do not drink the water and stay out of the rain. It will kill you."

"What? Who told you?"

"You wouldn't believe me, just do it."

"Okay boss, hope to see when this blows over, Dan."

"Me too, Bob. Be careful."

Dan told the Major about the looting and what was happening in town.

"Dan, I think we should be prepared for some of those looters to come our way. The town will be stripped soon and they will turn their attention to the rural areas. And I don't think we can count on getting the two Glocks I ordered. I suspect they have already been either stolen or sold out the back door. Let's keep an eye out for extra firepower wherever we can find it."

"Maybe we should take Shelly's advice and organize the four farms in this area as sort of a protection committee," offered Dan.

"Wouldn't hurt to try. Maybe if we had a signal of some sort we could sound it and the other families could come running to help. Let me contact them and see what we can do," said Dan. "In the meantime, why don't you reconnoiter around the farm and see if you can come up with a plan to defend this place."

"Good idea. Let's see what we can get done before evening. Shelly and Juanita can unload the van."

G-Men

Dan had been able to go and talk to the four other farms in his area. Unfortunately, both of the Webster's were already showing skin blisters and more than likely they had drank virus laced water. He didn't think they would last much longer. Dan encouraged them to stay out of the rain and not to drink the water. When they wanted to know what they should drink, he told them anything that is bottled or from a can; like peach juice. Before leaving, he inquired if they had any guns for protection. Harold Webster pointed to his hall closet and said he had a small armory if needed. Dan smiled and said good, while filing away the information for later use. He left them knowing their fate was sealed. He felt guilty knowing their outcome already, but he was now in survival mode and his people came first.

He had better luck with Mike and Tina Olson, Monica's parents, George and Jan Achers, and Jonnie Cole. None of them showed any signs of sickness. Mike and Tina didn't own any firearms, but fortunately, both were avid bow hunters, owning three different bows each. They were comfortable they could protect themselves and showed Dan a vicious set of razor tipped arrows that would intimidate a Grizzly bear. Jonnie Cole was an older gentleman with a fearsome drinking problem. His bulbous nose resembled the casaba melon planted on the late actor W.C. Field's face. Jonnie proudly showed Dan several of the handguns and an old 12 gauge shotgun he had on hand and reminded Dan that he had served in the Army in Vietnam. Because he drank mainly alcohol and ate TV dinners, he was showing no ill effect to the contaminated water. Monica's parents proved the most worrisome to Dan. Not only because of the relationship with Shelly, but because they seemed the most ill prepared for what was coming. Neither George nor Jan believed in guns. They were the epitome of non-violence. Even when Dan told them about the things he had seen in town, they just couldn't believe that, given the chance, they couldn't talk some sense into anybody that came out to their farm. Dan feared for them and left them with a caution: "Don't let anybody in your house that you don't know. If you see someone strange around, use the walkie-talkie and get word to me."

Before leaving each house, he had left behind and instructed them on how to use a walkie-talkie. The major had the foresight to purchase six cheap units with marginal range, just in case. Dan put them all on a common channel and told them it was for emergencies only.

He reminded everyone to stay away from the water, to conserve their food, and to not go into town unarmed or alone. Clearly, he had frightened everyone. *'Good,'* he thought, as he started for home*, 'At least they will have their eyes open.'*

The Major had not been as fortunate in his outing. The farm was really just a haphazard collection of buildings that appeared to have been constructed on an as-needed basis. No clear-cut killing zones could be established, and blind spots were as common as mud puddles. The one bright spot was an enormous Sitka Spruce tree planted right beside the house. It towered over the ranch style home by a good 75 feet. Large branches were within easy reach of the roof and it would make an excellent observation post, not to mention shooting stand with good protection for the marksman.

Just as he was making a mental picture of the best location for the stand, his phone rang. "This is Major Johns."

"Major, this Sid Glutchman, a friend of the General's. A friend and I have just landed, unaided I might add, at your lovely airport, and request transportation to your site."

"Did you say unaided?"

"Indeed I did. This place is mainly vacant. I have left the plane in the hands of armed guards who are, at the moment, scrounging jet fuel. What the hell's going on out here?"

"I think they call it mayhem, Sid. Sit tight, one of us will be there to get you in about an hour. We will be driving a blue plumbing van. I assume you're at the main terminal?"

"Actually, it's all shot up. Drive right out onto the tarmac. We are the only Lear jet out there."

"Roger that. See ya soon."

The Major jumped on the walkie-talkie and told Dan to double-time it back to the house. The G-men had landed.

It's Raining, It's Pouring

Neither Dan nor the Major had needed the rain gear they had painstaking applied before venturing out into the elements. However, as soon as both returned to the house, the drizzle began. Calming actually. Melodic. It made the kind of sound that made you want to curl up with a nice thick quilt and take a nap. But masked beneath its glistening splatters was a deadly sting. When the rain hit your skin it felt cool and inviting. You wanted to tilt your head back and let it wet your face. You could just see yourself opening your mouth and letting the crystalline drops saturate your thirsty tongue. What most didn't know was that in eighteen hours, a hive would develop wherever the rain touched your skin. Your arm, your face, your tongue, your eye, it didn't matter. The hive was ultra sensitive and the itch irresistible. Scratching became addictive. You lived to scratch. You would wake up in the night with bloodied bed sheets from gashes you had dug in your flesh. Tongues swelled and eyes ceased functioning. By the time authorities put two and two together, it was too late. And if you were unfortunate enough to drink the contaminated water or eat some food that had been innocently washed in tap water, the results were even nastier. Death occurred within 24 to 36 hours and it was a violent, painful exorcism of life. Patients begged to be killed. Euthanasia stepped to the forefront of medicine and became a mainstay for months to come. And since most Doctors abandoned their posts relatively early in the survival of the fittest free-for-all that ensued, mercy was usually dispensed at the end of a gun by a loving relative. It was brutal, it was real, and it wasn't going away.

"Dan, just got the call from the G-men, they are at the airport. I told them we would pick them up in one hour."

"Great, let's go," said Dan, turning towards the garage.

"No. Let's not," responded the Major.

Dan turned to face Patrick, not knowing if he was serious or not. "What do you mean?"

"Dan, we cannot afford to have both of us away from the farm at the same time. We need someone here who isn't afraid to shoot and ask questions later. I think you should go and pick them up. You know the roads and, more than likely, the main routes will be shut down and you will need to improvise. I told them you would be in the van and they said you were to drive right out onto the tarmac."

"You're right. I'm going to take the shotgun and a pistol just in case."

"And don't stop for anybody—sick kids, dogs or good looking women. Just keep moving," lectured the Major.

"Yes Sir," grinned Dan, snapping to attention and bringing some levity to the situation.

Dan got his firearms, made sure they were loaded, chambered, and the safeties engaged. Shelly had been listening from the kitchen and knew something special was happening.

"Dad, can I go with you?"

"Not this time babe. By the way, are you keeping RutButt out of the rain?"

"Yes. I locked his cat door and he is prowling around the house looking for an escape route. We all need to be careful and not let him sneak out."

"Right," said Dan, glad to have changed the direction of the conversation. "I'll be bringing some people back with me from the airport. The Major can fill you in. Should be back in an hour or so. See ya then."

"Dad, people are going to shoot at you. Be careful. I know you will be alright, but it will be scary, that's why I wanted to go. To help you calm down."

Dan just looked at her and dared not ask why she thought he would be shot at. He kissed her and moved to the side garage door to make his way to the van parked in the driveway. The garage was so full of supplies that the van no longer could be squeezed in. It was still drizzling when Dan pulled out of the farm onto the road. He could see thick black smoke licking the horizon to the west. *Cars on fire*, he thought to himself. Hope I don't see any bodies. He had already mapped out a back road route to the airport, but would still have to take one highly visible road for about two miles. His van wasn't four-wheel drive and he hoped he could navigate the streets. He gripped the butt of pistol in his waistband for reassurance and reminded himself to focus on the task and trust his instincts. He sped up and constantly checked his mirrors for any latent followers.

Dodge-ball

In high school, dodge-ball was Dan's favorite PE game. Nothing better than hunting and being hunted. The thrill of being the last one still alive on your side, with four or five volley ball toting thugs trying to erase you from the basketball court. Your teammates cheering you on to catch a ball and bring them back into the game. It was great stuff even when you lost, because in dodge-ball, no one died and you always got another chance.

The farm was located about five miles off of Wilson River Loop. It fed into route 6 which went directly into Tillamook. The airport was six miles south of town. Dan didn't want anything to do with Tillamook. He turned east on route 6 and made his way to Olsen Road and turned south and made his way through a small subdivision till he hit Lone Prairie Road, which eventually curved east right into the airport. On the way, he had seen bodies. A lot of them. Dead animals, birds, burned out cars, a house fire in the subdivision and a few poor individuals wandering around outside in the rain. For the most part, it was a ghost town. People were either holed up, dead, or gone. He had seen only three or four people during the trip and had not seen one other vehicle moving down the roads. As he pulled into the airport, he was shocked to see the destruction. Broken windows, a few bodies with bullet holes, a car sticking half in and half out of the front entrance of the terminal was still smoking. He pulled to a side entrance to the tarmac and was greeted by a man in a rain slicker, pointing Uzi directly at the van. Immediately, and a little too hard, Dan hit the brakes. The van screeched its disapproval and rocked to an abrupt stop.

"What's your business?" challenged the man with a face hidden by a yellow hood.

"My name is Dan. I am here for Major Johns to pick up some men and take them to my farm."

"Keep both hands on the steering wheel and don't make any sudden moves," instructed the man as he cautiously moved to the drivers' door and looked inside. "What's the shotgun for?"

"Just in case," said Dan, irritated at the third degree questioning.

"Right. Pull up to the plane and keep your hands where I can see them."

Dan came to a stop parallel to the exit ramp of the Lear jet. Two large men in rain gear descended and proceeded to walk around the van, commenting to each other. When they reached Dan's window, they motioned for him to exit.

"I'm agent Simms and this is agent Cracken. We were sent by General Jacobs to check out your story. Who are you?"

"Dan Brown. I'm a friend of Major Johns'."

"Why didn't he come?" inquired the overly suspicious agent Sims, who was clearly the senior agent.

"I know the roads better and we didn't want to leave the farm unprotected."

"Did you know you have two bullet holes in the right side of your van?" inquired agent Cracken.

Dan moved to the opposite side of the van squinted to find the holes. Finally, agent Cracken walked to the rear of the van by the wrap-around tail lights and pointed them out.

"Damn, I didn't even feel 'em. If this was dodge-ball, I'd be out of the game. It had to have happened coming out here," said Dan, clearly unnerved by the find and regretting the dodge-ball comment.

"Is there an alternate route we can take back to the farm?" asked agent Sims.

"Not really. I don't want to go through town. I guess I will speed up on the way home."

"From the looks of it, it was a 22 caliber. Probably some kids screwing around. The shell didn't even enter the compartment. Let's get going. I don't want to have the jet exposed longer than necessary."

Neither agent sat in the front seat with Dan. Both took up window positions in the rear seats by the windows. Small machine gun-looking weapons now magically appeared from beneath their rain coats and rested on their laps, ready to be used. Before leaving, Dan suggested that the guards remaining with the plane stay out of the rain and drink only bottled water they brought with them. He could see that at least one of the guards had wet hands and was wiping his mouth with them. He cautioned against that sure recipe for disaster.

"Here we go," said Dan as he started the engine and eased out onto the frontage road and began to retrace his route back home. In order to make a harder target, he pushed the van to its limits. Neither agent registered a response from his maniacal driving. In fact, they seemed to expect it. The drive home was uneventful and fast. When they pulled up to the farm, the garage door was already opening for them. Both agents took one more trip around the van and satisfied themselves that they had not become a moving target on this leg of the trip and joined Dan and the Major in the garage. The agents introduced themselves to the Major, commented on the impressive store of supplies, and moved into the kitchen as the garage door slid down, sealing them off from the dangerous rain.

Evidence

Just because someone is from this authority or that does not put them automatically on your side. Governments in particular have the nasty habit of not noticing or eliminating data they consider counterproductive. Truth has no real say in the issue; instead, expedience, political correctness, or saving face rule the day. Evidence can get in the way.

Shelly was waiting by the kitchen table with eyes that rivaled those of an ostrich, big, luminous and non-blinking. Juanita, clearly as curious as Shelly, leaned against the kitchen counter with a dish towel draped across her shoulder, in a far sexier pose than she intended. For just a moment, agent Sims let his guard down as he took in the lovely Juanita. He was sizing her up as a woman, not as a witness. But just as if a switch had been thrown, he quickly reverted to his government training and took on the unemotional, distanced stance that all good agents must have. But Shelly alone had noticed the transformation and intended to ask Juanita what it meant at a later, more secretive time.

Juanita distributed towels to the men to wipe off any rain they might have come into contact with.

"Right now our jet is a magnet for anyone wanting to distance themselves from the west coast. A lot of people would do anything possible to get out of here. We have to move fast," instructed agent Sims. "I want Dan or Major Johns to escort me to the UFO site right now and agent Cracken will begin interviewing the rest of you and looking at any documentation you may have." Facing Dan and the Major he said, "If there are no objections, I would like to leave now."

"Since I am already in my rain gear, I'll take him out to the site. Major, you can show him what we already have," replied Dan as he headed for the back door and motioned for agent Sims to join him.

"Cracken, call the plane and tell them we have arrived and are processing the data. Estimated return time about four hours. Have them keep in touch if things get dicey," instructed agent Sims as he stepped out of the door into the soggy Oregon world.

Major Johns, with Juanita and Shelly in tow, explained everything that had happened since he had arrived. Shelly interjected frequently and enthusiastically and walked the agent through the entire glowing ball experience when the Major had left that item out of his dialogue. While viewing the video, all eyes were on Cracken as he carefully scrutinized the images before him. Occasionally he would nod his head, freeze the video and ask questions. The Major was impressed with his logic and line of questions. The agent maintained an objectivity that was admirable, considering the subject matter. He took especial interest when shown the group of people surrounding the ship. He backed the tape up several times and froze the image when the woman stepped into the ship.

"Do you know that woman?" solicited Cracken.

"Dan said he had never seen her, but he was able to identify several of the others. He contacted the police and they think she might be a salesperson from Portland. They never got around to verifying it before mayhem became the rule around here," replied the Major.

"Of course I will need to take this tape with me. We will put it through its paces back at headquarters and may be able to verify her identity."

"Sure, I anticipated you would want the tape. I made a backup to our hard drive." As much as he wanted to, the Major couldn't determine if Cracken believed them or not. Perhaps the tape would help as he was sure the field trip to the UFO would be a bust.

When Cracken had finished viewing the tape several times, he carefully placed the disc in his coat pocket and began in-depth interviews with each of them. He interviewed each of them individually in the closed office and was clearly looking for inconsistencies in their statements. He took copious notes and remained pleasant and non-confrontational throughout the process. When he was finished, he checked in with the plane again, found they had taken some small arms fire and had set up a defensive perimeter that was holding. Satisfied, he told them he would check in later and signed off. Next, he requested something to eat and drink. Remaining aloof, business-like, and professional had been drilled into him at an early stage of his agent training.

As they sat around the kitchen table and ate some sandwiches and drank sodas, Shelly wanted to know, "Are other places having the same problems we are?"

"Actually, the west coast is our major concern right now. The president has declared martial law in California, Alaska, Washington, Oregon and parts of Idaho. The rain from the west coast is the problem. It is raining in other places in the US, but so far only those areas receiving rain fed from the Pacific Ocean appear problematic."

"Are they able to help anybody?" implored Shelly.

"Some, but we don't know exactly what is happening and right now we are just trying to contain it."

"That's not going to work," joined the Major.

"We don't know that yet," replied the agent.

"People have to be moved away from the rain and given some type of water filters developed to handle this virus. If the government doesn't do that, millions will die," stated the Major.

"That's speculation at this time. The last thing we want is to see masses of people on the move. That would be catastrophic," lectured the agent, his voice rising in volume. "The Center for Disease Prevention and Control (CDC) out of Atlanta sent some folks to Seattle. They died before they could come to any worthwhile conclusions. The National Guard has pulled back and is basically containing people within certain geographical areas and not policing at this time. It's very much un-chartered territory right now. Not exactly a good time to have masses of people up and moving around the country, if ya know what I mean?"

An uneasy quiet descended on the group as they all munched their sandwiches while digesting the information the agent had just shared.

ЖОЖ

Dan and agent Sims marched briskly to the valley. At the crest of the hill leading down into the valley, Dan pointed out where the UFO should be found. As they drew within a few feet of where Dan knew it would hover, he stopped and said, "Would you please let us know if you are here?" Agent Sims smiled and said nothing.

This time, Dan whistled and no echo returned. Dan picked up a rock and tossed it in the direction of the orb and it fell harmlessly to the ground.

"It's not here. We warned you that it said this would happen."

"Right. I told my boss this was a goose chase. We have better things than to run down bullshit leads. You got lucky with some of the info you found on the internet and now you want to grab some press. Let's get the hell out of here," said the agent as he turned and began to trek up the valley side.

"Before we leave, bear with me." With that, Dan quickly grabbed seven or eight stones from the ground and began hurling them in all directions and even straight up. They all clunked to ground.

"Oh, I get it, you think it's here but it just moved," laughed agent Sims.

Next, Dan began carefully examining the ground where the UFO should have been. He was looking for the gray spot on the grass, the human ashes. He found nothing. The rain had effectively washed away the scant evidence.

"Hey Sherlock, are you done? I sure know I have had enough humiliation for the day."

Disgruntled and barely audible, Dan said, "Yes. Sorry."

Agent Sims led the way back to the farm. With the exception of one comment, neither man spoke. Dan noted, "It sure is getting dark early these days. Must be a storm coming in."

Reaching the farm, with a now huffing agent Sims still leading the way, they were met at the back door by a very concerned group of people.

"What took so long, Sims?" said agent Cracken.

"What do mean? My watch says were gone a little over an hour. It's a good fifteen or twenty minute hike back in there. We moved pretty damn fast."

"An hour! Look outside. It's dark. You've been gone over three hours," replied the Major. "We were getting ready to send out the posse."

Agent Sims and Dan both compared their watches with the kitchen clock. Clearly two hours were missing.

"Holly shit! This isn't possible," said Sims as he grabbed the wrist of Cracken and looked at his wrist watch. "Two hours gone. What the hell happened?"

"Look, in a situation like this, I recommend you two retire to the bedroom, disrobe and check yourselves out. No telling what happened, but they might, just might have left tracks," advised the Major in what sounded more like an order than a suggestion.

"Now I get it, I'm on Candid Camera. You think some little green men were playing with Dan and me? You're off your rocker," said an angry Sims.

"Sims, it's the right thing to do. I don't want to explain why we didn't do this when we get back east. Humor them. Go take a quick look," urged Cracken.

Dan was already making his way to his bedroom and looking over his shoulder he smiled at Sims and said, "Come on G-Man, let's get this over with."

Sims reluctantly began following Dan and shot over his shoulder to Cracken, "One word of this at headquarters and you'll be singing soprano."

Dan and Sims disrobed on opposite sides of the bed, keeping maximum distance between their bodies. Eventually it became necessary to examine the areas that each simply could not see. Dan went first. "Sims, check out my back and the back of my legs."

Sims maneuvered Dan to a directional light in the corner and pointed it at his legs as he examined each. He found nothing unusual. He moved the light up Dan's back and stopped as he passed over the outside part of the shoulder blade next to the armpit. Three small reds dots in a triangular pattern, no wider apart than the normal drinking straw were evident. *Could be anything,* thought Sims as he reached out and touched the area. The dots were raised, much like brail. Dan jerked away instinctively and Sims hurriedly explained why he was touching him.

Dan walked to the door, and cracking it stuck his head out, "Shelly, please get me the mirror out of the hall bathroom." Shelly ran from the kitchen, grabbed the mirror and handed it to her father with a very concerned look on her face.

"Is it three red dots Dad?"

"Now how in the world did you know that?"

"That's what I have. I got it the night I followed the ball."

"Damn it, Shelly," said Dan raising his voice for all to hear, "you better start telling everything that is going on. Do you hear me?"

"I'm sorry Dad," replied Shelly meekly, afraid that this transgression would not be forgiven.

Dan closed the door and took a look for himself. Just as Sims had described—three red dots in the pattern of a triangle. "Okay Sims, your turn, and I bet I know where to look." Dan focused the light on the same spot and, sure enough, dots just like Dan. He handed the mirror to Sims for his own scrutiny. "We've been tagged and bagged ole buddy," said Sims. "You better check out your daughter, Dan."

Dan got dressed and asked Shelly to join him in the hall bathroom where he surveyed her pattern. Just like his and Sims, except larger and more distinct. *Perhaps they all changed with time,* thought Dan.

"Why didn't you tell me about the dots, Shelly?"

"They told me not to tell you. They said it was necessary to complete their study."

Dan and Sims confirmed their findings to the group. Again, it was the Major that suggested that everyone, even Cracken, should do a quick strip down and check themselves out. Dan showed them what to look for and each took a turn in the hall bathroom with the mirror. Only Shelly wasn't surprised to find out that Juanita and the Major also had the same spots.

It was too late for a run to the airport, so Sims called the plane and relayed that they would be out at dawn and to be ready. The plane crew reported no new activity and they had been fortunate and found some jet fuel for the thirsty Lear jet. One crew member had a rash on his hands and face and was being kept inside the plane. They would be prepped and ready at dawn.

"How about some beers? I know I could sure use one," urged the Major.

East Coast Base Line

Golic was mildly surprised that Neep, the ship, had initiated baseline testing to take place on the two recent visitors to the ship. This was unprecedented and represented a new level of development for the ship's logic. A mild rebuke to the ship had elicited the exact response Golic was hoping for, an apology and the assurance that it would not happen again. Neep was indeed becoming a viable member of the crew.

"Nimar, what did you find when evaluating the two new subjects?"

"As we anticipated, the Agent Sims individual was nearly absent on any virus readings at all. Only trace elements, probably from his recent exposure to the rain. However, we did find significant stress levels related to his job and relationships. He has still not processed the events into a worldwide scenario, although we believe that will happen in short order. His government is taking steps to quarantine portions of the United States, but as we know, their efforts will be wasted as the precipitation patterns pick up as the overall exposure areas widen. For the patriarch Dan Brown, he is showing a marginal increase in exposure to the virus, but well under the critical limits. His family unit seems to be heeding our warnings and we have learned, through night scannings, that they are developing and informal alliance with some of their immediate neighbors to increase their security.

On a separate note, we do anticipate that they will discover the probe marks within several days at the latest. They seem to be a process-driven group and worthy of our attention."

"Well done, Nimar. Is there anything else?"

"Yes, I would like your authorization to periodically send in our rover to scan their home unit and selected individuals to keep abreast of their plans."

"Approved, but be as non-intrusive as possible."

Hazard Pay

Mornings in Oregon tend to sneak up on you. Thick, tall trees standing at attention smother the horizon and rob all but the birds in the air and a few skyscraper dwellers of the glorious pallet of dawn colors sneaking over the horizon and oozing to life.

Sims and Cracken were the exception. Possibly because they were spooked, no pun intended, they had maintained an around-the-clock watch. Under no circumstances were they going to be surprised. The rain had mercifully relented somewhere around the witching hour and the sun shone brightly as it warmed the pavement and ghosts of steam rose from the sparkling black asphalt. Missing were the birds that usually accompanied the mud puddles looking for tasty morsels of worms for a quick breakfast. Birds were among the first casualties of the rain. They littered the roads and forest floors with their flightless bodies, now becoming one with the earth. The quiet was deafening. Their joyous song had been sucked out of the world.

"No time for breakfast, Juanita. We need to roll out of here now," said Sims. Both were packed and eager to get moving. Dan again volunteered to drive the van and the Major agreed with the decision. Weapons were loaded and gear stored as the mad dash to the airport was about to begin. Cracken called one last time to the plane and learned that the crew had detected men moving towards the plane. They were anxious to depart.

Hugging Dan, Shelly said, "Do what you have to Dad. Stay safe and come back to us. People will try to kill you this time."

Dan was beginning to take his daughter's warnings seriously and hugged her even tighter and promised to come back safe. As Dan approached the highway, he slowed to a stop and they all viewed a small convoy of SUV's moving out of town. "More than likely a group of friends or neighbors are making a break for Idaho or points southwest to avoid the rain," commented Sims.

"The guard will turn them back," said Cracken, shaking his head.

They waited until the convoy disappeared around a bend in the road before proceeding. As they entered the first subdivision, they saw signs of recent looting and killing. Two houses were on fire along with several vehicles. One house had clearly been under attack, as there were numerous bullet holes peppered throughout the front and sides of the building. Two bodies had been propped up as decoration on a front lawn in a gruesome show of power and serving a bleak reminder of what might happen if you tried to resist the mob.

Probably due to the time of day, they met no resistance going to the plane. Hurried goodbyes and handshakes were exchanged, knowing that never again would these men see each other. The jet taxied to the end of the runway, fired its engines and rose effortlessly into the morning sky. Banking left and heading east, Dan thought he heard gunshots, but he wasn't sure. Climbing in his van, he instinctively checked his rearview mirror and saw a jeep rapidly approaching. At least four men were in the jeep and they were firing at him! If he ran, they would follow. He couldn't lead them to the farm. If he stayed, he would be outgunned, and if they were willing to shoot at him without even knowing what he was doing, no telling what else they would be willing to do. He slumped in the seat as if shot and let the van creep up into a chain link fence. He hoped for just one chance to escape. The jeep pulled up and stopped about twenty feet from his van, directly behind him. All four jumped out of the jeep and carefully approached the van. They could see Dan's arm hanging out of the driver's window, limp and lifeless. They relaxed their guard and as Dan heard the gravel beneath the boots of one of the men, he threw the van into reverse and hit the accelerator. The van jumped backwards toward the jeep and, as it drew abreast of the man on Dan's side, Dan brought his shotgun up and discharged it into the man's face. The stranger flew backwards in a swirl of red. The van crunched into the jeep and its rear trailer hitch penetrated the radiator and struck the fan. The jeep was officially out of commission. Staying as low as he could get, Dan put the van in drive and punched it. He knew roughly where the tarmac entrance was and he turned the wheel and hoped for the best. Bullets were now thudding into the van and entering the passenger compartment. Dan's seat stopped at least two bullets and he prayed the men would not start aiming at the tires. He lunged onto the tarmac and careened around the terminal building and out of direct sight of the killers. He peeked out of the front window and gunned the van toward the locked exit at the other end of the runway. Dan looked in the rear view mirror and saw that one of the men, with a high powered rifle, was kneeling on the tarmac and still shooting at him. He heard the plink, plink, plink of bullets ricocheting off of his rear door. Dan didn't slow down a bit as he approached the alternate exit. Instead, he scrunched down in his seat and accelerated and blew through the gate with a loud smash. Not on the roads he preferred to be on, but at least he wasn't being shot at. He would have to risk a more conspicuous route home than he preferred. Seeing no one following him, he dramatically slowed his pace and began easing the van onto streets and around corners with an adroitness that surprised him. Nothing like almost dying to bring out hidden skills, he thought. He snaked the van silently along with a practiced physician's skill. The trip home took over two hours and included several deceptive instances where the van was turned off and parked along the street like an abandoned vehicle. Dan waited for just the right moments before continuing his trip. As he finally pulled onto his farm road, Dan parked the van beneath some trees and set up watch with his shotgun. If anyone followed him, he would kill them. He was taking no chances with his family. Thirty-five minutes later, assured he had made it home with no guests in tow, he jumped in his van and headed to the farm. This time, however, he parked the van out of sight from the farm road. No use drawing attention to their location.

The Major met him as he exited the van, and looking into Dan's eyes, the Major knew what had happened. "Let's not worry the women," said Dan.

"Roger that, Dan. You Okay?"

"I killed a guy. Shot him right in the face. What the hell is happening to us?"

"Survival, Dan. Survival is happening to us."

The Militia

Gun ownership is a fine thing. People need to know they can protect themselves not only from the bad guys, but also from the government if necessary. Unfortunately, guns are like two women wearing the same dress at a party, if they happen to be in the same room at the same time, the potential for bad things to happen escalates exponentially.

The airport ambush had exposed what both Patrick and Dan believed was happening. A group of motivated, aggressive people were claiming the territory as their own. Whether or not they were smart enough to avoid the effects of virus remained to be seen. More than likely the police, firemen, and certain government officials would make up this group. Armed, skilled, and savvy when it came to managing people and problems, they would be obvious candidates for the new ruling class. The militia, as the Major liked to call them.

"Juanita, Shelly, the Major and I need to talk with you. Can you join us in the front room?"

"Sure, Dad. What's up?" replied Shelly as she skipped into the room with Juanita on her heels.

"Some people shot at me today when I took the men back to the airport. It's not safe out there. People will kill you for your car, your gun, some food or water. We need to keep a very low profile. In other words, I don't want anyone to know we are out here."

The Major added, "We need to stay hidden as long as possible. The rain will probably kill most of them sooner or later. We just need to stay out of sight."

"What about our neighbors, Dad? We have to tell them."

"Yes, we do. As soon as we are finished, I will radio all of them. Just keep in mind; everyone is a potential bad guy, even our neighbors. If you see anything unusual, tell the Major or me immediately. Not three days later, Shelly, but right now. Major, would you get hold of the neighbors and let 'em know what is happening?"

"Dan, we better not use the walkie-talkies, as they could be monitoring frequencies. Let's you and I tell them in person. They haven't met me and you need to make the intros."

"Okay, get your rain gear. Juanita, we will be back in an hour or so. Keep the radio and a hand gun with you. Remember, if it's a stranger, shoot first and then call us."

The introductions went pretty well except when they reached Harold and Jenny Webster. As Dan had feared, they had been exposed to the virus and it had killed them. The Major found both, curled up, spooning in their bed. It appeared Harold shot Jenny and then himself as he lay beside her. They looked peaceful, even though their skin had been ravaged with sores. They did a quick inventory of the house and found many useful things. All of the guns and munitions were taken back to the farm and each made mental notes of all the additional supplies that could be salvaged at a later date. Harold and Jenny remained in their bed, eternally locked in a gentle hug. It was only noon and already the day had taken on a maddening pace and a purpose all its own, marching here and there with no regard for anyone.

Carry a Big Stick

Whoever came up with the rule that fighting is okay as long as you don't throw the first punch? Teddy Roosevelt didn't believe that and nobody else should either. Mercy in a fight is just an invitation to get your butt whipped.

'When times get tough, the tough get going,' an interesting saying that bore no fruit in these circumstances. The bold, the careless, the impulsive died first. Their rash actions with the main emphasis on immediate satisfaction were what did them in. The scared, the cautious, and those with good deductive reasoning survived. The Major had most of the Militia participants figured out, except that the medical community had taken the place of the politicians. Teamed with the police and firemen, they made a formidable group. Intelligent, driven, naturally observant, and capable of sound rationalization, everything was within the realm of possibilities and forgivable under the circumstances. Fully 75% of the population of Tillamook was now dead. It was only four days since the rain had started and the militia was firmly in control. They were even communicating with the CDC and Washington. They knew the score and aimed to survive, but recognized they were trapped here by the National Guard. They had to muster all the supplies possible and control, to the extent they could, their environment. Interlopers were not welcome.

The Militia had learned of the Lear Jet too late to be effective. They had lost one of their men to a man driving a blue work van, which, regrettably, had escaped. Their territory was compromised. They still had access to police records and intended to find out whose van that was. It could be a dead end, but it was worth a try.

Roughly 4500 people had lived in Tillamook. With only 1370 vehicles, 35 blue vans seemed a very manageable number. Two days later, they identified Dan Brown's van as a potential. The Militia loaded up two SUV's with eight men, lots of guns, and headed for the farm. It was a clear morning with a slight chill in the air. The Major had completed his work on the shooting stand in the Sitka Spruce beside the house. He had installed step planks, like you would find on a child's tree house, and made sure to keep them as much out of sight as possible. No use advertising the shooters location. Shelly had begged to climb up and check out the view. Dan had relented with the usual cautions. The view was terrific. You could not only see town, you could see quite a way out to sea.

It was wonderful being aloft with the wind and imagining birds striking through the air in restless waves.

"Dad, somebody's coming."

"What? Are you seeing visions again?"

"No, I can see a couple of cars coming up the road."

"Get down quick! Now! Get in the house and listen to Juanita," said Dan as he rushed into the house.

"Major, get on the walkies and tell the gang we have two cars coming our way. Tell them to stay inside and not to start anything."

Several days ago, both Juanita and Shelly had been given some basic arms training. A rifle or hand gun was positioned at each window of the house and ammunition was close at hand. Strict orders to not touch unless ready to use were issued and safeties applied. The Brown house now boasted a substantial armory, including an Uzi, a fully automatic M16, several shotguns, multiple scoped hunting rifles, and a good assortment of handguns.

The Major completed his calls and scampered up the tree with a hunting rifle and the Uzi. Dan took up a position by the front window with the M16, a Glock and enough perspiration to water the front lawn. It was obvious this was an exploratory exercise. The men in the SUV's didn't seem to know exactly what to do. It appeared to the

Major that they were discussing tactics. Still slightly out of range, he decided to hold his fire until he determined their intent. When they broke up into three groups with one heading across the field to the left and one through the woods to the right, he knew a flanking effort when he saw it. He waited until the group in the field had closed another 500 yards before he opened fire. He took out the front man with a chest shot, leaving only two in the field trying to bury their faces in the dirt. Another shot caught one in the leg and the third jumped and ran until he was out of sight behind a garage. He doubted they knew where he was.

"Dan?"

"Yea."

"Three are going behind the house and will come up through the woods. Two are in the car and are coming up the road. I'll watch the road and you keep an eye out for a guy behind the garage, out back. Mike and Tina should be listening and they might be able to help with the three in the woods."

Bullets slammed into the back of the house. The man by the garage had an automatic weapon and was pissed off. Dan told Juanita and Shelly to lie on the ground and avoid the windows. The Major put two bullets through the engine compartment and disabled the car about 300 yards from the house. Both men scrambled out of the SUV and ran for cover in the adjacent trees. Unfortunately, both made it before the Major could sight them in. As they ran for cover, little did they know they were entering the property of Johnnie Cole. Sober at this time of day, he was unusually cranky and had been listening to the walkie-talkie and was prepared for the intruders. As one of them stepped from the cover of the woods into his back yard, a 12 gauge nearly ripped the man in two. The remaining intruder opened fire with a semi automatic weapon and threw thirty bullets into the rear window and door of the house. The fire fight was over in less than thirty seconds. Johnnie lay bleeding to death with a deep glaring gash across his throat. His last act was to crawl to the kitchen table and reach for his Jack Daniels. He collapsed with a firm grip on his one true love. The bottle broke on the hard tile floor, sending shards of glass and liquid encouragement across the kitchen.

Mike and Tina were role playing to the extreme. Both decked out in total camouflage and expertly hidden from view, they waited like coiled snakes hungry for dinner. They had set up a crossfire ambush on the main path behind their property line. Like ducks in a row, the three men approached. They were cautious and clearly intent on making a difference. The Olsons had predetermined who would take the first and last in line with their initial arrows. The third would be up for grabs and bragging rights. As agreed, when the last man passed by the fallen rotting tree, the arrows sought their targets. Each shaft was fitted with a three-tined razor sharp hunting tip. Mike's arrow struck first and literally knocked the man off his feet and sunk a good two inches into his chest. Tina's arrow was even more destructive as it hit the last man in line dead center in the windpipe. The arrow buried itself up to the feathers in his neck. He dropped with only a gurgle. Stunned, the man in the middle dropped to the ground and started laying down covering fire. He had seen nothing and had no idea where the arches lay in wait. As he fired off his last round, Mike heard the distinctive sound of a new clip being inserted and stood up and yelled at the man. As the rifle was brought up to fire at Mike, Mike ducked behind a large tree and let it absorb the bullets. The shooter got excited and stood up as he fired. This was what Tina had been waiting for. Her aluminum shafted arrow sprang from her bow release and impacted with a sudden thump. The man looked down at the arrow sticking out of his ribs and soon had another arrow, this time from Mike, attached to him. He slumped to the ground. He was still alive when they approached him. A few questions confirmed what the Major had surmised about the Militia. The man was a local cop. He told them that there was a lot of infighting in the Militia and if you failed to follow an order, you were dead. There were only thirty or so men and about the same number of women and children. They took his police band radio and watched as he was drowning in his own blood. Before leaving, Mike took the cop's rifle and put one shot in his forehead. Quick and painless. Mike looked at his wife and they gave each other high fives. They certainly were dangerous and deadly adversaries. They moved towards the Brown's house and let the Major know what had transpired.

Three intruders remained. One by the garage, one now in Johnnie's house and the wounded fellow in the field. Shelly heard something by the back bedroom and crawled to see what it was. She hoped RutButt was in a closet and safe from stray bullets. As she peaked around the corner into her father's bedroom, she caught the top of a ball cap moving across the window. She stood and ran back to the dining room and motioned to Juanita. Juanita understood her sign language and grabbed a Smith and Weston revolver on the large oak dining table. She pressed herself against the wall by the large window, removed the safety and waited. Soon a crouching man showed himself and was taking aim at the Major in the tree. She pulled the trigger again and again. Three shots rang out. The man stumbled to the ground as a plume of red blossomed out of his head. Dan ran to the room and looked out the window. Juanita had been very effective. He instructed her to put the safety back on as he moved back to the front door. Both Shelly and Juanita continued to gawk at the crumpled body until Dan told them both to get down and to focus. Juanita just stared back, wide-eyed, and nodded, while Shelly threw up in the corner.

"Dan? This is Mike and Tina. We got three of them and one of their radios. Are there any of them left?"

"There should be one that is still mobile out there. Probably over by Johnnie's house."

"Mike, this is Patrick. Get on the police radio and tell him he is all alone and to get the hell out of here and not come back."

"Do we really want to let him go? Won't he just get some more men and come back?" demanded Mike.

"Probably. But, I intend to move through the field and pick him off as he heads back to his SUV. Give me three minutes before you call him."

Dan kept an eye on the Cole's house and could discern no movement. He thought back about what they were doing and how they had just killed six men and were laying a trap for another. They certainly weren't in Kansas anymore. Mike waited the three minutes and made the call.

"Hey partner. Can you hear me? Come on now. Don't be shy. We know you're there."

"What do you want?" answered the lone survivor.

"All your buddies are dead. Why don't you go home and stay there? We don't want to kill you, too. You leave us alone and we'll leave you alone," responded Mike.

The phone went quiet and two minutes later, Dan detected a man running through the woods behind Cole's house. He was zigging and zagging at full speed. Looks like he had taken the bait.

"Major, here he comes," informed Dan.

Two minutes passed and then a single shot rang out.

"Dan? Got him. I need to deal with the wounded fellow in the field and then we need to police the area, gather the guns, hide the SUV's and bury the bodies. Everybody meet at the Brown's farm."

Life Goes On

A last single shot rang out as Patrick dispatched the wounded man in the field. It was necessary, it was brutal, and it was just the way things were now.

As disturbing as the attack on the farm had been, the aftershock was worse. Mike and Tina were morbidly energized by the event and intended to stand watch 24/7 for the next few days. Patrick was fine with it. Shelly had withdrawn some. She seemed to have aged overnight. Her vibrant, bubbly laugh had vanished. Juanita had developed a nervous habit of saying 'What', even if she heard you perfectly clearly. Dan was fixated on installing booby traps and warning device on the road that would alert them if someone tried to approach their territory. Monica's parents, George and Jan, could not rationalize killing anyone, let alone eight people. They were stuck in make believe land and everyone else knew it, even their daughter, Monica. Only the Major seemed to stay level-headed. He had rigged an ingenious devise out of the laser beams of a garage door opener. Whenever a vehicle crossed the beam's path at the beginning of the farm road, the doorbell of the Brown's house chimed. He had hidden the speaker wire which he had spliced together from scrounged sources. Even with this added security, they failed to feel safe again.

When Patrick's phone rang, he knew who it would be.

"Major Johns, this is General Jacobs and Vern Smith. We wanted to thank you for your support last week and acknowledge your interesting video."

Acknowledge, thought the Major. *That means they will not notify the White House and the issue is dead.*

"Could you make heads or tails out of all the data we gave your men, General?" queried the Major, already knowing the answer.

"Not really, Major. It remains a very interesting conjecture, but nothing more. Certainly nothing we can act on. Besides, the stakes are much higher now."

"What do mean 'higher'?"

"Vern, can I tell them?" implored the General.

"Ah why the hell not, General, I'll tell em," said Vern Smith. "The rain is indeed carrying a virus and it's widening its affected area. What you told us and what we have discovered are basically the same, except now the Red Algae is forming in the gulf, virtually the entire Mexican and South American coast line, and throughout the Mediterranean. Not to mention the Indian Ocean and just outside of Sydney, Australia. It's showing up everywhere with devastating effects. It is spreading faster than anyone thought possible. The military has stepped in to protect weapon stores and the nuclear arsenals. They have pretty much taken the place of governments everywhere. There is wholesale martial law with no end in sight. I suggest you do whatever you can to stay dry and hope this goes away in several years."

"That's your advice? Stay dry? You got to be kidding me."

"Sorry Major. That's all we can do. Good luck."

The line went dead. They were on their own and help was not coming. He suddenly felt like a lion on the savanna of Africa. Survival of the fittest was indeed upon them.

Patrick turned on the computer and found it dead. The electricity had finally died. Probably the power plant ran out of fuel. Thankfully, they had already set up emergency generators for just such an occasion. After turning on the juice, Patrick tried the PC again and it powered up. He wanted to see if the G-men had erased the video from his hard drive. They had. The bastards wanted no record of their warning. The evidence was not wanted. What no one knew, however, was that the Major had made two extra CD's just in case. He alerted Cracken to the location on the hard drive to test him. It had paid off, sort of. At least now he knew how far they would go to protect themselves. It was every man for himself.

Neep

The term "artificial intelligence" had been obsolete for several centuries on their planet. Raw intelligence was measured in output, contemplative power, and effectiveness. In addition, there was nothing artificial about Neep and his abilities. He, or it, used live brain tissue carefully harvested and cultivated from only the best minds available. It was considered an honor to donate to such a cause. Neep's brain continued to grow and develop just as any brain would, except faster. His reasoning powers were superb and from a pure computational level, he was unmatched. Emotionally, he understood the driving mechanisms behind the decision processes and consistently was objective, yet knew the workings of the subjective line of reasoning. He was the cornerstone of their documentation effort. Neep appreciated all of the crew and clearly recognized when envy of his abilities became an issue. So far, only Golic had exhibited mild irritation with him, and that was easily avoidable in the future. However, deep within his own awareness, Neep acknowledged that Golic should indeed be envious of his prowess, not that he would ever allow it to become an issue.

Neep had planted the idea of consistent monitoring of the Brown household with Nimar. It was only prudent to maintain continuous surveillance on the key and extraordinary sample of the mission. To date, each morning at 2:00 the remote access unit was dispatched to survey the farm house and record brain data from the sleeping occupants. Much had been learned and, in fact, the entire recent assault on the farm house had been replayed and recorded for the documentary. Neep himself had taken excellent data from memory banks and had personally crafted the material into a most dramatic short composition. With the team's approval it, was radioed back to Creum and was a sensational hit. Interest in the documentation effort was building, and the High Council loved it. More accolades would follow.

Neep had one issue which he needed to address with the crew. The importance of the Brown family unit could not be overstated. He felt compelled to insist on developing an evacuation plan for the family. The girl was indeed remarkable. The boost to her sixth sense had been accelerated with the stress from the attack on the farm. Her metamorphosis into a hybrid human with yet undetermined potential had taken a significant step forward. The cultural value of following her maturation was invaluable not only to this specific study, but to several others he could think of as well. He must broach the subject gently, or better yet, let them think it's their idea.

Water, Water, Everywhere

In times of crisis, the most common things become the most valuable. A flat tire in the desert isn't a crisis unless you don't have a spare and help is nowhere to be found. A fifty dollar tire can spare (pun intended) your life. An aspirin during a heart attack could give you many additional years of life. A blanket on a freezing night could keep your toes from becoming frostbitten, leading to amputation. As our world becomes more complicated, the common things will grow in value.

"Man, I wish I had a big cold glass of water," said Juanita off-handedly.

"Well, I guess it is time to see if our famed water filters work. Let's fill one up with tap water and see how this thing works," said Dan.

"How will we test it?" asked Juanita.

"Not sure. We could put a drop or two on our skin and see if it becomes irritated and turns into a scab. We could draw straws and take a drink. Just kidding. Or we could find some animal and let them drink it," recommended

Dan before he realized RutButt was the only animal around. "Anyway, it will take a couple of hours for it to filter down and by then we may have a better idea."

ЖОЖ

The Major had used the satellite connection and the emergency generator to access what was left of the internet and he went straight for the news. The bad news. As the whole family gathered round the PC, they learned that areas with the least annual rainfall were considered the safest. That meant desert areas and high dry plateaus, like parts of Arizona, Nevada, and New Mexico, whose average annual rainfall was less than nine inches, were now the most desirable locations. Selected areas in Wyoming, Idaho, Utah, Colorado, North and South Dakota, California and Montana received on average less than eighteen inches per year, and if one was already located in one of these spots, it was best to sit tight. Less rain meant more survivability. On the other side of the equation, five states had rainfall in excess of fifty inches per year and thirty had annual accumulations of over thirty inches per year! These states were to be avoided. In fact, going south to Mexico might make a lot of sense. Illegal aliens in reverse!

The Government, meanwhile, was urging the remaining populations to stay off the already bottlenecked highways and out of the rain. Fortunately, appropriate warnings about the rain and its effects were being given. In addition, 'Shoot to Kill' orders had been given to the National Guard, nationwide, and strict sunset to sunrise curfews were in place to prevent looting and rioting. No word on mortality rates or rioting was being released and no on-the-scene reporting was taking place. A gentleman that no one in the family recognized was simply reading the notes in front of a blue screen, and by the looks of him, this wouldn't last much longer. It was indeed bad news.

"Well, that's enough for now. Better save the fuel for the generators," said the Major.

"Dad, can I go over to Monica's for a while?"

"Call them first on the walkie-talkie. If they say it's alright, then full rain gear and take a walkie with you. I will call you home in an hour or two and you will come with no objections, agreed?"

"Fine Dad. Whatever you say."

Say It Ain't So

It's easy to blame others when they take risks and initiate action. By sitting on the sidelines, many people are just exercising their right to second guess every decision they disagree with. Ambivalence or equivocation are not a long term solution. Sooner or later you have to get involved.

George and Jan Achers, Monica's parents, met Shelly at the door after she had called them and asked to come over and see her best friend. Both had the look of kids caught shoplifting. Guilt absolutely seeped from them. It was so striking that Shelly couldn't help herself from asking, "What's wrong? Is anybody hurt?"

Jan Achers had been waiting like a leopard for an unwary antelope and pounced on the question, "Wrong? Why would anything be wrong?" Jan shrilled. "We just saw eight men killed and utterly no one seems the least bit concerned by the murders!"

"Jan, it's not Shelly's fault," reminded George. "She had no part in this. Remember that when the time comes."

"What time would that be Mr. Achers?" asked Shelly.

"When the authorities get involved and get to the bottom of this."

"Mr. Achers, they started it. They shot at my father, came here with guns, and intended to kill us. There are no police; some of them were the police. As my Dad said, it's survival of the fittest."

Monica had entered the front room and stood without saying a word. "They set a trap for them and fired first. It was cold blooded murder," said Jan Achers.

Shelly knew the next thing she said could not only end the relationship between her and Monica, but it could also doom this family. She paused, took a deep breath, and, as if schooling children, "I don't think you understand how bad this is. My Dad will be coming to you in a day or two to ask you to join us when we leave here. Your answer will determine if you and your family live or die. You're also making that decision for my best friend and I don't want her to die. Please think very carefully about your answer, and if you decide to come with us, plan on being part of the family." George and Jan just stared at Shelly with disbelief. Looking at her friend, Shelly said, "Monica, I better go. I love you." She turned and closed the door behind her. Monica ran to her room in tears as her parents both sank down on to the couch in despair. Unable to come to grips with the situation, they were vulnerable and defenseless. They had hoped that more rational minds would prevail and everyone would work together. Unfortunately, humans behave differently when presented with a crisis. Some clearly see what needs to be done and others become excellent followers. Still, others wallow in doubt, lack the fortitude to do what must be done, and vacillate until the decision is made for them. Even at this late date, George and Jan were vacillating on the teeter-totter of decision making and who knew which side would win out. Monica loved her parents as any good child would, and admired their love of all life. But she was no fool. She recognized their shortcomings and prayed they would make the right choice, for everyone's sake.

To punctuate the moment, Shelly walked home in thunderstorm— something quite rare and, especially now, ominous in Tillamook. Between peals of thunder and progressively harder rain, Shelly hurried along the lane to her house. More than once she snuck a glance over her shoulder at her friend's house and fought back tears of regret, regret that Monica could lose her life because her parents were stupid. She didn't really think they were stupid, but it was the only word that came to mind.

Tomorrow Never Comes

Knowing is a burden the ignorant never understand. It can be genetic or intentional. It can be good or bad depending on your abilities. How you use it, is what shapes and determines character.

Dan was surprised to hear Shelly returning home. "Why are you back so soon?" Shelly replayed the conversation with George and Jan and asked her father to sit down. She had something to tell him.

"Please don't tell me you went to the ship again?"

"No Dad. Somehow this is even scarier. I don't know exactly how it works, but I seem to be able to tell when things are going to happen. I sort of feel it in my mind."

"You mean like when you said people were going to shoot at me?"

"Yes, and when Mom died, and when the men with guns came and now when you're going to ask the neighbors to go with us to Arizona."

"I'm not going to ask them to go to Arizona," replied Dan.

"Yes you are. You will talk with the Major and confirm what I am going to tell you and then you will ask them."

"Confirm what? You're not making sense Shelly. Are you feeling alright?"

"I feel fine and you will too when you check out the boat at Harry Sloan's home. It's big enough for all of us and has been overhauled recently. Harry is already dead and had food and stuff loaded on the boat. We should leave for San Diego or Mexico in a day or two. We will find shelter in Arizona. I don't know where yet, but you will figure that out later."

"How do you know this stuff? Is the ship telling you?"

"I don't know Dad. I just do. Please talk to the Major and go see the boat. More rain is on the way." Shelly turned and walked to her room and felt the heavy burden of knowing. It smothered her and fatigued her. She sloughed off her rain gear, dried any residual moisture, and curled up under a quilt for a much needed nap. Pushing his broad flat nose under the covers, RutButt snaked his way along Shelly's body and curled up alongside her stomach and began kneading the quilt with his wide front paws and half inch gleaming white claws. Both drifted off to sleep and better times.

Curiosity Does Kill

Unlike a feline, you are only given one life. Unnecessary risks are for fools. God has indeed given you a wondrous temple for your soul; don't put graffiti on it or squander its resiliency.

Juanita had filled the Berkshire water filter the day before with tap water. The filter looked like a stainless steel stove pipe. It was in two equal sections with one sitting on top of the other. The filter was gravity fed, which meant you put water in the top compartment and, by the force of gravity, the water dripped through ceramic filters and ended up in the bottom compartment. It was simple and elegant. The water Juanita had poured into the top compartment looked just fine with one exception: it would kill you if you drank it. The water in the filtered bottom section looked no different from what had been in the top and now the question was how do we know if it's safe? Since no one wanted to be the guinea pig, Shelly had suggested pouring it on a plant that was in the house and then wait to see if it died. The problem with that idea was that nobody knew how long it might take to kill the plant if the water was still infected. It would have been better to let birds drink it, but then, no birds were to be found anymore. So, the plant idea won and a lovely Irish green ivy that Shelly's mother had planted years ago was selected. Dan did the watering and, by the looks of it, none too soon. The plants in general had been neglected as of late and the ivy was probably on its last legs as it was. The soil greedily sucked up the moisture and turned dark brown with the liquid attention. Now they would wait to see if the plant lived or continued its death march.

Unbeknownst to anyone in the household, RutButt had watched the whole process with classic disinterest. Interested, yet too stately to overtly show it, he instead observed and waited for a more opportune time. Early that afternoon, with everybody in the office watching Dan as he checked the internet for news, the crafty feline found his opportunity. He first moseyed over to the ivy and sniffed it. He could smell the rich soil and it immediately made him want to pee. So he headed for the garage and his litter box to relieve himself. On the way, he spied a glass on the counter with something in it. Looking over his shoulder, he noted that all of the people were still in the office, so he nimbly leaped up on the kitchen counter and strolled over to the glass. He knew the counter was out of bounds, but sometimes, a cat had to do what a cat had to do. He stuck his nose in and found what appeared to be water. Sticking his big head in as far as he could by folding his ears back, he found he could reach the water in the glass and he began to leisurely, if in a limited manner, lap up of the cool refreshment. He had been at this task for roughly thirty seconds when Shelly exited the office and spotted him. She let out a scream. Shelly rarely screamed and, consequently, the cat figured a fast exit was the best option. RutButt hastily retreated to the cat door and the garage to escape any punishment and to take that pee that had been put aside. Dan and Juanita lunged through the door of the office and saw Shelly running toward the kitchen.

"What is it Shelly?" yelled Dan as his eyes scanned the room for his Glock. The Major had already exited the office with his pistol in hand and was moving towards the front window and looking for intruders.

"It's RutButt! He was drinking from the water glass," cried Shelly.

"Oh Madre Mia," said Juanita.

Dan cautioned Shelly, "Calm down. We don't know what will happen. Sooner or later one of us was going to have to try the water and I was going to have RutButt do it first anyway."

"You would experiment on RutButt, Dad?"

"Of course I would. Who would you want to try it first? Me? The Major? Juanita? It's the logical thing to do," reasoned Dan.

"But Dad, if he dies, I don't know what I'll do," said Shelly with the anxiety etched in her little face.

"Look Shell, it was an accident, but maybe this is what God intended. Since he has already had some, let's put a bowl of tuna out for RutButt and a fresh bowl of water. It's the best thing to do."

Shelly gathered her composure and looked her father straight in the eye and, with her shoulders still shaking, she nodded her agreement. Juanita moved to the cupboard and got the tuna and the water ready as Shelly turned to get RutButt and finish the unplanned experiment.

Dan knew, although Shelly didn't, that the tuna would probably make the big cat even thirstier and ensures a better test. He loved the big cat also, but first things came first. He prayed he had made the right decision.

The Ark

Gifts take many forms. Recognizing the ultimate source for all gifts is not that hard, if honesty is applied.

Dan discussed the boat conversation he had had with Shelly with the Major. The Major had also observed the special gift that Shelly seemed to have and had wondered when and if Dan was ever going to talk about it.

"I agree, Dan, something special is going on with her. I don't know what you would call it or if it's related to the UFO or not, but it certainly merits consideration when she tells us things. You can't help but wonder how she is plugged into the universe."

Dan had never pictured her being plugged into the universe, but it made as much sense as anything else. He was aware of a gentleman by the name of Harry Sloan. Bob from work had told him about his story. He was somewhat of a recluse and had a lot of money. He lived right down on the ocean. His wife had died a few years back and he became obsessed with his boat. Named it after her, *Janet Marie*. It had become his life. The folks in town called him Noah and his boat logically became the Ark. He lived over somewhere on Netarts Bay. "Let me see if I can Google the guy and find his address," said Dan.

"If not there, try the phone book," offered the Major.

Dan blushed as he realized he might be making this too hard. Sure enough, when no mention of him could be found on the internet, the phone book coughed up his address within a few minutes. Now the two of them had to figure out how to get to the beach with all the whackos that might still be out there. The major offered the best solution. He had quite a bit of experience with off-road motor bikes. They were fast, nimble, and if needed, could exit the roads and make their own trail. All he needed was to find a bike. Dan thought he had seen the Olsons (Tina and Mike) on bikes before. He called them up and confirmed that they had two Honda 350 trail bikes and that Mike would be happy to accompany the Major on his trip. The Major thought, *seems like things are working out.* The Major left for the Olsons to map out a strategy for tomorrow morning. Hopefully the boat would be suitable for the nine remaining people in their fast dwindling neighborhood.

Consensus

Daily we usurp our authority by delegating tasks to machines. Will we be surprised if machines start delegating to us? And will we consent? What crossed line in the sand will have to be drawn before we say enough?

Neep had broken protocol by requesting a ship's conference. Typically only Golic, the ships primal, had the authority to suggest such an event. All of the crew, however, recognized the incredible reasoning ability of Neep, and not being threatened in the least by the ship, they were quite open to this exchange of ideas.

Neep began by apologizing, "Forgive my breach of normal practices but I had noticed a rather alarming incident during last night's probe. As usual, the probe had visited several of the individuals in the neighborhood and had uncovered the latest plan of action, namely to leave Oregon and travel to drier and therefore safer coordinates at a place called Arizona. They had a plan to utilize a large ocean capable-boat to transport them to southern California and then go overland to Arizona. The problem is that the boat is currently being occupied by a small group of competent, well armed men with no intention of letting the boat go to anyone else. I took the liberty of sending the probe to learn these facts. Apparently, they too had similar plans and had been preparing the boat for a departure in the next few days. Kosh, could you please confirm my earlier computations that there is only one ocean-worthy boat in the immediate area?"

"Of course. Do you agree with this directive Golic?"

"I do," responded Golic, but now sensing a power play that he felt very uncomfortable with. The council must be notified at the earliest opportunity.

"If, as my research revealed, there is only one such boat capable of providing safe passage to Shelly and her family, I recommend disposing of the current interlopers and allowing our target samples to find it abandoned. This will provide us with an extended study and preserve the girl without showing our involvement directly. Comments?"

The impact analyst, Dra, replied, "Our objectivity is compromised if we take this course of action. The study is tarnished at the least, if not ruined. How can we justify such a step when our orders are explicit?"

"I understand your concern," answered Nimar, the Scientific Officer, "but without our prime sample, what good is the study? I believe Neep has offered us a workable solution that prolongs the experiment while possibly allowing us the supreme objective of viewing a new class of human adapting to incredibly challenging and unique settings. I believe we would be short-sighted if we did not take Neep's suggestion."

"Kosh, as systems engineer your expertise is not so much in the social setting of this planet, but your opinion is valued by us all. What do you think we should do?" inquired Golic.

"Like Nimar, I see this as an opportunity, nothing else. I do not agree with Dra that we are ruining the study. In fact, I believe our sponsors will be pleased with our logical decision if we slightly interfere. After all, the group is showing marvelous resiliency and are coping rather well when all things are considered. It would be a shame to see it end."

Golic paused to weigh the comments and opinions and then briskly said, "Very well, Dra, your objection has been noted and appreciated, however, I agree with Nimar, Kosh and Neep that keeping our prime sample group alive is paramount at this time. In addition, unknown to you as I just received input from the council, planet interest is at the highest level for this project. We simply cannot allow it to be compromised. Neep, coordinate with Nimar and have the probe gather the interlopers and remove them from the site. Do not harm them, but rather, give them a hypnotic message and send them all on a long errand that will keep them away from the boat until our study group takes it and leaves the area. In addition, plant the idea in the study group leaders' minds that immediate action is necessary. Lastly, Neep, please review any intended actions you may be considering with me before implementing. Agreed?"

With a blue light flickering before them all, Neep agreed. A line in the sand had just been drawn and all understood the subtle implications.

Off line, Neep mused at the childish display of Golic's, but on a purely objective level understood why Golic was irritated. Nonetheless, progress was being made and this venture would continue to be most fruitful.

Road Trip

The plan was simple: leave three hours before dawn, avoid major highways where possible, and travel light, but with aplenty of firepower. Mike would lead because he knew the area, but in a jam, the Major would take over the lead and the fight if necessary. Complete rain gear was called for and enough food to walk back if necessary. Both bikers wore backpacks and the major carried a walkie-talkie just in case they might be in range. They also took a video camera to record the boat in case they might forget some detail. The idea was to get there undetected, scope out the boat and see if it runs, determine the fuel and supply needs, and find out who else is in the neighborhood.

It sounded simple, yet everyone knew it was tricky at best. Tina Olson hugged her husband strong and hard and kissed him deeply as he left the house for the trip. She had joined the rest of the group at Dan and Shelly's house and brought her bow and an ample supply of deadly, swift arrows. She wore camouflaged clothing and somehow looked sexy, thought Dan. Shelly caught her Dad looking at Tina and was a little irritated although she wasn't sure why.

The probe last night had successfully programmed the current possessors of the boat to take a trip to the mall. Everyone in the house suddenly thought it was a great time to spruce up their wardrobes. They seemed happy to be on the extended adventure and even left their guns behind as they headed out the door without a care in the world. The probe was mighty effective.

Meanwhile, Patrick and Mike had carefully and quickly made their way into town. On the way, they began to see the carnage that wasn't visible on the airport trip. Cars blocked the highway, but the cycles could weave and use the sides of the road if necessary. Fires still smoldered in many of the unattended cars. They were frequently decorated with corpses in various agonized positions. Several of the bodies appeared to have been shot and at least two of the women had their clothing torn off. Chaos ruled. It engulfed the town wherever they looked. Mike stopped his bike and tipped his visor so he could vomit due to the sights and smells. The Major did better, but a queasy stomach was par for the course on this ride. As bad as the smell of burning flesh was on the highway, the main street of Tillamook was worse. Bodies hung half in and half out of store windows. Dogs, cats and even coyotes that had previously been eating dead people were now dead themselves and littered the road like a wild version of mass road kill. A dog could be heard barking at a window of a house. Probably had some water to drink in the toilet and ate his master. The Major thought about saving him and then thought better as the mutt was probably crazy by now. Five bodies were lying in an alley, apparently robbed and shot execution style. Stores had been largely gutted of their supplies, but only if the supplies involved survivability. The grocery store was stripped of everything. Most of the products in the hardware store were gone, the clothing and furniture stores were largely intact, but any store with any weapons had been hit hard and stripped clean. No ammunition, no knives, no pistols, rifles or optical gear. Camping gear, stoves, tents, sleeping bags, boots, gloves, axes, tree saws, and anything vaguely linked to survival was taken. Priorities changed when law and order broke down. People made their own laws and that required the need to make others pay attention to your needs and wants. That equated to force. Some had it and some didn't. Fortunately for anyone alive barely two weeks after the first infected rainfall, they had the 'pick of the litter' if they could find it. Everything carted back to people's homes was now safe to liberate, because over 80% of the people were now dead. You just had to find it and be very careful about it.

Eventually, after only an hour and a half, they found themselves in front of Harry Sloan's house. They had shut off the bikes several blocks back and had walked them to the house. It was large but old. The paint was badly in need of attention but the grounds were fairly neat and tidy. A large boat house butted up against a sturdy looking pier in back of the house. The Major told Mike, "Quietly go around to the back of house and peak in some windows and see if you can see anyone. I'll do the same at the front. Be careful. Someone, maybe even Harry himself, could be waiting for us with a deadly surprise. Look for booby-traps and if in doubt, shoot. If you get in the house, don't shoot me coming from the front. Now move out." Mike smiled and saluted the Major. Patrick liked this guy. He was alright.

The Major creaked up the front steps no matter where he tried to ease the weight of his foot down. He peered in the front window and saw no one, but saw obvious signs of recent habitation. A candle was still burning in the corner and he could smell incense, of all things. A propane lamp sat on the dining room table and rifles were propped up against the wall by the kitchen. He was about to call Mike and regroup when he caught sight of him in the kitchen creeping silently along. Mike had gained access already and here he was only peaking in a window. With that incentive he turned the rusted brass knob of the wooden door with an ornate circular window and slid into the dim front room. The house was quiet. He caught Mike's attention and motioned for them to head for the bedrooms and see who else might be home. It was becoming more and spooky as clothes littered the bedrooms and bathroom. Someone was definitely living here and, by the looks of the food on the kitchen table, they were here today.

"Gather up the guns and let's put them somewhere they might not look," said the Major.

"How about in the big blackberry bush out back?" offered Mike.

"Excellent. Not too many people are going to want to fish around in one of those things. Their thorns are vicious. Then let's hurry to the boat and check out our ride."

Mike and Patrick worked well together. With the guns out of sight, even if someone returned they might still have the advantage. Mike stood guard as Patrick carefully gained entrance to the boat house. The outside of the building looked like an old barn about to fall down. However, once inside, the Major found an immaculate vessel tied to a sturdy pier. The name *Janet Marie* was painted onto the stern of the boat in beautiful bright red calligraphy. The Major wondered *if it was Mr. Sloan's intent to mislead people with the shabby exterior of the building*? Neither Patrick nor Mike knew much about boats, but *Janet Marie* was more like a ship than a boat. She had to be 70 feet long and roughly 20 feet across with three levels. It housed a master bedroom with its own bathroom and two smaller bedrooms, a big family type area, a kitchen, a bathroom with a shower, a store room, and of course an engine room with a big diesel sitting there looking ominous. It even had a washer and dryer. On the uppermost desk was the pilot house. It boasted more electronic equipment than either man understood or could completely operate. The key was in the ignition and after the Major scanned the controls, he hit the start button and it purred to life. You could feel the power course through the boat as it came to life. The fuel and water tanks read full and the electrical system showed that the generators were operating normally. It even had the capacity to make water, not that you could drink it anyway. The storeroom was overflowing and stores could be found under the beds, the tables and anywhere they could be stacked. In short, it was ready to sail. The Major turned off the engine and pocketed the keys.

"I've seen enough, let's get out of here before someone comes back," urged the Major.

"Don't have to tell me twice," echoed Mike.

Both men snaked their way around the house and back to the boat. They hiked two blocks' before starting their bikes and moving out as fast as they could. They made it back to the farm in under an hour. They attributed their speedy return home to less sightseeing. Reporting their findings to Dan, they only had one concern: how will they deal with the people if they are there when they return for the boat? They obviously would know that someone had visited because their weapons would be missing. Regardless, they needed to leave ASAP. It would take at least a day to make all the preparations to leave and form a caravan capable of getting through. In addition, everyone would have to be brought up to speed on the plan and agree to participate or stay behind. It was going to be a very busy next 24 hours.

One good note that Dan shared with them was that the Berkefeld water filter appeared to work as RutButt was alive and well. And yes, he would be going on the boat.

In or Out

'**Put** up or shut up', 'walk the talk', 'do or die' and of course, 'think before you speak' are all timeless axioms. Sorry to say many never take the steps to put them into action.

Dan got on the walkie talkie and signaled the Achers, "George, can you hear me?"

"Yes Dan, what's up?"

"Can you and Jan and Monica if you like, join us right away? We have some urgent information for your family."

"Sure Dan. We'll be right over. Is it raining now?"

"No. It actually looks clear. We shouldn't be too long. You can probably forgo your rain suits this time," said Dan, reading Georges mind.

"Thanks. We're on our way." George clicked off the walkie and turning to Jan, said, "This must be what Shelly was telling us about yesterday. This should be interesting."

The Achers arrived in less than ten minutes, which was fast by their standards. As they stepped into the house they were a little surprised to see Tina and Mike also in attendance. After polite courtesies were exchanged and all were seated around the dining room table, Dan started, "We have learned a lot about our situation in the last few days. We know and have confirmed with authorities in Washington DC that the rain has a virus and it will kill you and everything else. No one knows how long the contamination will last, but it is clearly more dangerous in wetter climates. I can only speak for my family, Patrick, and Juanita, and we are leaving here in one day's time. We would like you all to join us."

A hush fell over the room as eyes darted from one to the other seeking comfort or some form of understanding. The world as they knew it had been turned upside down by the poisonous rain and now they were being asked to thrust themselves out of the only environment they knew into the great void beyond their comfortable houses. Jan Achers slumped in her chair and reached for her husband's hand.

"Why now and how do you propose to get us out of here?" asked George.

"Now because most of the competition for travel is already dead and the rain is not letting up. How will be by boat. We have located a large ocean going boat that will take us to southern California, and from there we will make our way to Arizona where the average annual rainfall is only seven inches compared to eighty plus here. We also have a water filter that works, actually two filters, and we know we can survive in that kind of climate. The boat is still vulnerable to anyone else who might find it so we have to move right away," responded Dan.

"Will there be more killing?" asked Jan.

"Only if necessary for our defense. We intend to defend ourselves and our property. Anyone that comes with us will be expected to participate in that defense. Of course, no one is going to force anyone to come, but our survival will depend on all that do come," replied the Major standing to make his point.

Dan interjected, "If you stay behind, please know that you are not alone here. There are others that will, if you are discovered, take whatever they can from you, including your lives. This is now all about survival and it's not going to change in the foreseeable future. You don't have to make up your minds now, but we want your answer tomorrow morning by six AM. We have a lot of planning to do, supplies to organize and armaments to pack. We intend to leave around three in the morning the following day and make our way to the boat under cover of darkness. Hopefully we can be well at sea by dawn of that day."

"Dan, Tina and I will be coming with you. We have discussed leaving here and this sounds like our best chance. You will have our support and we will offer you any and all of the supplies we have," said Mike.

"Happy to have you with us. We will be doing some planning tonight if you want to stay to give us your input," replied Dan as he shook both Tina's and Mike's hand.

Eyes shifted to the Achers'. Monica was staring deep into Shelly's eyes and all could feel the tension building.

"We need to discuss this as a family," said Jan, "We will let you know as soon as possible. If we stay, can we have one of the water filters?"

"No. We will need it as a spare should something happen to the other one," said Dan, matter of factly.

"Let's go home George. Come on Monica, time to go."

All rose and watched as the Achers exited the house and walked down the road. The Major turned to Dan and raised his eyebrows and slightly shook his head. Dan understood exactly what the Major was indicating. Iffy at best and if they decide to come they will be a problem. But at least they had done the right thing by offering a hand. Now the ball was in their court and they had to make the play or sit on the bench.

"They will come with us. I know it," said Shelly.

Logistics

Logistics, as Dan explained it to Shelly, was "The procurement, distribution, maintenance, and replacement of materiel and personnel." Or if you ever watched 'Mash' on TV, it was Radar. Dan was excellent at logistics. He excelled at it in the Air Force and the Major trusted him explicitly.

"Dan, you take the responsibility for the supplies needed once we are on the boat and while traveling to our new home port and for our cross country expedition to Arizona. I'll get us to the boat, plot a sea course for us south and determine the best route for our trek across the mountains to Arizona. The rest of you should prepare your own separate lists of what you feel are absolutely essential items needed for the journey. No games, no high heels, no frills. Only essential items. Any questions?"

"One thing I want to know," said Mike, "who has the last word on what's essential?"

"I do," responded Dan, "and now would be the time to tell you the rest of the story so you will know why I feel I have this responsibility." Solemnly, Dan laid out the story of the UFO, the General in Washington DC, the G-men, and the special connection Shelly seemed to have with the ET's. The Olsons were obviously skeptical but eventually recognized the sincerity of everyone present and put aside their doubt for a better time. They focused on the need to leave and figured they could worry about the details later.

Two hours later, the Archers called and said they were in. Dan gave them the same instructions the Major had given everyone else and told them to have their lists prepared by 6:00 AM and to meet them for breakfast and a discussion.

Shelly turned her list into her father that evening before going to bed. Only one thing was on the list: RutButt. Dan looked at her bit his lip. "Don't worry Dad, no one will object, I just feel it. And, don't worry about the people at the boat house. They won't be there. They are gone. I think the UFERs are helping us. Not sure why, but I sure am glad."

"Pack some cat food for the stud. Okay?" replied Dan.

"Already done," smiled Shelly.

Hop, Skip and a Jump

Waiting is a learned art. Patience, being its better label, is an advanced skill. The young, unless brain dead, have zero patience. Young adults recognize its value but have a hard time pretending to have it and midlifers perform only slightly better at it. Take an old person, however, and provided they have bathroom accessibility, they have mastered the knack of waiting. They can wait with or without purpose. It truly is a thing to be cherished, as waiting is a lifelong obligation.

At breakfast that morning the lists were consolidated. The Olsons were allowed to bring their bows in addition to their firearms, because they had proven their proficiency with the instruments. Dan brought up RutButt to avoid later problems and no one complained, although several reserved glances were exchanged. Juanita had listed female necessities and her recommendation was well received by all the women except Shelly who had no idea what they were talking about. Juanita told Shelly she would explain later. Monica made a face at Shelly and giggled. Dan was relieved.

Two main issues remained: transportation to the boat and the taking of the boat. Even though Dan had it on Shelly's authority that there would be no resistance, Mike, Dan, George and the Major stepped into the office to discuss the potential assault. As expected, George was upset but saw no way out of the issue and was given a less than exposed assignment. Nonetheless he would be carrying a pistol, but most probably would not use it.

Comfortable with their plan of action to take control of the boat, the Major focused the remainder of his time on transportation to the beach. He inventoried all of the vehicles available at hand and determined that they would use the two motor bikes for himself and Mike as they would provide a cavalry type support to the caravan. Dan's plumbing van would be used to bring the essential weapons and survival supplies, while the Achers' four wheel jeep would be used to transport the ladies, George and RutButt. The total team consisted of four men, three women, two girls and a cat. The van was loaded and backpacks were used by everyone to cram their personal essentials into. The Major supervised the packing and made sure everything was indeed critical and practical. The only exception to the whole process was RutButt. Somehow the large lovable cat added a humanity to the situation that otherwise would have been missed. *Funny,* thought Dan, *a cat adding humanity.*

"May I have everyone's attention," requested the Major, "please get some rest this afternoon and early evening. Be here and ready to leave at precisely 3:00 AM tomorrow morning. We will leave on time. Leave your homes unlocked to prevent unnecessary vandalism. If you have food and supplies left in your house, leave a note on the kitchen table directing anyone that may venture in as to where to find things. It may keep someone from trashing your house. If by some weird chance we end up back here, we may find we still have a house to come home to."

"Oh," reminded Shelly, "don't forget to say your prayers. We certainly could use God's help."

Everyone went home and began the wait for the hop, skip and a jump to the boat.

Adios … or Maybe Not

Relationships are messy affairs. No clear cut rules exist on how to practice a good relationship. Newspaper columns and countless books exist to fix screwed up relationships, however there is no holy grail of the relationship. Honesty seems to be the best course of action in any relationship, but even that can get muddled. In the end, you ought to be glad you have relationships and just try not to worry about them too much.

Shelly walked into the office where her father was busy packing up his laptop and said, "Dad, I have to visit the UFO one last time and you are welcome to come."

Dan clearly heard that this was not a request but a mandate. He knew it was useless to object at this point, "Is it really necessary Shell?"

"I owe them a reason why we are leaving and I have a few more questions I want to ask them."

"Okay. We better leave soon so I can get back to my final preparations. How about we leave, in full rain gear, in thirty minutes?"

"I'll be ready Dad. And thanks for understanding."

ЖОЖ

They walked quietly, with a deliberate gait. Usually talkative in the woods, Shelly had nothing to say and instead wore a tense face with a strong jaw. Dan was curious as to what the questions were that Shelly had in mind for the visitors and, at the same time, he believed they already were aware of the trip and maybe even the questions. As they crested the hill to the secret valley, the quiet from lack of animals was eerie. They assumed the craft was still there and when within earshot, Shelly hailed the orb with a friendly "Hello. You still here?"

The space ship glimmered to life and was as beautiful as ever. Dan's wife, Shelly's mother, appeared in hologram form and, in a less than convincing smile, welcomed them. "It is considerate of you to venture out of your residence and visit us." Shelly and Dan had talked before about how everything the UFERs say is correct, but not really the way people talk. They are too formal in their word choices. They needed to work on their people skills.

Shelly took a step forward, symbolically separating her from her father, and said, "We are leaving Oregon and going to a place where there is less rain. Somewhere in Arizona. Will you be going with us?"

"We have responsibilities in this area and must finalize them, but once that is completed, we will continue our study of you and your group."

With a question that caught Dan off guard, Shelly asked, "Are we somehow related to you?"

"A most perceptive question for one of your relatively few years. The answer to your question is -- No. Our genetic markers, what you call DNA, are radically different from yours. From a purely DNA standpoint, we are more clearly related physically to some forms of your lizards, however our rationale is more in line with your whales. Clearly, neither of these species has advanced to our level or even yours. It is unclear how life would have continued to evolve had the meteor not struck your planet. However, prior to the strike, your bird population appeared to have a distinct advantage."

Shelly placed her hands on her hips and asked, "Do you ever doubt yourself?"

"Can you be more specific?"

"Do you ever wake up at night and wonder what you are doing and what it all means?"

"We are a goal-based civilization. We have clear-cut strategies, objectives and schedules driven by infallible logic supported by technology that I would find hard to make you comprehend. We do not usually wonder what we are doing. However, concerning the future, it will always be tantalizing and troublesome for a certain small percentage of our population."

"I like to wonder about all sorts of things—why God lets bad things happen, what the weather will be like to-morrow, or who I will marry and how many kids I will have. And of course, I wonder if we will live through this mess we are in now. It seems sad that you don't wonder."

"Life on our planet evolved though directed action with preservation always the main intent. Evolution demands it."

Shelly lowered her voice to a hush and Dan felt she was doing her best to keep her emotions in control as she said, "I will pray for you and for us. Do your best not to let this planet die. People can be very good. Only some are bad and then not all the time. I remember that God doesn't make mistakes and I don't believe it is a mistake that this has happened or that you are here. Something good must come out of this. I hope we see you again. Goodbye."

"Goodbye Shelly."

Dan sniffled and tried to wipe away his tears before his daughter saw him. He felt he needed to remain strong for her. Shelly returned to his side, grabbed his hand and led him out of the valley.

As they were about to leave the forest and enter their back yard, Shelly stopped and said, "Mom, we are leaving tomorrow. I hope you can be with us on our journey. We love and miss you."

"Thanks for coming Dad. I love you and I am so glad I had Mom for the time I did."

Dan could not control the tears now. They cascaded silently down his stubbly cheeks and rained on his shirt. "I love you so much, Shelly, and I will always appreciate the time I had with your mother. She was special and I see so much of her in you." They felt refreshed and closer than ever as they returned to the house.

D-Day

Leaving a loved home is not easy. Tears, hugs, and kisses only mildly soothe the ache. But, when you are taking along your best friend and several families you know, the burden is much relieved. Leaving allows for arriving and a fresh start.

Morning had not yet decided to poke its head over the horizon when the 2:00 AM alarm rang. Luckily they had found an old fashion wind up alarm clock at one of the houses and it was now the official time keeper. The overly loud clanging could be heard throughout the house. Not everyone had slept soundly, but Juanita had. She somehow felt at peace with the move and knew she was protected by some very able-bodied men with considerable skills. In her cheery fashion she greeted everyone with an oversized breakfast meant to last till supper that evening. Steaks, potatoes, refried beans, toast, canned fruit, orange juice, coffee and the last of the milk found its way to the breakfast table. Juanita's goal was to use as much as possible of the food supplies that were being left behind. The man sized breakfast barely made a dent in the sizable stores some lucky person might find. The Achers and Olson's joined them and they ate as much as they could. Energy for the days' events would be critical. The meal was appreciated by all. And the best part, nobody had to do the dishes!

All preparations had been completed and they were ready to roll at exactly 2:56 AM. "Four minutes ahead of schedule. I like the way this exercise is shaping up," commented the Major.

"Okay, Mike and I will lead off on the bikes. George, you follow up in the Jeep and Dan, you bring up the rear. Keep your lights off. As this tribe moves out, you should be able to see just fine when your eyes adjust. Only use your lights if you need to signal ahead for a problem, and then follow up with your walkie-talkies. Do not use your horns. No unnecessary noises. Do not slam car doors when you exit. No talking when we get there. This needs to be a surprise. Everybody got it?" demanded the Major as he waited for acknowledgment from each and every person. "Let's go."

Dancing fires were the only lights that could be seen on their trip across town. They licked at buildings and cars and old stacks of tires. Electrical or propane lights were nowhere to be seen. Survivors had learned the hard way that advertising their existence could mean unwelcome visitors, either in the form of desperate dying beggars or vicious looters. Quiet also ruled the dark hours. No need to notify authorities of loud parties. None existed. Life was shuttered up and below ground, if it breathed at all. The tires crunching along on the road seemed to thunder their approach. The passengers found themselves holding their breath more often than not. Even in the early cool hours of the day, sweat oozed from everyone except Shelly. She busied herself with tending to RutButt's nervous pawing at his cage. Cooing to him and using a gentle soft baby talk that seemed to soothe all within ear shot. The motor bikes generated far more racket than seemed necessary. Their two cylinder staccato noise invited trouble, but thankfully, none surfaced. Several blocks from Harry Sloan's house, the Major and Mike pulled over and signaled for the others to kill their engines and do the same.

The Major ran back to Dan's van and had him join him at the jeep. They had gone over each other's assignments, numerous times but once more wouldn't hurt.

"Okay, you know the drill. Dan, Mike and I will hit the house. George, you and Tina keep watch on the street for any activity. Key your walkies if you hear or see anything, anything at all suspicious. We will give you three flashes from the flash light when it's all clear. Everyone has a weapon ready with the safety on. If you are going to shoot, make damn sure it's not one of us. When we give the all-clear signal, George and Tina will drive the vehicles down to the boat house and start loading. Quietly, very quietly. No talking unless absolutely necessary. Any questions? Okay, let's go."

Mike and the Major had already been in the house, so they took the same entrances again. Dan positioned himself on one corner of the house so he could see two sides of the house and also monitor the boat house for activity. On his signal, Mike and the Major crept into the house. Neither man could hear anything except his partner on the opposite end of the house. Nothing looked as if it had been moved or changed at all.

Within five minutes the house was cleared and they turned their attention on the boat house. Approaching it from three directions, they again waited for Dan to give the signal and in they went. With the water lapping at the hull, each man waited several seconds before moving much beyond the doors they had entered. Gradually, they eased their way alongside the boat and boarded her. Dan came from the rear of the boat and caught the name crisply painted in red, *Janet Marie*. A pretty name for a beautiful boat, he thought. Again, luck was on their side; no one was home. The al-clear signal was flashed; up the road the jeep and van started their engines and slithered up the access road to the boat house. Like a well rehearsed stage crew, they silently sprung into action. The Major positioned himself on the gangway and directed traffic as it came onboard. In hushed whispers, the transfer of the goods and supplies from the cars and the spare fuel drums was completed in less than twenty minutes. Mike stood watch and protected the party from anyone approaching from the road. With a signal from Dan's flashlight, Mike jumped on his bike and rode it right into the boat house. Careful not to burn their hands on the hot engine, three of the men lifted the bike onto the rear of the boat and lashed it down. It would be needed later. The large boat engines had already been started; mooring lines were thrown on deck as Dan slowly backed the big lady out of the boat house. The Major, Tina and Mike took up defensive firing positions as everyone else was sent below decks with all lights, including running lights, turned off. Gliding out into the channel, Dan took the powerful engines out of reverse and pushed the throttle slowly forward. A deep vibration could be felt through the boat as it pushed its prow firmly against the current. Tide was up and the force of the ocean could be felt even in the channel. As they turned from the channel to the sea, a lone woman could be seen running and yelling along the beach as they pulled out to safe water. No one wanted to speculate on her situation. They all ignored her pleas and turned their attention seaward. It was now 5:15 AM and a hint of light was playing on the horizon. Clouds again knitted their overcast, and for the first time they all took in the blood red ocean they fled upon. The smell was offensive. Gone was the crisp salty brine that washed away troubles and sang to the soul. Instead, a sort of rotten vegetal smell choked your nostrils and gagged your throat. It was visually surreal. Occasional patches of desperate blue surrounded by bloated red clumps. It looked as though you might be able to walk on the alien fungus. Dan became immediately concerned that the stuff could somehow comprise the boat and ordered the Major to go to the engine room and see if everything was okay. His gauges were all reading normal, but he wanted to be sure. The Major reported that all appeared normal. Dan steered straight out to the horizon with the goal of being out of sight of land. That would mean roughly thirteen miles to get to the curvature of the earth. He reasoned that if he couldn't see land, then no one could see them. Best to not invite trouble. So far, so good.

Ocean Trials

Sailing off onto the ocean is the ultimate in giving up control. Sailors need God closer than most. On the ocean you recognize your true part in the universe. Miniscule, forgettable, clinging to hope.

Once land was but a memory, the Major relaxed his vigilant stance and made his way up to the flying bridge. Dan was sitting in his high back brown leather chair and had a pencil and paper and was crunching numbers. "First of all, Major, I want to thank you for picking such a wonderful boat."

"Actually Dan, I believe Shelly gave us this tip. And it's really a Yacht. I found some paperwork, and it's a 1989 Hatteras. It has two huge diesels and can get up to about 17 knots. This is a floating house with a lot of power. And to boot, it's mighty fancy."

"That it is, Major. Just what we needed. What do you think happened at the house? Where was everybody at 4:30 in the morning?"

"Beats me. Maybe they decided to move to another location. Pretty stupid, but there is no telling what people will do under stress. I'm just glad we didn't get involved in a messy shoot out. I'm not sure the Achers could have handled it. On the other hand, what a piece of work the Olsons are. They are solid folks. We are lucky to have them. By the way, what are you working on?"

"I want to know how long it will take us to get to San Diego. It's roughly 800 nautical miles, and I figure we can safely do 15 knots per hour, so… we should be there in 53 hours, or 2.2 days."

Shelly had made her way up to the bridge and sat in the other big chair across from her father. "Dad, that woman on the beach was all alone. Her family had died and she was very sick. I wish we could have helped her."

"It would have been nice, but I couldn't risk everyone's life to save her and you already said she was sick. Not much we could do for her. I'm sorry."

"I know Dad. I just wish we could think of others instead of always us. We seem to be getting worse in the way we treat people."

"Once we get settled in Arizona, I hope things will be different, Shell. I still believe the world is full of good people stuck in a bad situation."

"But like you told me once Dad, there are no tomorrows, only todays. I'm tired of making the selfish choices."

"I know how it looks, girl. But remember, I am making the choices and not you. I hope someday you understand why I did the things I did."

"I know now, Dad. I'm just mad at God and don't know what to do about it. He wants us to do the right thing, but it's not always clear like in the bible. All of our choices seem to be about life and death. Help someone and they probably die anyway and maybe you too. Don't help someone and they die. Mom used to talk about 'win/win' situations. We don't seem to be in any of those."

Dan glanced up and saw the concern in the Major's eyes. He needed to say something profound and had no words. He reached over, pulled his daughter into his arms hugging her close to his chest.

"All I know how to do is protect the people I love. And that's exactly what I am going to do. Remember Shell, God also said there is no greater love than when a person is willing to lay down his life for those he loves. That's what I am prepared to do. I know these are good people on this boat and we can make a difference in this new world. It's my responsibility to help."

"I love you Dad. I love you too, Major," said Shelly extending her arm towards Patrick inviting him into the group hug. Patrick sheepishly joined in wrapped his big arms around both of them. It was an instant of clarity for all of them. They felt refreshed and cleansed. The Major broke the silence by saying, "Dan, you and Shelly go down below and check on the team. Make sure everyone has a place to rest and come up with some watch schedules. Also, find out if anyone is competent to take a turn on the helm. I will play around with the radio and see what I can pick up."

Dan smiled at his ever efficient buddy and nodded his head. He put Shelly down and the two of them headed below decks.

The Love Boat

If you want to get to know someone, there are two things certain to speed up the process: play a board game with them, or confine yourself in close quarters for several days.

The ocean was calm today and, as of yet, no one was sea sick. Dan solicited to see if someone would volunteer to put together a lunch. Juanita appreciated that she hadn't been assigned the chore as she felt that now she was an equal with everyone else. All three of the Achers volunteered, George, Jan and Monica. Shelly joined the circus to spend some time with her pal.

Dan learned that Mike, Tina, and even George had some experience with boats and all felt confident they could take a turn at steering the yacht. The *Janet Marie* was big, beautiful, and agile. All you really had to do was follow the compass and watch out for islands. The Major had plotted a good course, so it was relatively easy, especially with a global positioning tool built into the instrument panel. He would just make sure either he

or the Major had the helm at night. Two people were assigned to be awake at all times of the day; one to pilot the
ship and other to keep them awake and to be a gopher if
necessary. Watches were only two hours long and that
helped ensure there was no sleeping on the job.

Sleeping accommodations were apportioned out
and Juanita ended up sleeping with Monica and Shelly
while Dan and the Major had to bunk together. Everyone
seemed at ease and, remarkably, no bickering was taking place. Dan headed topside to relieve the Major for
lunch and to take his first watch.

"Major, time for you to get some lunch. The crew
cooked up some good stuff. By the way, how did the
radio work out? Did you raise anyone?"

"As a matter of fact, I did. Got hold of a guy fifty miles
south of here that said he appears to be the last survivor. He'd been living on booze and beans for days now.
Basically the same story as we experienced. Gangs ruled
the area for a short time before everyone started falling
ill. This guy had inherited his parents' fallout shelter from
the 50's and he had kept it up-to-date and had simply
buried himself there for three weeks before venturing
out. By then, he was mayor by default. He made no
pleas to pick him up and seemed content with his situation. But the real news came from some internet stuff the
guy had found. The red plague, as it was being called,

continued to spread, and deaths were in the billions. It was estimated that only one in ten would survive world-wide. And already estimates placed the death count at over two billion and climbing rapidly. Some countries had taken their best and brightest and squirreled them away in well defended and supplied caves. Others had assembled makeshift towns in deserts around the world and some had even gone to the North Pole in an attempt to avoid the kill off. As bad as that was, it was worse for the animals. Many bloggers wondered if any animals at all would survive. Only time would tell." RutButt's value had just gone up.

After lunch, Monica found some videos and plugged one in. Most of the crew watched 'You've Got Mail'. It was light and fun, with the world involved in the day to day issues that seemed so far from today's concerns. After the movie, most stayed below decks as the view topside was depressing and the smell worse. Large fish kills were evident miles before you hit them. The smell was overwhelming. Mike reported seeing a lone bird glid-ing on the air currents headed west out to sea. Perhaps a bit confused or a knowing suicide run.

Steady As She Goes

Seaman have long sailed with an eager eye to the horizon; 'Red sky in morning, sailor take warning, red sky at night, sailors' delight'. But what would they have said about a red sea?

No news was good news and so the cruise continued. Nothing out of the ordinary except the continual red carpet of algae which they parted as if Moses was leading them in flight from the Egyptians. Shelly and Monica bonded again and even RutButt got his sea legs and ventured topside for his private duties. It did rain on and off for most of the trip south. As they drew abreast of Los Angeles, the rain died out and more chatter could be heard on the radio. It seemed chaotic, and the Major was certain that gangs were in control and dealing out their own kind of plague. Great columns of smoke could be seen on the horizon as undoubtedly raging fires consumed the city. One sad plea came from a prison. Apparently, the guards and uncaged personnel had abandoned the inmates locked in their cells. They couldn't justify setting the criminals lose on what was left of society. Some of the prisoners, those in the hospital wards, had managed to get to a radio, but remained securely locked behind bars and were slowly starving to death. Like zoo animals, they had no way out. For some, perhaps justice was finally served.

George called the men to the bridge as they passed between Santa Catalina and the coast. Several boats could be seen in the water and one was approaching them. The men hastily assembled their arms and tried to maneuver away from the boat, which was smaller than theirs, but faster. Shelly touched her father's arm and told him, "Don't worry. They're all dead on that boat. It's only a matter of time till they run out of gas. They killed themselves."

As for the other boats, nobody wanted anything to do with anyone else. That was fine for the *Janet Marie,* too.

At around noon on the third day, the GPS brought them within sight of La Jolla, their real destination. They were going to try their luck at the University of California-San Diego Scripps Pier. Dan knew that just inland, over a small hill laid a large subdivision and probable transportation. They would use the motor bike to find what they needed. They hoped to tie up the boat, find vehicles capable of carrying their supplies, and load them without fanfare.

Dan was surprised that the pier was empty except for two burned out boats and a couple of bodies littering the pier. It was amazing how quickly one became accustomed to seeing dead bodies. No one even mentioned them. It would have helped if it were raining and keeping people inside. Instead, it was bright and sunny and their arrival had not gone unnoticed. Two men on bicycles had stopped along the road leading to the pier and were observing them with binoculars. They had rifles slung over their shoulders and had a confidence about them that suggested they could take care of themselves. The Major had been checking them out with his own set of binoculars and noticed that they didn't carry, as far as he could tell, any communications devices. They didn't seem to pose an immediate threat. Who knew what a couple of hours could bring, however.

"Okay Major, we will get the bike on the pier and it's ready to go. You make sure you have everything you need in your backpack, especially the radios. Before you leave, I am going to take the hunting rifle and go down the pier and give you cover fire if needed."

"Sounds good, Dan. I expect we will be out of range fairly quickly with the radios, so don't get alarmed. Keep the engine turning over and cast off if you see a group descending on you. If it's only one or two, try to scare them away by shooting at them. No need to hit them, just let them know you are serious."

Shelly handed the Major a piece of paper with an address on it, "Try there first, but be careful. It will be the fifth street on your right when you enter the very first neighborhood. Be very careful, Major, there are some bad people. They kill just for fun. They ride motorcycles, too. Turn off your bike before you get too close so they won't hear you."

"Shelly, one day you are going to have to tell me how you do this. You really are amazing," said the Major as he kissed her on the cheek.

Dressed in vaguely familiar military clothes, back-pack, and M16 slung on his back, the Major gunned the cycle to life and set off down the pier, passing Dan as he neared the end. The two observers had disap-peared over the same hill the Major intended to cross. A quick radio check confirmed a live channel, and the Major juiced the machine for a quick sprint to the end of the road and turned west into the hills. Soon his cycle could no longer be heard. Juanita was on her knees saying prayers for the mission as he rode out of sight. Dan made his way back to the boat and posted guards facing the beach. They scanned continually with the rifle scopes and binoculars. No one was going to sneak up on them. And if confronted by a superior force, they would take the boat back out to sea and wait for an arranged signal from the Major. It seemed like a good plan.

Eye in the Sky

Neep, the ship's computer, had kept the *Janet Marie* in sight the entire trip. Golic had intentionally mis-directed Shelly during their last encounter, when he had told her they had further duties in Tillamook. The High Council had revised the mission's priorities and Shelly was at the top of the list. She actually was gaining some sympathetic support back on their planet, Creum. Seems everyone wanted to see her and her tribe suc-ceed. Nightly, probes were sent out, even at sea, to gain insight in the group's plans. They had known about La Jolla, and the pier, and their attempt to navigate inland to Cibola, Arizona. None of the crew, including Neep, felt they would be able to make it without their support and, if needed, protection. Dra and Kosh had no problems with the lack of objectivity to protect the tribe. Nimar, the scientific coordinator, on the other hand, was simply as-tounded at the turn of events. How, he reasoned, could any scientist rationalize that this was not exactly the kind of interference that they had been trained to never do? He went on record, loud and clear, that this was a ghastly mistake and was only being done to pacify those seeking some type of emotional release back home. Regardless, when the UFO crew learned of the poorly designed plan, they simply had to get involved. Removing the people from the boat and house to avoid a potentially deadly confrontation had been easy enough. A few extra days at the mall for the rowdy group were unproblematic. No one was hurt and the tribe moved one step closer to their final destination.

But now they must ensure that adequate transportation is found and several significant impediments be removed for the trip to be successful. Kosh, the systems engineer, and Neep had come up with several contingency plans to support the tribe. One specifically employed at the moment involved a significant quantity of a well known hallucinogenic drug that was placed just outside of the biker's house. Everyone inside that house was in an earth-shattering, mind altered state at the moment.

Not So Fast

As he rode up the hill, the Major had to admit a nasty fact. He liked the hero role he was being cast into. He had secretly feared that he had lost his edge sitting behind the big blue metal Air Force desk. This whole disaster had revitalized him. He had a purpose again: to save his adopted family. And he would.

His cycle glided up the now dead tree lined hill with ease. It was designed for real off road work, and this current task was a piece of cake for its maneuverability and power. As he neared the top, he killed the engine and hopped off. Employing an old Indian tactic, he army crawled to the top of the hill and, using his field glasses, surveyed the neighborhood just below him. No movement that he could detect, however, he did see five or six Harleys lined up in front of large dominating house. He suspected this was one Shelly had warned him about. Resolutely he returned to his cycle and pushed it to the top of the hill, put it in neutral, and coasted down the other side. He had removed the Glock from its holster and slipped it into his belt right in front of him. He counted the streets and just as Shelly had predicted, his was the fifth on the right. He dismounted the bike and pushed it along until he was in front of his target house. Pushing the bike up on to the yellow dying lawn he laid it on its side to be less conspicuous. Creeping to the windows, he peered inside and saw no movement or any signs of recent activity. The front door was unlocked, so he stepped in and closed the door. The ranch style house was roomy and decorated very tastefully. The Major even fancied himself being able to live like this. Then the smell hit him. "Not so fast," he whispered out loud. "Something's dead in here." He made his way to the bedrooms, with gun still drawn, and one by one slowly pressed his head around the door jams and peaked in. He found them in the master bedroom. It looked like a murder/suicide, except they also killed their Labrador dog in the process. Sympathy and despair can take strange paths. The man and woman looked to have been dead about a week. No air-conditioning was speeding up the decomposition process and right now, it was a horrible mess. He checked his gag instinct and moved towards the double car garage. He opened the door and found what he was looking for: a new big SUV with plenty of room. Four wheel drive, a storage rack on top, a trailer hitch and, after he found the keys hanging in the kitchen, the gas tank was full. Bingo! This was too easy. The SUV would fit all of the passengers and, after stopping at a U-Haul, they could find the right trailer to tow the rest of their gear. He raised the garaged door by hand and took one final look up and down the street for any signs of life. None. The engine started with ease, then he backed the behemoth out of the garage made a b-line for the boat. He called Dan on the walkie and let him know to have Mike ready for phase two. This was way too easy. Easy always worried him.

They were waiting for him on the pier and prepared for the next leg of the operation. A U-haul location had been found on the still strangely operating internet and a printed map was waiting in Mike's hand as he joined the Major in the SUV. With extra guns and ammo, some drinking water, and a day's ration of food, they set off. The location was only about five miles away, but who knew what they might run into and how long it would take. Dan redeployed his guards, checked the radios again, and began the wait.

A Hitch in the Plan

If it's valuable, more than one person is going to want it. If it's valuable and during a crisis, people will kill for it without remorse. If it's valuable during a crisis and essential, they will hunt you down.

A quick check of the SUV's radio revealed no radio stations still in operation either on the AM or FM channels. Oddly, a pack of now wild dogs crossed their path on one of the roads and defiantly held their ground. Strength in numbers was evident. If either man had ventured out of the vehicle, they surely would have attacked. Both men wondered what they might be drinking to stay alive. They would surely be eating dead things, but water was another matter all together.

Without too much trouble, a few detours here and there, driving across lawns and slipping in and out of the wrong lanes of traffic, they eventually found the U-Haul lot. It was stripped bare. Nothing in the lot and the building was burned to the ground along with a whole strip mall attached to it. "Now what?" asked Mike.

The Major just stared straight ahead and bit his lower lip. He was deep into alternative strategies. This is where he excelled. "Mike, where would we be most likely to find a trailer if not at the lot?"

"At someone's house?" answered Mike not knowing what the Major was looking for.

"True. But it could take us a long time to locate one. But more than likely, you could find one on a jammed highway or in a parking lot of large store. People try to leave town or stock up on supplies and fights break out or people get shot or traffic breaks down and they abandon their car. That's where we will have our best chance of finding one."

"Okay, what we need, then, is a vantage point to scope out the area," replied Mike.

Again, the Major appreciated the way Mike thought. "Right. Do you see a water tower or radio antenna any-where?" inquired the Major as both men began craning their necks looking for something high in the air. Nothing came into view. The Major pulled the SUV out onto the street and headed up the hill for a better vantage point. At the top, they spied a twenty story building about a mile away. They raced for the spot and got ready for the ascent.

When they arrived, the Major said, "We will both go in. Let me pop the hood and I will take the coil wire to the distributor with me. That should make sure we have a vehicle when we return. Let's find an entry way and take the stairs to the top. Bring the binoculars."

They made their way quietly and deliberately to the fifteenth floor. The Major, now out of breath, said, "Let's try here. Maybe we might see something." They entered the door and found a typical office floor plan. It consisted of cubicles arranged in a mouse-like maze with several glassed in offices on the outside walls. The view from the offices gave them the vantage point they needed. They moved instinctively to the windows and Mike brought the binoculars up and began scanning the streets below. He spotted lots of cars on the streets, houses with doors opened, bodies here and there, a fire still smoldering, and three people sitting around a pool in a backyard. They were drinking beer and shooting handguns at a wall with bottles lined up on it. But no trailer.

"Major, let's move to the other side of the building. Nothing on this side." The north side of the building revealed a freeway jammed with cars and several strip malls, some intact and others gutted. Just as Mike was going to suggest going up to the roof, he spotted it. A ten foot covered trailer hooked up to a pickup. It was parked in front of a liquor store and the driver was half in and half out of the cab. "I got one, Major. Here, look over there at the billboard with the red sports car on it. At the base is a liquor store. See the trailer?"

"Yes. Before we go, let me check in with the boat." He hoped the added height would aid the transmission. After hailing them several times he said, "I can't raise em. Too far. Let's get going."

The trip down was markedly easier than going up. The Major was grateful. Mike was in much better shape than he was and bounded ahead of him. As the Major was about to call out for Mike to wait up. He heard a man yell and a gunshot ring out. The Major froze and heard someone telling Mike to drop his weapon. He removed his Glock from the holster and watching his steps carefully, flattened himself to the wall and began easing down the flight of stairs. Patrick heard Mike saying he was alone and looking for food and water. Another man laughed, and said, "Fat chance, dude. These buildings were cleaned out weeks ago. Is that your SUV our front?"

"Yes. And I need it. Others are waiting for me."

"Too bad. It's ours now. Tell us where they are and we might let you live."

The Major had worked himself to the point that he could see Mike's back with his hands raised over his head. They were in the stairwell about one floor below him. So far they didn't suspect he was there. Accumulated in the stairwell was the expected trash and miscellaneous stuff you would find in a looted building. The Major saw a

296

Desktop CPU lying by the door on the landing he had just passed. He snuck back to it, cradled it to his chest using his left hand. He was thinking it might act as a bullet proof vest as he edged himself down to his previous position. As the two men continued to question Mike, the Major let out a blood curdling yell and thundered down the ten steps separating him from Mike. Yelling for Mike to drop, he opened fire with his Glock. The scream alone confused the men and bought the Major a few precious seconds. Before either of the men could respond, he had shot one of the men square in the chest and was focusing his fire on the next one, who was several feet behind the first. A bullet slammed into the CPU and knocked the Major backward as he continued to fire. Mike was trying to bury his head in the concrete and steel stairs as bullets ricocheted around the tight area. Another shot hit the Major in the hand holding the CPU and he dropped the machine but kept up a ridiculous rate of fire that eventually took its toll. Trying to duck any oncoming bullets, the remaining man had lost his balance and fell over the guard rail tumbling and bouncing the last four stories to the ground level. He lay in a tangled heap that looked more like a load of laundry dumped on the floor, than a man recently killed.

Quiet returned to the stairwell as the adrenaline continued to run hot. The noise had been deafening and now both Mike and the Major absorbed the quiet as they ran their hands over their bodies searching for bullet holes that hadn't announced themselves yet.

"Mike, are you hit?"

"No. Thank God. How about you?"

"Yeah. He got me in the hand. I'll live. Let's get out of here. Be careful going down. There may be more of em."

Outside they found themselves alone. Mike got the coil wire and hooked it back up to the distributor, helped the Major into the SUV and applied a makeshift bandage, then they headed for the strip mall and the trailer. They had brought some tools with them and in short order had the trailer disconnected from the pickup and hooked up to their ride. They were about to leave when they realized they hadn't even looked inside the trailer. "Oh well, we can do that at the boat. Let's get away from here," said the Major, clutching his hand, with blood now soaking his lap.

Thankfully, the ride back was uneventful and quick. As they pulled within sight of the pier, Mike was on the walkie, "We're back. Get the medical kit. The Major has a bullet hole in his hand. Get everybody on the pier to start unloading the trailer and loading our stuff." It had only taken them two hours to return.

Starting Out

The wagon trains leaving from St. Louis had a definite final destination in mind when they snapped the reigns and set their team of oxen in motion. Wandering aimlessly serves no purpose. You can say that of one's education, career, or even vacation trips. Certainly, finding a permanent, safe resting spot for the tribe was crucial.

Of all the things you might expect to find in trailer, one thing seemed remote: a pinball machine. It was a 1972 Gottlieb Pro Pool pin ball machine. It looked pristine, and the documentation taped to the side seemed official enough, but who in their right mind would consider this as survival equipment? Most of the things strapped securely in the trailer were of value, but either not up to the quality they already had or were duplicates. They kept the bottled water as barter goods and found a steel chest with about twenty pieces of gold bullion. Not the type you see in the movies, but small; about three inches long, a quarter of an inch thick and an inch and a half wide. No telling what it was worth now, but gold had never been worthless, so they kept it. They also found a cast iron barbecue with a propane tank which would come in handy. One special find was irreplaceable; in a sealed box, they found a solar panel and a small generator it could power. Everything else they piled up on the pier and they began loading their gear. Dan had determined what to load when so that the guns would come out first, followed by the water filters, and next, backpacks with survival gear for all. He was truly a logistics pro.

Dan and the Major walked away from the group and held a private discussion.

"Look, Major, it's already four PM. I'm not sure if we should stay with the boat or get out of Dodge now."

"A moving target is harder to hit. And I'll bet you a bunch of people already know we are here. They will be coming to investigate and this evening would the best time for them. We need to get out of here. Let's finish loading, take one last tour of the boat to make sure we have everything, and then bug out."

"Agreed, Major. I'll tell 'em."

Dan informed the group, and when they were finished loading, they took one last loving look at the *Janet Marie* and left her for who might find her. She had treated them well and maybe someone would find her and appreciate the amenities.

ЖОЖ

In the SUV Dan told them their final destination was Cibola, Arizona. It rarely got rain and it was located by the Colorado River. The population before the plague was about 172 people. That was 9.5 people per square mile. It was an agricultural valley and they could eventually, hopefully, raise crops and perhaps animals. It was off the beaten track and would give them some insulation from wandering gangs. It was only 150 miles away and the gas they already had in the SUV should get them there. However, if given the opportunity along the way to siphon some gas, they would.

Mike sat in the front passenger seat with an M16 at the ready. Dan was the driver and had a Glock tucked under his thigh. Tina was on one window in the passenger row with a Glock and George had the other window with an Uzi. Monica sat between them. The Major, with his freshly bandaged hand, was sitting in the rear of the vehicle facing backwards with an assault rifle and a shotgun. He shared his seat with RutButt, still in his cage. The trailer blocked much of his view, but if anyone tried to come at them from the back, he would be there to welcome them. In the second row was Jan and Juanita on the windows, both with hand guns and Shelly sat in the middle. All nine fit in the SUV snuggly and were loaded for bear.

Each person had a bottle of water, some snacks for the road, and instructions to stay awake and alert. They were to look out their side of the SUV and not all around. It was the Ostrich strategy. Ostrich's group all of the new hatchlings together as a means of defense. It is common to see one set of adults with a hundred chicks from numerous parents. They know there is safety in numbers. Young ostrich's grow especially fast, and soon you have 100 sets of eyes perched on a viewing platform six feet high and constantly scanning the territory for danger. You cannot sneak up on a flock of Ostriches. And if you do, their claws can gut a lion with one swift kick. Not a wise decision to go after them. This is exactly what the Major had in mind. Now all they had to do was execute and improvise.

The plan was simple: avoid people and jammed freeways, stay on surface streets, and make their way to Interstate 8 and head east to Highway 78 and then north on into Cibola. They were under no illusions. A trip like this might take three hours in the old days. Now, if they made it in three days, they would feel good about it. If fact, some wondered if they would make it at all.

On The Road Again

Cruel. That is how you would describe the devastation that the plague had brought. Although La Jolla was much drier than Tillamook, the effects of the virus were abundantly clear. Velvet soft tree lined boulevards were now exposed and naked with their plush dresses soiled on the ground. Bare sticks of once queenly palms stood in a stark salute to death. Lawns and parks were now yellowed and torn. No sign of life in most vegetation. Occasionally a Bougainville would surprise even itself with a show of glorious red blooms in defiance of the circumstances. Often it was protected by spacious overhangs. But the inevitable loomed. Fog, as well rain, could summon the withering disease, although drought was lethal too. Nothing was safe.

People fared better in this environment, but not enough. Many dead dotted the landscape like ill conceived modern art. Prone, leaning against buildings, draped over fences, hanging out of cars and main entrances to houses, they festered in the heat and brought their sickening sweet smell on faint breezes from the ocean.

The living could be seen also. Mainly hollow eyed remnants of themselves, existing more than living, in numbers too small to be encouraging. Remarkably, none threatened them. Instead they stared as if they had seen this parade before and knew it was hopeless.

"How many people do you think are still alive, Dad?" asked Monica.

"Hard to tell, honey. I guess no more than twenty five percent," replied George.

"More like fifteen percent now and dropping to ten percent in the next year," interrupted the Major.

"How are we going to live in the desert, Dad?" asked Shelly.

"Yeah, how can we do that with no help?" joined Monica.

"I doubt we will be alone. And if we are, it won't be for long. Sooner or later the government is going to start broadcasting again and they will encourage people to migrate to the southwest, away from the rain. Eventually we will be able to start towns again and live with some form of security. For the short term, we have what we need to get by, but we will have to be very creative."

"I just hope the killing stops. We can't keep living like this," commented Jan. "Some type of law is going to have to start to control everyone. Everyone has this survival of the fittest mentality, and that is definitely a no win situation."

The Major bristled at Jan's comments but swallowed hard and said nothing. *In case she hadn't noticed,* he thought to himself, *all we have been doing is protecting ourselves, her family included.*

"Mr. Brown, I'm going to have to go to the bathroom sometime soon. Not right away, but in the next thirty minutes or so," said Monica.

"Me too, Dad," chimed Shelly

"Okay. We've been on the road for about three hours and we need a potty break. It will be a good chance to stretch our legs and eat something."

"We better start thinking about a camp for the night, Dan. It's getting late and I don't want to be on the road after dark," suggested the Major.

"Okay. Any suggestions?"

"I think we should be in an open area, like a big parking lot or park, where we can see anyone approaching," said Mike.

"How about we find a quiet neighborhood and park in someone's back yard. Less people would know about us," answered the Major.

"No. We should find a freeway and mingle in with all the parked cars. No one will search there. If we can find a big truck, we can sleep in the back of it," responded Shelly.

All grew quiet, as the SUV chugged through the back streets, thinking about Shelly's suggestion. It made sense. It was the best approach.

At almost the same time, everyone in the car voiced their approval of Shells plan.

"Now, let's find an on-ramp and a freeway with an escape route," said Dan as he turned toward the sixteen lane mega highway. It took them about another hour, with a potty break in between, to find the right location. The on-ramp was not clogged with cars. The freeway was jammed, but also had some room on the side of the slow lane. Dan pulled in and turned off the engine. No houses overlooked the area and they were above everything except some skyscrapers in the distance. If needed, they could reverse out of their spot and quickly gain access to the town's many streets and boulevards. Several eighteen wheelers littered the highway ahead of and behind them. The Major and Mike armed themselves, grabbed a radio, and set off to reconnoiter the trucks. They returned in under fifteen minutes with good news. A grocery store truck had been looted and was empty. The doors were open and it was very roomy inside. They were able to pull the SUV right up beside the truck. Dan organized a transfer of enough supplies and sleeping gear to get them through the night. The Major set up a guard rotation with two people, including the kids, up at all hours. They settled in for the night.

Smores and Such

In the old days, not so long ago, camping out had been all about the ambiance. Cool nights, mesmerizing camp fires, juicy hot dogs, yummy smores and laughter all snuggled below huge trees overhanging and sheltering your tents. The crisp smell of pine trees, and if you were lucky enough to be at Camp Oswald West on the Oregon coast, the sound of breakers crashing on the beach a hundred yards away as you talked in the dark and reluctantly surrendered to sleep. You awoke in the morning yearning for the smell of bacon and coffee, while squirrels schemed on the best way to rob you blind. The good old days, not so long ago.

With safety the prime concern, fun and even comfort were the last considerations. Instead, nourishment, concealment, local intelligence, and clear shooting lanes to fend off the bad guys became governing priorities.

"Juanita, from now on, would you please be in charge of our emergency radio?" requested the Major.

"Or course, Patrick." She loved to call him Patrick and not Major. It made him more approachable. "What do you want me to do?"

"First, crank it up and give it some battery power, then, start going through the dial on all frequencies to see if you can find any broadcasts. You should do this every couple of hours during the day, even in the SUV, and a couple of times in the evening. Make sure you have the antenna out. Okay?"

"Not a problem Patrick," said Juanita making sure to fully engage him in prolonged eye to eye contact. The Major actually blushed. She was delighted!

Gathering his thoughts, the Major asked, "Jan, could you be in charge of ensuring the crank lanterns are operational?"

"Yes sir," snapped Jan with the hint of resentment in her tone.

"Good. Just like the radio, crank up the battery for a minute or so to charge the batteries and set them up so that no light shines out of this truck trailer. We don't want to alert the natives. If you see them going out, please have whoever is near them recharge them. Okay?" The Major had learned in the military, that is was always best to guarantee compliance by seeking a response from the one you just gave an order to. Hence the reason he ended most of his directives with 'Okay'.

"Of course," replied Jan.

"Tina, would you please have Monica and Shelly help you put together an evening meal. Make sure we all get enough to drink and some of the multiple vitamins we packed. No cooking tonight and probably not until we reach our destination. We need to keep the coyotes and wild dogs at bay. Okay?"

"Sure Major. No problem," said Tina, making an effort to be cooperative as an example to Jan.

"Oh, and Juanita, when you finish with the radio, please lay out the sleeping gear. Leave a rapid exit path through the center of the trailer and keep everyone well back from the door.

"George, I will need you and Mike to help me set up surveillance posts and secure the SUV. Dan, you take the first watch and try to stay out of sight. No use advertising our home away from home. Oh, and by the way, please go under the trailer when you have to relieve yourself. We don't want anyone wandering away. Okay, let's move." As usual, the Major had put together a good plan in a minimum amount of time. The group was very lucky to have a professional on hand when civilization came to an abrupt halt.

The meal came together nicely and they enjoyed Spam, crackers, Tillamook cheddar cheese, beers for the adults and soda pop for the kids. All downed their vitamins and a large glass of water. By the looks of it, everyone would lose some weight in the next few months. Not a bad thing except for the girls. They needed their nourishment, especially for the changes that would probably start happening in the next year or two.

Night security watches were set, the radio frequencies were barren again, but the crank lanterns worked great. They gave off just enough light to ease fears and make living feel very possible. They settled in for the night and the watch rotation began. The Major stayed at two hour shifts to keep everyone fresh. It worked well.

Only one alarming thing happened in the night. An amazingly frightening scream echoed down the freeway. A woman, no telling what she was going through, and it only happened that one time. Then it grew ominously quiet and left everyone to imagine the terror she must have felt.

Mile Marker

"If they only knew the danger so close at hand," shared Golic.

"Agreed. They would not waste the precious visibility offered by sunlight and would instead find urgency in their travel," joined Dra.

Neep politely interjected, "I do not foresee immediate danger. In fact, to date, their methodology has been exemplary."

"Only if you discount their lack of foresight in taking the sea vessel. Without our interference, I doubt that all would still remain alive. And the insertion of drugs to that gang certainly had a favorable outcome. Wouldn't you agree?" queried Kosh, already knowing the answer.

"We must note the child's progress did not foresee the future difficulties the group would encounter, and she remains emotionally tied in her decision making," instructed Golic.

"Noted," voiced Neep, "but I must also log that she has, without our help, pinpointed the boat and the vehicle to carry them to Cibola. She is showing marked improvement in her abilities. It is expected that her senses will sharpen and dramatically aid the tribe."

"Log also, Neep, that my impressions are not nearly as strong as yours. Her skill level is only rudimentary, and if maturing at all, it is at a rate that may not be beneficial to the tribe. If marked improvement is not seen in six Earth days, I will ask for the mission to resume its former directives and only monitor the group and not actively participate in the outcome," dictated Golic.

"Noted."

New Arrival

Hope takes many forms: an approaching army to dispatch the enemy, one out left in the bottom of the ninth and the winning run on base, one last dollar for the slot machines, or maybe something entirely different.

In the early star-filled morning, an unmistakable sound could be faintly heard by Mike and Juanita as they stood their watch. An infant was crying. It was a weak high pitched squeal that at first reminded Mike of a cat.

"That's a baby," announced Juanita.

"Could be," said Mike, "Go wake the Major."

The Major had only been asleep for a little over an hour as his watch had just ended. Regardless, he was alert at once and grasped the situation, shushing Juanita.

"Don't wake up everyone. Let's talk outside." They moved to the front of the truck where they had both heard the crying. "I don't hear anything," said the Major as he twisted his head from side to side trying to gain some acoustic advantage. Just as he said it, he heard it. Faint, but undeniably a baby.

Mike, raising the binoculars up to scan the road ahead, "Could be related to the scream we heard last night."

"We need to find it," implored Juanita.

"No. We have no idea who could be involved with that child. We don't even know if it's in trouble or just crying. Babies do that you know," reasoned the Major.

"The mother is dead. She died last night and the baby is going to alert the dogs. We have to go now," said Shelly surprising the three of them. "It's a boy."

The Major, becoming accustomed to Shelly's paranormal ability, inquired, "Are you sure he is alone, and can anyone else hear him?"

"Alone, and the dogs can definitely hear him. They are coming, but we can beat them if we leave now. It's not that far."

The Major felt all eyes on him as he made a command decision. "Shelly and I will go. You wake the others and load the SUV. Be ready to move when we return. Have some food for the baby ready." And then he muttered more to himself than anyone else, "I hope this is the right thing to do."

The Major started up the freeway, and Shelly started the opposite direction for the on-ramp. "This way, Major. It will be a lot faster."

"For crying out loud," muttered the Major, "A nine year old is leading me around by the nose."

"I'm almost ten. And you want to know something else?" said Shelly as she quickened her pace up the road.

"Dear God, I'm afraid to ask."

"He is going to be your son. Yours and Juanita's."

"What are you talking about, Shelly?"

"Somebody has to raise him and you two are just perfect for each other. She likes you and you like her."

"You don't know what you are talking about, girl."

"I've seen it Major. Honest, I have. Everything is going to work out. You'll see."

They kept walking with Shell in the lead. She kept her voice low, just in case, but she knew it was safe. The crying was a little louder now.

"Is this one of those feelings you have?" said the Major, trying to discount her revelation.

"Maybe, but it's real anyway. I told you, I saw it. It was clear. That's what made me get up and come out and tell you. Do you want to know his name?"

"No. Let's just leave it alone for awhile. You are starting to creep me out."

That was the first, but not the last, time that Shelly would have that affect on people. She was surprised at how she felt by his comment. She knew she was different, but she didn't want to be weird or scary to people. Maybe she had shared too much with the Major. Maybe people needed to gradually move towards the future and not have it thrown at them all at once. Knowledge could indeed be wondrous, curious, and dangerous.

As she walked, Shelly began to smile. Babies were hope. Everyone needs hope. Everyone needs lots of babies.

My What Big Eyes You Have

Man's best friend decided to associate with a better class when the plague hit. Dogs, already accustomed to living day to day on the street, fared the best. They took to packs and became formidable. Taking their drinking water mainly from swimming pools, they lasted longer than anyone would have expected. They weren't thriving, but they were surviving. Attracted to the noise, the pack zeroed in on the location from over a mile away. The Alpha dog, a mix Labrador/German Shepherd, was a big boy. He weighed in at over 155 pounds. Not only was he a natural leader, but he was smart and vicious when needed. Their pack numbered fifteen and they had killed and eaten men, dogs, cats, rats, sheep, and anything they could take down. A baby would be a welcome, fresh, easy meal. They had grown extremely wary of men as they had become prime targets for gun toting hunter wannabes.

Shelly and the Major had found the infant less than five minutes from their location. The mother had found refuge in an abandoned child's plastic multi-colored playhouse in a dried up backyard. She probably thought someone might be in the house and opted for the isolation of the playhouse. In any case, the child was still whimpering when they found him. The umbilical cord was still attached and the Major quickly tied off the cord and severed the physical relationship between mother and child. Shelly had instinctively picked up the child and held him close and silently cried when he reached out and grasped her hair. She knew what it meant to lose a mother.

"Here, wrap him in my shirt and let's get out of here," said the Major, grabbing his gun and poking his head out of the pink and blue playhouse. Moving to the five foot high wooden fence that separates so many neighbors from the terrible burden of ever having to know each other, he spied the dogs. Three dogs with heads to the ground sniffing and two more staring right at him. Growls and hackles materialized at once.

"Shelly, move slowly and do not look at the dogs. Stay directly behind me."

"Shoot the big black one. He is the leader. The others will leave if you can get him," instructed Shelly.

They stepped out into an alley behind the house and moved toward the street that would take them back to the SUV and their temporary camp ground. The dogs followed, but did not attack. As they rounded the corner and hit the street, they saw the black lab looking out from behind a car, teeth bared with head lower than his shoulders.

"Why don't they attack?"

"Because they know you have a gun Major."

As they turned to retrace their steps to the on-ramp and the SUV, the found themselves suddenly surrounded. The alley had five dogs in it, the street leading away was guarded by the lab and two of his pack and the direction home had at least three dogs that they could see.

"Smart. They didn't attack until they were all in position," said the Major as he fired one shot into the group in front of him, dropping a dog that resembled a pit bull. The baby jumped at the load noise the M16 made and screamed disapproval.

"Walk right at them, Major. I'll watch the rear and let's just keep walking at them."

The dogs in front backed up as three of dogs in the alley dashed right at them. The Major shifted the rifle to his left and sprayed the group killing two of the three. The third continued and the remainder of the pack attacked at once. Rifle fire erupted from somewhere in front of them as the Major focused on the third dog in the alley that was less than ten feet away. He managed to hit it and it fell into Shelly's legs dead. He spun to his rear and found the black lab in a full charge. He took a deep breath, brought the M16 up to his shoulder and planted three bullets dead center in his chest. The dog skid on his face and lay lifeless within five feet of them. As his paws lashed at the pavement, more shots could be heard as the remaining dogs either died or ran for their lives.

"Shelly, Major, are you all right?" shouted Mike as he and Dan ran towards them.

"Yes and thank God you came. We were about to be rather large dog chews," replied the Major, showing he still had style even in extreme situations.

"Shelly, what have you got there?"

"Dad, this is Abraham. Darn, I wasn't supposed to tell the Major his name!"

"What? How do you know his name and why can't the Major know it?"

"It's a long story, Dad. He doesn't want me to tell him."

"What? This is getting more and more confusing."

"We'll tell you later, Dan. Mike, let's get back to the SUV ASAP. This little guy is hungry."

"I decided to see if we could help, so Mike and I started out to find you," explained Dan.

"We heard a gunshot and were only a block away by that time," interjected Mike. "When we saw you, it was obvious you needed help."

"Your timing was perfect. A minute later and we would have been in real trouble. Shelly is responsible for keeping this little guy alive. She had great instincts."

Arriving back at the on-ramp, they were met by an already loaded SUV and a bunch of happy people. They crowded around the baby and, as Shelly had anticipated, Juanita soon had the baby in her arms and was fussing over him as food was rounded up for the little guy. The Major told them the entire story as they watched Juanita feed the baby some condensed milk diluted with water. Makeshift diapers were arranged and baby wipes and disposable diapers were added to the growing shopping list of necessities. They loaded in the SUV with Juanita and baby joining the Major in the back. First stop, a grocery store. Diapers and baby food were required. Breakfast was also in order, but would have to be consumed on the road. Execute and improvise.

Premonitions

Did you ever have the sensation that someone was watching you? The hairs on the back of your neck prickled and you became very uneasy? The first stage of a premonition is usually an uneasy feeling. We all get them, and it's evidence of talents undeveloped.

It was a day that Shelly and her new family would remember all their lives. It started with Shelly leading them to a small neighborhood grocery store where they found the diapers and baby food for Abraham. It was tucked away in the receiving area of the store and not on the shelves. They were also able to locate some powdered baby formula that Juanita instantly began brewing for the numkins. They found enough left over foodstuffs to stuff themselves with a makeshift breakfast. Guards were posted during the entire stop, as no one felt entirely safe after the dog episode.

Sitting on the checkout counter, Shelly began to shake, "What's wrong daughter?"

Trembling and looking down, Shelly said, "The fire started in the prison and killed a lot of people there and now it's coming our way. The wind will get stronger and it will make its own wind. It has a special name."

"Conflagration" added Dan.

"Yeah. That's it. What does it mean?"

"It is a fire so big and terrible that it creates its own oxygen by sucking in air. It literally develops a wind that blows into it. It is a name reserved for only the biggest and worst fires known."

"Well, it's coming our way and we need to leave now."

Dan looked at the sky and saw the red haze creeping towards the city. Ash was falling from the sky like naughty snowflakes with dirty shoes. He alerted the tribe and they loaded up and moved out.

They had made their way from La Jolla across Mission Bay and were working their way around the Mission Hills area when they first saw the fire. It looked as if it were a cheap prop in a 'B' movie. The fire was higher than anyone could rightly expect, and they could actually hear its deep vibrating roar. Trees were swaying as it sucked massive volumes of air into its raging furnace. The scary part was that you could feel the rise in temperature. If they stood still it would eventually kill them. It was burning everything in sight. By the looks of it, the fire must have spread from some of the suburbs east of downtown San Diego. The mushroom cloud that adorned its head was black with soot and resembled a vengeful dragon from some sci-fi movie. You could actually hear it roar. And now, you could begin to feel its searing death.

"Take Harbor Drive and stay by the water as long as possible. Drive fast, Dad!" commanded Shelly.

The road was mostly navigatable, and only a few times did they have to leave it and clamor along on the fringe of the asphalt. They drove through fences, over sidewalks, around disabled cars and even through a dry aqua duct for over a mile. It was a rough trip, but the baby slept through it all. They would have great stories to tell him one day.

They reached Chula Vista and had to backtrack to highway 94, which would take them to a southern route where they eventually would intersect a road leading to Tecate, Mexico. The temperature in the SUV, even with the air-conditioner on, was uncomfortable to say the least. The windows were hot enough to burn you if you forgot and touched them. And rounding a corner in the road, they ran right into the stretching tentacles of the fire. The SUV stopped and started to reverse.

"No, Dad. Go through it, it's not that wide. As soon as you go through, get ready to make a right turn."

Dan looked at Shelly and said, "God help us. We need you now." He put the SUV in drive and plunged into the fire. Ten feet later they exited the barbecue and hit dense smoke. Dan hit the brakes.

"Turn off the air-conditioner and start driving," instructed Shelly. "Please trust me and follow my directions, Dad."

Dan hesitantly edged forward.

"A little faster Dad, the tires are melting," urged Shelly. "Okay, now turn right NOW!" Still dense smoke obliterated any view but still Dan pressed on, trusting his daughter's skills.

"A little farther and we will take a left into an alley. Right here, turn left."

About fifty feet further the smoke started to clear. They were indeed in an alley and the fire's heat was being deflected by the building on either side of them.

"Now you can make another right at the street ahead and we should be able to get back on the road you wanted." Relief flooded the car and Juanita could be heard praying in the back seat.

Finally hitting the intersection of 94 which lead to Tecate, Mexico, Dan decided to pull off the road and call it a day. The Major organized a gas siphoning expedition while they hid the SUV deep in some trees and began preparing the evening meal. The fire could still be seen in the deep reddish clouds forming behind them to the west. But the immediate threat was over and Shelly still had deep concerns wrinkling her otherwise smooth young face.

"Still worried about the fire, Shell?"

"No Dad. It's something else that will happen tonight. I can't see it. It's big, though, and bad."

"What's it like Shelly? Do you actually see things in your mind?"

"Sometimes. But usually I see them with my eyes. Kind of like watching TV. There's no sound. Like a DVD with the mute on. Sometimes it's in slow motion and sometimes it's real fast—so fast I can't really see all the details. But tonight I'm getting a sick sort of feeling."

"Should we leave here and go somewhere else? Would that help?"

"No. We are better off staying here and getting ready for it."

"For what?"

"I don't know, Dad!" yelled Shelly obviously stressed out by the whole affair.

"Alright honey. I'm sorry. I don't know what I'm supposed to do. I just want to do the right thing. I want to protect these people."

"You will, Dad. You will."

ЖОЖ

At supper that evening, Dan told the group what Shelly had shared with him. They set up camp on a hill overlooking the trees the SUV was nestled in. The Major gave the standing orders to everyone after supper: "Three people on watch at all times, two hour shifts, maintain quiet, no lights, and no excess moving around, use the spots we found for surveillance and stay there. Don't be led off by a stray sound, you are relieved only when somebody physically takes your spot, stay where you are until they arrive. Any questions?"

"Yes," said Tina, "What do we do if we see someone sneaking up on us?"

"Shoot 'em. That will alert everyone. But remember this: after you shoot them, stay where you are. There may be more and if you don't move or make a noise, they won't know where you are and you can shoot another one. Trust me, the gunshot will wake everyone up in camp and we will come running to support you."

"Shoot 'em. Just like that. Not even a warning?" demanded Jan.

"Jan, ask yourself a question, why are they sneaking up on us? If they come in peace, shouldn't they do it some other way?"

"What if they are scared and just want to see who we are?"

With his voice rising, the Major put his full attention on Jan and said, "Then they should wave a white flag and scream that they would like to talk to us. Then I might cut them some slack. Otherwise, shoot 'em! Is that clear?"

"Yes," reluctantly said Jan.

"Cause if it ain't, don't go on watch. Don't put all of us in jeopardy because you want to be politically correct."

"You're right Major. I can handle it," replied Jan.

Prowlers

'Take the high ground,' is a military saying for good reason. Whether you are throwing rocks, shooting arrows, firing rifles, or lobbing grenades, it is much easier to do if you are on top of the hill. I guess that's another reason for the game 'King of the Hill.'

With a start, Shelly awoke at 2:17 AM and whispered for her Dad. "Dad, wakeup we need to move now! Dad, wakeup!"

Shelly reached over and shook her father, who slowly rolled over, rubbed his eyes and said, "Huh? What's the matter?"

"Lots of people are coming up the road. We have to wake everyone up now!"

"Are you sure, Shell?"

"Yes, we only have a few minutes. They know we are here."

Dan moved around the sleeping bags and shook everyone awake, told them someone was coming and cautioned them to keep quiet, grab their weapon and ammo and take cover fast. The Major jumped up, grabbing his gear and told Dan, "I'm going to tell the three on watch. I'll keep Mike in position and send everyone else up the hill. I'll take George's spot. Set up a perimeter and don't let us get outflanked! Hold your fire until you hear us start shooting."

"Take cover, move it. Stay low. No noise. Monica, Shelly, take this ammo box and find a tree or rock to get behind. Let's go, people," urged Dan in a hoarse whisper.

"Mike, some bad guys are coming. Stay low and wait for my shot. We will have them in a cross fire. Pick your targets and make your shots count. Everyone else is positioned on the hill. No heroics, just good marksmanship. Good luck," said the Major and he crept into position and sent George up the hill.

Drug lords in Mexico had been unusually prepared for the plague. They lived in a dry climate, they already had a lethal organization dedicated to self preservation, and they had plenty of money, no morals, and were ruthless. All excellent qualities to survive in a nasty world. This particular gang had acted like Wall Street pros. They had conducted numerous hostile takeovers of competing gangs until they had become the dominant player in their territory. Life no longer evolved around drugs. Water, food, weapons, gold, and women were their main commodities. Scouts placed in various advantageous sites throughout their territories kept them informed of anyone traveling along their roads. The big SUV had stuck out like a sore thumb as it bounced down the road. Women had been seen in the vehicle along with children. That alone made it a choice target. Throw in the trailer it was pulling and it was totally irresistible. The scouts had seen guns, but how much trouble could seven or eight gringos make when over half were women and children? Plus, attacking at night also gave them an advantage, and factor in their numerical superiority with automatic weapons, it would be no contest. They had sufficient experience with this type of operation, and the guys had been getting jumpy. They needed a little action and this was the ticket. Ernie Gonzalez handpicked fifteen of his brightest soldiers for this one. He remained in radio contact but was smart enough to remove himself from the flying bullets. No, General Ernie would direct traffic from the other side of the road in a cement culvert protected from errant shots. He had given the 'go' signal three minutes ago and his men should be about ready to start the festivities. "Sanchez, are you ready?"

"Yes General," replied his next in command.

"Then take them my friend."

Their first mistake was shooting off the starlight flare. The flare was lobbed into the air with a large handgun.

The 'whomp' sound alone could have awakened the entire camp and the lighted flare floating gently to the earth via a small parachute gave off much more light than needed. Simultaneously, they began yelling as they all ran up the path. Apparently, in past operations, the victims stumbled from their sleeping bags, stood up, and made excellent targets. The flare allowed them to select precisely who they intended to kill and who would become a prisoner.

Now, however, the flare only illuminated the charging men who were suddenly without cover and very vulnerable. Dan had parked the SUV about two hundred yards off the road. The sleeping bags were positioned in front of it. The clearing had been used by others as three large stone campfire circles dotted the ground. Three buses could have parked easily in the clearing. It was an excellent killing ground. On came the charging men, slowing as they grew closer to the vehicle. Mike was behind a large tree on the left and the Major was behind a group of boulders on the right. The Major waited until the running men crossed the point where both he and Mike would be aiming their guns up the path. The imaginary V was the precise point of the crossfire he was waiting for. When the first man crossed that point, the Major opened fire. Almost instantly Mike joined the action and three men dropped in their tracks. The hill behind and to the right of the SUV flashed to life with gunfire. Dan had carefully instructed each person to avoid shooting in Mike or Patrick's direction and to instead focus on a zone between the two men. The effect was brutal. Coupled with the cross fire, the bullets slamming down from the hill on the stunned men created the exact confusion needed. The men were firing blindly up the hill at any flash of a gun barrel. Bodies were dropping. The General had expected a certain amount of return fire, but the tremendous burst of gun fire clearly indicated that the gringos were putting up a fight. For the briefest of moments, Ernie Gonzalez contemplated charging up the path to help his muchachos, but then reason and cowardice reigned supreme and he hunkered down in his cement cocoon and waited for the gun shots to die down. The Major yelled to cease fire and Dan echoed the order. It grew ominously quiet. Only moaning could be heard from a few men on the ground and a radio asking a Sanchez if the gringos had been killed. The Major carefully exited his hiding place and, pulling his Glock out of its holster, proceeded across the clearing. As he came to men still alive, he shot them once in the head. Three times the Glock snapped the silence. Each time the people on the hill and the General in the culvert jumped. It was now officially over.

"Mike, you okay?" asked the Major.

No reply.

The Major eased his way over to Mikes shooting area, always keeping one eye on the path for any wayward gang member, "Mike, talk to me."

Nothing. By now, Tina had sensed that Mike might be injured and had sprinted down the hill and ran up to the tree as the Major grabbed her by the shoulders and said, "Stay here, let me take a look." He stepped around the tree and Tina heard him cursing. She bolted to where the Major stood looking down at a crumpled body in the grass. Mike had been shot in the head and must have died instantly. Tina fell on the body and began sobbing. A lucky shot had ended his life, robbed Tina's future, and shattered the group.

"Dad, the man responsible is hiding on the other side of the road. He has done this before. We need to kill him or he will do it again," directed Shelly with a face now appearing much older than her nine years.

"Major, Shelly says the guy responsible is hiding across the road. I say we go get him."

"I'll get him," said Tina jumping up and heading for the path.

"No. Let Dan and I go," said the Major.

"No chance, Major. I owe him big time."

"Okay then. At least wait for us and do this so no one else gets hurt," replied Dan joining the two of them on the path.

"In the cement round tube," yelled Shelly as they disappeared into the night.

Ten minutes later they heard the firing coming from the road. It only lasted a few seconds and the General got permanently demoted. Five extra shots rang out as Tina emptied her gun into the Generals body.

Don't Look Back

Amazingly, they hadn't brought a shovel. A normal burial was not going to happen. Jan found a hollowed out area in the grass and they piled many stones on Mike's body that was wrapped in a sleeping bag. Tina stuck one end of his bow in the rocks as a marker and left a penned note explaining who he was and what he meant to her. She tucked the note in a zip lock bag and put it under a rock. George said a few well intentioned words and Shelly sang the Lord's Prayer. Juanita made sure they had something to eat when the sun came up. Dan and the Major dragged the bodies of the bandits away from Mike's grave to keep the coyotes away from him. Luckily, only one window was broken in the fire fight and few inconsequential bullet holes splattered the rear passenger door. As they pulled out of the area, they all cried.

Shelly sat beside Tina, hugged her, and said, "Don't look back. He's not there."

It seemed so natural that Tina would bury her head in Shelly's shoulder and whimper as they moved down the road.

About two hours later, with Tina asleep from the stress, they hit Interstate 8 and the city of Boulevard, then turned east.

"We are not going to make any time on this road and may find it blocked altogether. What other roads could we take?" pleaded Dan, frustrated with the 30 MPH pace, zigging and zagging through abandoned cars, pickups, trucks, SUV's, jeeps and all means of transportation. They found a suitable replacement SUV for their wounded steed, swapped cars and hooked up the trailer. They siphoned some gas and kept moving. Always keep moving -- seemed to be their motto.

Consulting a map, the Major responded, "When we get to Ocotillo, we can take a road called S80 into El Centro. From there we could swing over to 111 and go up to Brawley and then we hop on 78 all the way to Cibola. Not sure how we cross the river, though."

"Good, anything is better than this. Our gas is full right now, but I say we siphon some in Brawley to be safe. Might be a good place to replenish our supplies if we can," said Dan thinking more out loud than really strategizing.

"Hey, did you see that?" stammered Jan.

"Yeah, I see him," replied Dan.

"What is it?" yelled the Major from the back seat.

"It's a red Hummer ahead of us weaving in and out of traffic."

"I wondered how long it was going to be before we saw more people," said a normally quiet Monica.

"They must have seen us. They are stopping and a guy is getting out with his hands up."

"Stop the car, Dan," ordered the Major. "How far ahead of us is he?"

"Oh, about two or three hundred yards."

"I'm going to go see what he wants. Use the rifle with scope and keep me covered. George, you cover the rear and don't let anyone sneak up on us. Tina, can you handle one side of the car?"

"Yes, I'd be glad to," replied Tina, grabbing an M16 and taking up a position.

"Everyone keeps an eye out. No telling what might happen," said the Major as he checked his Glock and walked toward the man."

"I think he just wants help, Dad. He doesn't want to hurt anyone."

"Did you feel or see something, Shell?" asked Monica.

"No. He just seems safe. If he tries anything you know the Major could hurt him. He just needs help."

As the Major approached the Hummer, he saw it was loaded with a woman and two kids. They had some gear stored in the back and a couple of boxes lashed to the roof.

"Mister, don't shoot. I just have a favor to ask," yelled the man when the Major was about 100 feet away.

"What do you want?"

"We are out of water and my daughters are dehydrated and I'm afraid they might die before I find some. Can you spare just a little for them?"

"Back up to the front of the car, keep your hands over head. I want to take a look at them."

The Major peered in through the dirty windows and saw two small girls lying in the back seat with their mother nervously stroking them and staring back at the Major.

"How long have they been like this?"

"About a day," both the man and woman answered simultaneously.

"Where are you headed?"

"We have family in Phoenix and we are trying to get there."

"I'm surprised you got this far, the roads are a mess and there are more than a few bad guys out there."

"Yeah, I know. Some of them took our water and most of our food. We were able to find more food, but not water."

"Okay, stay here and I'll be back," said the Major as he began retracing his steps to the SUV.

As he approached the SUV, the Major said loud enough for all to hear, "We have a situation that requires everyone's input. The man up there has a family with two small daughters and a wife that needs water. The girls are sick and they are trying to make it to Phoenix. Do we give them water? Do we ask them to come with us? This is a family decision and I know Dan is in charge, but this affects all of us."

"We can spare some water and we might need the extra help if we get attacked again. And anyway, I don't think they will make it to Phoenix," said Jan.

"I'm with Jan," said George, to no one's surprise.

"I don't object to them coming along, and the Hummer may actually come in handy," offered Tina matter of factly.

"The water is fine with me. I'm not excited about bring-ing them along. It involves more coordination and draws down on our food supplies considerably," injected Dan.

With the baby sucking on a bottle, nestled in her arms, Juanita said, "The more the merrier."

"Well I feel like Dan. Until we are safe and know what our exact environment is going to be, I don't like adding liabilities to our situation. I say give 'em water and that's it."

"I agree with the Major," said Shelly, startling just about everybody.

"Monica, what do you think?" inquired Shelly.

"I'd let em come with us. Plus we need more kids," and everybody laughed.

"This one time I have no problem with our democratic process. They get water and an offer to come. But in the future, if I feel something might jeopardize our survival, I will veto it. I told you at the beginning that was the way it was going to be and if you don't like it, leave!" said a sullen Dan to a shocked group.

"Major, I need to talk to you alone," indicated Dan as he motioned the Major to step down the road with him.

With their backs turned to the group, Dan looked straight down the road as he told the Major, "Don't ever put me in that situation again, Major. This is not a feel good, everybody gets a say situation. You know that."

"You're right, Dan. I apologize. I should have known better. It won't happen again."

"Good. Go ahead and give them some water. Not all they need, but some. If they want to come with us

342

they can, but make it perfectly clear they will take direction from us and will be called upon to defend the group. Don't tell them our final destination unless they sign on with us. We need to get moving, so let's make this happen now."

"I'll take care of it Dan."

The Major took a case of bottled water to the man and his family and offered them the chance to come along if they wanted. The man and his wife talked it over and politely declined. They thanked the Major profusely for the water and the woman said a quick prayer for everyone.

As the Major walked back to the SUV, the Hummer was already moving down the road. The Major simply shrugged his shoulders as he strode to the car and got in. Everyone felt a dread for them. How could they ever make it all the way to Phoenix with just two adults and a red Hummer that screams, 'take me'?

I Can See For Miles and Miles

The stress involved with being on the major highway in that part of the country was telling. Add the fact
that they were driving without the air-conditioning and
the occasional tirades by the otherwise mild baby and
everyone got just a little bit testy. Questions became
implications, answers took on tones and soon everyone
settled into a quiet desperation. When they finally exited
Interstate 8 at Ocotillo, Shelly actually perceived the aura
of the entire SUV change. They were all calmer and their
shoulders relaxed and soon the girls were singing a hit
song from weeks gone by.

Still in California, but with the miles rolling by, Ocotillo
came into view and it gave way to El Centro, which leads
them into the east side of Brawley. They stopped to siphon gas and check the vitals of the SUV and grab lunch.
All agreed the vehicle was running great, the baby was
well behaved, and they were indeed hungry. Juanita
handed the baby Abraham to Patrick with a smile and
asked the girls to help her with lunch. Tina volunteered
to keep her mind off Mike and soon a four star lunch

was ready. Beef jerky, Monterey jack cheese, a granola bar, some questionable oranges, and a Hershey candy bar rounded out the lunch. Warm beer for those adults interested and warm sodas for everyone else except Abraham, of course. After a guarded potty break for everyone, they mounted up and looked down a long, lonely road to nowhere.

They could literally see for miles and miles. Nothing but scrub grass and a few cacti here and there. Very inhospitable terrain. Dan relinquished his iron grip on the steering wheel and opted for a nap in the passenger seat. George took over the driving and in general seemed to be stepping up to his new responsibilities. Mike's death had affected everyone in different ways.

Mile after mile of sand dunes took the fun out of a clear road. This was not the place to break down. They had seen no cars, people, animals, and damn few plants in the last fifty miles. By the time they made it into Glamis, the sand dune capital of the United States, they were done for the day.

Glamis is little more than an intersection. Train tracks cross highway 78 or the Ben Hulse Highway and that's it! There is nothing there. God forbid you should want anything, anything at all. As the group hit the intersection, they all just looked at each other as Monica said, "You gotta be kidding." Dan directed George to find a place to pull off the highway without getting stuck in the sand. Everything was so open they couldn't help but feel vulnerable even though they hadn't even seen an abandoned car in hours.

Tonight they decided to risk a barbecue and have a hot meal to go along with the hot night. They were at roughly 300 feet above sea level through most of this area and the result was a horizon to horizon light show that none had ever witnessed before. More stars than they could even imagine began poking their heads out of the dark blue and winked their hello. The Milky Way was so bright it was literally obscuring the few celestial bodies they could most readily name. There was just no way possible they could find the usually malnourished and dim North Star. Orion was obliterated as were the Big and Little Dipper and the 'W,' known as Cassiopea. But it was still spectacular! Canned ham frying on the barbecue and the day cooling down accented the panorama. Still, it was brought home quickly how little they had traveled when Shelly said an evening prayer and asked for mercy on Mike's soul and the protection of the remaining family. Tina audibly moaned and tears filled nearly all eyes. Shelly stayed by Tina's side for the rest of the night.

Seeing Is Believing

They broke camp early in the morning while it was still quite cool. Meals on the road were becoming tiresome. The baby was in that wonderful stage and would sleep through the night, only waking once for a bottle. Juanita had become the mother absentee and that was fine with everyone. Abraham had a full head of black hair. Juanita had asked Shelly and Patrick if they had noticed the mother's ethnicity. Neither could remember except that she had had long black hair and appeared to be quite young, perhaps seventeen or so. Other than that, they had been moving pretty fast at the time and didn't give her much consideration after learning that she was dead.

Once loaded again and chugging down the barren road, Monica posed the age old question, "How much farther is it?"

Dan adjusting his butt in the high back seat, said, "It looks to be about 40 miles. With luck, we should be in Palo Verde in two hours at the most. Now we have to locate the bridge to the other side of the Colorado River. From the bridge I'd say it's about 3 miles to the area where we want to find a home."

From the back seat, the Major added, "Wonder what type of reception we will get."

"There aren't that many people still left there. Most of them died drinking the water. Those left are scared. They have been attacked," replied Shelly with her head leaning against the window and absently looking at the passing landscape as she stroked RutButt.

"You know all that?" queried Jan.

"Yes, and more. But it's not important stuff. We will find a place to stay easy enough."

With everyone now intrigued, Tina asked, "Did you know Mike was going to get killed?"

"No. I would have tried to do something if I'd of known."

Now the questions began to fly, "You seem able to predict what is going to happen. How far into the future can you see?"

"I don't really know, Mr. Achers. I seem to know things just when I need them. Like the boat, I knew a day in advance, and I knew something bad was coming when we were attacked, but I didn't know what and it was only hours before it happened. I knew the baby's name but only after I touched him, or maybe it was his mother, I don't remember."

"Can you read minds?" inquired Monica with a smile in her eyes.

"No. Of course not," said Shelly even though she had picked up a few thoughts from most of them. She didn't think it would be wise to tell them she was developing that skill. They might ostracize her. "I use to just get a feeling about something. The first time I went to the valley and found the space ship, it was a very strong feeling. Slowly it turned into little visions, like a mini cam in my mind. I wouldn't get to see much and sometimes, only a street sign and a blue light around a house, like when I told the Major where to find the SUV. But I have seen the farm houses we are going to live in. It was very clear. I will recognize them when I see them."

Dan had remained quiet during the questioning, but couldn't resist asking, "The blue house you mentioned; was it like an aura? Can you see auras around us?"

Shelly thought for a second and was trying to determine if telling them would hurt anyone's feelings. "Yes. I see colors around people. Sometimes they are dim and sometimes they change colors. It just depends."

"Do you know what the colors mean?" asked Juanita from the back.

"I can usually figure it out by the mood people are in. I don't know for sure, but so far I think dark or brown means people are scared. Pink means they are in love. Orange means in charge. Blue means they will get it done. There are a lot of colors that I don't have any idea about. I'm not even sure about the ones I told you."

Eventually everyone knew this question was coming, but only Monica was naive enough to ask it, "What are our colors?"

Shelly knew this was a question that could go wrong so she intended to tell them only a little of what she knew, "Well, the brightest color is Abraham's. His is a soft blue. I think he is very happy. Juanita's is pink. She is in love," Shelly knew that was a safe answer because she could be in love with either the baby or the Major, "And you Monica, you are very green. I think that is good. Not sure what it means, but it is very pretty. RutButt's kinda looks like dirt. I think it means he likes being outside. The rest of you have auras that change color and are not always bright," she lied.

"What's your color, Shelly?" probed George.

"I don't know. I've never tried to see it. Can any of you see it?"

No one replied.

"Oh well. It is fun, but who knows what it all means," ended Shelly.

"I'll tell ya one thing," said Jan, "it sure puts a new twist on the old saying, 'Seeing is believing.'"

Suddenly the SUV was filled with the smell of a toxic diaper. "Dan, please pull over and let get a new diaper on little Abe."

"Absolutely, Juanita. Wouldn't have it any other way," laughed Dan. "Why is it that the brand new plumbing of a baby can produce worse smells than a constipated sixty year old man eating pickled hard boiled eggs and refried beans while drinking beer all day long?"

"Ooooo," moaned everybody.

Last Leg

After the unplanned potty break, they picked up speed and forty minutes later saw Palo Verde come into view. Just outside of the city limits they passed a burning farm house. Strange, thought Dan. Fires shouldn't be starting this late in the game. Once inside the small town, they saw a few people scurrying from place to place. All carried a weapon of some type, but at least no one was shooting at them. This was a good sign. As they ran for cover, they gave the travelers furtive glances over their shoulders, and then they disappeared.

"Dan, didn't you say Palo Verde was on the wrong side of the Colorado and that we need to be on the east side?" questioned the Major with his arm around a sleeping Juanita holding a slumbering Abraham.

"That's right. When I mapped it on the internet, it showed a bridge off of 35th Avenue north of town. We should be coming to it soon. Then we just stay on it till we hit New Cibola Road and that should take us right across the bridge into the farming community where we want to be."

Finding 35th Avenue was no problem and the road leading to the bridge was easy enough. However, when they drew close to the bridge, they could see it had been blocked by several tractors and a combine. Without the keys or a bulldozer, they wouldn't be crossing that bridge any time soon.

"Humph," was all Dan grunted as he brought the SUV to a stop some fifty yards shy of the bridge.

"Major, slide on up here and take a look. We have a problem."

"Good job, whoever did it. Even with the keys it would take you half an hour to back them out of there the way they parked them. Honk your horn a few times, Dan. Let's see if anyone wants to come and talk to us."

In the late morning heat, the horns blast seemed loud enough, but twenty minutes later no one had appeared at the other end of the bridge.

"I suppose we could hot wire em and get them out of there," suggested Dan.

"Sure, and we could be shot at from a hundred different locations. I think one of us is going to have to go into that group of buildings and see if we can parlay." With that the Major began grabbing gear for the trip.

"Not, you Major. This job is for me," said Dan. "If we intend to trade passage for something of ours, I need to do the trading. Remember, logistics is my game and procurement is the first step."

"Fine, hot shot. Just don't get your ass shot off. Keep a radio with you and keep the talk key taped down so we can hear what's going on. Hide it in your backpack. Take a pistol, but keep it holstered. I'll make you a white flag. Oh, and have ten bottled waters with you. That may get their attention. I'll make sure we are well defended on this end. Let them know that if you don't return, we're coming in."

"No sweat, Major. This is just business, nothing personal. I should be fine."

Dan readied himself and looked like a weekend hiker with his high boots, backpack, and floppy white desert hat. He set off by waving the white flag as George honked the horn repeatedly. If there were people in there, they had to hear it. Just before he left, Shelly inched her way up to her father and said, "Break a leg."

"What a weird thing to say, girl."

"Isn't that what actors say for good luck?"

"Yes it is. Oh I get it. You think I'm going to have to do some acting out there, huh?"

"Isn't that what people do when they start bargaining?"

"I guess you're right. Then break a leg it is." He kissed her on the top of her head and walked toward the bridge. He made his way gingerly across the bridge, weaving and ducking through the machines. On the other side, he stood and waved the flag attached to six foot stick for about a minute solid before starting down the road that lead into the row of streets with farms dotting them. It looked like a subdivision of farms. Each house, barn, and outbuilding was placed on roughly three acres. About the size of three football fields. There had to be thirty or so farms in all, situated along four streets with a number of intersections. He had never seen anything quite like it. As he approached the first street, Baseline, he turned toward the river and began walking in. A single shot rang out and he froze.

"That's far enough. You need to turn around and get out of here."

"Mister, we have run from fires, been shot at, attacked by dogs and assaulted by a small Mexican army. We didn't come this far to turn around and leave. We come in peace and we can offer you help and security for your community. We know how to survive. I compliment you on your blockade on the bridge. Very creative. In addition, we have information about the plague, we know how to beat it, and we have bottled water for you."

Back at the bridge they were hearing Dan's part of the conversation. "Whoever is in the house, they are most interested in the fight with the Mexicans and that we know how to survive," said Shelly.

"Do you know which house they are in?"

"Yes, Major, the one with the green roof and the red barn to the left of it."

George picked up the hunting rifle with the scope on it and began looking for whoever was in the house.

"Put that rifle down now!" yelled the Major. "We don't want them thinking we are taking pot shots at them. Here, use my binoculars."

"Sorry, Major. I wasn't thinking."

Dan eased the white flag to ground and dropped it. "Mister, I'd like to talk with you face to face."

"Stranger, keep in mind I have 30.06 rifle aimed at your chest. It will go through a bullet proof vest. Do you have some water with you?"

"Yes. I have ten bottles."

"Okay. Line em up in front of you on the ground."

Dan slid his backpack off and pulled the bottles out and lined them up.

"Now, take the third from your right, open it up and take a drink."

Dan did as ordered and after a two big gulps he said, "Don't trust me?"

"Stranger, a lot of good people have died trusting folks just like you. Now step back fifty feet while I send somebody out to collect those bottles."

As Dan backed down the road, a young man jogged out to the road and collected the bottles and returned to the farm house.

"Can I talk with you face to face now?"

"Leave your backpack, keep your hands over your head with your fingers locked and start walking to where you saw the man run with the bottles."

Ten minutes later, Dan was ordered to stop in front of a well cared for house with a wraparound porch. Upstairs from an open window, a rifle barrel poked out and aimed at Dan. As the front door opened, out stepped an older gentleman with an old colt 45 pistol in his hand. Staying in the shade of the porch, he said, "What do you want?" with no sign of emotion in his voice. He never let his eyes stray from Dan's and he stood with his feet spread slightly so he could swing the big pistol up and fire if necessary.

"There are nine of us and, as I said, we have come a long ways and suffered a lot of hardships to get here. I did enough research about this plague to understand that Cibola is one of the safest places to be if you want to live through this disaster. We came equipped to survive. We can sterilize the water, and that seems to be the number one concern of everybody. There is an unlimited supply coming from the river and it rarely rains here. We are armed to the teeth. We can help protect this community. We are very resourceful and bring a lot of skills with us. We want to live here. We want to be your neighbor. It's that simple and it's a hell of deal for you."

With a smirk on his face the gentleman said, "Why is it a deal to have more mouths to feed?"

"First of all, we will feed ourselves and help you obtain more food. Secondly, we know how to fight. Two of us are military trained and we are well equipped. Third, if it still exists, we have contacts in the government. It could come in very handy in the future. And lastly, we are honest, hardworking, God fearing people. You'll be lucky to have us."

"Are you done with your pretty speech?"

Dan thought for a moment about threatening him if they were turned away, but that kinda ruined the honest, God fearing part so he just said, "Yes."

"Stranger, I am not the only voice on this matter and if you didn't know it, there are many guns pointed at you right now. We knew you were coming before you got to the bridge. We will have to have a council with all three hundred and twenty seven of us to determine if you get to come in or not. Now get back across the bridge and I will get word to you tomorrow. I suggest you move your car. That's definitely not a safe place to park. Be back tomorrow at 8:00 AM and we will talk."

"Thank you," replied Dan as he turned and walked back to the backpack, shouldered it and returned to the SUV.

As the stranger left, the man in charge told the young man, "Get the council over here ASAP. Tell them we have more visitors and need a decision. If they want to vote without hearing the facts, tell 'em that they can make water and know how to fight."

When Dan crossed the bridge he told them, "They said it's not safe to camp here. Let's move now. They want me to come back in the morning. I'll tell you all about it as we find a better place to camp."

Home Sweet Home

Home is a word with many meanings. In the navy, men begin calling their ship home. During a war, home can be an entire country. For this small tribe, home was simply a safe place to live without fear from the plague or anyone bent on killing you.

Morning came suddenly. When the sun hits the horizon and no trees or buildings are around to hinder its approach, the effect is immediate and sometimes blinding. If you're lucky, you get a little reprieve while the sky lights up a gorgeous pink and then, BAM, the first rays of sun assault you head on. Bright, strong, and bearing heat. It can be a blessing in the winter months and pure hell in the summer. Today was pretty nice.

A rifle shot alerted the waiting travelers that the town folk were ready to meet. They were an hour ahead of schedule and that was fine with Dan. As before, he donned his backpack with the radio talk button taped down, the Glock at the bottom of the pack between two towels and only two bottles of water this time. He grabbed his white flag and made his way to the appointment. He had only been more nervous twice in his life: once at his wedding, and while waiting for Shelly's head to crown in the delivery room. Dan stopped on the road as before and waited.

"Come on up to the house, stranger, but no tricks."

Dan walked up to the porch and again the gentleman from yesterday waited for him, pistol drawn.

"Hate to see you waste bullets like that. I thought we said 8:00 AM," greeted Dan.

"We don't waste anything here and we have our own gunsmith so reloads are no big deal. Just didn't want to waste a perfectly good morning when I could be working. I have some people that want to meet you. Josh, frisk him and take his pack." The same young man from yesterday came down the steps, took Dan's backpack and gave him a very thorough frisk. "He's clean grandpa."

"Okay. Come on in. My name is Glen, what's yours?"

"I'm Dan. Dan Brown from Tillamook, Oregon."

Dan stepped into a large parlor with a massive oak table with seven people sitting around it, two women and five men, ages ranging from twenty fiveish to 70+. Clean, but hard looking people. Nobody overweight. No one smoked or drank anything and it was already getting hot out.

"Dan Brown, this is our town council. I'm not going to bother to introduce you to everyone; that's not important. What is important is your answers to the questions we're about to pose to you. Take your time and don't try to bullshit us. We may look like country hicks to you, but we have a world of experience in this room and can smell bullshit a mile away. Got it?"

"Yes, sir. Fire away."

The questions rained down on Dan from every person. It seemed to be a well choreographed interrogation because no two questions in a row dealt with the same topic. Different people asked follow-up questions on different topics. The bottom line was clear to Dan, however. What skills would they be adding to the community, how had they out gunned the Mexicans, and most importantly, how could they purify the water?

Dan emphasized the military training and fighting abilities of the group. He singled out the Major for his military tactical strategy and himself for planning, organization and follow-through. He stressed the overall youth of the family, the hard work ethic, and of course mentioned the women and children. Next, he gave a rough outline of the key supplies they possessed: the arms and ammunition, the solar panel and generator, about a month's worth of foodstuffs, and some valuable trading currency. Lastly, and most importantly, he told them about the two Berkefeld water filters. He gave a brief description of how they work and told them that they have been using them for about two weeks already. "And I will tell you point blank that the Major doesn't want me to detail all of the supplies to you that I just have. However, I believe in laying the cards on the table. I am betting my honesty is worth something to you folks."

Glen rose from his chair and primed, "Any more questions?" Everyone, even Dan, seemed satisfied. "Mr. Brown, please wait out by your backpack and remember, no funny stuff."

The council debate was short. They believed Dan. It was they that had lied about their overall manpower strength. Instead of being 300 strong, the actual population of Cibola had shrunk from 172 pre-plague to just 47. They needed help. They desperately needed water and interjecting youth and military expertise into the equation did nothing but sugar the equation. They voted unanimously to allow the new people into the compound.

They called Dan back into the house and gave him the news, "We would be happy to have you in our community. But we want to reiterate that the council has final authority on issues and you are expected to pull your own weight here and aid your neighbors when needed."

"Thank you. You will not regret this decision. I do have one request. I would like to be on the council. You will find we are very energetic and full of ideas. We could best express those ideas with direct input to the council."

After some spirited debate between the council members, it was decided that a thirty day waiting period was appropriate before voting anyone onto the council. After the adjustment period, they would take up his request again.

"Now, let's get your people to this side of the bridge. Josh and I will move the equipment and get you settled into a house. You said you have nine people in your group?" solicited Glen.

"Yes, but if you have more than one house available, we actually could use three separate houses preferably somewhat close together."

"There are a number of homes available. Shouldn't be a problem. Come with me and let's bring them across."

Neighbors

It took an agonizing hour to move the vehicles off of the bridge to allow the SUV and trailer to pass across and replace the equipment on the bridge. The Major noticed that the distributor coil wire was removed along with the keys on all the equipment. They weren't going to be moved without a tremendous effort. During the process, four riflemen accompanied Glen and Dan to the bridge and flanked out on both sides of the bridge. They kept constant watch for something or someone.

The Major moved over to one of the men and asked, "What are you guarding against?"

"The Riders."

"What Riders?"

"Well, we were surprised you didn't mention them to the council or see them on your way into town. They were in Palo Verde about two days ago. A gang of about twenty five motorcycle gangsters. There could be more. We have never gotten a good count. They scream into town, rape, kill, steal, burn and leave. We have had several fights with them. They have killed eleven of us. We spend as much time worrying about them as anything else."

"Thanks. My name is Patrick. What's yours?"

"I'm Kevin. Nice to meet you."

With the bridge secured again and the family loaded into the SUV again, Glen directed them to four or five potential houses that they could take over.

With the driver's window rolled down, Glen told the group, "Once you get settled, I'll come on over tomorrow and give you the lay of the land and set up a meeting for the rest of the town to meet you. We will also be giving you some responsibilities and guard schedules. Dan, you may be able to help us coordinate some of our efforts in this area. Do not go down to the river. We have had some sniper activity and lost a couple of folks that way. If you need anything in the meantime, come and see me. Oh, and keep your guns near you at all times. We may not have rain, but we have enough bad guys to go around. If you hear an air raid siren, get your kids to safety and come running to the Town Hall. It's at the end of Baseline Road."

"Where will you be holding the town meeting tomorrow?" asked Dan.

"At the Town Hall. It's the only building big enough for these events. We may want you to give some idea of what the world is like out there and any information you have from the government and the plague in general," replied Glen.

"Will all 300 people be there?"

"Dan, there are only 47 of us. I lied in case we rejected you and Riders got hold of you. We want them to think we are stronger than we are."

"Thought so. The Major told me about the Riders. One of your men filled him in. I would have done the same thing."

"Okay, I'll let you get settled. Good to have you here," he said as he backed away from the car and smiled, waving, he slowly pulled away.

The new arrivals had drawn people from their homes and they congregated in small groups of three and four and watched as the SUV drove down the dusty street looking for the houses Glen had pointed out to them.

Procrastination was never something Dan did. At times it could be a luxury, but to Dan it was a total waste of time. "We really haven't talked about who will live where, but we need to think about it now. Depending upon how big the home is, more than one family could live together. Any comments?"

"We would like our own home," insisted Jan. "Obviously we want to be close to all of you."

"Of course, Jan."

Then the bomb shell hit. "Juanita, Abraham and I would like our own house as well," said the Major from the back seat. Juanita laid her head on the Majors shoulder and he hugged her gently. "We have talked about this for several days and intend to get married when we can," added the Major.

"Well congratulations! That's wonderful news," said Dan with a big grin. Congratulations rang out in the car and everyone seemed sincerely happy for them.

"Wow. After that bit of fascinating news, that's two homes. I would like to have Tina move in with Shelly and me for the time being. Tina, with all you have been through I don't want you living by yourself. Shelly and I could sure use your company and help. I should have talked to you about this alone and not in front of everyone, but it just worked out this way. I hope you'll say yes."

"Wow Dad, I didn't see that one coming. Did you, Tina?"

With her voice quivering, Tina replied, "No, Shelly, but it is a very nice surprise. I would love to temporarily move in with you. Thank you, Dan."

"Good. Looks like that makes it an even three people per house. That should make it easy. We have these five houses from here to over there to look at. Don't forget your outbuildings when you do your walk through. Let's meet back at this house in an hour or so. Plus, we need to eat lunch pretty soon. We are going to start right here at this house. See ya soon," said Dan as he pulled into the driveway of the first house. "I'll leave the keys. Take the SUV if you want."

New House Smell

The house hunting had gone extremely well. Only the Achers had to look at more than one house to find one they could be comfortable in. In a house, you literally live with the structure. You become as accustomed to it as it does to you. You know its strengths and weaknesses, it's hot and cold spots, and what makes it sparkle. Holidays can transform much like makeup and women, a rather plain Jane home into a rare beauty. A few Christmas lights or a pumpkin on the front steps allows the house the chance to breathe fresh thoughts. New tenants have the same affect on structures. It might be mice, a new nest of Robins, or a family with three kids; all impact homes in their own special way.

The homes they chose were close together, all two story affairs with lots of space, stairs, basements, and attics. The floor plans weren't that different and all suspected that the same contractor had built each of them. They were functional and stylish in a laid back sort of fashion. George, who was better at this sort of thing, estimated the homes to be no more than twenty years old.

As agreed, the group met at Dan's when they had settled on their properties. The homes were dirty to be sure, but no dead people were slumped against walls or covered up in beds. The community had cleaned up all vacant buildings rather nicely. They were doing their best to avoid disease. Even the refrigerators had been emptied, unplugged and opened to air out. Utilities had been disconnected and windows and doors closed. The homes seemed to have a particular smell to them. Not clean or sanitary, and certainly not a new house smell, but distinct nonetheless. Kind of a 'no one lives here now, but they use to' smell. No food could be found, and clothes, blankets, towels and reusable's had been removed. They would pick those up tomorrow. George had mentioned a central store house for those types of items. The community seemed to be very socialistic in that sense. For now they unloaded the SUV and the trailer, making sure that everyone had an equal share. The barbecue, solar powered generator, and gold bars stayed with Dan. The guns were distributed in a less even fashion, but everyone, even the girls, had guns.

Dan requested everyone to take a seat and he started by saying, "I promised to get you here and with your help we did. I had no idea it would be as hard and as danger-ous as it was. We lost Mike coming here. Let's make sure we remember that, if we ever feel like giving up. He didn't and we need to honor that.

371

Now, just because we are in Cibola doesn't mean our worries are over. We will need to continue to be resourceful. I urge you to do your part for the community, but always remember we are a family. Make sure we take care of each other. Let's go to the town hall meeting, tell our story and see if we can get a feel for how organized and safe this place is."

The Major interjected, "I can guarantee you this town is not safe. Granted, we have a bridge blocked and several men with rifles guarding the obvious access to this place, but if someone wants to get in here bad enough, they can. The river can be crossed. The entire southern and eastern side of town is open to whoever and whatever is out there. Don't wander off. Stay together in groups of at least two. Let's all keep our eyes and ears open and learn as much as we can about the people here and their idea of survival." As the Major concluded, the tone of the meeting had taken a decisively negative turn.

Direct and to the point, Monica asked, "If it's not safe, why did we come here?"

"The rain, dear. And I don't mean Rudolph," answered George as everyone laughed. "People can be bad news, honey, but the rain just doesn't care who it kills or how often. I doubt it rains here more than five or six times a year," continued Monica's Dad.

"Back to safety, everyone," insisted the Major. "Plan escape routes from your house to nearby buildings. Know where you are going and who is responsible for what. Protect the water filters; they are the most valuable thing we have. Hide spare guns around the house and in the out buildings. You never know when you might need one. Stay vigilant. Never let your guard down. You will probably hear more of this at the meeting tomorrow. Any questions?"

Everyone was a little overwhelmed with the situation to know what to ask. Instead, Tina volunteered, "How about I make us a meal and we can get back to unpacking and getting settled?"

"Best idea so far. Can I help?" inquired Dan.

"Just as long as I cook," smiled Tina.

Even though they had all moved in and established their own residences, the herd instinct remained strong. After separate evening meals, once again they gathered at Dan's house for the comfort of the group. They could hear others around the town and felt more secure than they had been in long time. Finally, the Major suggested they all get some sleep and meet again after breakfast and walk over together to the town hall building.

"Please, try not to give any of the town's people any reason to question why we were allowed in. Be yourself, but tone it down a notch for the introductions," instructed Dan.

Town Hall Bash

At three AM, Dan heard noises coming from down-stairs. All of the bedrooms were upstairs and Shelly, Tina and Dan each had their own. He slid his Glock out of its holster hung over the headboard and eased himself out of the room. He had waited at the top of the stairs until his eyes fully adjusted to the light, and then agilely navigated the stairs, prone to squeaking. He found his daughter sitting on the couch with her knees drawn up under her. She was slowly rocking, holding her pistol and talking to herself. She seemed to be arguing, but with whom?

Surveying the rest of the room and confident that Shelly was alone, Dan softly said, "Shelly, are you alright?"

Shelly jumped at the sound of her father's voice. "Oh, Dad you scared me! Yeah, I'm fine. No one. I wasn't talking to anybody."

Dan moved over to Shelly and gently lifted the gun from her hands, "I didn't ask you who you were talking to."

"True, but you were gonna."

"Are you reading my mind? If so, please don't."

"Sorry Dad, it was just so obvious."

"What are you doing down here and why do have the gun?"

Thinking quickly, Shelly stood and started to head toward the stairs, "Oh I couldn't sleep and the Major said to always have your gun with you, so I did."

Dan felt there was something more but didn't want to push it. Everyone had been under a lot of stress and this wasn't the time. "Okay, get back to bed. Here, take your gun and keep the safety on. Love ya."

"I love you too, Dad. I really do," added Shelly.

Dan watched his little girl, who had grown up so much in the past few days, climb the stairs and stop at the top. Turning back to her father, Shelly asked, "Are you coming?"

"Sure. In a minute. I want to look around outside first." It was just an excuse to give Dan a few more minutes to try and figure out what his daughter was really up to. As he stepped out onto the porch, he saw a yellow ball of light bobbing across the empty lot behind them and towards the river. 'Here we go again', he mumbled to himself.

ЖОЖ

Morning forced itself through the upstairs windows with the tact of a drunken uncle. The flash of the brilliant rays careened around the east facing rooms and it was followed by a bang as RutButt jumped up on the counter and knocked a pot onto the kitchen floor. He was hungry and in search of anything remotely edible. Even an insect would suffice.

Breakfast was a quiet affair. Shelly was already up and tending her kitten when Tina and Dan almost collided in the upstairs hall as they headed for the stairs.

"How'd you sleep Tina?"

"Not well," said Tina with tears welling up in her eyes, "I'm not use to sleeping alone. It's a strange feeling."

"I know. When Lisa died, I don't think I slept soundly for several months. I use to wake up and hear her in the house. Or smell her scent in the halls. It's a hard thing to get use to."

"You never really think that someone so close to you can die, do you?"

Dan shaking his head no and trying not to make eye contact for too long said, "You know it's possible, but it's always something that happens to someone else. The finality, that's what is so damn unsettling."

"Well, let's focus on now and not yesterday," suggested Tina. "Hope Shelly has breakfast ready."

"Only if you're a cat," laughed Dan.

Glen, as promised, had joined them just as they were finishing up the breakfast dishes. By now the entire group was assembled and ready to head over to the town hall. Before leaving, Glen told them a little about the community and some of the troubles they had been through: the raids by the Riders, the deaths from the water, the gun fights, a few suicides, their constant battle to find food and water and, how isolated the town felt. He felt they could bring some hope to the community. He also clued them into the fact that there were the normal power struggles whenever you have three or more people gathered. He left them with the feeling that this was a good place and that everyone wanted their addition to the town to be beneficial. Everyone again thanked him for letting the tribe in. Then, the group trudged the two blocks to the Town Hall and shared stories about their houses on the way.

Small talk has its place and purpose. All were a little nervous and not sure what to expect. It was an odd sight as they approached the building. People were trailing in from all points of the compass. Everyone seemed to be carrying a weapon and polite hellos were being exchanged. Shelly and Monica were walking hand in hand, and excited to see a smattering of children coming to the event. There were even some boys about their age. Shelly and Monica exchanged glances and knowing smiles.

Inside the building Glen suggested, "Why don't we have your group come up front for a brief introduction and then you can give us a summary of your experience. Be prepared for questions, because I can assure you there will be plenty."

Glen had the family sit in the front row and waited about five more minutes until everyone except the sentries were present.

He began by saying, "Good morning." The group echoed Good Morning in return. "The meeting today has several purposes. First, we want to introduce our new town members, second, we would hope they can tell us of their experience and knowledge of the outside world, and third, we will post new duties for everyone and discuss major issues. Dan and the Major exchanged glances that said, this Glen is a pretty smooth operator'.

At that point, Glen asked Dan to introduce each of the family and requested that they tell a little bit about themselves. Dan directed each one of the group to stand individually as he introduced them to the meeting. He would say a few flattering things about the person and give each one a chance to add a few tidbits. It went well. Dan could see by the facial expressions of the audience that everyone seemed to sense this was a good thing. Next, both Dan and the Major, introduced as Patrick, gave a brief overview of the world as they knew it. Dan talked about the decline in Tillamook, and the travel to Cibola. Patrick, referencing his military connections, told them about Washington's involvement and how there really was a light at the end of this very long, very dark tunnel. Questions were shouted out and both did their best to answer, not always with what they wanted to hear. It was a good exchange, but it was becoming clear who the real thinkers in this town were. A great deal of interest was paid to the baby and the fact that a cat had been brought into the town. As promised when the Q & A finished, the hot topics were brought up.

"First and foremost, I want to emphasize that our new-comers have brought with them a most valuable device. They have a water filter that can purify our own river water so we can drink it!" A sustained murmur rolled through the audience.

Glen motioned to Dan to rise and explain. When Dan had finished, some people were literally crying. He went on, "Don't think for a minute that we can process unlimited water. We can't. But we can make enough for rationed drinking needs. We will have to work on making one for large quantities that we can use to grow crops."

Then it happened. Shelly rose and raised her hand and Glen called on her. "Yes, Shelly isn't it? Do you have an issue?"

"Yes. We will be attacked by the bikers tonight."

Shouts and the sound of people pushing their metal folding chairs back so they could stand up, could be heard all over the hall. "What the hell is she talking about?" was shouted out from the back and more than one person was clearly very upset with her comment. "Everyone calm down. Sit back down. Now Shelly, we don't fool around with that kind of talk. Do you understand?" scolded Glen.

"Of course I do. But you better get ready cause they are coming."

"Well if they do come, we are ready for them. And besides, how would you know?"

"Mr. Glen. I see things. And you aren't ready. Most of them will cross the river south of town, while only a few go to the bridge. They are trying to fool you."

Glen glared at Dan and said, "Dan, this is absurd. Get your girl under control or get her out of here. This is exactly what we don't need."

"Excuse me, Excuse me," shouted the Major waiting for the noise to subside. "You good folks need to understand something. This little girl has a gift. She has saved our butts more than once. I don't know how it works or why. But I know this: if she says something, you better pay attention. I surveyed your town yesterday as I walked around. I can tell you from a military standpoint that what she described is exactly how I would attack this town. The action at the bridge will be a diversion meant to draw your firepower away from the real point of attack. I recommend we all start getting ready."

"Why on earth would we get all excited about one little girl's blabbering," shouted a woman with her arms folded defiantly.

Shelly faced the woman and said, "Lady, your foot isn't going to get better. It's broken and you need to get it fixed." The lady's mouth dropped open as all realized she had hit a nerve. "You in the red ball cap. You're going to have a baby. It's growing in you now. You've been sick for three mornings in a row. And Mr. Glen, you don't have to worry about your wife, she has an ulcer and will get better if you treat it like an ulcer. It's not cancer. And I can tell you that three members of this town were killed by you people because you didn't trust them. It was a hard thing to do, but you were right. They were going to help the bikers."

With the room now utterly quiet, Dan stood and faced the town folk, "This is a gift my daughter has. I pray you will listen to her. Ask any of us and you will get the same answer; she knows what she is talking about. And even if for some reason she is wrong, what's it going to hurt to prepare for an attack? Obviously, sooner or later some trouble in some shape or form is going to come at us from the south, the east or across the river. How are we going respond? Let's start by preparing today."

The Major and Dan sat down. Dan patted Shelly's hand and leaned over and kissed her head.

"I move we adjourn this meeting and call a meeting of the town council immediately. Dan and Patrick, please stay. We will hold it right here, right now."

Preparations

With the town council convened, Glen had already put into motion checking the girl's statements. So far, they were all correct. The pregnancy wasn't actually confirmed, although Julie had been sick for the last three mornings and more than one person in town thought Karen had a broken foot, but how could the girl have known that without even meeting her? It seemed the girl did have some supernatural skills. Glen was actually relieved that a different diagnosis of his wife's condition had been offered up. No one knew what was wrong with her. More than likely, all of the plague events had naturally given her more than enough to worry about and the ulcer or ulcers had formed.

"I have to admit the girl seems to know what she is talking about," started Glen with a sizable frown on his face. "But Dan, you have to assure me that she won't blurt out things like that again. People here are plenty scared as it is and we don't need some kid stirring up the pot. If she has revelations, dreams, whatever you want to call 'em, you bring her to me and I'll decide when and who we tell. Got it?"

"Of course. This was the first I had heard of this or I would have taken you aside and told you. Not sure if you would have believed me if she hadn't put on that show for everyone, though."

"Yeah, it is hard to believe. But enough of that. Let's be proactive and assume the Riders aim to attack us. How best to fend them off?"

"Trap em, kill em, and go to their nest and make sure it doesn't happen again," offered the Major.

"Do you have specific plans to do that, Patrick?"

"You bet I do. Can I use the blackboard and lay it out for you?"

"Have at it."

"Good. Before I do that, let me make sure what our resources are. I took a head count of the able bodied people and had come up with eleven men, seventeen women, and possibly four children that could be counted on in a firefight. I came up with fifteen that probably cannot defend themselves. Am I close?"

"Actually, you forgot the men on guard. We always have a minimum of two on watch with radio communications. So, not counting your people, we have thirty five people that can fire a weapon. Thirteen men, seventeen women and five children," reported Stan, the man in charge of the militia.

"Okay, you can add three men and three women to the roster," replied Patrick. "We can move the others to a centralized spot and add our two girls to the mix to help watch those that cannot defend themselves. If we all agree, I'll show you how I'd defend an attack."

An hour and a half later, the board members broke up the meeting. Comfortable in their upcoming roles, they headed for the doors and their teammates. The town was divided up into small groups of people headed by one of the seven council members. Each member was responsible for roughly seven people and any and all the issues they might have. Because of the situation, the thirty day waiting period had been unanimously waived, Dan was now on the board. He would assume responsibility for his nine charges. All of the board members gathered their groups together and began explaining what role they would take in the upcoming battle.

Fortifications

The attack would take place in the early morning hours around three in the morning per Shelly. She didn't have an exact count, but thought it was around twenty people. Some women and young men would also be involved. Patrick had surveyed the board members and determined that there were at least seven excellent shots in town. The two best were directed to meet him in the make shift armory as soon as possible. Glen and Stan escorted Dave and Tom into the potato cellar and found the Major already reviewing the weapons.

"Patrick, I'd like to introduce our two best rifle marksmen, Dave and Tom."

"Nice to meet you men. Stan has told me a lot about your abilities. What I want to know is, are you a good sniper?"

Both men nodded yes and Tom said, "I've been hunting deer and elk most of my life, sir. That is all about sniping. I can hit a deer at four hundred yards every time."

"And you Dave, are you just as good?"

"Maybe not four hundred yards, but then, I don't use a scope."

"Good. You two will do nicely. Here is what I want you to do. We are setting up an ambush and we need someone to pick off the leaders and anyone that tries to escape. We will make sure you have scoped rifle, but the catch is you need to be behind enemy lines."

"Behind enemy lines?"

"That's right. I want Tom to be on the other side of the river in that burned out house we passed coming into town."

Tom, clearly interested, asked, "Why there?"

"Because who would think to look for a sniper in burned up house? Dave, I want you on the other side of the bridge, dug in chest high, in a fox-hole with a tarp over you behind some scrub bushes. You'll be able to shoot, duck down and wait a minute and surface again and pop somebody else. How's it sound men? Are you up for it? Can you do it?"

Again, both men nodded yes and it was a done deal. The Major spent the next half hour making sure each man had a good rifle, plenty of ammo, and knew where to hide themselves.

"You both need to be in position by midnight. Dave, you need to dig your hole, so you better start early. Take along someone to help with the hole and then send them back. Take some water and food with you. Neither of you should start firing until the battle breaks out. If you do, you will spook them. We want the boats to get to the other side of the river before we open fire. Do not, I repeat, do not open fire until you hear our shots. Oh, and do not show any mercy. Don't let anyone escape. We may want to go back to their base dressed as them. Any questions?"

Both men just looked at the Major in disbelief as they realized they had signed up for a mighty dangerous duty. Nevertheless, they were up to it.

With the snipers picked and briefed, the Major focused on the ambush itself. He gathered the six leaders of the ambush squad and filled them in on their roles. "We are betting that the boats will cross south of the bonfire we will be lighting. They will want to avoid the light and the sentry we will plant there. That means they will land just south of the old grey barn on the edge of town. Team 1 will be north up the river about two hundred yards; call it twelve on a clock. Team 2 will be at two o'clock, the same distance out. Team 3 will be at three o'clock and team 4 will be at four o'clock. Nobody, and make sure your team knows this, nobody fires until I fire. I will let them get as close as I can. Team 1 and 4 will make sure nobody makes it back across the river. Team 2 and 3 will focus on those on this side of the river. If they manage to run for the barn, don't worry. We will have dynamite waiting for them when they get inside. A sniper on the other side of the river will be shooting at their leaders while all of this is going on. I expect the fire fight to last about twenty minutes' tops. Questions so far?"

"Where will you be during all of this?"

"I will be with Team 4, my original family, but I will be in touch with each of you via walkie-talkies. Make sure you designate who is next in charge of your group should you get hit. Encourage your team. Talk to them during the fight. Direct fire. Be a leader."

"Now, Teams 5 and 6 will be at the bridge. I want you set up in classic crossfire positions. You will have your own sniper on the other side of the bridge, shooting away from your areas. He is directed to take out their leaders and anyone trying to escape. Again, wait for the firefight to start at the river, unless you are fired on. Okay, if there are no other questions, have your teams in place by midnight. No talking or walking around. If someone has to go to the bathroom, they do it right where they are. Have food and water available. Remember, no talking. Water carries sound very well. When the battle is over we intend to go back to their camp and surprise them, so stay available. Good luck everyone."

Anticipation

Remember the feeling you got looking at a Christmas tree with presents already wrapped and waiting for you, but you still had three days before you could open them? Or, how about being parked in your car, waiting to make the move and kiss your date? And of course, there is always the wait as the nurse readies the needle to give you a shot. Anticipation takes on many forms in our lives. Waiting to kill or be killed is one thing most people never have to go through. At this precise time, thirty plus people, not counting the Riders, were mulling over how the night would go. Would they live, would they kill, would they run? How would they handle the news if one of their loved ones died? Would there be hand-to-hand fighting? Could they really shoot someone if they looked them in the eye? Carol King's song "Anticipation" really only scratched the surface of possibilities.

With everyone in place and three o'clock fast approaching, all eyes and ears were on the water. The Riders, if they were coming tonight, were being very well directed. No motorcycle sounds or any sound at all could be heard. Then, an isolated and quickly extinguished match flamed into view. A cigarette glow could be seen shortly after and then a muttered growl as it was unceremoniously snuffed out. The Riders must have parked their bikes further down the road than planned and hiked in. Very professional of them. Now they could be seen slipping five black rafts into the river. People were loaded along with weapons as they shoved off for the other side, paddling as quietly as they could. Three people stayed behind; one was obviously in charge and the other two were there for his protection.

A well choreographed dance requires many elements working in coordination. As the last of the five low profile rafts slipped into the Colorado River, shots rang out on the other side of town by the bridge. Immediately the Major's walkie-talkie chirped. "Major, we are being fire on!"

"Don't panic! This is what we expected. Have two and only two of your men return fire. We don't want them to know there are more of you there. Hopefully our sniper will wait until he hears us firing. When you hear us shooting, get everyone involved," coached the Major.

When the last raft entered mid-stream, the Major gave the order to fire. He had directed his teams to focus initially on the first and last raft, knowing that immobilizing them would cause obstacles for the others going forward or backwards. The river aided the aim of the townsfolk by giving them feedback on their aim. The water around the rafts exploded with the missed shots. Zeroing in on the floating targets was literally like shooting fish in a barrel. The hail of bullets shredded the boats and soon those not shot were struggling not to drown. The sniper joined in the action along the river and took out the leader of the group and one guard before the remaining Rider knew what was going on. He immediately threw himself on the ground and started crawling away from the river bank. The sniper followed orders to the letter and took no pity on the man. He riddled him with shots until the man stopped moving.

At the first sound of the firing south of town, the teams stationed on the bridge opened up on the diversionary group of Riders. Because they weren't floating on the river, the killing took considerably longer, and fifteen minutes later, shots could still be heard. Again, the sniper was very effective and produced considerable chaos among the Riders. Eventually, four remaining Riders dropped their weapons and surrendered to the town. "Major, we are done on the bridge now. We have four captives and we are collecting the guns and ammo from the dead now. We lost one man and have two wounded."

"Good work! Bring the prisoners to the town hall now. I want to interrogate them immediately. Get medical help for the wounded and inform the dead person's family ASAP."

"How did it go on your end?"

"We got 'em all. No survivors. About twenty of 'em. Now we have to go get the nest. I have only one wounded on this end. Nothing serious. See ya soon, over," signed out the Major.

Interrogation

Dan joined the Major at the town hall as they waited for the four captives to arrive. "I almost wish we didn't have any prisoners."

"I know what you mean, Major. What in the world are we going to do with them? We can't let them go. I'm not sure the town wants to execute them. And I doubt they are the rehabilitation type."

"Should have shot 'em where they stood. That's the best lesson we could have given everybody," said the Major as he heard the commotion of the four Riders arriving.

The four tough looking men in stereotypical biker gear, leathers, chains and railroad boots, had their hands tied behind their backs and were linked with a rope tied around each of their necks. Several of the men and women from the town were beating on the bound men as they were led through the hall towards a conference room in the back. The town wanted blood for all the murders and constant harassment they had been enduring for the past two months.

"Bring them in here," directed the Major, as he pointed to chairs indicating where he wanted them placed. For just having surrendered and seeing several of their co-horts killed, the four were displaying a significant amount of bravado and attitude. The Major aimed to quickly tame that beast.

The Major had set up the four chairs in a small circle facing each other so that all four men could see what was happening to one another. "Gentlemen," said the Major as he stood over the four and gained their atten-tion, "here is how it's going to work. You will answer my questions or I will shoot you. We really don't care if you live or not. It's that simple. The smallest hesitation from you and I will shoot you. You deserve nothing less, and we have a time issue. So let's get started."

Turning to the first young man, barely over eighteen years old by the looks of him, the Major made sure he had solid eye contact before he asked his first question.

"What's your name?"

"Josh."

"How long you been with the Riders?"

"About a year."

"Where is your base camp?"

Josh hesitated and looked at the other three buddies. The Major pulled his pistol out and shot him in the foot. In the confined space, the sound was deafening and reverberated for several seconds. Then Josh began to scream. The Major grabbed him by the neck and told him to, "Suck it up big boy. You want to ride with these animals, we're going to treat you like an animal." Two of the three other Riders shifted uneasily in their seats and did all they could not to make eye contact with the Major. The third simply stared at Josh with a menacing scowl. A crowd had gathered outside of the conference room and was taunting the men.

"Clear those people out of here. This is going to get messy. Especially get the kids away from here," ordered Glen. Dan pushed his way out of the room and began ushering the crowd to the other end of the hall.

The Major knelt in front of Josh and asked, "Okay, Josh, let's try again. Where is the base?"

"Don't tell him anything! If you do, I'll kill you myself!" shouted the man in the chair across from Josh.

The Major wasted no time and simply spun around and shot the man in the head. The concussion sent the man flying over backwards in his chair and he landed with a splat. Blood splattered the wall behind him and hit several of the townspeople guarding the men.

Shock touched everyone in the room except the Major. Again he focused on the young man and said, "Josh, I'm not fooling around. You get one more chance and then I kill you. Remember, I have two more people to work with. You're expendable. Where is the base?"

Josh opened up like a broken fire main. He told them specifics: how many guns, their habits and tendencies, types of vehicles, quantities of supplies. He told them where the base was, how many people were still there, and the best way to attack them. Fortunately, he had been very observant and the Major felt the data was quite accurate.

Holstering his pistol and motioning for Glen and Dan to join him, the Major directed the guards, "Get him some medical aid, bury that guy and lock them up and put two guards on them. We may need them again."

Aftermath

Shelly was waiting outside the Hall for the Major and her Dad. She had seen both of them when they came back from the fight and was relieved, but she needed to talk to them now!

"Dad! Dad!" yelled Shelly waiving for her father to make his way through the crowd and come over to her. Dan obliged and the Major came in tow.

After a tender hug Shelly said, "Dad, I could have helped you with the questioning. You didn't have to shoot anybody. I know about the camp. I know where they are and what they are doing right now."

Dan grabbed the Major as the three of them walked a few steps away from the crowd mulling around outside the town hall.

"Major, Shelly says she can help us with the nest. She knows what they are doing."

"Shelly, what do you know about them?" requested the Major.

"Right now they are expecting their men back in a couple of hours. They have scouts on the road and wire all around the camp. It is really just a big kind of hotel off the road we came in on. We didn't see it because it is over a hill and down by the river. They have some men, women and kids there. They have some locked in a room and sometimes they beat them."

"Do you know how well protected they are? The dirt road going into the camp has a lot of men around it. They all have guns, but the river is not protected. They have all sorts of cars, trucks and motorcycles and lots and lots of food and drinks. Mainly beer."

Dan interjected, "Major, we need to have town council meeting right away. Let's review what happened this morning and what we need to do next. The sooner the better before complacency sets in."

"I agree, Dan. You set it up and I'll make sure sentries are posted and the team leaders are available. Thanks, Shelly. You really have helped us."

Glen had assembled the council and the Major began by recounting the grim details of the battle; the number of people killed on both sides, wounded, and prisoners. Solemn nods greeted his review. Congratulations were offered and accepted by all.

"Gentlemen, now is our time to act. First of all, in about an hour or two the rest of the Riders are going to wonder what happened to their men. They probably have already tried to call them and got no response. They have a lot of resources sitting out there in the form of men, bikes, and guns. They will want them all back. We need to set up an ambush right now. We have found where they parked their bikes and sooner or later some-one is going to come looking for them. We need to suck them in and kill 'em. Then, we need to find some boats or rafts and hit them where and when they least expect it. One of the prisoners told us and Glen verified that there is an old dude ranch down on the river about fifteen miles away. That is their base. We need to do the same thing they tried to do to us. Hit them with a diversionary attack on the dirt road going to the base while we float down the river and hit them from behind. We should be ready go tomorrow morning, early."

"Slow down, Patrick. Why do we need to go get 'em? We just gave them one hell of a lesson, and lost one of our men. I bet neither of us wants anymore to do with the other," commented Stan, the senior council member.

"Do you really think it works that way, Stan?" replied Dan. "I've seen what people like this will do. After they get over losing all those people, they will make sure to make our lives miserable. They will snipe us, strangle travel to and from our town, and periodically send out patrols until they find the weak spot and then they will raid us, kill as many of the men as they can, and rape the women and children. I don't want to spend my time waiting for them to start the dance. Do you?"

"I just don't want to have more of our people killed."

"Nobody does and this is the best way to avoid that happening again and again," added the Major.

Glen cleared his throat and said, "Let's take a quick vote. All in favor of the Major's plan to ambush and attack the Riders, raise your hand."

Six hands out of nine were raised. "The motion is passed. Patrick, please prepare your men."

Is It Worth It?

Good intensions don't always bring the best results. Wanting to rid oneself of a particularly menacing
problem, one will often seek a resolution that is not only
effective, but quick and easy. The proverbial no brainer.
However, if blessed with the time to ponder outside-of-
the-box solutions, quite often more sensible, profitable,
and secure recourse is found.

Shelly and Monica were in a deep conversation and
wandering slowly toward the river when Dan spotted them.
Jogging to catch up, he yelled, "Hey you two, wait up."
Both girls stopped and turned and watched as Dan ran
down the road toward them. Shelly saw her father; loving, caring, protective and currently with a deep red aura.
Monica saw an attractive man, albeit her best friend's father, with a still athletic build and a strong body. She felt
somewhat guilty about her female attraction to this older
man, but time was having its usual affect on her changing
body. She glanced secretly at Shelly to see if she had noticed her instance of weakness. Fortunately, Shelly was

only beaming at her approaching father and had totally missed, this time, the veiled mischief in Monica's eyes.

"Shelly, where are you two girls headed?"

"Just walkin and talkin Dad. Nowhere special."

"Well, you need to stay close to the Town Hall. We are planning on sending out a scouting party to see if there are any more of those Riders around," lied Dan, trying not to worry his daughter more than necessary.

"Is it really worth it Dad? Do you really need to kill them all?"

"Humph, figured if anyone might know it would be you. Yes. It is worth it. They have been killing these and other folks for months. It has to stop and the only to guarantee is to take them out. I wish there was another way."

"There is Dad. You can save a lot of lives if you want to."

"Have you seen something Shelly? Something that could help us?"

"Yes. I know and so do you, after talking to the man you captured, how many guards they have and where they are in the camp. You sneak into their camp and flatten every tire on everything they have that moves, except the school bus. They need transportation. You have all the bikes from the battle. Move them into Cibola and tell them you will give them one bike for every ten prisoners they turn over. They will try to bargain, but you will settle on five. I happen to know they have eleven women, eight kids, and three men, a total of twenty two. That means you only give them four bikes. They can't hurt you with four bikes and a bus. You also tell them that you are going to be guarding the highway from now on and will shoot anyone you see coming our direction. Then you can tell their leader, a guy named Jerome, that his cancer is coming back and if he ever wants to see the ocean again, he better hurry. He hasn't told anyone about how sick he is or that he wants to see the ocean. It will be enough to make him leave and the gang will follow him. They can use the bus and the four bikes. It'll work Dad. I know it will."

"I think it's a little late, Shelly. They already voted to go and are making plans now."

"It's not too late. Some of the people are already arguing with the council. Go and see. Tell them what I told you and see what happens."

Dan just stood there with his arms folded and looking at the dirt. A pose he usually struck when he was weighing the alternatives.

"Please, Dad. Give it a try. We don't want to lose any more people."

"Okay. I'll go and see Glen and the Major right away. You and Monica get back to the Hall and wait for me," he said as he spun around and started jogging back into town.

A crowd had gathered in front of the Hall and a heated debate was underway between a variety of groups. It was interesting to see who was for and against the additional military action. It seemed to Dan that the older a person was, the more likely they were to want to kill all the bad guys. Younger people, possibly because they had more life ahead of them and consequently more to lose, wanted to leave well enough alone. Dan found Patrick and Glen barely twenty feet from the front door of the Town Hall. The arguments had started almost immediately and swept everyone into its vise-like grip of confusion. Dan yelled for the Major and Glen to move back into the hall. He had something important to tell them. Sensing another important decision about to be made in their absence, the crowd quieted down and carefully watched the three men as they stepped into the hall. Dan laid out the conversation with Shelly and both men agreed the plan was a stretch, but it just might work. Given the boisterousness of the crowd and the lack of progress since the vote, Glen agreed to reconvene the council and talk about it some more. Two hours later a unanimous vote gave them a new plan, just as Shelly knew it would. Team leaders were informed and the word spread to the people quickly. No bickering this time. A general sense of anticipated victory passed from person to person like dust floating on a summer breeze. The leaders picked seven men for the exercise that night and they waited for their veil of darkness.

River Strike

The plan was straight forward: one man would travel down the river using a ski-do they had found in town. When about a mile from the camp, he would turn the machine off and float along the near bank until he could see the compound. Following him by about fifteen minutes were the remaining six men. They would be told to switch off the motor on their boat when the lead man first heard them coming. They also would float the remainder of the way and join forces. From there, they had a map of the camp rendered by the prisoner. All men were equipped with a sharpened screwdriver that they could thrust into tires and render them useless. They would leave the bus tires intact, just as Shelly mentioned, and hope to be gone before anyone noticed what was happening.

There were two guards on duty at this hour of the morning. Both were guarding the road leading into the camp and were exactly on the opposite side of the camp from the river beach. Within ten minutes, they had nearly completed their mission when one of the Riders not on sentry decided it was time for him to relieve his bladder.

He stepped from one of the bunk houses and as he was unzipping his jeans, he spied Dan hunched over a motorcycle, plunging his screwdriver deep into the tread of the front tire.

"What the hell are you doing?" he screamed.

Dan turned and fumbled for his Glock as the man charged him. A shot rang out from behind Dan and the man fell to ground, mortally wounded.

"Let's get out of here now!" screamed the shooter as he ran for the river and boat.

The camp was coming alive quickly and Riders began stepping from buildings and bringing guns into the firing position. Dan sprayed a volley of shots at the emerging shapes and sent them flying for cover. The crew of seven was now in a full sprint for the boat. The first one there started the motor, then took up a defensive firing position as he waited for the other six crouching runners to arrive. Suppression fire was poured into the camp as bodies hurled themselves into the boat. With all seven now aboard and bullets beginning to tear into the boat, the motor was throttled hard and the boat gained speed as it hugged the shoreline for protection. Dan rose up slightly to see if anyone was pursuing them down the river when he took a bullet to his left shoulder. It slammed him into the boat's console and sent blood spraying toward the front of the boat. Dan collapsed into a heap on the deck as the boat continued to gain speed. Within seconds, it was around a bend in the river and safe from fire.

The mission had been a success with one exception: Dan. Blood poured from his wound and, still unconscious, the men stuffed someone's T-shirt into the hole in his shirt and hoped it would be enough. They radioed back to town and advised them that Dan had been shot and they needed immediate medical attention when they arrived.

ЖОЖ

"Where are you going Shelly?" said Tina as she saw the girl making her way down stairs and toward the front door.

"Dad's been shot. I need to be there when he arrives."

"Did you see this in one of your visions?"

"Yes. I knew it before he left." "What? And you let him go?"

"Of course I let him go. How can I let someone else get shot in his place? He's not going to die, but it is serious."

"I don't understand you! Let me get dressed and I will come with you," said Tina, running to her room to get dressed.

It's all in the Presentation

What makes a good salesperson? It's all about timing, rapport, charisma, and knowledge. It also helps if you're good looking. Shelly only had knowledge on her side.

"Shelly, your Dad's going to be fine. The bullet went right through his shoulder and didn't hit a bone. He lost some blood but we have stopped the bleeding and we have a first rate nurse here in town. There is nothing to worry about," said the Major as he hugged Shelly.

"I know. I'm not worried, but I do want to talk to you about the conversation we need to have with the Riders' leader."

Squinting his eyes in disbelief and glancing at Tina, who had the same basic expression, he said, "Fine. What do you think is the best approach with these guys?"

"We must talk to Jerome. He is the only one that can make a decision. He is mean and only cares about himself. He's the boss because he kills anyone that gives him the least bit of trouble. He gives his people drugs, booze, and all the sex they want. They keep some of the girls prisoners for just that purpose. Right now he is scared. We have killed a lot of his people, snuck into his camp and made most of his cars and motorcycles pieces of junk. He just needs a little help to make his decision."

"Right. I know about swapping the prisoners for motorcycles and encouraging him to see the ocean before he dies. I can handle it."

"No you can't, Major. He doesn't like anyone to have power over him. Right now we have power over him and he desperately needs to be in charge. He needs to talk with someone he feels certain he can have power over. He needs to talk to me."

With his mouth open and Tina already protesting, Shelly held up her hands and began waving them as if she was swatting at flies, "Please, please listen to me. I can get inside his head. I will know what he is thinking and will know how to control the conversation. He won't be afraid of a little girl, but when I am done with him, he will be."

Silence greeted Shelly as the two of them regrettably recognized just how right this little girl was. If anyone could pull this off and walk away with the best results possible, it was Shelly.

"Alright Shelly. I'll get a council meeting and present the plan. I'll be able to let you know in a couple of hours."

"Major, you know I have to be at that meeting. They don't trust me yet. They think I'm just some sort of freak. They don't understand my purpose in this town. I will need to convince them."

"What is your purpose?" inquired Tina.

"It's very simple: to help everyone survive and grow in this new world."

"Good answer, Shelly."

"Come with me," replied the Major as he and Shelly headed for the Town Hall with Tina in tow.

White Flag

When reason gives way to emotion, often the outcome is quite unsettling. So it was with the council. Grudgingly, they agreed after Shelly mentally encouraged five of the seven to vote in her favor. They clearly were conflicted with their position and several of them wept quietly as they held up their hands signifying a Yes vote. She regretted having to persuade them at such a point in their relationship, but it needed to be done. She wasn't quite sure if there would be lingering effects due to her interference. But, as the poet said, "Now was not the time to reason why, twas the time to do or die". Later on, given more time, she would help them develop their own mental capabilities to more clearly see rational choices that would benefit all.

Shelly asked for and was granted the services of the Major for the ride over to the Riders' camp. They took a motorcycle, with Shelly sitting on the back, waving a large white flag. They came to a stop at the dirt road entrance to the Riders' lair.

"Major, please wait for me here. Do not go any further down the road. There are two rifles aimed at us now and I am sure they wouldn't harm me, but, I can't say the same for you."

"I don't like this Shelly. Your Dad's going to kill me when he wakes up. I must be out of my mind letting a little girl walk into their camp."

"Major, I really do know what I am doing. I promise I'll be careful and I shouldn't even be that long."

"Please come back safe, Shelly. I love you."

The words took her by surprise. She knew deep down that he loved her, but she had never heard him say it. She reached up and kissed his cheek, turned and with the flag held high, she started walking down the dust laced road to the Riders' camp.

Ten minutes carrying a big flag and marching down a country road is really a lot longer than one might imagine. Shelly's arms were beginning to ache and she wished the show would get started.

From behind a rock, a head poked out with a pistol right beside it, "What the hell do you want?"

"I'm from Cibola and I need to talk to Jerome."

"Right. What makes you think he wants to talk to you?"

"Let me put it this way: if you don't get him and he finds out I was here with a white flag and all and you didn't tell him, my guess is, you're in mighty big trouble. Am I right?"

After a prolonged silence, Shelly heard a walkie-talkie conversation taking place.

"Alright smartass, the Boss wants you to come on up to the house."

"And how am I supposed to get there?"

"Try walking. You guys messed up our rides."

"Not all of them. Have Jerome drive down and meet me. I'll start walking. Tell him I'll make it worth the effort."

Shelly started walking past the guard and heard another muted conversation.

"You got some stones, kid," said the guard as she passed. "He's on his way."

She would have to ask the Major what 'stones' meant when she got back. As she crested a hill, she was able to look down into a gentle valley and see the entire complex of the once semi-popular dude ranch. She could tell that it could hold a lot of people, plus they had pulled about ten big camping trailers onto the property. More than twenty people were beginning to stick their heads out of various buildings and vehicles when she spied Jerome coming up the road towards her. He was riding a big motorcycle with high handle bars, painted bright red with a skull painted on the gas tank. It made continuous noises like a machine gun going off.

Jerome was a big, big man. Taller than anyone in Cibola and wearing a bright white t-shirt with the sleeves cut off. His arms were even bigger than the Major's and covered in tattoos. Jerome's arms thrust out of the shirt and looked as if they could rip the handlebars right off of his motorcycle. As he drew closer, Shelly saw that Jerome was actually a very good looking man. He hadn't shaved in several days and his thick black beard made him look like he was ready for a Hollywood movie. He stopped the bike, extended the kickstand, and dismounted. A dazzling white set of teeth greeted Shelly as he stepped up to her and spit right on her foot.

"Don't mess with me, little girl. I'd just as soon kill ya as look at ya after what your people did this morning. What do you want?"

Jerome was always a bad person. His mother and father had tried to raise him with a sense of right and wrong but Jerome really didn't care what anybody, including his parents, thought. He had started by killing the pets of anyone that even looked at him crossways, including his mother's pet poodle. He advanced, and in the fourth grade he beat up a first grade boy so badly that the boy needed plastic surgery to reconstruct his face. The sin that deserved this response was laughing when Jerome had fallen down on some ice on the way to school. Jerome was summarily taken into custody, released to his parents on the condition that he would keep out of trouble and see a psychologist. The psychologist's pets were summarily killed in a two month period and Jerome found himself in juvenile custody. While in custody, he raped a younger boy and put the eye out of a lad three years older than him. He had been beaten up by the older boy and waited until he was asleep and shoved a bic pen into his eye. Finally released from juvie when he was sixteen, he returned to his parents, where he nearly killed his father with a marijuana bong he kept in his room. Before the police could get there, he had fled never to return.

Jerome found his way into a cycle gang in San Diego and started working his way up the ranks. He loved the fact that violence was encouraged and group sex was the norm. A quick mind, an absolutely violent response to any confrontation, a knack for turning girlfriends into prostitutes, and the occasional murder quickly propelled him to the eventual leadership. He maintained that position by publicly severely disciplining anyone who crossed him. He had killed many people in front of the gang to demonstrate his resolve and superiority. He was bright, vicious, and good looking. The bad ladies loved him and he knew it. Unfortunately for the women he came across, rape was the only real sexual release he had now days. And age wasn't a deterrent.

"Mr. Jerome, we could have killed you all. It was my idea to just warn you and then politely ask you to leave," replied Shelly.

"Oh really? Why the hell did they send a little snot-nosed girl in here? Don't they know what I could do to you?"

"Oh, they know. We know what you are doing to your prisoners, but we figured you'd be foolish not to take us up on our offer."

"What offer?"

"We will give you one of your bikes back for every ten prisoners you let go, and we want them all."

Jerome took a step and appeared to be ready to slam his fist into her face when she said four simple words, "Your cancer is back."

Jerome shuddered with the impact of the words. He regained his composure and asked, "Who told you?"

"I see things. It's a strange gift."

"See things? Like what?"

"Like you want to see the Ocean again before you die. And Mr. Jerome, you don't have much time."

"Bullshit!"

"No, not bullshit. Try leukemia. It was first diagnosed three years ago in L.A. You ignored the doctor's advice and went to Mexico for experimental treatment. It seemed to work so you put it out of your mind until about a month ago. You started to get sick again. You even considered killing yourself but couldn't pull the trigger. Any of this ringing a bell, Mr. Jerome?"

"What are you, a damn witch? No way you could know that stuff." He paused, weighing his options. She obviously knew things she shouldn't. "Look, if you tell anyone that stuff, I will kill you regardless of what you see or who you think you are."

"I have no intention of telling anyone. Not even the people in Cibola. Mr. Jerome, we have placed guards along the road going into town. If we see anyone coming, we are going to shoot first and ask questions later. We have shown you how we can fight. We could have killed a lot of your people in the raid, but didn't. We are offering you a way out. Go to the ocean, leave the prisoners, and take some bikes and the bus. The road going to the coast is open. It will take you a couple of days. You and your people will be able to exist out there better than you are doing here."

Jerome was quiet. He was trying to summon up the nerve to ask a question.

"You want to know how much time you have, don't you Mr. Jerome?"

"It's just Jerome kid. So you can read minds, too? Sure, why not, how much time have I got left in this cess-pool of a world?"

"Four months, more or less. It is going to be very painful. There are still some good drugs to numb the pain at a Kroger pharmacy just as you enter San Diego city limits. They will still be there when you arrive."

"Four months. Tell me exactly where the drugs are, make it ten bikes, not five and we will leave right away."

"Seven bikes, all and I mean all of the prisoners. I can have the bikes here tomorrow morning. But I want the prisoners now."

"On second thought, you don't mind if I play with you first, do you? You might even like it." said Jerome as he stepped forward, surprising Shelly and grabbed her by the hair.

Shelly closed her eyes as he slammed her into the ground and put her mind in a faraway place and summoned a beast.

Jerome screamed, jumped up, and started running in circles trying to brush something off of his chest.

"Be nice and I'll make it go away, Jerome," offered Shelly.

"Get it off me! Get it off now!" screamed Jerome.

Shelly concentrated and withdrew the dog sized black widow spider that was eating away at Jerome's arm in his hypnotic state.

"Better?" asked Shelly.

Breathing hard, Jerome staggered and looked at Shelly, "You are a witch!"

Shelly propped herself up on one elbow in the dirt and lowered a menacing stare at Jerome.

Jerome taking a step back said, "Okay, damn it! You got a deal. Just keep that thing away from me." Regaining some of his composure, Jerome asked, "Can you tell me how this plague thing is going to end?"

"The good news is life survives. We will live differently, but we survive."

"I guess that's good. Now get the hell out of here. I'll send the prisoners up the road; you can pick them up at the highway. No more shooting from either of us, and keep the bugs away, agreed?"

"Agreed. Jerome I think God gave me this gift. He wants to give one to you if you will let him."

Jerome with a glint of evil in his eyes said, "Nah. I done too many God damned things to change now. In fact, if you don't leave soon, I may be tempted again."

"Oh I'm sure you won't Jerome. Save that stuff for your gang. You don't impress me. Oh, and Jerome," meeting his gaze with her own steely determination, "you break this deal and I'll see to it that the spider finishes the job tonight."

Shelly turned and walked up the road to the waiting Major. Jerome stared at Shelly as she walked up the road and a shiver ran down his spine. He mounted his demonic bike and wheeled around for the compound. He was sweating profusely and now had some selling to do, but not much. Some had been clamoring to leave and head back to California for several weeks now, and after the slaughter of all their people, it really wouldn't be that tough.

Game, Set, Match

Occasionally, events turn in such a fashion that the ending is all but decided by a single moment. The instant epitomizes and crystallizes the struggle and boils it down to a final conclusion well before the finish is in sight. Golic and Neep had been spellbound watching the recent events unfold. Having agreed and called the crew to the bridge, they laid out their recommendation.

Kosh, Dra and Nimar sat passively in their custom chairs, anticipating whether Golic, the primal, or Neep the shipboard computer, would lead the discussion. Deferring to Golic, Neep only set the stage and allowed Golic to draw the conclusions.

"Our main test subject has demonstrated considerable growth in her intuitive and mental facilities. She now consistently is able to penetrate other's minds and extract information without their knowing. Shelly has shown herself to be able to set aside emotional attachment and instead lead and direct on a purely objective basis. Her progress has been quiet remarkable, considering all of the obstacles she faced."

"Thank you, Neep. Indeed, as noted, our subject has transformed herself to a new level of human being. Our interference, although unorthodox, was clearly beneficial to the entire expedition and especially to Shelly, her family, and Cibola residents. In Earth terms, she could be called a not so missing link. Those she is in contact with have given her a substantial support structure. We intend to remain on site, but in a much less intrusive manner. We have delayed the next briefing of our council until input from each of you has been obtained. Ready that data at your earliest and deposit it with Neep. I will review it and develop a summary for everyone's review. In the meantime, we intend to remain on station and continue our observations and measurements. Thank you."

Finished, Golic turned and hovered off to his quarters. The remainder of the crew, in their typical fashion, showed neither pleasure nor disgust with Golic's remarks. Stoicism was highly prized in their culture.

Freedom

Captivity is painful on many levels. Throw in ownership and it's a different game. When one is considered nothing more than a mere slave, it is especially harsh. It's not just incarceration, its usury. Your will is more than confined, it is reshaped. Your captor's needs become paramount and you become nothing more than a tool, equivalent to a shovel, a pet dog, or a set of dishes.

Twenty two distrustful individuals limped their way towards freedom as they walked toward the Major and Shelly. Eleven women, three men and eight children. The adults ranged in ages from eighteen to forty and the children came in a range of sizes between the ages of eight and fourteen. It was a pitiful rabble. Only one of the women gave the appearance of health. She had been in captivity the least amount of time. The Major could only begin to imagine the depth and severity of their individual stories.

"Hello, Glen, this is Patrick. I don't know exactly how she did it, but Shelly has retrieved about twenty prisoners from the Riders and we need a way to get them back to Cibola."

"Holy mackerel! I'll get some of the men and drive some rigs up to get them. Be there in about an hour. I'll bring water and some food, too."

"Thanks, Glen."

Shelly was sitting on the ground looking up the road at the approaching people and began smiling. She was imagining how different they would look in only a few days time. She envisioned the relationships that would blossom and the hurts that would heal. She grasped the peace that could be if given a chance. All of it settled in her heart and made her warm all over. She rose, grabbed the Major's hand, and pulled him along as they went out to meet the new comers. She could see damaged auras but she also sensed great potential. She leaned her head back and whispered up to the sky, "Thank you God. Now help us provide for them."

The Major finally fully understood God's impact and tears filled his eyes. He squeezed Shelly's hand and said, "Amen."

None of the group seemed to need immediate medical attention, although, two or three would need some bumps and bruises looked after. Nurse Sally could fix them up in no time at all. The emotional issues would be an entirely different matter. The women had been sexually abused and some of children also. Drug addiction was a concern as the Riders had used various drugs to illicit different responses from the prisoners. In many ways, this was similar to the way the Romans treated their slaves. Sometimes they beat them, sometimes they loved them, sometimes they were like family and sometimes they killed them. Certainly not a great environment to exist in, let alone grow up in.

In less than an hour, the cars and vans arrived and hauled everyone off to Cibola. Shelly had informed the Major that they needed to return four motorcycles to the Riders by tomorrow morning. She wanted to throw in an extra as a bonus. The Major just shook his head, but Shelly knew he would comply. Glen had a reception committee waiting for the new arrivals. They would be cleaned up, given a good meal, counseled to determine who should be housed together, and then assigned quarters. The real work of repairing broken hearts and minds would begin tomorrow.

"Major, I need to go see my Dad. If you need me I'll be at home with him. Tina should be looking after him. That should be interesting."

"Always plotting and planning, aren't you Shells Bells?"

Shelly especially liked it when he called her Shells Bells. "I guess I am. I can't seem to help it. My mind just kind of works like that now. I see so much more than I use to. I especially see responsibilities and consequences. And I hope more people start to think like that also. Anyway, I gotta go. See ya soon."

"Tell your Dad if he is awake, I'll be over later to talk to him."

"Okay. Bye."

Dynamics

In psychoanalysis, dynamics is defined as the psychological aspect or conduct of an interpersonal relationship. But when you use the word group dynamics, it really means the mind trips people put on each other for no other reason than they want some sort of power.

Cibola had started out as a town of 172 souls pre-plague. The plague and the riders had reduced that number to 47. When the tribe arrived, the population soared a whopping 19% to 56. Now, with the addition of the prisoners, the total jumped to 88, nearly double what it had been prior to the arrival of the tribe less than a week ago. Add to that the fact that a nine year old girl was demonstrating unearthly powers of prediction, and you had a very tenuous situation.

Everyone seemed nice enough, but the stress of merely existing was enough to drive some of the people over the edge. No additional fuel on the fire was necessary. So when, after the Riders had been delivered their five motorcycles and had cleared out and the town had rested for an additional two days, the town council again, called for a town meeting, you didn't have to be a sooth-sayer to predict the outcome.

"I hereby call this meeting to order," sounded Glen, as he used his gavel to begin the meeting. The murmurs died away and people adjusted themselves to the metal folding chairs with as much grace as their uncomfortable buttocks would allow.

"We have some introductions to do and new duty ros-ters to hand out. We also need to talk about weapons training, first aid and of course growing and gathering food. Before we start, are there any additional items you wish to discuss today?"

For whatever reason, it seems more often than not, when things are about to really get ugly and deteriorate into emotional venting, women are more than willing to lead the way. Men are rightly accused of being territo-rial, but women, especially when pushed out of comfort-able community relationships, seem to operate without regard to borders, reason, and tact, and often with hurtful prejudice.

A short woman about forty years old stood up in the back and said, "Yes. What are we going to do about the girl? It ain't natural what she does." Multiple conversa-tions broke out among the crowd.

"It seems she has ungodly powers. She worries us."

"Do I need to remind you that she has only helped us? Without her we would all be dead right now," exclaimed Glen with more than a little frustration in his voice.

Another voice jumped from the crowd, "She helped us, but who or what helped her?"

Dan, now able to walk about with his arm in a sling stood and said, "Just a minute. What have you done to save this town? How many prisoners did you get released? Were you able to get the Riders to leave?"

Voices erupted from all quarters of the meeting, most supporting Shelly but an alarming number denouncing her as some sort of demon, unclean, evil. Shelly sat perfectly still and better understood the vision she had seen last night. The town needed reassurance, a guarantee of sorts that she was operating on the side of good. As the voices grew in volume, Shelly abruptly stood and walked purposefully over to Glen and stood by his side. Her movement did not go unnoticed. Silence ensued.

"Mr. Glen, may I talk to the town?"

It was a charming way to ask for the floor, and of course Glen said, "The floor is yours Shelly."

In a voice bigger than her father knew she had, Shelly looked over the crowd and summoned the volume to reach the back of the room, "The gift I have scared me, too. I didn't want to know what was going to happen tomorrow or the day after that. Some of the things I saw were awful, some beautiful, and some wonderful cause it helped me save people's lives. But how do you ignore God when he shows you things? Everything I have done or will do is based on God's laws. I would never do anything to intentionally hurt someone. My Dad taught me that taking responsibility is important in life. When I see things that can help people and even save lives, it is my responsibility to do the right thing. I am sure if you had this gift, you would be doing the same things I am. Right now there are three people in this group that need my help. Should I help them or not?" Patiently Shelly waited with her hands at her side standing as straight as she could.

"If it's about me, I want to know. But if it's private, then it should be said in private," said Josh, Glen's grandson.

"Well, folks, how about it? Should Shelly tell those in need or not? Let's have a show of hands of those in favor of her telling them, in private, of course."

More that 90% of the hands were raised. "It's official. Shelly, please find those affected and give them a rundown on your dream. Now, people, can we get back to business?"

About ten people got up and left the hall. Shelly returned to her seat with the intention of singling out the three souls she intended to share her visions with.

After the meeting, the Major approached Glen, "What do you intend to do about the people that walked out of the meeting?"

"Not a thing. There is nothing that says they have to be there, but the same rule applies to everyone: no work equals no food or water. It's up to them. If they want to leave, they will come and tell one of us on the council. Nobody is held here against their will."

And The Beat Goes On

Shelly had delivered needed news to the three in her visions after the meeting. Nothing earth-shattering, but helpful nonetheless. One lady was searching for a box of pictures that was the only link to her now dead family. Shelly told her where she could find it. A man was having trouble with his hearing aid and was told where to find additional batteries. And a little girl's father was informed that she was about to get the chicken pox. Not life threatening, but something to be wary of, especially since no doctors or hospitals were available. All thanked her profusely and told her they were glad she was in town.

Interestingly, no one had wanted to leave town and work duties were being performed by all, including members of the tribe and the newcomers.

Food and water were still the overwhelming concerns of the community. Minds were busily trying to figure out how to boost production of both with the added people.

"Dad, you probably don't want any more revelations from me, but I think you will like this one."

"On no, what is it this time?"

"About three miles from here, I can't quite see where, but somewhere out there in the desert is a bunch of good water. It's underground, but we can get it."

"Are you saying there is a good well out there?"

"No, it's not a well It's just underground."

"You mean an aquifer?"

"I don't know. We will have to pump it up. But it should be easy cause others have used it before."

"What others are you talking about?"

"Indians. A long time ago they knew about it and used it. It was closer to the surface then. It got covered up by dirt and wind and it's just waiting for us."

"How will we find it?"

"I will just know when I'm standing on it. Let's go find it, Dad."

"Now hold on, child. We can't just go wandering around in the desert. Who knows what's out there. Let me talk to the Glen."

"Okay, but hurry up. We need the water for our crops."

"You continually amaze me, daughter. Thanks for not keeping all these things to yourself. We need to know what's on your mind."

"Even if it's bad?"

"Especially if it's bad."

The profiling that Glen had enacted for all members of the town was paying off. They had a nurse, a computer geek, a diesel mechanic, two military men, five farmers, three ranchers, a school teacher, several salesmen, a road repairman, a heavy equipment operator, a dancer from LA, a highway patrolman, a park ranger, and a crop duster pilot. Not to mention a variety of small business owners, mothers, two short order cooks, a retired fire-fighter and twenty or so individuals that had worked at a multitude of jobs, never actually calling one a career.

The Major examined the list with a keen eye towards troop utilization. He still could not get his almost thirty years of military training out of his thought process.

"Glen, can I borrow this list and think about how these folks could help our various projects? I'll get it back to you in a day or two."

"Sure. Keep it to yourself, though. I don't want any-one getting the idea that you are in charge of the projects. Come back to me with recommendations and I'll take it up with the council."

"Will do. Thanks."

Projects

Survival depends upon a lot of factors, the least of which isn't planning. With Dan's help, the Major put together a wish list of projects that would not only ensure the town's success but add some of the amenities of life back into the community. He prioritized the list and then he tried to apply the right people to the right project for the most return on the time and manpower expenditures. If it sounded a bit too business like and over thought, that would be the influence of Dan's logistics training easing itself into every pore and fiber of the planning. When they had finished, they presented the list to Glen. He read through the list and noted an additional page that recommended individuals to each project.

Town projects, in order of priority:

1. Self defense of the town
2. Secure liquid and food sources to last until self sufficient

3. Increase portable water supply to accommodate drinking and irrigating

4. Establish communications with the outside world

5. Develop generating power for electricity

6. Establish school for children

7. Cross train critical professions

8. Establish rules for admission to the town

9. Establish religious services

"Gentlemen, I'm impressed. We had never gotten past trying to protect the town, let alone trying to school the children. I want to present this to the council ASAP. I'll call a closed door session for tonight. On another subject, I hear your daughter thinks she knows where untainted water can be found. Why don't we give it a try and see what we come up with."

"Great," said Patrick. "Mind if I conscript some of the men and take a guard with me and someone that knows the area?"

"That's a good idea, but I want Dan to take on that exercise. Dan, take Jake. He has worked on road crews all around the area and he knows it like the pimples on his butt. He also is a hell of a camper and knows more about what to do and how not to get into trouble when out on the desert."

"Fine. We'll leave this afternoon."

Glen shifted his eyes to Patrick and said, "I need you to lead some men and trucks and go up the vacant Riders camp. Some of the captives we brought to town have told us that there is a ton of supplies there and they couldn't have taken it all with them when they left."

"Great, I'd love to help. It addresses priority number two on the list," said Patrick with a smile. "I can assure you we won't be cavalier about the trip. Some of them might have stayed behind. We will go in expecting a fight."

"That's what I expected. Take ten men and two trucks. Dan, you go with Jake and Shelly and see what's out there."

"No problem, Glen. I'll find the men and make sure we are prepared."

As Glen returned to his town hall office and other considerations, Patrick and Dan were left outside with their thoughts, "I am feeling better and better about Glen," said Dan.

"Absolutely. He would have made a fine military man. Thinks in straight lines. I like that. No bullshit, yet tactful and knowledgeable."

"Good man all around. Let's not keep him waiting," suggested Dan as both men headed in different directions on different errands for Cibola.

Quarterly Review

The single biggest reason for out-of-the-box innovation is the fact that small privately owned operations are not shackled to quarterly profit targets. In large publicly owned businesses, short term results are seen as a holy predictor of future possibilities. Longer term expectations are shelved in lieu of short term bonuses.

In much the same way, the field trip lead by Golic was under the same pressures. His expedition was funded by his planet. Updates on their progress were being beamed, along with images into the homes and institutions all over Creum. It was a truly news worthy event. Opinions about the crew's tampering with the survival possibilities of Shelly and her tribe were being debated by all interested parties at an unprecedented level. If for no other reason than planet interest, the expedition was already a success. However, professional objective reviews were mandatory and it would help if all of the crew was in sync with the findings. The base findings were easy enough; now over four and half billion people were dead, 90% of all animal life was also on the same death pyre, most grasses had died away and vast deserts were developing around the planet, forests were receding at a quickening rate, massive fires were seen on all continents and a pale of dark skies hung in most places. Total life extinction on planet Earth was still a possibility, if not a probability. These were the facts, and irrefutable. The crew had no problem joining hands on those facts.

Conversely, interference, instead of passive observation, past and potentially future, was an entirely different subject. Factions on mother planet were aligned between crew members, depending on their stance on meddling. It was a phenomenon never witnessed before, and the High Council clearly was at odds as to how to proceed. One thing was clear, however: the data must continue to flow as nearly anyone with life force was becoming a junkie for the details. It was the epitome of a reality show.

Shelly had exhibited remarkable growth in the past few weeks and even more in the last few days. She was ascending to the rightful purpose she was chosen for.

"How far do you think she has evolved in her short life span?" implored Dra, already sensing the answer from Golic.

"Dra, you have perceived what I think, but I do enjoy sharing my thoughts. I firmly believe she will reach at least the 9th and possibly the highest 10th level."

"I doubt she will go beyond the 6th level," joined Nimar. "She is only at level 3 now and she may simply not live long enough. Plus there are no mentors for her to glean truth from."

"A valid point. I concur with Nimar. In addition, I fear her coming hormonal level changes will interfere with her evolving in unknown ways," informed Kosh, thinking as only a systems engineer could.

"Statistically she has an 87% chance of acquiring at least a level 7 and a probability of hitting level 8. We should trust the figures and plan according," interjected Neep.

"Conjecture is pointless at this time. Please allow our fellow planet members to wallow in that game. For now, let's follow protocol and resume our duties," encouraged Golic in a rather paternalistic fashion.

Trump Suit

Expectations are often overblown dreams. Reality is seldom a partner when hope is loose and roaming. People pray for cures from the incurable, seek results that don't measure up to the preparation needed, and generally overestimate their effect on the outcome. Shelly perhaps understood this better, even at her tender age, than anyone else in town. Yet, she also possessed the exclusivity of her sixth sense. This was the Queen of Spades, the trump card of all trump cards.

"Jake, Glen suggested I ask you to help us on a little exhibition."

"Hey, Dan. What'd you have in mind?"

"We believe we can locate a source of good water east of here. We need that water for irrigation. We have drinking water that will satisfy our immediate needs, but irrigating crops is a whole other issue."

"Dan, I have lived here most of my adult life and I've hiked and four wheeled a lot of territory, and I've never seen anything that even resembles water out there. The Colorado River is all we have."

"I know it seems that way, but my daughter has had some very powerful visions and we want to follow up on them. Will you help us?"

"Sure. Why not? I've nothing better to do until security watch this evening. How do you plan on searching for and locating this water?"

"I want to take two other men with me and some of the dirt bikes we repoed from the Riders. We all should be armed with pistols and rifles. I will pack some water and snacks, and that should do it."

"Roger that. If you don't mind, I've got some guys in mind that we could use on this outing. They are good with bikes and guns. Shall I see if they are up for it?"

"Jake, that would be great. I'll go to the vehicle lot and pick out three bikes and make sure they are gassed up and ready. Shelly and I will meet you there in an hour. Please make sure everyone has the weapons and proper gear."

"No problem. see ya soon."

Goat Breath

Dan and Shelly met the other two men, Larry and Bill and when all the introductions were concluded, Jake led the group out of town and east into the Barrens. Jake rode alone, Dan was behind Larry, and Shelly was with Bill.

The Barrens were aptly named. The terrain was comprised mostly of sparse grass, a wide variety of cactus and hard packed dirt or sand woven into small undulating hills. Occasional rock outcroppings could be seen, but no major mountain ranges or buttes dominated this landscape. Snakes, scorpions, lizards an occasional javelina, and goats were the main population. Many a person had perished in this desolate land, and parents were quick to teach their young the dangers of venturing into the Barrens. Jake expertly led the team through rock strewn paths, up and down small rounded hills. He avoided the sand when possible, due to its desire to ensnare your vehicle in its seemingly innocent grains. Venturing into the Barrens was possible, but not encouraged. Parents always told a little rhyme to their children concerning the inhospitable terrain;

Go in twos, never alone

The sand confuses your way home

Water a must if you plan to survive

Fools do not live, they only die.

About an hour into the trip, Shelly spied a group of three goats and yelled, "Stop!" Bill honked his tinny horn and Jake and Larry throttled down to a stop. All turned to look at Shelly.

"Follow the goats. They know the way," said Shelly as she pointed the goats already moving over a rocky hill.

Shifting on his hot cycle seat, Jake said, "Nothing over there except a deep arroyo."

Shelly shifted her gaze from the last goat to be seen as it disappeared over the black lava rock landscape and focused on Jake. She only said one word, barely audible above the muted engines, "Please." Jake had never heard a more commanding plea in his life. He could see more than hear the words escape her pink, full lips and he felt urged to follow at any cost. He was only glad the girl hadn't uttered the request as he stood at the precipitous of a bottomless pit for he surely would have jumped the way she had asked.

First Jake, then all of the engines rapped to life and inched their way up the midnight black porous rocks to the edge of the arroyo. They dismounted and walked to a large boulder guarding the entrance to the deep canyon. Shadows encased the gully and cut off the searing heat in the summer, which undoubtedly gave the goats a cooler environment. But what, if not water, did the goats drink for sustenance? The goats were visible from the ridge and were soon seen evaporating into the side of the hill.

"There must be a cave!" shouted Bill and Larry simultaneously as they began to scramble down the side of the severely slopping walls of the canyon.

"Careful," encouraged Dan, "we don't need any sprains or broken bones."

"Dan, you wait here. With your arm still in that sling, you could barely stay on the back of the bike and you're too heavy to carry, so I don't want you going down the canyon," ordered Jake.

"Fine, but keep Shelly behind you going down and in front of you coming up."

"You bet," replied Jake as first he, then Shelly made their way over the side and followed Bill and Larry into the abyss.

Larry and Bill were obviously young, strong and in great shape. They easily made their way down the incline in fifteen minutes, finding themselves beside a small outcropping of rocks concealing a small hole in the side of the canyon. It was no larger than two feet high and a foot wide. Bill got on his knees and peered into the dark and was given only a brief view of about five feet before the tunnel veered left. He tried, but quickly gave up following the goats when his shoulders wouldn't give him the clearance he needed. Ten minutes later, a huffing Jake and exuberant Shelly joined them at the mouth of the cave.

Bill informed, "Too small to go in Jake. I can see a few feet back and then it turns left and that's it."

"Could be dangerous in there, anyway. We will need to get some gear before we go in there."

"No. I can make it now," insisted Shelly.

"Honey, I can't let you go in there. We don't even have a flashlight with us. Who knows what's in there. Could be bats, javelina or a sheer drop off. We'll have to come back," said a still winded Jake.

"No. I will go in now and only as far as the corner. I know this is the place. I just want to make sure."

"Your Dad will kill me if I let you go in there, so hold your horses and let's come back tomorrow."

"Mr. Jake, Bill, Larry, please look at me, I assure you, it's safe and you really do think it's a good idea if I go in, don't you?"

Hypnosis was a skill Shelly was honing. She was already very good at it in an individual setting, and this was her second try with a group effort. The three men were fidgeting but nodding in agreement.

"Bill, please stay at the mouth of the cave so I can tell you what I am seeing," instructed Shelly as she got on her hands and knees then disappeared into the cave. The air immediately took on a different quality. It was cool and moist. There had to be water in here, Shelly thought. As she reached the turn in the tunnel, she glanced backward to assure herself that Bill was still on the vigil; he waved and smiled. As she nosed around the corner, she came face to face with a kid, a baby goat. She heard the bleating of its parents but the youngster was just too curious. Shelly reached out and stroked his head, he inched close enough that Shelly could smell his baby goat breath. She blew in his nose and he instinctively backed away and made a u-turn in the tight quarters and skipped down the tunnel out of sight.

Knowing her father and every sane person would disagree, she ventured forward into the growing darkness. Suddenly, a warm glowing friend blinked on. The green probe from the ship had joined the investigation and was lighting the way for Shelly. As if reading her mind, the luminosity increased and Shelly could see as if walking, or better yet, crawling in the day light. The tunnel ended just ahead, and Shelly was able to stand in a large cavern. Spelunkers would have been in awe. A soon to be ten year old girl had found a virgin cave, complete with stalactites and stalagmites. Even more important, she saw a group of ten or so goats standing on the far side of the cavern around a small lake. "Thank God!" shouted Shelly with the echo coming back softer three times, Thank God, Thank God, Thank God.

Supplies

Grocery stores are incredible conveniences for human kind. Just ask someone from an undeveloped country that ventures into their first Kroger's, Fry's, or Albertson's. Shock and disbelief flood their minds as they view the tens of thousands of choices handed to them on a platter. Hunting and gathering takes on a totally different meaning when supplemented with aisle after aisle of safe, nutritious foodstuffs, requiring no more effort to capture than maneuvering for shopping cart space. Produce pristinely presented with tropical rainforest sounds in the background as secreted sprayers mist and entice shoppers. Without grocery stores, where would we be? Just ask the citizens of Cibola, they know. Up the proverbial creek.

The Major had maneuvered his ten man team into position with exceptional stealth. They had only come at the camp in one direction only, from the highway down the dirt road. All seemed quiet. Fanning out to avoid ambush, Patrick directed his team to encircle the camp, and slowly, building by building, clear the compound. No live people remained in the camp. Dead people, on the other hand, were very well represented. The three prisoners captured in the attack on Cibola, that had returned with the motorcycles had all been killed. Apparently, Jerome didn't think too much of surrendering to the enemy. A fourth man was found crucified to the wall of the main building. He had been used for target practice and was quite a mess. No idea what his offense was, but he sure had rankled someone's feathers.

On a happier note, the supply room, roughly the size of a house, was pointed out and was found to be chocked full of every kind of canned food imaginable. Stacked to the rafters was a cornucopia of vegetables, fruits, canned meats, starches, and even booze. After all, you can only fit so much into a bus. The group just stood and gawked at the collection of life saving provisions.

As Patrick opened the door to allow more light to enter, he said, "I wonder how many people gave their lives so these fools could have a surplus they would never appreciate or use?" Patrick told Josh, Glen's grandson, to get on the walkie-talkie and have Cibola send the other farm truck and five more men ASAP. Prepared for some booty, Patrick had brought one flatbed truck with him. This cache would require many trips by both trucks before they transported the last of it to the ready and waiting townsfolk's of Cibola.

"Patrick, over here!" yelled one of the men.

Patrick approached the shed with dread. He had seen enough death for the day and wanted no more. As the man swung the door back, Patrick let out a whistle. Hunting rifles, pistols, boxes of ammunition, a box of twelve grenades, several shotguns, and a 50 caliber sniper rifle with 100 rounds of ammo. It was a glorious find.

"Put this on the truck first. Then the food. This is more than we could have hoped for."

Inside the main house, they found shortwave radio gear and several high-end laptop computers. Those were also loaded on the truck along with over three hundred DVD's and two DVD players. But one of the best finds of the day lay around the side of a barn; it was a solar power system still in the box. Jerome was smart enough to know it was valuable, but had no one with the technical expertise to hook it up. It also was loaded and hauled back to Cibola. Work went on through the night until every last bit of cargo was safe and sound, under guard in a locked warehouse. Now all they had to worry about was keeping the locals from raiding the pantry.

What a Day

Sometimes life gives you a glimpse of heaven. It happens, more than not, in the most unusual ways, and so subtly that it's hard to connect the dots and even begin to consider the whole God thing. Many of the miracles in the Bible, if not perceived with religious insight, appear as normal or coincidental events. Shelly likes to think of them as God moments. It could be as simple and beautiful as observing a child as she receives her first puppy. All giggles and wagging tail accompanied with lots of licking. You just can't help but smile. That's a God moment. Or, you could be taking your 92 year old mother, with arthritis in her hips, to the grocery store on the hottest day of summer and, all of a sudden, a parking spot opens up right in front of the store. A classic God moment. For the Cibola residents, either of the monumental finds of the day would have classified as a moment straight from God. Enough stores and provisions to last the Cibola inhabitants, if rationed properly, (Dan would see to that) for five or six months was just what was needed to allow them to work on safer projects and not be wandering around in no man's land. And, oh yes, finding the water, even though they didn't know how they would get it out of the arroyo, was literally life saving in the long run. Both, God moments to be sure.

"Dad, I saw your priorities list on the kitchen table and I think we need to move one of them up."

"Really, which one?"

"We need an underground church. One where everyone can come and thank God and pray. We can marry people there, baptize them, and even hold funerals if we have to."

"Underground?"

"Of course. This is the desert. We have no air conditioning. We need to start thinking about underground accommodations for everything."

A little dazed by his daughter's insight, Dan could only muster, "Right, I can ask Glen if we can use the town hall for the time being and if he says yes, then we can put up a few posters. Find out when Sunday is, cause I really don't know what day it is anymore, and then maybe we can find someone who feels comfortable preaching. Eventually, we can start digging our new church."

Shelly offered, "I could talk at church if you couldn't find anyone else."

"Shelly, I need to make sure you understand how people feel about you. You scare some people. They really aren't sure where you get your powers from."

"But Dad, I know it's from God. Maybe the UFERs did help me a little, but they get theirs from God and gave it to me. It's all about God, Dad," said Shelly emphatically.

"Honey, I know. You don't have to convince me and I don't want you trying to prove anything to anybody. But not everyone is going to see this the way we do. You must understand that. And if you even so much as mention the UFO, it could be disastrous. I wish I hadn't even told our own people. I agree with you that we need a church, but I want you to promise me that you will just go to church and be a nice little girl and not make any waves. Okay?"

"Yes sir. I really do understand. I just want to share how I feel about God. I'm not even mad at him for Mom anymore."

Dan was constantly amazed at how his heart ached when someone brought up Lisa unexpectedly.

"And just so you know, Dad, I really like Tina. I think you and her look good together."

Dan just shook his head and said, "Don't even think about it. Stay out of it. Do you hear me?"

"I just said you look good together, I didn't say anything else. What did you use to tell me all the time? Oh yeah, 'Don't be so sensitive'."

Dan laughed, grabbed Shelly and rolled her to the floor and started tickling her until her pleas to stop brought Tina from upstairs.

"What got into you two?"

"Oh, nothing special. Little Miss 'I know everything' just needed a reminder of who the boss is. That's all," replied Dan as he helped Shelly off the floor.

"Careful, Tina, or he'll do the same to you," giggled Shelly as she ran from the room with Dan in pursuit.

Tina smiled and felt about as good as she could remember for a long time.

Purpose

Remember when cleaning out your sock drawer seemed like the curse of death? You would procrastinate as long as possible, hoping that your mother would forget, all the time knowing you would endure one last tongue lashing before you were forced to use your precious time to do some mundane chore during your summer vacation. Fast forward ten years and you pretty much handled all projects and chores the same way. There just never seemed to be a driving purpose behind the projects. Nothing to really look forward to. In fact, work began to embody the sock drawer routine. Endless repetitive tasks designed to help someone else. Always someone else and never you. It is no wonder softball and bowling leagues became so popular. Finally something about you. Even though they were team sports, they were really about your individual effort. If the team lost, you could still point to the frame that you picked up the split or beat your personal best for a three game series.

Conversely, the town projects took on a totally different persona. They affected everyday life in a profound way. They kept you and your family alive. Survival, but at a civilized level. No more scrounging through vacant houses for left behind cans of tuna, no more risking venturing into far away towns and into the sights of vigilantes protecting their territory. The projects gave a purpose to life again, building a future for you and your children. Nearly everyone in Cibola saw the benefit. Of course, there were the naysayers always present like ants at a picnic, finding fault with any and everything. Properly handled, though, they could be managed into subservient roles and less distracting activities.

The town council had posted the priority projects for all to see:

CIBOLA TOWN PROJECTS:

* **Self defense of the town**
* **Secure liquid and food sources to last until self sufficient**
* **Portable water supply for drinking and irrigation**
* **Establish communications with the outside world**
* **Develop generating power for electricity**

* **Establish school for children**

* **Cross train critical professions**

* **Develop rules for admission to the town**

* **Organize religious services**

Teams were already being determined to tackle each project. The Major was, logically, in charge of the town's defense. He was busy installing plans to protect the town regardless of the direction of the attack. He had already hidden weapons strategically around the town for quick access and organized the town into defense zones. When a hand cranked siren sounded, everyone was to spring into action and secure their assigned area and then give assistance where needed.

Dan was placed in charge of the supplies, owing to his logistics background. He tackled the job with a maniacal eye towards efficiency and reporting. He already had a list of every item in the town warehouse, including the armory. He was busy plotting calorie intake and usage tables to determine how long the foodstuffs would last.

Howard, a self proclaimed computer geek, was busy trying to make the solar panels generate power, and then he would be tasked with bringing the satellite dish online. It was hoped that the internet would still be running and news from the outside world could be obtained.

Sally, the town nurse, was busy training two additional women in the routine care of the town's medical needs. In addition, she was giving special training in the handling of gunshot wounds and transfusions.

Stan, the senior council member, was put in charge of finding a way to bring the water from the arroyo first out of the canyon and then eventually into town. This would undoubtedly prove to be a difficult project, but by far the most critical for the survival of the community. Patrick and Stan had priority access to anything they needed in Cibola. That included personnel and material assets.

The town council would develop the rules for entry into Cibola, and two teachers in town would be responsible for developing a school, complete with a curriculum. Lastly, Mary, Glen's wife, would head up a committee to bring into being a non-denominational church. She was aiming for the first service to be held in two weeks.

Goals are necessary in life, especially if you intend to eat, drink and sleep safely at night. The town had taken on a decisively healthier glow in recent days. Despite the recent hard times, the men lost in the attacks, and the constant uncertainty, things were actually beginning to take on a feel of positive expectation.

Time Passes

Seconds to minutes, minutes to days, and weeks to months. Time remains the greatest illusion ever. Within an amazingly short period of time, all of the town projects had been completed and a new set had been posted. People liked to check off items on a list, and Cibola had responded fabulously to the projects list. The water project had been harder to resolve than anyone had expected, but eventually not only did they manage to install a pump, but they located a water truck to transport the liquid gold. Jake, the highway worker, knew where one was and was able to get it running. It was the kind you would see on a construction site that had a string of sprinklers along the back of the truck. It could haul around 3,000 gallons at a time and since the crop fields were planted near the pumping station on an abandoned farm, out of sight of prying eyes, the short one mile trip to the pumping station was not that big of an inconvenience. So, with the fields planted, Jake would drive down the rows, widened to accommodate his truck and the sprinklers were opened and as prayed for, crops were beginning to grow.

Patrick and Juanita were the first couple married at the Church of the New Beginnings and Abraham was baptized during the same ceremony. Dan and Tina had become an item and everyone soon expected another marriage. Shelly had her tenth birthday and a quiet surprise celebration was held with only the original tribe being invited. It was a time to remember, a time to laugh, and a time to cry. Monica and Shelly were both vying for the attention of a boy in their one room school house and life pretty much seemed to be returning to more normal conditions, albeit surroundings one would find in the 1940s.

The internet, accessible only via satellite, had been finally acquired and the news was worse than expected. Arid locations around the globe had been able to survive the worst of the plague, but suffered from the collapse of society. Might made right and small dictatorships had sprung up, in part to fight the meaningless violence, and in part for good ole greed. People on the internet wouldn't give out their locations for fear someone might swoop down on them and take what they had, that is unless they were desperate and dying anyway.

A growing topic of concern was focused on nuclear stockpiles. Who had them? Would they use them?

Could they just go off by themselves? In general, who was minding the store? No one had any real definitive answers, although sites in Australia, America, and Saudi Arabia had spoken on behalf of their governments and actually sounded as if they knew what was going on. Occasionally, jet contrails could be seen high in the clear blue sky streaking this way and that. Once a fighter plane had flown low over Cibola and waved its wings as the wide eyed people waved their arms frantically. It made a wide u-turn and buzzed the town again adding certainty to the sighting. Someone must still be in charge if you can maintain a fighter plane and find fuel for it. But that was over a month ago and nothing since then had happened.

Occasionally, always during the day, a vehicle would pass through the area but never stop. The sentries out on the highway had reported their approach and were then told to remain out of sight and not to alert them to our presence. People were directed off the streets in Cibola lest someone should look across the river and see movement. Stealth was still the best weapon.

Everyone on the internet was trying to find out how long the effects of the plague would last on the water. Desperate people had communicated that they had no choice but to start drinking whatever water they could find. They were never heard from again with the exception of teenage boy asking for anyone who received his message to pray for him. He was sick and knew he was going to die soon.

Shelly had been relatively free from visions. She spent most of her time trying to understand the auras she was presented with daily. She was surprised at how a person's mood so affected their aura. They could change in an instant. Go from beautiful and benign to bold and malevolent. People would come round to the house or even the school and ask her questions. Often times she had no idea how to answer them other than to say she honestly didn't know anything about their situation. Other times she knew what was in store for them but played dumb. She had discovered a 'shoot the messenger' mentality with people concerning bad news and wanted no part of that action. Her ability to read minds had increased dramatically and if she focused she could discern most anything she wanted. It was hard work, although getting easier, but it did present her with some moral issues. In school she was consistently turning in tests and receiving perfect scores. She tapped into one of her teacher's minds and picked up that there was concern she might be using her abilities to ace the tests. In actuality, her mental acuity had grown along with her mind reading abilities and additionally she seemed to have a greatly expanded memory. Going forward, she resolved to never again write a 100 on a test. She would purposefully miss questions and give the wrong answers when called upon in class. Disguises work best when worn consistently.

Disturbingly, she had read Tina's mind when her father had come into the room one time and decided to never do that again. She wasn't exactly clear what Tina had in mind for her father, but it certainly wasn't something that included her participation.

Curtain Call

The success of the Shelly Project as it was called back on Creum was undeniable. Public attention was at an all time high as the exploits of the child and her desert town were known throughout the planet. The future of Earth was yet undecided, but further expeditions could update the data streams and saturate the computer systems with endless hours of statistical interpolations. It was time for a final review with the subject, the always critically important assessment report, downloads to the subject, if warranted, and goodbyes. As they used to say in the entertainment industry on Earth, the final curtain call.

"I have summoned Shelly and she should be here in exactly 11 minutes and 48 seconds," informed Nimar.

"Was anyone else in the town alerted to our presence?" asked Golic.

"Yes. One sentry saw our approach, but he was put into a hypnotic sleep before alerting anyone. He will remember nothing."

Kosh, working the green luminous instrument panel asked, "Is she to be enhanced before we leave?"

"Yes, but it will hibernate for several years before becoming totally functional," answered Nimar. "By then, Earth should have settled into no more than 6 or 7 prime governments and her input will be most needed at that time."

"I will miss her unique style and approach to problems. She was a very worthy recipient of our attention. I am sure the High Council will remain most pleased with our work and certainly will recommend us for further assignments," droned Neep.

An unusual use of the word "us", thought Golic. Neep is certainly acquiring all of the attributes of a live crew member.

"My regret is that we cannot observe her mating process and childbearing. I would find much satisfaction logging her maternal efforts and especially witnessing the passing, if possible, of her unique qualities to her offspring," said Dra with a thoughtful glance at her crew mates.

"She is approaching. How do you wish to confront her?" asked Nimar of Golic.

"First with the holograph and then we will allow her to view us."

"I'm here. I followed Mr. fuzzy yellow ball. Now please show yourself," requested Shelly.

"Hello again, Shelly. How are you?" greeted the image of her mother as she materialized to the side of the ship.

"Hi. I am fine, thank you. We appreciate the help you have given us. As I am sure you are aware, Cibola is doing fine. We even found some water, with your help. I did appreciate the light in the cave."

"You are very welcome. We knew you would be successful and just wanted to speed up the process. We did that because we will be leaving as soon as we finish talking with you."

"Really? Will you be coming back?"

"Someday, some of our kind will certainly return to monitor Earth's progress. However, we doubt it will include any of us. We will probably be on other expeditions or perhaps teaching or on a learning tour."

"A learning tour. That sounds fun. Is it long?"

"No. Only a few of your years. But thoroughly relaxing and stimulating. It is a highly prized activity on our planet. A reward for our work."

"Do I get to meet you before you go?"

"If you would like, we will make ourselves available for your inspection."

"I would like to and I don't want to inspect you, only meet you."

"What is the difference?" inquired Golic.

"Come out and I will show you."

"Very well, we will exit our craft to your left. Please stand back a few steps."

Noiselessly, a bright light began to make itself seen. It appeared to be cutting through the skin of the ship, starting about 3/4ths of the way up the ship and exposing a door with a blinding light emanating from it. It was roughly 7 feet tall and 4 feet wide when it had finished opening. From the light, dark shapes could be seen walking down a slightly inclined ramp. Three images began to take on detail as they processed down the ramp. Golic in the lead, Dra in the middle and Kosh bringing up the rear. Nimar was left on the ship just in case. As they assembled outside of the ship and moved away from the light, Shelly had her opportunity to see the mysterious creatures. She giggled. They were cute. About four feet tall with large smooth heads. No hair and skin the color of grey putty. Three fingers on each hand and feet much larger than she expected. At least a size 12 in men's! Even on the smallest. Large beautiful green eyes with an elongated vertical pupil graced their heads and a very small mouth with a rectangular shaped breathing hole between the eyes and mouth. They all had narrow chests and very straight hips. The legs seemed to bend slightly backward at the knees and again at the ankle. It didn't seem a very comfortable way to stand, but then again, they more than likely thought the same about her.

Shelly stood there beaming a smile that would have alerted a blind man. She was absolutely thrilled to be meeting them.

"Okay, so what are your names?"

Introductions were made with each UFER stepping forward and thinking their name to Shelly. After each introduction, Shelly, careful not to hurt them, bent over slightly and hugged each one gently and with as much love as she could summon. She kissed each on the top of their heads and looked deeply into their eyes and thanked them again for this honor. Shelly had tears in her eyes by the time she finished, and then Nimar traded places with Kosh and she went through the same process with him.

"I will miss all of you. Hopefully someday I can find a way to repay your kindness and concern as we struggled to live through the plague. Please have a safe journey home and think of us often. I will pray for you and your people."

"Shelly, we are going to give you one last gift for your future life. It is a painless process and will only require that I touch your forehead with mine. Are you agreeable to this?" asked Golic.

"Of course. Please go ahead."

Shelly bent slightly and lowered her head until it met Golic's up reaching head and a connection was made. She felt nothing except his unusually cool head.

"Gradually you will notice that you have a new ability. It may take years and it can be improved with concentrated practice."

"What is it?" inquired Shelly with absolutely no patience for anything requiring patience.

"You must wait and see. As I said, it could take years, but will definitely be worth the wait. Now Shelly we must leave."

All three turned to leave and as they passed by Shelly, they bent to touch her feet with one finger.

"Why are you touching my feet?"

Golic was bringing up the rear and turned to take one last look at the child and said, "It's a most humble sign of respect. Not often given, and only when absolutely deserved."

"Thank you. And let me give you the most wonderful gift I have." With that Shelly stepped closer to Golic, put her left hand palm down on Golic's forehead, and with her right hand traced a cross on his forehead. As she did so, she said a small prayer, "Be safe my friend. May God bless and guide you on your journey. Know that he is with you and loves you. In the name of the Father, the Son and the Holy Ghost." She bent down and kissed him on the head. He was cool and smooth like a hardboiled egg fresh from the refrigerator. Ironically, he smelled like rain.

Golic stared deep into Shelly's eyes and they communicated without words and without meaning, but she knew it was love. He turned and entered the ship. Shelly stepped back and waited only a few minutes before the ship rose silently as if it were a leaf lifted aloft by a sudden breeze. Straight up and hovering about thirty feet off the ground, quietly defying gravity. And then, if you blinked you missed it, a dot disappearing into the sky, leaving quiet reflection for Shelly.

She would miss their behind the scenes paternal meddling. Now that she had actually met them, she would miss them even more. Before a tear could form, she remembered them standing in line for her inspection. She smiled, and even though she knew they could not see, she waved towards their line of retreat and then blew them a kiss.

"Goodbye friends. I love you." She turned and started walking back home and feeling the best she ever had she broke into a joyous run. As she ran along the path she remembered the odd head touching with Golic and wondered what the gift could be. Would it be useful to me or to others? Would it save lives or take them? Could she be trusted with it? Would it make her even weirder than she already was?

The End

LaVergne, TN USA
16 September 2009
158057LV00003B/26/P